Praise for Martina Reilly

'Martina has the wonderful knack of combining sensitivity for a serious subject with a big dose of humour' *Irish Independent*

'Martina is one of the best' *Irish Examiner*

'A cracking read – warm, splutter-out-your-tea funny, and unputdownable. I loved it' Sarah Webb

'Reilly has a wonderful comic touch, both in the way she draws her characters and in her dialogue … a brilliant read' *U magazine*

'A rollicking good yarn' *Evening Herald*

'Hard to put down, laugh-out-loud funny, perfect holiday reading' *Woman's Way*

'Clever, frank and funny' *Bella*

'Like Marian Keyes, Reilly takes a cracking story, adds sharp dialogue and buckets of originality' *Scottish Daily Record*

'We love Martina' *More*

'Has all the elements of an excellent read: mystery, drama and romance' *Woman*

'Martina Reilly's characters are so well observed' *She*

Martina Reilly, formerly known as the author Tina Reilly, lives in County Kildare with her husband and two children. Catch up with Martina on her website www.tinareilly.info, on Facebook or on Twitter @MartinaReilly

Also by Martina Reilly

Things I Want You to Know

MARTINA REILLY

HACHETTE
BOOKS
IRELAND

First published in 2014 by Hachette Books Ireland
First published in paperback in 2014 by Hachette Books Ireland

Copyright © Martina Reilly 2014

The right of Martina Reilly to be identified as the Author of the Work has been asserted
by her in accordance with the Copyright, Designs and Patents Act 1988.

A CIP catalogue record for this title is available from the British Library

ISBN 978 1444 794 427

Printed and bound by Clays Ltd, St Ives plc

Hachette Books Ireland policy is to use papers that are natural, renewable and
recyclable products and made from wood grown in sustainable forests. The logging and
manufacturing processes are expected to conform to the environmental
regulations of the country of origin.

Hachette Books Ireland
8 Castlecourt Centre
Castleknock
Dublin 15, Ireland

A division of Hachette UK Ltd.
338 Euston Road
London NW1 3BH

To all my friends, especially Irene, Imelda,
Kathleen, Margaret and Mary.
So proud to know you all.

PROLOGUE

NICK

The day is clear and startlingly bright and it makes the view of Dublin from the top of Three Rock Mountain stretch out before us like a forever. On a day like today, that view doesn't end, it just disappears into the horizon in a hodgepodge of browns, greens, yellows and blues.

'It's beautiful, Nick,' Kate says, awestruck.

I think *she's* beautiful. 'Yeah, isn't it?' I point out various landmarks to her but she's barely listening.

'It's like, we can see so far ahead here, we should be able to see into the future.' She grins at me. 'What do you think?'

I come behind her and wrap my arms around her. I let my chin rest on the top of her head. Kate is tiny, small-boned and delicate but a powerful runner. She beats me every time. She's also an incurable romantic. 'I think you're right,' I grin. 'I can see into the future right now.'

'Yeah?' She stares ahead. 'What can you see, then?'

'Us.'

'Yeah?'

'Having hot sweaty sex in the next five minutes.'

Like I knew she would, she laughs and belts me. 'You've a one-track mind, Nick Deegan,' she scolds good-naturedly.

'Just about you.' I nibble her ear. Truth is, I wouldn't be able for sex having just run seven miles, four of them up a mountain.

'Well, you'll be sad to know, I don't see that in the future,' she says. 'But I can see us flying to Barcelona to do the marathon and rocking it.' We've entered the Barcelona marathon. Kate convinced me but I'm dreading it.

'But right now, in our future,' Kate goes on as she brings her hands up to mine, 'I can see us running home, getting rid of Larry, nice and all as he is, putting Emma to bed, and then me feeding you popcorn and seducing you in front of the telly.'

'Keep talking,' I say, with a small grin. 'I like the sound of this future.'

'I can see you unbuttoning my top and sliding your hands inside and—' She stops. 'Aw, maybe I'll just show you.' She wriggles out of my arms and starts to jog on the spot. 'D'you want to start running into the future so I can show you?'

'How does a four-minute mile sound to you?'

She laughs delightedly and I run after her and catch her up.

I wish we hadn't run. I wish we'd just stayed in the present, my arms tightly about her. I wish the future had never come knocking on our door.

FOUR YEARS LATER

NICK

I watch from the table as Larry, my best mate, pauses in the doorway of the canteen. Looking around, he spots me and raises his hand in a half-wave. I smile back and he lopes across the room towards me.

'Hey.' He plants himself on the chair opposite and grins. 'Tomorrow, eh?'

'Tomorrow.'

'All packed?'

'Uh-huh.' In the two months I've been here, I haven't really unpacked.

'So things are good, then?' Larry shifts on the chair and scratches his face. He has this unfortunate skin condition. When he's nervous, his face breaks out.

I evade the question a little. 'We'll soon find out when I get home.' Saying the word 'home' makes me nervous and incredibly happy all at the one time. I just want to be with Kate and the kids. Especially now. I swallow hard; I'm not going to think about it. Not yet. Not while she's still hanging in there. 'Any news yourself?'

'I've a story that'll make you laugh,' Larry grins. 'Just let me grab some food.'

Larry tells stories to make me laugh every week. They mostly revolve around his disastrous record with women. I watch him head towards the food counter. The food here is awful but Larry would eat anything and the hotter the better. He arrives back with some sort of red curry with extra chillies heaped on top. Forking it into his mouth, he chews in appreciation. 'So, I'm at this work thing,' he begins after a second, jabbing his fork in my direction, 'and I meet this woman, about thirty or so, not bad-looking, and I tell her my name. I say, "I'm Larry Donaldson." And you'll never guess what happened.'

'You got laid.'

Larry laughs and has to mop his mouth. 'Nah. She grew all saucer-eyed and she pulled me away from the rest of the guests. I'm telling you, Nick, I really thought I was in there. Then she says …,' Larry pauses for the punch line, "… How's Donald?"'

'What?'

'That's what I said. I said, "Donald who?" And she said, "You said you were his son. Larry."'

I start to laugh. 'Larry, Donald's son?'

'Yep. Not the brightest star in the sky.'

We're still laughing when my phone rings. It's not a number I recognise. 'Hello?'

'Nick,' the person at the other end says, 'it's Marcy.'

Marcy. My heart flips. Marcy is my wife's best friend but we've never got on. Now though, it's the anxious tone in her voice that makes my heart beat a little faster. Something has happened, I know. Something awful. I block out the thought even as it forms. It can't have. I was going home tomorrow. I had six months to prove to Kate that she could trust me. That the kids could trust me.

'What's wrong, Marcy?'

At the other end of the phone, Marcy swallows.

'What?' I ask, filling in the dead gap of silence.

'It's … it's …' She stops and gives an uncharacteristic sniff.

My whole world sort of crumbles at that sniff. It's as if the walls of the canteen open up and things start to fall downward. Larry suddenly seems miles away. I press the phone harder to my ear. I can't utter a word. I know what she's going to say. Like a deer in rifle sights, I stand poised between one life and the next, unable to influence my fate one way or the other.

'She wants to see you, Nick,' Marcy says in a wobbly voice, 'but I think you need to hurry.'

That's not what I thought she'd say. My heart lifts a little. 'Kate? Now? But I'm going home tomorrow.'

'Please hurry,' she says. Then adds, 'We're on our way to the hospital.' She hangs up. I stare at the phone like I've never seen it before.

'Nick?' Larry asks, his voice shattering the shock. 'Everything all right?'

Standing up, I gulp out, 'I have to go. Kate—' I can't finish the sentence. They told me she had eight months. At least.

I grab my jacket and as I'm zipping it up, Larry asks carefully, 'Is Kate OK?'

I shoot a glance at him. He's scratching away on his face. I can't say the words so I make for the door.

Larry grabs my sleeve. 'Come on, I'll drive you.'

I don't want him to. I don't know how long it will take before my calm slips and reality hits me. I hate reality; it's like being waterboarded. 'It's cool, I can get a taxi.' We both know I won't. An hour later, I've been checked out of St Michael's Psychiatric Unit and am on my way to the hospital.

Larry doesn't say much on the way. He knows, I think, because he drives at speed as I mentally will him on. He passes out cars and earns annoyed 'beeps' from motorists. Finally, just before the turn in to the hospital, he says, 'The kids'll need you when …' He lets the sentence hang. He sounds like Dr Phil. He shuffles about in his seat and sniffs and wipes his nose. Then, without saying any more, he turns in through the gates and I see the building looming up ahead.

I'll be useless, I think. I've been in treatment for the past two months and for the last couple of weekends I've had supervised visits with my kids. But the plan was for me to go home and for Kate to be there to train me in. What will I do if she's not there? But that won't happen. This is a blip, I think. They gave her eight months two months ago. She can't die. Not yet. I'm not ready. Not ready in all sorts of ways.

'I know you think you'll be crap,' Larry says, 'but I think you'll be great.' A pause. 'You used to be great, and all Emma and Liam need is for you to be there.'

I can do that, I think. I can be there. I can take some more time off work in the garage, Danny won't mind. I can be a full-time dad. I can do this.

'And me and the guys are always at the end of a phone line,' Larry adds. He means our poker-playing friends – Danny, Davy and Peter.

'She's not gone yet,' I gulp out, and press my fingers hard into my eyeballs. I lay my head way back on the seat. I blink. But it's no use. Kate is dying and I'll be in charge. I can't manage without her. I just can't. I can live without her if she's in the world but if she's gone … A tear slides out and runs down my face.

Larry coughs some more and, hiking his arm around his head, he scratches his chin on the other side. He always does that when he feels awkward. Without saying anything more, he parks the car outside the hospital door and we both jump out.

* * *

Marcy is in the foyer. It's like she's waiting for us. I come to a complete stop and watch with slight horror as she comes towards us. I know what she's going to say and I can't bear to hear it. She's red-eyed and appears devastated. She stands in front of me and I know. I just know. I'm too late. Too late as always.

'She's gone,' Marcy hiccups out.

And my head can't take it in. So I say, 'Gone where?'

Marcy says nothing more for a beat, then as if there is a wedge in her mouth that the words have to squeeze by, she says, 'Gone to heaven, Nick.' And then she is gasping and choking, big heaving sobs.

'Oh, shit.' Larry lays a hand on my shoulder.

Gone to heaven. It sounds so childish. So lovely. Much better than 'she's dead'. I can't move. It's like a moment suspended in time. I'd offered to move back home when I heard Kate was sick but she said no. Very gently. Very softly. She said that I had to get my head sorted before I moved back in. I had initially protested but she told me there was no way I'd get to keep the kids full time if I didn't sort myself out. I'd been doing fine, I thought. To prove her wrong, I'd gone to the doctor and to my horror he had approved the admission to St Michael's. I'd talked and talked, had nightmares but worked hard and I was to be checked out tomorrow. A new Nick. One she never got to see.

Marcy is still crying and I notice that she looks shorter than usual. I realise with a shock that she's walking around in trainers. She normally wears six-inch-high stilettos which bring her to my nose and just under Larry's chin. Funny how you notice these things in the midst of everything. I wonder next if she'll hug me, but then think that she won't. 'Sorry,' she says. Her blue eyes are red and puffy. She scrubs a hand over them and black trails in its wake, smearing over her cheek.

To my surprise, Larry enfolds her in a hug. She doesn't resist, but instead she clings to him like a drowning woman.

'How—?' I falter.

Marcy looks at me, Larry's arm still around her shoulder. 'She just … she couldn't breathe,' she gulps out. 'She wasn't great this morning but she kept saying she was fine. You know the way she was. I took the day off to be with her, I didn't think she was well. Then about an hour ago, she got really bad. I got her here as quick as I could. I really did and she kept asking for you, Nick, and—'

'Hey.' Larry hugs her tighter. 'Come on. It's OK.'

'The kids?' I ask.

'Liam is asleep, a neighbour is with him, and Emma is on a sleepover, so you won't have to tell them until morning. Kate …' Her voice sounds strangled. 'She's … she's upstairs in the room they took her to. Number three, St John's .' Her voice is soft, not the abrasive tone she normally reserves for me.

I don't wait another second. I leave Larry with his arm still around her as I take the steps two at a time, looking for St John's. I find it and am directed by a sympathetic-looking nurse to Room three. Once outside, I have no idea what to do. I'm not sure that I want to see Kate dead. Life has always pulsated from her, that to see her so still, that might destroy me. I can't let it, though. Emma, my eight-year-old, and Liam, my two-year-old, need me. I drag a hand over my face and slowly push open the door. A lamp throws its soft light over everything. I take a step into the room and the smell of illness leaks into my mouth. I swallow hard and turn to look at Kate.

My Kate.

Her face is alabaster white, almost melding with the sheer white pillow. Her hair, dark, fans out on one side. And she is so still. Her eyes are closed, her hands, with her brilliant red nail varnish, are almost shocking to see. I go nearer. She looks so small, so frail, not the Kate I remember. Not even the Kate of two months ago when she'd ordered me to sort myself out. That Kate had been the Kate I knew. How could she have changed so much, so soon? The last time I saw her was back then and she promised me that if I worked hard, she'd be around when I came out of hospital. There was no urgency, she said, she'd be there. And my poor heart had lifted in the hope that I could undo all the damage I caused. I reach out and touch her cheek. It's still warm and it cracks my heart. I kneel down beside her and lie my head alongside her and cup her head in my hands, wishing I could wrap myself up in this moment and never leave. Wishing she'd always be warm and that I'd be able to hold her.

'I love you, Kate,' I whisper, with such an intensity that I feel it could just bring her back. I hold my breath, waiting, but there is only the light and the stillness and the voices from the corridor. 'I'm sorry about Jack,' I go on, 'and …' Even now I can't say it, so I just add miserably, 'and all the rest of it.' A tear slides out and I blink it back. 'I failed you, I know, but I won't fail the kids. I promise.'

Oh, God, the kids. I wish it was me that had died. They'd be so much better off with Kate. I am, it has to be said, a complete and utter deadbeat. Not in the drinking, wasting-his-life-away kind of deadbeat. But an emotional deadbeat. I wasn't always like that, I was fun once. Or at least Kate thought I was and then I had a sort of breakdown, only it wasn't the sort of breakdown where they cart you off to hospital and pump you full of drugs and talk to you and suddenly you can get on with your life. Nope, this was the sort that happens to a coastline where the sea erodes pieces away, bit by bit over time, and then hey, you look one day and everything has changed and there is no way to put it back. Ever. And so I had to go. I've spent the last two months trying to glue myself together for the kids' sakes so that I could move in and take care of them because Kate was sick. Only she wasn't meant to go just right now.

I stay, lying bedside Kate until Larry comes up. He knocks, then stands awkwardly in the doorway. His trousers are horrendous, I notice for the first time ever. Thick brown cords. A yellow shirt. Blue trainers. Larry scratches his face. 'D'you want a cup of tea?' he asks.

The absurdity of the question almost makes me laugh. 'No, why would I want a cup of tea?'

'Coffee?'

'No!'

Larry flinches and I feel bad. 'Sorry, Lar, it's just …' I don't have the words to convey it. Instead I look at Kate. There are no words for the loss I feel. It's the loss of her, of her life, of whatever plans we might have made. It all unfurls like a sheet in the wind, only to blow away. God, she's beautiful. The first time I ever saw her in her luminous orange-and-green Docs, I wanted her.

Larry walks cautiously into the room. He stands at the end of the bed. His hands dangle uselessly, he heaves a great big sigh. Eventually he murmurs, 'She looks peaceful.'

I can't take it. The way he talks as if she's dead. My shoulders start to shake and I bury my head in the crook of my elbow.

Larry's hand patting my shoulder is a comfort.

EMMA

When your mammy dies it means that everyone feels sorry for you. Only they never say that, they just sort of look at me and Liam – that's my little brother, he's two and a half and the cutest baby brother in our class in school, everyone says so – and sort of shake their heads and say things like, 'God help them' or 'They'll miss their mother.' Sometimes they crouch down and say, 'How are you?' in a high voice that is like they are talking to babies.

I'm eight. I'm not a baby so I just look at all those people and I tell them that I am fine, thank you very much. That's what Mammy always told me to say when people ask, 'How are you?'

Daddy says he will mind us now. I had been hoping that Marcy would mind us or maybe even Nana, but instead it's Daddy. And after Mammy goes up to see Jesus and God he moves into our house with all his things and the night Mammy gets buried, I see him crying in front of the TV only he says he isn't crying, he's laughing at some funny thing on and what am I doing up? He doesn't wait for me to tell him, he just lifts me up in his arms and asks me if I want something to eat. He feels like something to eat, he says. So I tell him I'd like pancakes. I said Mammy made us pancakes all the time on a Tuesday morning and I would like some now. It was a lie, which is not nice but I am making my first confession soon and all my lies will be wiped away. Daddy says he doesn't know how to make pancakes but he could do me some French toast if I want. I say OK.

Then he makes me some French toast and finds some syrup in the fridge and the two of us sit at the island in the kitchen and eat and eat and he smiles at me and I smile back at him.

He is OK, I suppose.

Not as nice as Mammy, though.

I miss my mammy.

NICK

I lie awake and think about the last few weeks. The funeral, the burial, the flowers, cards and condolences all sort of blur. Bits stick out. Like telling the kids. Liam is only two, so he doesn't really understand. He misses Kate without actually knowing what it is that's gone. That's worse than anything, I think. Emma just looked at me and asked if she was going to live with Marcy now. That hurt. There was a time Emma followed me around, chatting away about her day. Now she barely talks to me and when she does, it's usually to tell me that I'm doing stuff wrong. I think she's really mixed up, the poor kid. She hasn't cried at all, though everyone says to leave it, that it'll happen when it happens. She has bad dreams but she doesn't want me to hold her or anything. She's always been independent. Or wary of me, I'm not sure which.

Kate would have enjoyed her funeral. Larry had done one of the readings and said, 'Peace be with you' instead of 'This is the word of the Lord.' Peter had started to laugh and tried to make it look like he was crying. Larry had reddened up like a pepper. Then, at the end, Marcy, who had come with her boyfriend, a big weightlifter-type, insisting on singing 'Wind Beneath my Wings', completely oblivious to the fact that she was screeching. And Peter, who had only just stopped laughing over Larry, had started laughing all over again. Honestly, Marcy sounded like a cat being slaughtered as Kate's coffin was carried out. I didn't mind because Kate would have found it hilarious, and as I pictured her laughing, I swear my heart sort of broke. Poor Em tried so hard to be brave. Her little face was white and almost bruised-looking from the sheer effort of trying to keep it all in. I did wrap an arm around her and told her I'd mind her but she looked sort of doubtful and asked if Marcy could help. Her distrust stings like a whip, but I can't blame her, I suppose. I did leave her and Liam, after all. And what was worse, Liam was only six months old. I barely remember him being born, I was that far gone, though I know in the first few months of his life, I tried like crazy to be the dad he needed. It lasted six months. I left them then and it was one of the biggest mistakes I ever made but I wasn't thinking clearly. Hell, I wasn't thinking at all. But eight-year-olds are too young to understand all that. So I nodded and said that yep, of course Marcy could mind her too. She ended up in Larry's arms with Marcy rubbing her hair. I was grateful to them for being there; we chose Em's godparents well.

I found myself standing alone at the grave. Then my parents came and stood beside me and my mother sniffed and snorted and clung on to my arm while my dad harrumphed and thumped her on the back. Em refused to come near the grave and instead remained with Marcy. Liam, in Larry's arms, sucked a lollipop, and as for Kate's family, her mother and father died years ago. Eventually, near the end, Larry, Danny, Peter and Davy stood beside me too. I was never so glad of them.

After the funeral, when people had gone home, there was only Marcy and Larry left. Marcy, tears sliding down her face, had handed me a large scrapbook. 'Kate said to give it to you after her funeral.'

On the front, in Kate's handwriting, was written: 'Nick – The Things I Want You To Know'. All around the edges were pictures of Emma and Liam. Colourful tabs stuck out of the pages – a lot of tabs. Things like 'Bedtimes', 'School Lunches', 'Recipes', 'Dinners', 'Bills', 'Garden', 'Stories', 'Parent and Toddler', 'Timetable'. There were photographs on some of the pages and little pockets with things inside. Loads and loads of information that Kate had put together to give me when I'd moved back in.

I waited until I was on my own before hastily flicking through it. But just looking at Kate's writing, at the way she drew smiley faces over things, at the pictures she pasted in, cut me at the knees. I had to sit down and hold it and inhale its scent. But I haven't been able to look at it. I will, though, I will. But for now, to keep the pain at bay, I prefer to muddle along a bit.

This all plays like a loop in my head until the alarm goes off at seven thirty. Time to get Emma ready for school. I roll out of bed.

'Daddy?' Liam, who has taken to climbing into my bed at horrendous hours of the morning, holds up his arms. I hoist him up and hold him close. He's two and a half; I've missed out on most of his little life and if he wants to keep me awake all night so I can share time with him, then so be it. I love this boy, the warm uncomplicatedness of him. The fact that his hugs are hugs and his kisses are kisses and when he smiles it's *for* me, not *at* me. Though Em is only eight, she scares me. It's like she can see right into me, into the hopeless floundering dad that I am. She has the ability to crucify me with a look.

'Come on, Liamo, let's go make breakfast.'

I rap on Em's door as I pass and tell her to get up. She mumbles something from inside. I hurry past Kate's room, which used to be our room. I haven't been in there yet.

Ten minutes later, Liam is in his high chair, banging on it with his spoon. I'm microwaving some pancakes for the kids. Apparently, Kate cooked the kids pancakes in the mornings. I don't know how to cook them, so I buy the ready-made ones. Emma says they're not

as nice but she eats them all the same. I love to watch her slathering
maple syrup all over them and getting all sticky and gooey. Emma
slinks into the kitchen, her hair all scattered, wearing her yellow
dressing gown with the teddy on the front. Looking at my kids
always makes my heart ping. I find it hard sometimes to believe
that Kate and I made them, that they are ours but yet themselves.
It's bloody amazing.

Emma plonks into a chair. 'When are you buying my
Communion dress, Daddy?' She attacks her pancake with gusto,
using her fingers to tear it apart.

'Communion dress?'

Saucer brown eyes look up at me. 'Yeah, I'm making it in May
and Marcy said to make sure and remind you. The sooner the
better, Marcy said.'

I hand her some kitchen paper to wipe her hands. 'May?' That's
weeks away, but I don't want Marcy criticising me. 'Well, I guess
we'll go on Saturday, if you like.'

'I want a long one, with a veil and a bag and an umbrella and I
want white pearly shoes. Amy Murphy has white pearly shoes and
they're lovely. She got them in a special Communion shop. Will we
go to a special Communion shop?'

'Of course we will. That's where we're going to get a special
Communion dress, isn't it?' There are special shops for Communion
dresses?

'Uh-huh.' She slides her head to one side. 'Will you leave us
again? I asked Marcy and she said no but that if you did, we could
live with her.'

The directness of the question blindsides me. I sit in beside her
and say with conviction, 'I'm not going anywhere. And I didn't
really leave you, Ems, I just went to live somewhere else.' I think
of my dingy flat and wince.

'Yeah, you lived with that smelly man called Jack.'

How does she remember? She was only just five. 'He wasn't smelly, honey, he just needed a bath and a place to stay.'

'He *was* smelly. He smelt like chicken soup.' She wrinkles up her dainty nose. 'And he scared Liam because he yelled.'

'He had a nightmare. You yell when you have bad dreams, don't you?'

She shrugs. 'I don't scare people, though.'

I decide not to talk about Jack any more. 'Well,' I tousle her hair, 'I'm not leaving and you won't have to live with Marcy.'

'Aw.'

I'm not sure how to take that. She pops the last of her pancake in her mouth and lightly dances out of the kitchen.

I heft Liam from the chair. He's mushing up syrupy pancake between his fingers and I have to pry them loose, which makes him scream. Running his hands under the tap, I wash them clean and bring him upstairs to dress him.

* * *

We walk to the school. It's Emma's second week back since the funeral and the teacher said she seems happy enough. I had wanted to keep her out longer but apparently it's best for kids to have a routine. Em insists on dressing herself and she looks as cute as a button in her blue dress, which she tells me is called a pinafore. A white shirt buttoned up tight and a blue tie and cardigan complete her school uniform. She's wearing a white furry jacket with a fluffy hood and her good shiny brown boots because we couldn't find her school shoes this morning. Emma struts ahead of me like some kind of mini model.

I push Liam in his buggy. His look is not so successful. I'm still finding my way around his clothes and the best ways to dress him without him running off or wriggling away. He has very definite ideas on what he wants to wear too and I hate upsetting him. I catch him sometimes looking around and I think he's looking for Kate. I wonder what he thinks happened to her. He knows she's dead but he doesn't know what dead is. I think he feels like me, that a part of him has gone, only he doesn't know which part. Anyhow, tracksuit bottoms and jumpers seem to cause the least fuss and today he's wearing blue tracksuit bottoms which unfortunately seems a bit small for him and a grey jumper which is too big. At least I've remembered a hat, which I forgot one day and he kept crying and putting his hand up to his ear. But if I'm not watching he sometimes yanks the hat off and it gets lost on the way and he cries with the cold anyway.

I try to get to the school gates early so that I can make as quick an exit as possible. Sometimes I feel that all the other parents, who are mostly women, are staring at me. I hate being stared at. I reckon they either pity me as the widower or hate me as the guy who left. Either way, it's lose–lose. Up front, Em seems to have been joined by a little friend. Their heads bump as they discuss whatever it is eight-year-old girls discuss. She's got the sunny disposition Kate had, drawing people to her quicker than a free holiday giveaway.

She is running back to me, pulling her friend along by the sleeve of her jacket. 'Jane is my best friend ever. She wants me to come to her house today for dinner. Can I go? Can I go?'

'Hi, Jane.'

Jane peers up at me. She's got a squashed little face. 'Is this your dad?' She doesn't sound that impressed.

'Yep, I am. You want Em to go over to your house after school?'

'Yes, she does. Can I go, Dad, please?' Emma looks beseechingly at me. She'll throw a wobbler if I refuse. She's been doing that loads lately and I know it's because her little life has been thrown up in the air.

'Dad? Can I?' she asks, her voice hitching up a notch.

Surely I should meet Jane's mother to suss her out, though you can't always tell what someone is like from a first meeting. But maybe it's the responsible thing to do. And what are the travel arrangements? I've seen toddlers walking home from school on their own, which is downright mental.

'Maybe we should talk to Jane's mammy,' I say.

'She says it's fine,' Jane says firmly.

'See?' Emma's voice has grown a little cross.

I feel I'm being press-ganged. 'Well, …'

'Daddy, this is what girls do,' Emma says, her eyes narrowing.

Please don't freak out, Emma, I mentally beg. I attempt a smile. 'Well, …'

Just then a pretty blonde woman hurries up, also pushing a buggy. Her kid is asleep. He looks a lot cleaner than Liam. Her buggy looks like she just bought it from a catalogue. There are no banana stains or jam marks on that contraption. 'Hello, you must be Nick.' She places her hands on Jane's shoulders.

'Yes.' I give the woman a smile of relief. 'And you're Jane's mother?'

'I am. Jane was wondering if Emma could come over today after school. I can drop her back.'

'Please, please, please, Daddy.' Emma clasps her hands and hops from foot to foot. Jane copies her. Jane's mother laughs.

I find it quite manipulative but it works. 'OK. What time will she be back? She goes to bed around ten.'

'Oh, right.' The woman looks taken aback. Maybe it's rude to ask these things? The whole school gate etiquette is way over my head. 'Well, we'll probably have her back by seven, if that suits.'

'Fine. Great. Thanks.'

She falls into step with me as we approach the gates. We watch the girls run in, Jane blowing a kiss to her mother while Emma just waves at me. I wave back and watch until I can't see her any more.

'And how's Liam?' The woman, whose name I don't know and find I can't ask now, crouches down and tickles Liam under the chin.

He giggles. I grin.

The woman stands up and touches my arm. 'I'm sorry about Kate, she was such a lovely woman.'

I dip my head. This is why I hate the school gates.

'She always brought Liam to the Mother and Toddler,' the woman goes on. 'In fact, Kate and I set it up. Will you be doing that?'

Mother and Toddler? I'd heard Kate mention it once or twice, seen some reference to it in the book she gave me but I still can't bring myself to look at that book. Anyway, what happens at a Mother and Toddler session? 'Eh, I dunno.' I attempt humour: 'I'm not a mother.'

'Oh,' she smiles, 'that doesn't matter. It should be called Parent and Toddler really. It's on tomorrow morning, you should come. You'd be very welcome and it allows Liam to have fun too.'

'I'll see.'

'You'd like to go, wouldn't you, Precious?'

For a horrifying moment I think she's talking to me, but obviously she isn't, as Liam kicks his legs in glee. It's like he's saying that he does want to go.

'It's on in a room on the ground floor of the community centre at ten,' the woman says. 'Do come.'

I smile at her in a non-committal way and am kind of glad when she leaves.

* * *

After I drop Em to school, if the weather is good, Liam and I take a walk. There's a park and a playground and a motorway and quieter roads. I walk them all. It takes three hours. If it's raining, I put

Liam in his car seat and we drive. Sometimes we park at the sea and spend our time looking out. I suppose I do it to avoid going back to the house. I guess in time, the feeling that Kate will be there waiting as I walk in the door will abate, but at the moment, no matter where I am in that house, I think I see her, fleeting glimpses that are gone when I turn. I think I hear her. I go into the kitchen and I see us drinking wine over a takeout as Emma sleeps in her crib. I go into the front room and I see us watching box sets of *CSI*. Every room in the house was painted by Kate, the flowers in the garden were planted by her, she hung our wallpaper while I splattered her with paste. I was happiest in those early years before I made such a mess of everything. Liam was the result of desperate sex one night when everything was falling apart and both of us were powerless to stop the mess. It was up to me, but even now, I'm not sure if I could have stopped it. Neither of us was happy when we heard Kate was pregnant, but I wouldn't change a thing now. The minute Liam appeared and opened his eyes, we were smitten.

At twelve, I arrive back at the house. The hours from twelve to two thirty I fill with lunch and washing and tidying. I take as long as I can over lunch. At two thirty, I go to pick Em up, but today I have hours to fill as she's not coming home.

I give Liam some cheese and ham, and a banana for after. Emma says that's what you give babies for lunch, and as Liam eats it, I'm not about to argue. I will have to find out what else I can feed him, though. My thoughts turn to the book that Kate left me. Maybe she wrote something in that. I get as far as pulling it from the kitchen drawer before the panic sets in and I shove it back. I close my eyes and take deep breaths. Part of me desperately wants to read it, to connect with Kate, but the other part does not want the grief that will follow. The next time I need to know something, I will use it, I promise myself as I lift Liam's high chair into the television room and switch on the TV for him. Then I do what I always do to take my mind off the empty hours ahead. As he's watching some dancing furry puppets, that quite frankly would scare me stupid, I pull out a packet of cards and begin to memorise them. I call them out as I go and after a bit, I notice that, as the cards flip, Liam is staring at them in wide-eyed fascination.

'You like these, eh?'

He smiles.

So I put on a show for him. I rap out the cards and Liam's smile widens. Then he laughs, and his laughter is like a babbling brook in the middle of the desert. I swim in it, I drink from it and it nourishes me.

EMMA

Jane thinks she is great because her mammy is still alive. She keeps saying all the time I am in her house, 'My mammy got me a veil for Communion' and 'My mammy got me my Communion shoes.' I tell her that my mammy got me those things too, even though she didn't. She was too sick to get them. Sometimes I think Mammy didn't want to stay alive enough. If she really wanted to, I think Jesus would have let her stay alive because he listens to our prayers and he is our friend. Only Mammy and Daddy never went to mass, so maybe Jesus didn't know who they were and now he's only meeting Mammy for the first time. I hope he likes her. Everyone else does.

Jane is showing me her dress and she says when we go to my house will I show her mine? I tell her that my dress is a big secret. Jane says that that isn't fair and that I have to show her my dress and I say, 'Actually I don't.' She gets a bit huffy then.

I wonder why my mammy got sick and Jane's didn't. My mammy had cancer. She found a little lump on her neck and they did tests and little bits of the lump had travelled all over her body, like it was going on holidays. Some of the lump was in her liver and even some went to her brain. I remember Mammy telling me she was going to be very sick but that it didn't matter, that I was to still tell her all that was happening in my life. She pulled me up on the bed and kissed my face like she was tickling it and I laughed and Marcy laughed too.

I used to go up to Mammy's room every day after school. And every morning before school. Molly, my friend Laura's mammy, would collect me and bring me to school then. I used to be able to talk to my mammy and she was able to walk around and cook and bring us out like other mammies but then she got the lump and we just had to hug her.

But the hugs were very nice.

Anyway, after Jane mentions her mammy AGAIN, for about the five hundred and forty-third time, I tell her that she is just showing off having a mammy and she says she isn't. I tell her that everyone loves me loads 'cause my mammy died. I say that the teacher loves me loads and never gives out to me any more and that my daddy lets me watch all the cool teenager programmes, and she says that I am a liar and I tell her that I will show her. And I say that Daddy gives us pancakes in the morning 'cause he loves us loads more and that my brother Liam can mess up the house and Daddy lets him. Then she says, 'If my mammy died, would it be the same for me?' and I say to her that maybe it would.

'But I don't want my mammy to die,' she says.

That makes me mad, I don't know why, so I hit her.

NICK

Emma comes back at a quarter to seven. I've just got Liam into his pyjamas, which he is desperately trying to get out of as he seems to have become obsessed with not wearing any clothes. Opening the door, Emma bounces in and laughs at her brother's struggles. 'Look, Jane, Liam hates the pyjamas my daddy put on him.'

Jane laughs too.

The girls rush on into the television room and I have no choice but to invite Jane's mother, whose name I still don't know, into the house.

'She was an angel,' the woman says. For a second I don't know if she's talking about Kate or Emma. Then the woman runs a big red fingernail along the hall table and smiles after the girls. We both try to ignore the big streak in the dust her finger has just made.

Emma comes out of the TV room holding a banana skin between thumb and forefinger. Her nose is wrinkled in disgust. 'Ugh, Daddy, gross,' she says. She disappears into the kitchen and I hear the lid of the bin slam shut. Reappearing again, she says in a scolding voice, which amuses me, 'Jane says we should keep our house tidier.'

I laugh. 'Well, if Jane wants to come clean it, she can. That was Liam's banana for his supper.'

'Sorry about that.' Jane's mother looks embarrassed. 'Jane is a real little housewife. You should see her room, everything in its place.'

'She sounds like a Stepford wife in the making.'

She doesn't seem to take that as a joke. Instead she gives me a tight smile and calls her daughter. 'So, will we see you tomorrow?'

'Tomorrow?'

'Parent and Toddler?'

Liam has disappeared. I look around and see him pulling open a kitchen drawer. He starts flinging things all over the place. He's laughing loudly. 'Eh, I'm not sure.' I run into the kitchen and pick Liam up. He yowls.

'It's good for the children,' she says in a kind of no-nonsense way as I come back out, a wriggling Liam in my arms. 'It helps them to socialise. After what Liam has been through, it might be good for him.'

I feel I've just been given a lecture.

'Down!' Liam orders and I have no option but to lower him to the ground, whereupon he runs back into the kitchen and starts doing the same thing again.

'He's gas.' The woman smiles, though I think she doesn't really mean it. Then she heads into the room and tells her daughter to hurry up.

I stop Liam one more time by handing him a lollipop from the drawer.

'Daddy, can I watch *Glee* later?' Emma asks from the hallway, having followed Jane and her mother out.

'Is it over by ten?'

'You ask that all the time. Yes, it is.' Emma folds her arms and looks at me like a cross little madam.

'OK, then.'

'See?' Emma turns to Jane and, sounding triumphant, says, 'He *does* let me watch it.'

'Wow!' Jane is impressed, and I feel great about that. 'My mammy says it's not suitable, don't you, Mammy?'

Is it not suitable? I glance at Emma, who looks at me sweetly. She's gorgeous.

'Come on, Jane, out to the car. It's nearly past your bedtime.' Her mother is annoyed now, which is weird.

'Emma stays up until ten, why can't I?'

'Everyone has different rules.' She smiles at me apologetically. 'Let's go.'

Jane seems a little weird. One minute, she's all smiles and the next, she's cross. She stomps out behind her mother as Emma happily waves her goodbye. When we close the door on them, Emma surprises me by cuddling my arm. 'Sometimes Daddies have the best rules,' she says.

I wish we could just stay like that.

* * *

Both kids are in bed by ten thirty. I'd watched *Glee* with Emma and thought that maybe it was a bit advanced for her. But she told me she knew what gay and lesbian meant, that everyone knew and that if you didn't know you were a dork. I felt like a dork under her gaze so I said nothing else. Now, provided they don't get up, it's chill-out time. I pop open a can of beer and flick through the TV channels. The late-night poker games are great but if they aren't on, I normally head to bed. Larry calls over sometimes and we sit in silence. A good silence, though.

I've taken six months' leave from my job in Danny's garage to mind the kids and help them settle. When I was in the hospital, I managed to keep working some days, as I was let out. Anyway, six more months is as long as my savings will last. After the six months are up, I'll get a minder for them.

I normally head to bed about one. Sleep takes a while to come, and even when it does, I get woken either by a nightmare, or by Liam climbing into my bed at around four in the morning. I hear him as he hops out of his cot bed and pushes open his bedroom door. I welcome the pitter-patter of his bare feet on the floorboards as he enters my room. Liam and I don't talk, I just move over in the bed and open the bed covers. He hops in beside me with a giggle and I fall asleep to the rhythm of his breathing.

Another day successfully survived.

* * *

A couple of days later, as I'm pulling the door behind us on the way to school, my parents arrive. They have a habit of landing in without any warning, like fighter jets on a war-torn country. Their effect on the kids is the same too. All the order I have tried so desperately to maintain scatters like shrapnel. The sight of my mother and my father send my kids into tailspins of excitement, mainly because they arrive bearing enough sweets to feed us for a year. This is their first visit in three weeks, and I guess for them to hold off so long shows admirable restraint.

My mother is the main attraction, she's a bundle of fizzing energy. She's on every committee, appears in the local weekly paper at least twice a month, knows absolutely everyone and has a passion for collecting just about anything that can be collected. Her house is a warren of ornaments and useless knick-knacks. In years to come, she swears they'll be worth money.

Dad, on the other hand, plods along behind her, cigarette in hand, taking the world in and only talking when he absolutely has to.

'Nana!' Emma, her plaits flying behind her, throws herself into my mother's arms. I wince as Emma's hair comes loose. I'm not very good at that sort of thing and Emma, though she knows in theory how to make a plait, can't do it either. When she was in bed one night, I studied it on YouTube and even practised on one of her dolls, but it didn't make any difference. By the end of the day, Emma's hair has come unravelled like threads from a badly made shirt.

'Oh, darling, your hair!' My mother's laugh tinkles like spoon on spoon. 'Come here and let Nana fix it for you.'

Emma puts a hand up to her head and giggles a little. 'Daddy!' she says, without rancour. 'Look!'

I splay my hands helplessly. 'There's a brush on the kitchen table, Mam.' I unlock the front door to let them back in before glancing at my watch. 'But hurry or we'll be late.'

'Oh, Nicholas, you shouldn't put brushes on the kitchen table,' my mother admonishes with a smile, flapping her hands a little.

The minute she says it, I get a clear picture of just how bad our kitchen looks that morning. I'd have cleaned it when I got back with Liam later in the day, but Mam and Dad wouldn't know that. All they'd see when they walked in would be bread crusts and spilt milk and half-eaten bowls of flakes. Also, Liam has thrown every box in the presses across the floor because we played a game of hide and seek that morning. I only let him play it when we're really early. In an attempt to negate the damage, I stand in front of the kitchen door and offer to get the brush. 'You don't want to be brushing hair in the kitchen, eh?'

'What's wrong with that?' Emma asks. 'You do.'

I try to pretend she hasn't said anything. 'Go on out and I'll get the brush.'

'Come on, Ems.' My mother gently ushers Emma from the house and, heaving a sigh of relief, I dash into the kitchen to retrieve the brush, which is sitting right beside the butter. I almost slip on a spilled puddle of milk which had been in Liam's cup before he'd splattered it across the floor.

Back outside, I hand my mother the brush. 'D'you know what?' I say, trying to sound generous. 'Why don't you and Dad walk Emma to school this morning and I'll have a cuppa on for you when you get back with Liam.'

'Walk?' My mother peers at her stilettos. 'I couldn't possibly walk in these, Nicholas.'

'You can drive me, Nana,' Emma says, beaming. 'Daddy always makes us walk and I hate it. I much prefer the car.'

'Well, Daddy is right to make you walk.' My mother smiles at me over Emma's head. 'But all right, just for today, I'll drive you.'

'You can take my car,' I say. I pull the keys from my pocket. 'Their car seats are in it, make it easier for you.'

By the time I think of the state of the car it's too late. Keeping things clean takes so much effort these days. I find it hard enough just to wash the kids and their clothes, never mind concentrate on the house. I can't take back the offer of the keys now and my heart whumps as my mother takes them from me.

'OK, I'll do Emma's hair and off we'll go.'

'Will you collect me from school too, Nana?' Emma asks, and I desperately want to gag the child. It's not that I don't get on with my parents, I do. And they were great parents, they did all the stuff parents are meant to do: the stable home, the listening, the being there – and Larry, who lost his own parents early, adores them. But their ability to cope puts me to shame. When Kate and I split up, my mother and I had the most ferocious row, and while she apologised for interfering, things have never quite got back on track. They've never brought the subject up since but it lies between us, neither of us willing to dip our toes into it, much like dirty canal water.

I watch as my mother deftly arranges Emma's hair into a neat, perfectly parted pair of plaits. As she finishes up the second one, her fingers stop just as she is about to tie the band. She lifts the plait to her nose, closes her eyes and inhales. I feel vindicated, as I washed the child's hair last night. 'You smell like your mammy did,' she says, kissing the top of Emma's head as, with a flick, she finishes off the plait.

'Yum, 'cause Mammy always smelled soapy and flowery,' Emma grins.

My mother smiles over at me. There is such a look of sorrow on her face that I have to avert my eyes. Kate was the daughter she never had. I used to joke that my parents liked me but that they loved Kate.

'Now,' my mother says, all business again, as she zips up Emma's jacket. 'Away we go. Henry, you drive.'

Dad sits in behind the wheel and adjusts the seat to fit his bulk. He's a big man and it takes a while before he feels comfortable in moving off. Then with a 'beep' he pulls out of the garden, Emma and Liam waving wildly at me through the window. I try not to think of the dirt in the car, and once they are safely away, I get to work cleaning the place up a bit.

* * *

By the time they arrive back, the house is tidy enough on the surface. Scratch below that however and the truth will be revealed. I can only keep my fingers crossed that they don't attempt to open any presses as I'm not insured for concussion. I just can't seem to get stuck in to cleaning right at this time. Maybe it's a fear of what I'll find when I do. Pieces of a marriage all over the house. Of a life that was sidetracked.

'Kettle's on,' I say as they enter the hall, my mother carrying Liam. I take him from her. Dad deposits my keys on the hall table. 'Go on into the kitchen, I'll just switch on the TV for this guy.'

'TV?' Liam says. 'Yay!' He punches a fist in the air, which makes us smile. The poor little guy has started to screech a lot during our morning walks and even with the promise of an ice cream, he isn't happy. I think he just likes to be around familiar things. He's taken to curling up on the sofa and hugging a blanket when he watches TV now, like a protestor on a march who fears he's about to be moved on. I hand him the remote control and show him how to work it. I'm not sure how much he understands but the very act of receiving something colourful with buttons on it fills him with glee. He immediately starts pushing buttons all over the place.

I leave the door to the room open so that Liam can join us if he likes.

'So, how are you managing?' Mam asks as I pour coffee into mugs.

'Good,' I say, glad that my back is to her.

'I can see that,' Dad says staunchly. 'You've got the place looking lovely.'

'Thanks.' I deposit the coffee in front of them before sitting down. 'Emma likes to help out when she's in the mood. She polished the coffee table with Cif the other day.'

'No!' My mother covers her mouth. 'She must have ruined it.'

'She did,' I say wryly. 'It's tie-dyed now.'

They laugh, though it was a pretty expensive table.

'And on Saturday we're shopping for Emma's Communion dress.' I'm so glad I can tell them that because it sounds good. It sounds like I have stuff under control, when in truth I feel as if everything is racing away from me. I guess when I was out working all day, Kate did loads with the kids that I barely knew about. I know she let them help her bake, but as I don't know how to bake, I can't do that with them. I know there are recipes in the book she left me and I'll check them out. But one step at a time.

My mother manages a smile that doesn't quite make her eyes. 'That's great. I know Kate was so looking forward to doing that with Emma. And to think ...'

Dad catches her hand and they stay like that for a few minutes. I'm unsure what I'm supposed to do. If I acknowledge my mother's pain, where will it end?

After a bit, I say, 'Emma has made out a list of shops we have to visit, just like Kate always did.'

They smile. 'We'd like to buy it for her,' Mam says. 'If it's OK with you, of course.'

'Marcy already offered,' I say apologetically. The woman had rung last night, first to ask me if I knew about the Communion and then to tell me that I'd want to get my skates on as Communion dresses sell out really quickly. What did she expect me to do? Stop time? But I held my fire and she held hers. It showed admirable restraint on both our parts. Then she offered to buy it, as Emma's godmother. I had to accept. Kate would have. Then, to my horror, she offered to come with us. She said Kate had asked her to. Had I not read the book? I lied and told her that I must have missed that bit. She said it was on the second page. 'Kate spent ages working on that book, Nick.' She sounded cross. 'You better read it. It's important.'

I had taken a deep breath and hung up on her. Not my best move.

'Isn't Marcy the sweetest girl?' my mother is saying. 'That's her all over, thinking of something like that.'

'A lovely girl,' Dad agrees.

I make some noise that might be construed as agreement. Marcy is about as sweet as hydrogen sulphide.

'Kate was blessed to have her as a friend and didn't she sing so beautifully at the funeral?'

'She did, she did.' Dad nods.

I had never realised that my parents are tone deaf.

'And you, Nick.' My mother emphasises the 'you' and sounds a little like Oprah talking to a drug addict. 'How are you?'

'I'm good.'

There is a silence. It's loaded. They want me to say more. 'I miss her. Obviously.' Then, pre-empting what they must be thinking, I add, 'I know we'd split and everything, but, well ...' I stop. There is so much I could say but it won't come out. I want to tell them that even though I'd left her, she was my whole world, but it'd only sound hollow after what I did. I want to say that I had never planned on moving back because I didn't deserve to but here I am and I'm not sure I'm doing it right. I want to tell them that I'd change places with her in a heartbeat. All this I know, I just can't say it.

'We all miss her.' Dad swallows and nods. Patting his pockets, he pulls out a cigarette packet. 'I'll take myself off outside for a smoke.'

We watch him leave. I hold out the coffee pot and my mother pushes her cup towards me. We take some sips in silence. How on earth will I entertain them until Emma comes home?

'I was wondering, Nick,' my mother says, speaking as if threading her way from stone to stone across a pond, 'if you'd sorted out Kate's things yet?'

The question winds me like a punch in the gut. 'No!' She either ignores the anguish in my voice or doesn't hear it. Either way, I'm glad.

'Would you like me to?'

I glance towards the door where Kate's jacket, the blue one with the furry hood that she wore every day, is still hanging on a hook. 'No. Thanks anyway.'

My mother follows my glance and winces. 'I loved her too.' Her voice shakes and she sips some coffee, her hands wrapped around the mug like a lifebuoy, her painted nails gleaming. When she speaks again, she sounds stronger. 'I wish she was still here. But, darling, she's not.'

'Stop!' I stand up abruptly, fending her words off like blows.

'And she asked me to sort her stuff,' my mother says loudly. 'She told me what to keep for Emma and what to give away. Here.' I turn to see her opening her bag and taking a folded piece of paper out, which she gently opens up. 'She wrote it all down. There's a copy of this letter in the book Marcy gave you, haven't you seen it?'

I don't reply. Thinking of that book where it lies in the kitchen drawer hurts me. Instead, I stare at the letter, which she has placed on the table. I recognise the spiky, lopsided writing, the way the 'i' is dotted with a tiny love heart. I swallow hard.

My mother runs her fingers over the paper. 'And I can't let her down, Nick. She said after a couple of weeks to ask you if I could sort all her things.' A small smile. 'See here.' She points to a sentence. I flinch back. 'Read it,' she insists.

Reluctantly, I bend over the page. It's exquisitely, sweetly painful to see something that Kate has composed. It's a list of everything Kate owns and where it should go. My mother's fingernail brushes a line and I read.

Please, Violet, make sure to ask Nick if you can sort these things for me. I want someone to get use from them. Nick is a hoarder. He'll keep everything I possess until it falls apart and smells.☺ I know it'll be hard on you but it'll be harder for him.

I pull away and turn my back. So Kate did know that I'd find it hard to let her go, which means she knew I loved her. Something inside me shifts a little, like rolling a rock from a tomb so sunlight can penetrate part way.

'So?' my mother asks softly.

Reluctantly, I nod. It seems so fast. So sudden. But Kate was right. I never would have sorted her stuff. 'Just ... just let me go in one last time,' I manage to say. I can't explain but I need to go into that room, just once, on my own, before I can let anything go. I hadn't planned on doing it today, though.

'OK.' My mother dips her head and I see grey roots coming through the blonde she so rigorously maintains. Her hair isn't as neat and shiny as usual either, it sticks out of the bun, as if she doesn't really care what it looks like. I watch as she gently folds up Kate's letter. She takes her time putting it back in her bag.

***

I've told my parents that I'll need an hour and to come back at midday. That'll be time enough to clean out the room before Emma comes home from school. When they go, taking Liam with them, I take a deep breath, blank my mind and cross to the kitchen drawer. I need to look at the book and find out if my mother putting her belongings into bags is really what Kate wanted. I need to see what else she wants that I have refused to acknowledge. I need to do this for her and forget about me.

The book sits in the drawer, filling the whole space. I touch it with a finger, feeling the dread crawl in my belly. Finally, I pull it out. Then, hardly able to look at it, I carry it over to the table and sit down. More deep breaths before I gently open the first page. I start as I see a white envelope with my name on it Sellotaped to the inside cover. How did I miss that the first time?

I stare at it for a bit, unable to summon the courage to open it. What can it be? Maybe it's a letter from Kate telling me what a crap husband I was. I deserve it for everything I put her through, but then I think that a letter like that wouldn't be Kate's style. If she'd wanted to give me grief, she would have done it in person. What if it's a letter to say that she won't forgive me? That'd be hard to accept, but I owe it to her to read it.

I tear open the flap and a faint whiff of Kate comes from the envelope. My poor damaged heart flips in recognition, like a dog that expects a walk only to be disappointed. I sit for a second, unsure what to do, and then I pull the letter out. It's blessedly short and to the point.

Hey, you.☺ *Go to my room and look on the dresser.*
Kate. x

Of all the things she could have asked me to do, going there is the most painful. I ascend the stairs to the room. I've taken to calling it 'the room' in my head, because it hasn't been 'our room' in such a long time. 'The room' makes it sound as if it belonged to someone I sort of knew. Standing outside the closed door, heart hammering, I push down on the handle and venture cautiously in. The familiarity, yet alienness, of it hits me and I gasp suddenly, taking in the well-known, well-loved furniture and big double bed. It's dark, as the curtains haven't been opened, and it smells of stale air and old bedclothes. I flick the light switch and immediately everything is illuminated; yellow light spills across the floorboards, making even the neglected dusty pictures and ornaments shine a little bit. I can feel her, I think suddenly. It's as if she stepped out for a little while but will soon be back. Everything is waiting, poised for her return. Trinkets, makeup and bits of jewellery are scattered randomly on the dressing table. Things have fallen onto the floor.

There is a vibrant red scarf draped across the chair opposite the bed. Kate's coat, the one I bought her for her thirtieth birthday, the one she'd coveted every day for months, is hung across the back of the same chair, carefully, as if she'd looked after it well. I smile as I remember how I'd pretended not to notice her glancing at it each time we passed the shop window where it was displayed, how I'd feigned deafness as she dropped heavy hints about how that make of coat was supposed to be warmer than anything else and yet light enough to wear without feeling bulky. I'd been so delighted to buy it and give it to her, and I close my eyes now as I remember the rain of kisses she'd planted all over my face and neck. I pick the coat up and hold it to my face. It smells of her. I inhale deeply and close my eyes and rub my face in the softness of the fabric. I press the coat close to me and hug it hard. If longing and desire and sheer despair could conjure a person back, Kate would have walked in the door that second. I feel like absorbing the coat into me, letting it become part of me, just because she loved it so much. I sit on the bed, the coat in my arms, and rub the heel of my hand across my eyes as a tear slides out. Oh, Kate, where are you? Where—

There is another envelope on the dresser. Small and white with my name scrawled across the front of it. I cross over and pick it up. Inside, I can feel something small and hard.

I tear open the flap and extract a USB key. There's also a page with the username and password for the laptop written down. I sit for a second, unsure what to do, and then I leave the room, taking the computer with me. It hasn't been used since Kate died, it's lain beside her bed all this time, waiting to be turned on. But before I do anything, I need a very strong whiskey.

* * *

I flick on the laptop and key in the username and password. The home screen is a picture of Emma looking so much younger, sitting on a beach in her swimming togs. Liam lies on a rug beside a smiling Kate. I missed that holiday with them, having left Kate two months previously. Swallowing nervously, shocking myself with a gulp of Jameson, I insert the USB and watch as it boots up. There is one file entitled 'Nick – The Things I Want You To Know'. I press 'open', and as Kate's face, yellow and large-eyed, fills the screen, my heart catches and studders. I have an urge to vomit. It's as if I could touch her if I wanted.

'Kate,' I whisper as my finger traces the curve of her jaw.

Hey, you, she begins, and I jump.

Her face spreads wide in a grin, her teeth still sparkling white. *If you're watching this, I must be dead, so greetings from beyond.*

Her voice is weak but the fun is still there.

First off, right, thanks for wanting to be there for me when I was sick. I appreciated it, I did. There were a few reasons why I said no, though, and one of them was that I needed you to be OK for the kids. I needed you to go and sort your head out because they are what's important now. Marcy could look after me, but only you can look after our children. I really, really believe that, Nick, and I hope you do too.

If I could just turn back time …

By the way, I hope you're not drinking right now. I know you, I know you'll have a can or a glass of whiskey in your hand to help you along. What I have to say is important and I'm not wasting the last of my energy just so you can forget everything. Yes, I'm issuing you with a warning, put the drink down. Grab a coffee. I'll wait here while you get it. Press 'pause', though.

I do as she asks.

Ready? Grand. First off, the reason I'm doing this is to tell you that you'd better get your act together. You are now looking after our kids and I know they are as precious to you as they are to me.

Her face changes and big tears well in her eyes. She wipes them away furiously. I reach out and touch her face, my thumb brushing the screen. When she speaks again, her voice shakes and I so wish I'd been there when she'd made this. I want to run away but I won't.

I love those two little people with everything I have, Nick. I can see them, hear them, smell them when they aren't even around. I know every expression on their face, and their every gesture, no matter how small, tells me a story about their day. Leaving them, Nick, is torture to me. It's the worst thing about this dying business, leaving my children.

Her voice cracks like thin ice.

They're like the best books I'll never finish. You are responsible for how the story turns out. Jesus, Nick, make it good. They're so small, so defenceless. I would sell my soul to have an extra hour with them. An hour in which I could impart to them all I know, all the things they should do to keep their hearts and souls safe. If I lived until I was eighty, it wouldn't be long enough to tell them how much I love them and want for them. I won't even live much longer, so I'm depending on you, Nick. I'm depending on you to love them for both of us. Do not fuck up.

I press 'pause' and take a deep breath. I'd sell my soul for a drink right now. I drain my coffee and steel myself to listen again.

I want you to give them such a sense of self that they can be themselves. I know it's hard. I know you've had it hard, but so did I. I know how important it is to have a guide. I had my grandparents but it wasn't the same as having a mother and father. I hate to leave, Nick. I'm so angry. I wish I had the words to convey how I feel leaving them. The worry I have for them. The hate I feel for anyone who hurts them in the future, the people they haven't even met yet. I see it all in my mind's eye and it's like waiting for a car crash and being powerless to stop it. I know, with a chill, that my time with them is running out. Take loads of pictures of the kids, Nick. Hang them up. Tell them I'm there, watching over them. Kiss Emma, she will find it hard. She missed you so much when you left and now you'll be back and you'll have to make her trust you again. And she will if you do it right. She's such a loyal little soul. And Liam. Funny, madcap little Liam. Hug him every day. Tell them always that you love them. Tell them they are great people. Read to them. Sing to them. Play. Keep them safe. Praise them. Help them. Laugh with them.

I've put together a book. It's good that you're looking at me now, it shows you've opened it at least. Read the rest of the bloody thing! Do not shove it in a drawer.

'Oh, shit …'

On screen, Kate pauses and, once again, tears shimmer in her eyes. *I won't be there for them but this book will be me playing my part. Don't cut me out.*

'I will read it,' I whisper, and mean it.

I'm not telling you what to do. She laughs, and a lump the size of Everest materialises in my throat. *OK, maybe I am, a little. But you'll be great, Nick. Believe in yourself. I do. Plus, know that there are loads of people around who will be only too happy to lend a hand. First off is Larry, he's such a pet. For God's sake, use him. He's a bit useless at volunteering, he'll be a little unsure of his role, but I know he'll be around for you, so let him know what you want from him.*

And, of course, there are the rest of your card-playing buddies. Danny, whose wife is only dying for children of her own. She'd love to mind the two if you want to get out. And Davy is a little pet even if his mother is a bossy cow. And as for Peter, he's great with his grandkids and he did offer me a few babysitting sessions.

I never knew that.

Then there is Marcy.

I roll my eyes. Jesus.

Stop! I know you're rolling your eyes. I never understood how the two of you didn't get on. You're exactly the same, both of you. Anyway, Marcy has promised me faithfully that she'll tolerate you if you'll return the favour. She isn't as tough as she makes out, you know. A bit like you, if only you could see it. Marcy is easily hurt, she needs to be treated with care. Do that for me, please.

And don't forget your parents. They've made me feel like a daughter and they so desperately want to be in the kids' lives and they love you, Nick. And they worry. Let them have them the odd weekend. Ask them to babysit.

She pauses, and her expression changes.

Finally, and this is really important, Nick, there is one last thing I want you to do for me. It's a plan I have and it'll put my mind at rest. Don't laugh or roll your eyes or reach for the whiskey! It might seem a bit controlling and maybe it is, but I'm dead and I have no control, so indulge me. Kate takes a deep breath as if she's about to spring something awful on me. She often looked that way, usually when she was spending money we didn't have. *I want you, over the next few months, to go out with five women. Four women who are important to me, who I want to stay in my children's lives, and the last one who I believe will be important for you to meet.*

Fucking hell …

I've let each of them know that they'll be bringing you somewhere that means a lot to me. To us. Do this for me, Nick, please. It will start the Saturday six weeks after I die and thereafter every six weeks.

Next Saturday week? Jesus. I can't help but smile, though tears have been slipping down my face throughout. Flipping Kate! It's typical of her. Jesus Christ, I'm not great at the whole chatting to women thing. And if Marcy is the sort of person Kate picks for a best friend, I don't reckon any of these women will impress me much. But I know I will do as she asks if only as a connection to her one last time. I scrub my eyes and rewind the video as I've missed the last couple of seconds.

In the book there will be a section entitled 'Dates'. It's at the back. I've written a little comment for you after each date. Read them. Afterwards. Do not peek. I also want to say, Nick, just so you know, that we can only ever do what we think is best at the time. Once you do that, you have nothing to regret.

I wish I could believe that. If I could believe that, Kate and I would probably still be together.

She seems to gather herself, then she adds, *I love you, Nick. I always will.*

Then she reaches over and turns off the webcam and the laptop screen goes black before flicking to the home screen again.

'Love you too,' I say.

* * *

When my parents arrive back, I put Liam in front of the TV again. My mother has a roll of black bags with her and she shoves it a little behind her back as I glance at it. It's almost as if she is half-ashamed of having to do this job. Dad stands a little behind her, smoking furiously on a cigarette. 'You sure you're able for this?' he asks uncomfortably. 'There's no rush.'

I don't answer. When I turned off the laptop, I went back down to the kitchen and, composing myself, I thumbed through the book. I figured I could start off with a little flick through, sort of like getting my feet wet, before immersing myself in it. Pages flicked by. A picture of buns. Instructions on how to fix the cooker if it played up. The 'Date' section. All five dates marked by coloured tabs. Then I found the section entitled 'Disposal of Belongings' and read Kate's letter that she sent to my mother. Unable to protest, I lead my mother upstairs and push open the door to the bedroom. Somehow, I'm expecting it to have changed, but it's exactly the same as when I found the USB key. Kate's birthday coat is still draped over the chair, her bedclothes are crumpled and her makeup lies in disarray on the floor. The room is stuffy, the air old and dead. The first thing my mother does is open a window. 'Do you want to help, love?' she asks.

From my place in the doorway, I wave her on. 'Naw, it's fine. Go ahead.' I pause. 'I just want to keep that.' I point at the birthday coat and she nods.

I watch as she unrolls the black sacks and takes out sticky labels from her shopping bag. She's also got a pair of scissors and some rubber gloves and a bottle of Cif. She's going to wipe Kate away, I think in a mad moment before I get a grip on myself. But I leave just the same.

* * *

My dad is having a smoke in the back garden and I join him. The day is overcast but warm and the air smells as if it's been baked. It's the sort of afternoon that promises a wet night. Dad is standing against the wall of the house, puffing away. We remain silent for a bit.

'Emma still bossing you about?' Dad asks out of the blue.

'Yeah.'

He scoffs out a laugh, then says seriously, 'You can't spoil her too much, you know.'

I flinch. I'm not spoiling Emma, I just want her to smile. 'She keeps thinking I'm going to leave her.'

I wait to see what my auld fella will make of that.

'Yep.' He nods. 'I can see why she'd be worried.'

Thanks a bunch, Dad, I want to say.

'You messed up there all right, son,' he says. Then adds, 'But you're doing good with them now. Trust it.'

I dip my head. Trust it? Is he joking? I'll only trust it when they both grow up and become happy, secure individuals with no major hang-ups.

There is more silence. Then he asks, 'But why did you ever leave in the first place, eh? Leave a young baby, for God's sake.'

A fury that I thought I'd long buried rises up in me. It's the same fury I had when Larry asked me over two years ago. Can the man not see why I had to leave? Can he not understand? No one can, it seems. 'The kids were scared of Jack,' I say as evenly as I can.

'You could have left Jack,' my dad says calmly. 'Don't you know that?'

But the problem was, I hadn't known that. Jack was like the car I had to fix. If I could fix him, I could fix myself. Only thing was, Jack didn't want to be fixed. 'I couldn't …' I can't finish the sentence. I turn away and swallow hard. Things that are hard to talk about should be the first things we talk about, but instead they grow and grow until they almost disappear. Only they don't. They lie in wait and ambush you when you don't expect it.

I feel a hand on my shoulder. Dad has cast away his cigarette and is just looking at me. 'Maybe I should have told you,' he says. 'Maybe that was my mistake. Maybe your mother should have said. Maybe Kate should have fought harder for you. Maybe Larry should have beaten you senseless. But we didn't, Nicholas. So don't put all the blame on yourself.'

'I should never have left. I would have been here for Kate then. I would have—'

Dad cuts me off with a sigh. 'Maybe you leaving was better than you staying.'

'I'll never know.' My voice is breaking, damn it. It's the horror of finally confronting this thing that has haunted me since Kate died.

'No, you won't. But either way, you'd still be here now, so do your best for the kids.'

'I am.'

'That's my lad.'

We look at each other a while longer, then he gives me a final pat on the shoulder and turns away. I watch as he lights another cigarette.

***

It takes my mother three hours to sort everything out. When she comes downstairs, she's red-eyed. I ignore it.

'All right?' Dad asks her.

'Fine, thanks,' she answers, before turning to me. 'I've labelled the bags for the charity shops. Me and your father will drop them off on the way home.' She holds out some white envelopes. There are names on them. 'Kate wanted your friends to have these things. And there is some jewellery here for Emma. Give it to her when you think she'll be able for it. And she's given one of her rings here for Liam. Just a plain one he can keep.'

It's so final, hearing this.

'So can you drop those off with your friends?' she asks me.

'Uh-huh.'

'Now, I've cleaned the room, top to bottom. Stripped the bed and hoovered the floor. It's up to you what you do with it, Nicholas.'

'Thanks, Mam.' I drop the envelopes into a kitchen drawer and Kate's book seems to stare up at me. 'I appreciate it.'

'Anything, I'll do anything to help, don't you know that? I'll take the kids whenever you want, give you a break.'

I don't need a break from my kids. I don't think I ever want to be separated from them again. But I remember what Kate said about letting people help and so I nod. I'll just have to think of something to do when the kids are away from me. I just know I couldn't bear to rattle around the house on my own. It feels empty without Kate there, what will it be like without the kids?

'Now, I'm going to go in and say hi to my baby.' My mother peels off her big yellow rubber gloves and hurries in to Liam. Pulling him by the hand, she announces that she's bringing him off to the shops to get sweets. Liam almost hyperventilates with excitement. Twice in one day. He can hardly believe it. I find myself laughing despite everything. Bags of sweets can cure just about anything in his world.

'Would you like something?' my mother asks me on her way out. 'A choc ice?'

I haven't had a choc ice since I was about ten and it suddenly sounds like the best thing in the world to be eating. 'Go on so,' I tell her.

The smile she gives me makes me think that all I have to do is discover what my bag of sweets is.

* * *

Rule one, I read from Kate's book later that night, *don't spoil them. You will be tempted to. I was when I heard that I was dying, but spoiling them will only confuse them. They will feel sorry for themselves for far too long that way. They need to know that me dying is not a great tragedy for them, that they will cope. That their lives will still go on.*

I think of my dad's words earlier, but I really don't think I have been spoiling them. It's not as if I've taken Emma out of school and brought her away on a holiday or anything mad like that. Though the thought had crossed my mind.

Rule two. No pancakes in the morning.

Oh, fuck.

Do not be tempted to let Emma have pancakes in the morning. She will try to get around you, just like she has me for the last two years, but I have said no. She will tell you that everyone else has them. Believe me, they don't.

Rule three. Only school shoes to be worn to school.

Boots are school shoes, aren't they?

Do not let Emma wear her good boots to school unless she has new boots to replace them with. She has perfectly good school shoes under her bed. If you can't find them, because she hides

them, they are under her clothes in the wardrobe.
Shit!

*Also, don't let Emma – yes, Emma is the
negotiator, Liam hasn't got that far yet, you're on
your own there – watch the following programmes:*
The Simpsons, Glee, Revenge, Take Me Out.
*She will tell you again that everyone is watching
them. They are not.*

At this point I pour myself a drink. Of whiskey.

*Their bedtimes are, for Liam seven o'clock and
for Emma eight, except on weekends when it's
whatever time you like.*

Ten o'clock isn't so bad, then. Is it?

*Emma can wash her face and teeth herself.
Liam can't. Read Liam a story. Better still,* tell
*him a story. You were good at stories, Nick,
remember?*

*Also, Emma and Liam like to cook with me. We
bake on a Friday. There are recipes in this book.
Buns are easy.*

*And I bring Liam to Parent and Toddler on
Tuesday mornings. He loves it, though there is
a boy called Philip, who is three and a bit of a
bully, though his mother is lovely. Keep an eye on
Liam with him. I have a section on the Parent and
Toddler group in the book if you feel like getting
involved in it.*

*If you get a minder in for the kids, tell them
these things.*

*(I know a Parent and Toddler is not your scene,
I know you hate making small talk, but the other
mothers are grand. Really.)*

Emma is not allowed sweets in her lunches in school except on Fridays.

At this point I push the book away and heave an exasperated sigh. I cannot believe what an idiot I must be. Only that morning I'd sent Emma to school armed with three lollipops and some chocolate, so she could share with her friends. That child must be playing me for a fool. Though it makes me smile a little too. Wherever she is, Kate is probably rolling her eyes at what an eejit she married. I brace myself to hear how many other mistakes I've made so far.

Bath time is every second day. Emma's hair gets washed twice a week. Do not let her wash Liam's hair for him. She gets soap in his eyes. And Emma is making her Holy Communion soon. I had hoped to be there but I know now it won't be possible. Get her whatever crap she wants.

Marcy has offered to buy her dress so be sure and include her in the buying of it.

Marcy and me on a day out shopping. Shit!

I turn over the page to read more but find a large smiley with *Good Luck* beside it. I whisper a 'thanks'.

THE FIRST DATE

NICK

The last time Kate fixed up a blind date, it had been for Larry. Kate assured me that her friend Marcy would be ideal for him. Larry had looked at Kate, thought any friend of Kate's would be like her and readily agreed. Larry hadn't yet met his sporty, funny, gorgeous lesbian ex-wife and was game for anything.

And so Larry and I had turned up at a restaurant in town nominated by Kate. It was pretty upmarket and, to be honest, the two of us felt ridiculous as we were ushered to a table by a waiter whose French accent was so strong he sounded like he was putting it on. We ordered wine. Larry was feeling pretty flush because he'd just landed a big contract for one of his engine designs. Or something. I've never been quite sure what it is Larry actually does.

And then Kate walked in with Marcy.

Larry was the first to spot them and if I could have taken a photograph of his reaction, it would have been an instant YouTube legend. He froze, his wine glass halfway to his mouth. His eyes widened and his jaw dropped. 'I am so fucking screwed,' he muttered. He meant screwed in the awful sense of the word.

'Hey.' Kate leaned over and kissed me and then introduced Marcy to us. It was as if someone had dropped a bomb at the table.

Marcy smiled with enormous Angelina Jolie lips and slid in beside Larry, who was struck dumb.

She was incredibly sexy, there was no doubt about that, but it was scary sexy. A woman guys lust after but who in reality terrifies them. She was way out there in her figure-hugging leopard print trousers, her high shoes and her V-neck top that plunged like the Niagara Falls. Her lips, which were shiny, pink and enormous, dominated a face framed by masses of dark hair and cat-like eyes. Her voice was husky and she wore a lot of makeup. I'd imagine kissing her would have been like chewing through a whole tube of Max Factor.

Larry gave it his best shot. Unfortunately, he misfired and ended up shooting himself in the foot. He said later that he'd felt as if he'd been promised one thing from a shop and ended up with the wrong package. He felt he was holding onto a bull at a rodeo. He held on and on, telling jokes that fell flat, getting mixed up in his words until finally he crashed.

It started with his skin. In the course of a few hours, his face looked like something from the surface of Mars. Marcy freaked him big-time. So to bolster him up, I told Marcy that Larry was dead clever and was making piles of money designing engines. Marcy seemed impressed, so Larry spent about four hours talking to her about engines and explaining the differences between them. She didn't even attempt to look interested. Then Larry, sensing that he was losing her, drank too much and fell asleep on her shoulder.

Marcy shook him awake, but as she moved aside, Larry's head hit the table, causing him to yelp in pain. Marcy flounced off to the jacks, while Larry fell asleep pretty much immediately.

In furious whispers, Kate took Marcy's side and I took Larry's. Over my friend's sleeping form, Kate said that she couldn't understand how Larry had messed up so much. I told her that he hadn't, that Marcy had been to blame. She said that Marcy had been looking forward to the night, that Marcy was nice. Marcy nice? It was like calling a killer shark cute. Only when I said that to Kate, I didn't realise that Marcy was listening and boy, can the woman bear a grudge.

Unfortunately, through the years, Marcy, through Kate, has remained a constant in my life. When we married, Marcy was Kate's bridesmaid and Larry was my best man. When Emma was born, I nominated Larry for Emma's godfather while Kate nominated Marcy as godmother, which was grossly insensitive, I thought. The christening pictures are a study in hypocrisy, with us all smiling like loons.

Larry just avoids her now, as do all my friends. I wish it was as easy for me.

The worst incident with Marcy is one I'm sure she's forgotten about. It's probably a thing she never even thinks of. It was something I've never been able to ask Kate about because to be honest, what guy ever wants to appear like a loser?

But there was one awful night at work, when things in my life were going down in flames, literally. I rang Kate in a bit of a state and asked her to pick me up. I hated doing it; I was only short of begging her. As Kate promised to come over as quick as she could, I heard Marcy, in the background, berate her in what I can only surmise was meant to be a whisper. 'You've to look after yourself and the baby now,' she said. 'That's more important.' And to my horror, Kate came back on the phone and said that Larry would pick me up, that she was with Marcy and couldn't make it across the city.

I was crushed and hurt and unable to ever ask Kate why she had let me down. A small thing, but one which has continued to grow in my mind until I could hardly bear to look at Marcy without remembering it. At the time, I set out to prove that I was not a disaster. I was someone who could look after people too. And that all went wrong as well.

I carry my resentment against Marcy like dog shit on my shoe. No matter how hard I try to get rid of it, it's stuck there.

EMMA

I can't wait for tomorrow. I am going to get my Communion dress. It has to be really great because I told everyone in my class that my mammy bought me the best dress ever and that she bought me an umbrella and a bag and pearl shoes and a prayer book and beads and white socks. I told loads of lies but it's OK because I made my first confession then and I just told the priest that I told loads of lies and he forgave me so after that I didn't tell any more lies so that my sold will be all white and pure. I wonder what a sold looks like. I wonder where my mammy's sold is now. It's probably floating in outer space, looking down at us. Daddy said Mammy is there, all we have to do is ask her to be there and she will. I hope she isn't there when I am in the toilet. I say 'go away' to her then. But I hope she is there when I make my Communion.

My other sins were that I fighted with Daddy. Lots of times. One time when he shouted at me was when he tidied up and just stuffed all the things in the press and he didn't fold them. One of Mammy's very favourite tablecloths got all squashed up. I told him that he was doing it wrong and I pulled the things all back out. I didn't like the tablecloth being all squashed. He told me that I was bold and that I had to pick everything up. I shouted, 'No.' Then he looked real mad and I was afraid he might go away on us because he went away before when he got mad, so I said, 'You squashed Mammy's tablecloth.' And then I cried and he came over to me and tried to hug me but I pushed him off. He was the bold one.

Still, he bought me a lovely rubber and in class today, Amy Murphy told me that she liked it. It is in the shape of a strawberry and it smells like a strawberry. Amy said that my rubber was the nicest she ever saw. That was good because Amy normally has the nicest stuff in the class. Mammy used to say things like that didn't matter but they do and when I explained it to Daddy he agreed and bought me the rubber. I told Amy that her pencil, which is a Hello Kitty one, was the best I ever saw. She took her pencil out of her case and held it to me. 'Swapsies?'

I never heard of swapsies before. Amy explains it. For an eight year old she knows everything. But she is nearly nine. If I give her my rubber she will give me her pen. For a week. Like a lend. I didn't really want to, I prefer my rubber, but Amy has blonde hair and always has good parties, so I did. She said we can swap for a week and then we can trade back.

That is a good idea. At least I will get my rubber back.

At the end of the class, the teacher took me up and I thought that I was going to be in trouble because I slapped Jane again for talking about her mammy. I was right, everyone said so, Jane is talking about her mammy all the time now in front of me. When the teacher called me I thought of this and my heart started to go real fast.

My teacher is nice. She wears nice clothes and always has her hair done really good. It's all different colours like sun in it. Anyway, I went up to her desk and she said to me would

I mind if they did a prayer on my Communion day for my mammy in heaven.

First of all I thought I was going to cry, there was sort of a big lump in my mouth like as if I swallowed a big piece of bread, then the lump went and I just nodded to teacher. 'That's good,' I said, ''cause my mammy will be looking down.'

She asked me how was I feeling and I said I felt good. I was a bit hungry. I'm always hungry at two thirty because it is a very long day, that's what Mammy says. And Daddy says it now too.

She said she hoped I knew that if I was upset that I could talk to her. I said that I was grand.

Tonight I make a list with the Hello Kitty pencil. It is called 'Things to watch out for'.

This is it:

1. Daddy being sad.
2. Daddy staying in his room.
3. Daddy fighting with Larry and Marcy and Nana.
4. Daddy being cross. THIS HAS ALREADY HAPPENED!

I put it in the flowery bag Marcy bought me last year. Amy's pencil writes real nice.

NICK

Marcy arrives on Saturday morning, one week before my dreaded date, looking like some kind of an exotic animal let loose for the day. I had hoped she wouldn't be able to come with us as she works on a Saturday and I'd imagined today would be her busiest day but no, she arrived ten minutes early in leopard skin trousers and some kind of a floaty top. A big fake fur coat is draped over her arm and parrots dangle from her ears.

Emma and Liam almost combust with excitement on seeing her. I had kept it as a surprise for Emma because despite my resentment of the woman, they adore her.

'Marcy!' Emma shrieks, hurling herself at Marcy's legs. 'Are you bringing us?'

'We're all going together,' Marcy says, beaming. She hoists Liam into her arms. 'And guess what? I have booked a special lunch for us in a really nice restaurant where we can examine everything that you've bought.'

'Yay!' Emma dances about.

A lunch? To examine things? Can we not examine them at home?

'And after that, I'm bringing you into a special shop where we can pick out a new hairbrush to do your hair with.'

'Oh, wow!' Emma is on the floor with excitement. 'Because I want curls. Everyone is having curls.'

'Well then we need a brush for curls,' Marcy says with authority.

This is all beyond me. I would have gone in, got the dress and come home, which makes a lot more sense.

Still chattering, Emma hops alongside Marcy out to the car. Liam, in her arms, seems to have forgotten me. I lock up and pray that today is a good one, for all of us.

* * *

I'm rapidly discovering that shopping with Emma is pretty much like shopping with Kate. The discovery is bittersweet because I'm now dead beat looking at white dresses that all appear the same. Marcy and Emma, however, are exclaiming over the sleeves of this one or the neckline of that one. The shop we're in now is fifth on Emma's list of ten. Emma says to the sales assistant in her piping little voice, 'I'd like a long dress with a bag and an umbrella and a veil if there is one that matches it.'

She sounds so like Kate that I think my heart will shatter.

The assistant in the shop looks amused at Emma's declaration. 'OK, when is your Communion?'

'On May 5th.'

'Five weeks' time,' I say.

'Five weeks,' Liam repeats gleefully.

The assistant, whose name badge reads 'Clara', looks slightly concerned. 'Five weeks? Ouch, you've left it a bit late, haven't you?'

'It's twenty one whole days,' Emma says, maths not being her strong point. She starts to walk up the shop, pulling out dresses like a pro.

Clara turns to Marcy. 'It's just that we mightn't have her size in stock,' she says apologetically. 'And we only get deliveries once a week. Most of our dresses have been sold at this stage.'

'Oh, right. Is there a big demand then?' I say, wanting to be included.

Clara and Marcy smile. 'Pretty big,' Clara says.

'It's just …' I start to say, then find I can't go on. I look at Marcy. She looks at me and her eyes soften.

'We've loads of places to visit yet,' she says. 'We'll find something somewhere.' She turns to Clara and lowers her voice. 'We haven't been able to come before now,' she says.

'Well, I'll do my best for you,' Clara replies. 'I can promise that. And if we don't have whatever your daughter wants, I'll look up everywhere else for you.'

Neither of us say that we're not a couple. It's painful that this girl thinks it but even more painful to explain who Marcy is. I glance at my watch. It's two in the afternoon. We've been out since ten. Dresses have been hard to come by and Emma seems to have pretty exacting standards. She's seen nothing she liked and has refused to ask the shop assistants for assistance, declaring that the shops are rubbish. I've the beginning of a headache behind my eyes. Marcy has let Emma make all the decisions.

'Hey, I love this,' Emma calls, as she pulls out a long white dress. 'Can I try it on?'

My heart lifts up. Please let it be the one, I pray silently. That way we can grab this lunch Marcy has promised. I would kill for something to eat now.

'Of course you can, honey.' Clara hurries up the shop towards her. She's in her late twenties, I'm guessing, and pretty in a girlish way. Her hair is short, peroxide blonde and spiked, and though she is dressed conservatively, the Docs don't exactly blend. She does not look like someone who sells Communion dresses for a living. She takes the dress from Emma and studies it. 'That's my favourite dress too,' she confides, and I grin as Emma blushes with delight. 'Now,' Clara goes on, 'I'll give your mammy some white gloves to wear so it doesn't get dirty when she helps you into it.'

'She's not my mammy,' Emma says, and she sounds a little upset. 'She's my godmother.'

'Oh.' Clara flushes. 'Well, I'll give her some gloves, will I?'

'No way!' Emma shakes her head. 'I can do it myself.'

'You sure, Em?' Marcy asks.

Emma nods.

Clara looks doubtful. 'OK.' She carefully takes the dress from its plastic cover and explains to Emma how to put it on. Then she carefully carries the dress into the dressing room and helps Emma into the white gloves.

Emma pulls the curtain. 'Can anyone see anything?' she asks.

'Nope,' I answer.

'Nope,' Liam mimics.

'She's an independent little thing, isn't she?' Clara smiles. Turning to Liam, she asks, 'And have you got your clothes for the big day, little man?'

Holy Jesus, I'd forgotten that the rest of us would have to dress up. And would I have to invite anyone? I probably would. And then I'd have to book food or something. It suddenly seems overwhelming. It was bad enough organising the funeral, though in fairness, Marcy and my mother did that, roping in friends and relatives to do various things. One thing at a time, Nick, I tell myself. Get Emma sorted first and then worry about everything else.

I stand beside Liam's buggy, my mind dipping and diving, absently watching Clara tapping computer keys and making phone calls. Marcy prowls up and down outside the dressing room.

Eventually Clara looks up. 'She should be ready by now.' She calls gently, 'Are you ready yet?'

No answer.

Marcy and I look at each other and I move towards the dressing room. 'Hey, Ems, are you ready to show me?'

'No.'

She sounds weird. My heart flip-flops. I seem to be on permanent alert. I don't know what I would do if anything upset my kids. 'OK, will I give you another minute?'

Her voice is a whisper. 'Daddy, I can't get it on. I don't know how.'

'Will I—?'

'No! Daddies don't do that. Only mammies.' Her voice breaks, as does my heart. 'I want my mammy to do it.'

I stand outside the dressing room feeling powerless as inside she starts to sniff. Marcy places her hand on my arm and looks upset too.

Clara hurries over. 'Is there a problem?'

'She can't put it on,' I say. 'And she won't let me in.'

'I want my mammy!'

I rub my face and I have to turn away from Clara so she can't see my eyes. Closing them, I take a deep breath.

'Honey, only your godmother and daddy are here, so one of them might have to help you,' Clara says. 'Or I can. I can close my eyes and not look. I know all those dresses and the way they go on so I won't even have to look. If you can take it off, I'll put it back on you.'

I rub my thumbs into my eyes and bite my lip. Oh, Kate, where are you? How can I do this without you?

From the dressing room, Emma whispers that maybe Marcy could. Marcy pats my sleeve and heads into Emma, making a joke of some sort. I thank God we're the only ones in the shop. Ten minutes later, Emma, sad-eyed but trying to smile, steps out of the dressing room and I have to catch my breath. She looks beautiful. Like a tiny princess, her dark hair standing out against the dazzling white of the dress. The dress is a little long and the sleeves are a little big. She stands there and attempts a wider smile.

'You look gorgeous, honey pie,' I say, a massive lump in my throat. I pull out my phone and take a picture of her.

'It's a tiny bit big,' Clara observes, 'but if you like I can alter it for you, it'd be quicker than taking the chance on one in that size coming in.'

'Alter it?' Emma asks.

'Make it fit better,' Clara explains. 'Look, stay real still and I'll show you.' She goes off behind the counter and comes back with some pins. I watch as she nips and tucks, and whatever magic those pins perform, the dress looks even better than before, if that's possible.

'You like?' Clara asks through a mouthful of pins. She's on her hunkers and she straightens the bottom of the dress so that Emma can get the full effect from it. I feel unexpected affection for this stranger who's being so kind to my little girl.

'Yes,' Emma says shyly, swiping a hand across her face. Then her lip wobbles as she gazes at her sleeve. 'Oh, look, I've made it all wet and dirty now.'

'It's your dress, you can do what you like.' I attempt to cheer her up.

'I don't want a dirty dress on my Communion day,' she shouts at me. I can't summon enough annoyance to reprimand her.

'This lady will fix it all up for you,' Marcy says, hunkering down and cuddling Emma to her, 'and it won't be dirty, how about that? Do you want it?'

'It won't be dirty?'

'Not a bit. You'll be the prettiest girl in the church.'

'OK.' A big smile, which makes me smile. 'Are there shoes to match it here? My friend Amy has pearls on hers. I'd like some like that. And an umbrella and a veil. And a handbag.'

'I want handbag,' Liam pipes up, and he makes us laugh. So he says it again.

'You can buy really nice shoes in a shop down the road,' Clara says. 'The ones here are quite expensive. But if you look over there,' she points right to the back of the shop, 'see the umbrellas? You can have a look at them once we have the dress off.'

Marcy and Emma disappear back into the dressing room and I sit down on a chair. I'm suddenly tired. When they come back out, Clara shows Emma the rest of the Communion paraphernalia, which is ridiculous but necessary apparently and I shell out an enormous amount of money for it. I buy the shoes there too; I'd rather that then Emma have another meltdown in a shop.

Clara gives me a receipt and asks for my phone number. 'I'll give you a buzz when the dress is ready for collection. I do the alterations myself so it could be Monday.' She takes all the details down. She's left-handed, like Kate. Like me.

'Thanks for being so nice to Emma,' I say, once Emma is out of earshot. 'And sorry for her behaviour, she's normally a great kid.'

'She seems like a great kid,' Clara says generously. 'Enjoy your day.'

And again, the emotion that I'm trying so hard to avoid catches me unawares. I can only nod as I take the receipt.

Once back out on the street, Marcy is telling the kids to guess where she is bringing them for lunch.

Liam begins to chant, 'McDondals, McDondals', which makes us all laugh. I even find myself smiling at Marcy.

Then Emma slips a hand into mine. 'I'm sorry for shouting at you, Daddy,' she whispers.

It's a breakthrough of sorts. We haven't exactly been best buddies.

I stop pushing Liam and hunker down to her level. 'You can shout at me all you want, sweetheart,' I say, 'once you love me at the end of it.'

She wraps skinny arms around my neck. The first real hug she's given me. 'I nearly love you,' she says seriously, 'but I miss Mammy.'

Marcy turns away.

I kiss her cheek. 'I miss her too,' I whisper back. 'So how about we miss her together?' I have no idea what that means only that it sounds good.

Emma thinks so too because she nods. 'OK. You, me and Liam and Marcy all missing Mammy together.'

She makes it sound like a party. We smile at each other.

* * *

Emma takes it literally, because that night, after their bath, when they're all fresh and clean and damp-haired and sitting on the sofa, wrapped up in their dressing gowns, she asks me to find photographs. 'I want to look at Mammy so we can miss her,' she declares as she smoothes down her dressing gown and pushes dark hair back behind her ears.

I keep them up late on a Saturday because I love their company. The noise of them. The smell of them. They make me smile. Larry is coming over soon for a few drinks and I think I'll tell him about Kate's video. I haven't told anyone yet. I have tried not to think about it because it's just too painful and yet, I can think of nothing else. I'll need someone to babysit for these dates. Sometimes I'm tempted to look at the video again just for one last look, one last conversation, one last goodbye. But then I shy away from the pain of it. I've tentatively glanced through the book though and I've spotted some pictures in it. Still, I'm not sure I can face them, especially with the kids around.

'Would you not prefer to watch the TV?' I ask, hedging a little.

Emma takes Liam's face firmly in her hands and twists it towards me. Liam lets her. 'Me and Liam, we want to look at photographs.'

'Yes,' Liam says.

He'll make some strong, wild woman very happy some day, I think, amused. 'OK,' I say, 'let me get some pictures for you.'

Five minutes later, I'm on the sofa, Emma squashed on one side of me, Liam on the other. As I look down at their heads as they bend in towards Kate's book, both of them squealing when they spot their own pictures on the cover, I'm suddenly transfixed by a sweep of love for them. Two small, dark heads, two trusting little kids. As soon as I think that, the love ratchets up but the terror of messing up pulses underneath. I have to catch my breath and restrain myself from physically grabbing them to me and never, ever letting go. Just staying here forever, so that nothing bad can ever touch us again.

Emma looks up. 'Daddy?' Her eyes crease in concern.

I force a grin. 'OK, pictures of Mammy.' I find the section titled 'Good Times' and, as I look at the photos, I realise that Kate has taken pictures out of an album that Larry had presented us with on our wedding day. I'm certain my mother gave Larry the idea because making a photograph album is not a thing Larry would normally do. He'd have been more likely to buy some very expensive and ugly piece of china. But that album was a great gift. Kate had loved it. It chronicles me, then me and him, then me and Kate and him.

Emma squeals as she recognises me standing, gap-toothed, wearing a very unfortunate pair of tight swimming trunks adorned with blue dolphins. I'm about her age, on a beach on a grey day.

'That was on a holiday when I was a little boy,' I say. 'It was freezing but I swam in the water all the same.' I look like a frozen chicken from Lidl.

The next picture is one of my parents taken about twenty years ago. My mother sits at a piano, smile fixed, hands poised, while my dad, his arm resting loosely on the piano's edge, is pretending to sing. They do this all the time, stage pictures so that it looks really interesting. My dad is about as tuneful as a blowtorch. My mother was a piano teacher though. In the next photo, my dad has boxing gloves on and is pretending to punch my mother. She has her hands thrown up in feigned terror. Not exactly a picture to show strangers.

'Poor Nana,' Emma breathes.

I go into a long explanation about the boxing gloves being mine and that they'd come all the way from America and of how my dad wanted to try them on and how the picture isn't real and why men shouldn't hit women.

'Yes,' Emma says impatiently, 'but look at Nana's horrible dress.'

I laugh loudly. Liam joins in, laughing just because he can, and I tickle him for a bit.

Another page. Nostalgia and hurt and longing and love. Four youngsters in their early twenties. Kate in rock chick black, her hair spiked, attitude bleeding off her. Me, tall, not yet used to my new size, trying desperately to be cool and nonchalant, leaning against the wall of my parents' garage, pretending I'm smoking a joint. I'm wearing a tight T-shirt that shows off nothing and a pair of skinny black jeans that show off way too much. How did I walk in them? Larry is just being Larry, big cheesy grin and terrible clothes. He spoiled the image of the band we were aiming for but neither Kate nor I could tell him. The fourth guy called himself Rad; we never did find out his real name but that was cool too. He was our drummer. He was probably the best in the band. We were called The Black Forces of Destruction and we sort of fell apart when Rad told Larry he looked shit and Kate that she couldn't sing.

Emma peers at the picture. 'Larry looks nicer now,' she declares.

I guess he does too.

'You look nicer then.' Emma cocks her head to one side. 'Your face is all smiley.' I guess, despite the cool air I was aiming for, my daughter has just seen right through me. I was all smiley. Kate was there.

'And Mammy looks nicer then too.' Her little finger reaches out and touches the picture. 'She's looking at you, Daddy, see?'

Liam is staring transfixed at the photo. His eyes are wide and his little finger jabs at Kate. He looks up at me. I kiss him because I can't speak.

'Daddy, she's looking at you,' Emma says again. I can't see it at all. But I nod anyway. 'Oh, yeah, Mammy fancied Daddy a lot.' In truth it was the other way around. Kate dangled me on a string for a very long time.

'I think she did,' Emma says seriously, turning the pages.

There are more pictures, none of which are in chronological order. There's one of Larry at about twelve, smiling shyly at the camera, his hand in my mother's as she crouches down to his level. Larry is all dressed up. I'm standing on the other side, holding my dad's hand. 'That was when Larry made his confirmation,' I say. 'His mammy and daddy died when he was a little kid too. Just like Mammy's did. My mammy and daddy sort of took him under their wing.'

'He told me that.' Emma nods seriously. 'He said he knows how I feel and that I can talk to him anytime.'

Fair play to him, I think with affection.

'I told him thanks but I like talking to Marcy.' Emma shifts about on her seat. 'Can we call in to Marcy after school one day? Mammy always called in to her then. You never do.'

I give in, as usual, hoping that she'll forget. Turning more pages, I tell more stories.

When the doorbell rings, Liam, bored out of his tree, hops up to answer, running in front of me on fat little legs.

Larry stands on the doorstep, holding a twelve pack of cans. 'Hey, Liamo,' he says, 'want a can? I thought I'd call over for a session.'

Liam chortles.

'We're playing the "Missing Mammy" game,' Emma says from down the hallway, the book under her arm. 'So you can only come in if you want to look at pictures.'

Larry quirks an eyebrow at me and I say, 'Yep, we're looking at old photos of us all.'

'Well, why didn't you say so?' Larry pretends to glare at me. 'Pictures are my favourite thing to do. Here,' he hands me a can and, hefting Liam into his arms and throwing him over his shoulder like a sack of spuds, joins us on the sofa in the TV room.

He can remember different things to me, or sometimes we tell a different story about the same picture. Memory is a funny thing like that. It's liquid. It's personal. It's interpretation. It's personality. Larry's memories are sunshine. He makes the kids laugh. I enjoy the sight of Emma as she chortles loudly as Larry describes how we set up our band as teenagers. He does a brilliant impression of me on the guitar, all long hair, intense and unable to see the strings. 'And your mammy,' Larry says to Emma, 'she could sing so well. Even better than Rihanna.'

'Wow!' Emma is impressed. 'Even better? I never knew that.'

'A million times better,' Larry confirms.

And sometimes memory is a load of crap, I think. Pretend stories are much better. Kate wasn't a great singer at all but she looked good.

Larry winks at me over Emma's head and I grin back.

* * *

An hour later, over a few cans, I tell him about Kate's video. The room is dark, somehow I haven't turned on the lights and neither of us noticed the gathering gloom, like bad luck, creeping in. The only illumination is from the muted TV in the corner.

'Five dates?' Larry gawks at me. 'Five women?'

'Well, they're not date dates,' I clarify. I swirl my half-empty can about. 'I don't know what they are really.'

'Jaysus, I should have let Kate organise someone for me.'

Despite myself, I laugh.

Larry ponders for a second, before asking, 'I wonder will they be good-looking?'

Classic Lar. 'Who cares?'

'I can't see Kate setting you up with complete dogs, though.'

'She's not setting me up with anyone. It's not like that. Anyway, even if she was, I don't want anyone else.'

Then, as if a sheet has been shaken and let loose to float on the air, the silence descends. Larry and I watch the flickering TV images, seeing but not quite understanding what they mean. Eventually, Larry says, 'She must have really worried about things all the same.' As I look at him across the room, he adds, 'To organise it and all. She really doesn't want you to fuck up, does she?'

His words make me shiver. 'I won't, Lar. Not again.'

A moment of silence. 'Good to know,' he says.

***

The following Tuesday morning after I drop Emma to school, I push the buggy towards the local community centre. When Kate died, I vowed to do the best for the kids, and she did say in the video and in the book that this Parent and Toddler thingy would help Liam to be happy, so I'm all for it.

'Parent and Toddler group this way'. The sign is luminous yellow with a picture of a teddy on it. It's a freaky-looking teddy with overlarge ears and huge eyes, his paws outstretched. He looks like a zombie. I push Liam down a corridor, lit by a large fluorescent light. The floor is old oak and the smell of polish and age waft up, oddly soothing. Doors bearing signs saying things like 'Yoga Room', 'Karate' and 'Counselling Session, Do Not Disturb' adorn each side of the corridor. One of the doors has a small glass window and I peek in. It's full of women, dancing about in tight shiny trousers and lifting their arms about their heads while sweating profusely. One of the women glares at me and I pull away, feeling like a bit of a perv. I'd prefer being in that room, though, to going to the Parent and Toddler right now.

Larry laughed his arse off when he rang me this morning and I told him I was going. So I said, as if I knew what I was talking about, 'It's to help Liam socialise.' Kate had written that in the book.

'Great idea,' he U-turned. Then he added, 'Maybe it might help you too.' And laughed again.

Larry is in weird form lately. I can't put my finger on it, he's just not himself exactly. For one thing, he keeps dropping hints to Ems about her Communion present. That's not like him, his presents are usually crap and he knows it, so he always provides a receipt. I've tried asking him what he's bought, just so I can let Ems down gently, but he won't tell me. He's like a kid teasing his dog.

'Up, up, up,' Liam is chanting, and I think delightedly that he remembers this place from Kate. But I sadly overestimate his intelligence as he keeps chanting the word, even when we've arrived outside the Parent and Toddler door. It's not that it says 'Parent and Toddler', but I take it that the scary teddy bear outside is a hint as to what lies within. I've come deliberately late so that if it's not for us, I won't have to endure the whole thing. I can't think of anything worse than organised play for kids. But then again, as Marie, Danny's wife, said when I was talking to her the other day, I'm not a kid, am I? Maybe if I was a kid, Marie said, I'd think it was great. She has a point, I guess. Marie knows a lot about kids, even though she and Danny don't have any. Taking a deep breath, I push open the door and am knocked sideways by the wall of sound. Shrieks and manic laughter and wailing all compete against the backdrop of a TV blaring out happy-clappy tunes. Tiny tots are bounding around, some holding diggers and others dolls. Yet more tots are lying on the floor doing jigsaws or sitting at a table splashing paint everywhere. Two kids seem to be engaging in a wrestling match, and while they are laughing now, I reckon one of them will be screaming in about two minutes' time. And the room is painted in a garish red, guaranteed to send even the most passive child on a hyperactive bender. Big colourful posters showing dinosaurs and ballerinas are stuck up on the walls, lurching drunkenly. The alphabet is painted along the walls too but a few of the letters have faded badly. It's like a bad LSD trip.

Everyone looks up as I enter, which surprises me as the noise level in the room is of such ferocity that I'd imagine hearing any subtle sound would be impossible. I smile a hello, looking desperately around for another male. I spy one in the corner of the room and feel a whoosh of relief, but as he stands, I notice the red skirt and high shoes. Shit. So it's all women, then. Shit again. I'm not a woman's man, I don't do that whole fashion bra thing that Gok Wan seems so into, though if I could get a roomful of women prancing about in their bra and knickers and showing off their arses, I probably would give it a go.

'Nick! You came!' I turn to the voice and see Jane's mother hurrying over to me. What is her name? It's a relief to know someone, I guess. She crouches down to Liam. 'Hey, big fella, you ready to play?'

'Out!' Liam orders, straining his body against the straps of the buggy. 'Out!'

Jane's mother laughs as I hunker down and Liam wriggles free just as I've got the first strap off him. I watch as he hurls himself into the melee. I feel suddenly abandoned, as if I've come to a party where I don't know anyone and my best friend has gone off with some girl. I stand up and smile like a maniac.

'Everyone, everyone.' Jane's mother claps her hands. 'This is Nick, Kate's husband. Most of you will know Liam.' She indicates Liam, who has hurled himself at a box of Lego and sent it spinning in all directions over the floor.

'Hi, guess this is where it's all happening, eh?' I say and the women laugh. They probably laugh more than they should out of sympathy.

Liam is now turning around in circles in the middle of the floor, looking for all the world as if he's having a fit. I think he's even more overwhelmed at the noise of the place than I am. I watch as he staggers to a halt and plops down onto the ground, looking dazed.

I'm about to go over to him before he trips someone up, when Jane's mother touches my arm. 'Come over here,' she says. 'Would you like some tea?'

'No Scotch?'

'Sadly not, but we give free Valium on the way home.'

I laugh and follow her into a tiny kitchen, where even the presses are brightly painted in migraine-inducing orange. She brews me up a mug of tea and hands me a biscuit. 'Only because it's your first time, next week you'll have to wait like everyone else.' She says this as if I'm five and it takes a second to realise that she's serious. 'Now come and say hi to some of the girls. You'll get to know us all bit by bit, I'd say.'

I dutifully trot behind her and she pulls up a chair for me beside two other women, one very heavy and the other very heavily pregnant. 'This is Molly and this is Jean,' she says. 'Kate sat with them when she came.'

Jean looks like she's spent her life raiding the cookie jar. I know it's not politically correct to say it but the woman is spread across her chair like melting butter. She's not bad-looking, brown eyes. I'm a sucker for a brown-eyed woman and nice skin. Her hair is dark and glossy and tumbles over her shoulders but it is impossible to get away from the sheer size of her. She's like Mount Everest in the middle of the room.

Molly on the other hand, though she must be at least six months pregnant, is not as big as Jean. She's lying back in her chair with her hand on the small of her back. She looks like a Molly, red curly hair and freckles. I know her because Emma had a sleepover in Molly's house the night Kate died.

'Hi.' I nod, then don't know what else to say. I try to crunch on what is an incredibly stale biscuit.

'I recognised Liam the minute he bounded in,' Jean says, her voice like golden honey. 'He's such a happy chap, isn't he?'

'I guess he is,' I say back. 'Takes after his Dad.'

The three women laugh, again a little too much.

'I was so sorry I couldn't make Kate's funeral,' Molly says, shifting position on her chair. 'I had a bleed and was told to stay in bed.'

'Oh. Yeah. Right.' I shift about in my seat now. What does one say to a woman who has had a bleed? 'No worries.'

'She was such a kind woman,' Molly continues. 'She was the one who told me to tell my husband to wear looser underpants.'

'Why, did she object to his tight ones?' I quip.

Molly giggles and I like her immediately. 'No.' She flaps an arm at me before patting her belly. 'We weren't having much luck trying for our third.'

I find this all a bit personal, so I do what I always do: joke. 'Oh, right. Well, maybe better advice would have been to tell your husband to take his underpants off.'

The three of them laugh loudly. I shove the rest of the biscuit into my mouth and imbibe a large gulp of tea to get it to go down. I won't be eating those again.

A familiar yowl makes me jump. Liam is staggering across the room holding his head. 'Daddy! Daddy!' he howls. He buries his face in my chest.

'What's the matter, bud?' I hold him away from me and see a large bump rising on his forehead. 'Did you fall?'

'I'm so sorry.' An unnaturally skinny woman hurries towards

us, dragging a little boy by the hand. 'Say sorry, Philip, say sorry.'

'Bold boy,' Liam sniffles, still rubbing his head. I pick him up and cuddle him and look sternly at Philip. I want to thump him.

'Philip!' his mother says. 'Now!' Philip makes a face. 'Liam's mother is dead, Philip,' the woman says bluntly and we all flinch. The woman crouches down to her son and says, 'You shouldn't hit a boy whose mother is dead. Say sorry.'

'I'm sorry.' Philip trots it out with the air of one who has said it many times and for whom the words have lost all meaning. 'I hope you feel better soon.'

'Good boy.' His mother smiles at him. 'Now don't do it again, right?'

'OK.' Philip runs off.

'So sorry,' the mother says. 'Philip gets a bit excited with his lightsabre sometimes. He doesn't realise.'

I'm unsure what to do. I'd like to tell her to make Philip realise but that might cause a bit of unnecessary tension, so I tell her it's fine and she says that she's sorry about Kate, that Kate was great, before walking back to her chair.

I'll be keeping an eye on Philip, I think. I plop Liam back onto the floor. 'Now, buddy,' I say as I straighten his Ben 10 sweatshirt, 'you go off and play.' I lower my voice. 'And if that boy comes near you or tries to hit you, you come and get me, do you hear?'

Liam nods solemnly and I watch him as he bounds off again.

'Philip is a little brat,' Jean says as I sit back down. 'He always seems to be picking on some kid every week. His mother is too soft. You were lucky you got an apology.'

'Yes, I did ask her to try a star chart with him at one stage,' Jane's mother confides in a low voice, 'but she said that he just tore it off the fridge.'

'Star chart?' I look blankly at them.

'You know, when you give a child stars for good behaviour and if they get a target number of stars they get a reward,' Molly says.

'Oh.' For one moment I thought they'd have to memorise the solar system or something. 'Good idea.'

'It's fantastic,' Jane's mother says with the air of one who has discovered the secret to the multi-orgasm. She starts talking then about all the times she's used it and I zone out. She strikes me as the sort of woman whose house is like a military base camp.

A few seconds later, someone turns off the telly. The room is plunged into a semblance of silence, that is until Jane's mother hops up and calls brightly, 'Sing away!' She seems to be the one in charge.

The kids cheer loudly and all the parents stand up and there is a bit of calling out as mothers locate children. It's as if something great is going to happen, as if Messi is in the building and is going to sign autographs. So I find Liam, who is almost hyperventilating in glee, and next thing, Jane's mother instructs me to join everyone in the circle on the floor. Liam is looking at me with a big bright face. I grin at him.

'Sing away!' he says.

'Let's start with 'The Wheels on the Bus',' Jane's mother orders.

To my horror, everyone begins to sing and do the actions with their kids or, if their kids are too young, to manoeuvre their kids' arms into doing the actions.

Jesus H. Christ.

Sweat breaks out on my forehead. Pretending to be a wheel on a bus is not something I have ever aspired to. I swallow hard and look at all the unselfconscious mothers swaying and singing and taking such joy in it. I cannot believe Kate would have liked this. Liam yammers gustily along as my face flames in embarrassment. It's like some hippy cult all of a sudden.

'Come on, Nick,' Jane's mother laughs, 'get into it.'

I make an anguished face and some people mercifully throw me sympathetic glances.

'It's a bit embarrassing all right,' Molly confides. 'Sue can be a bit forceful.'

Sue! At last I know her name. And then I think that there are only so many sacrifices I can make for my kids. I see that not everyone is in the circle; some women, including Jean, appear to be making tea and I haul myself up to ask if I can help.

Liam starts to yowl and to drag me back down. His wails are disrupting the song and so I'm forced to sit again and feign singing 'The Animals in the Zoo' and 'The Animals on the Farm'. In fact, 'The Animals on the Farm' is pretty horrendous because every parent–kid combo has to think of their own animal and sing it alone for the rest of the group. I choose a snail for me and Liam. Fortunately snails don't make any noise.

A few women laugh but are soon silenced by a look from Sue.

'That's crap,' Philip pipes up.

'Philip,' his mother admonishes, 'that's not nice. If you don't agree with something, there are other ways to express yourself. You could say, "That's wrong" or "That's incorrect."'

Philip glances at his mother, then looks at me. 'No snails on farms,' he says.

'There are.' Some other kid sticks up for us. 'Snails live everywhere.'

'Shut up!' Philip pipes childishly but with force.

'Philip!' his mother snaps. 'Stop!'

Some of the kids giggle at the words and Philip smirks. I do too but I try not to.

Mercifully, we're allowed to keep snail and we get out of the sound-making part of the game. Liam is not a happy camper, however, and I feel a bit mean, though not so mean that I pick another animal. Tea and coffee follow the singing. It's served in the kitchen with nuclear-looking cake and the limp biscuits. The kids get some orange.

I stand with Jean and Molly, my lifebuoys in this sea of mysterious women. Sue is off organising the kids' drinks.

'D'you want a biscuit, Nick?' Molly asks, whipping a plate from a worktop. 'Get them now before they go.'

'No, thanks.'

'Well, I shouldn't,' Jean says as she reaches for a biscuit, and it's on the tip of my tongue to agree with her when I see that she really means she should.

Sue joins us. 'I'm on a diet,' she says. 'It's my third week and I feel that I'm doing really well.'

'I did think you'd lost weight, Sue,' Molly observes. 'What sort of stuff are you eating?'

'Or not eating,' I quip, which brings blank stares.

'Well, I bought these crackers,' Sue says after a beat as she fishes a wrapped package from her coat, which is hanging up behind her. 'You can have one in the morning, so this is mine now.' She unwraps the foil to reveal some sort of beige thing with air bubbles. 'Then you're allowed a normal lunch and then I can have another cracker in the evening.'

'Yum.' It's out before I can help it.

'I know they look a bit gross,' Sue says with a smile, 'but I've lost three pounds.'

The other two ladies 'ooh' and 'ahh' over this. I'm baffled. I know women diet, but really, two crackers and some lunch?

'If I get hungry at night,' Sue goes on, 'I just go to bed early to resist temptation.'

She is joking, right? But apparently not.

'I have no willpower,' Jean moans.

That much is obvious, though no one says it. Molly makes some flattering comment about how healthy Jean's hair is and then changes the subject by asking me about how I'm coping with work and everything. At this point the conversation moves off to something I can contribute to, the servicing of a car and where to go. I recommend Danny, of course. Then they talk about Kate, mentioning her casually, with affection. They say she painted the letters of the alphabet on the wall and I immediately love them. They tell me how she battled to get that room in the first place, how the caretaker in the building was so fond of her that he even got the room painted specially. Hearing this stuff cheers and hurts all at the same time. It's another side of my wife that I never saw. It's another part of Liam's little life that I never got to share. Not for the first time, I realise how much I've missed. I've barely seen my kids in the last two years and it was my fault. I did try but when Kate refused to let me, I didn't fight it. The little bit of remaining sanity I had knew she was right. It's only in the last year that I've tried to rebuild any sort of a relationship with them and even that has been erratic. Staying away from them was done out of love, though, I believe that.

After tea, everyone cleans up. Some people wash the cups, some people tidy the toys. All the kids sing a song about tidying up but do nothing. And finally, mercifully, it's time to go.

'Would you like to come for a coffee with us?' Jean asks as she wraps a scarf around her neck. She then drapes herself in copious amounts of material. I think it's her coat.

'Have you not just had coffee?'

They find this quite funny for some reason.

I watch them leave together, holding hands with their kids, chatting away happily. There's something nice about it.

I catch Liam and bundle him into the buggy. He has a huge grin on his face, his half-formed teeth looking so cute.

'Did you have fun?' I ask him, already knowing the answer.

He nods. 'Thank you, Daddy.' My heart melts.

* * *

On Saturday Danny and Marie babysit the kids for me. Larry had to cancel as he had to work overtime at short notice so he asked Danny and Marie instead. And of course he told them where I was going and both of them are finding it hilarious that Kate would arrange such a thing for me.

I watch as Marie dumps her overstuffed bag onto the kitchen table. It's frayed at the seams with all the stuff she has packed into it. Marie is a fine-looking woman for her age. She's in her forties, tall, with the curvy body of a high-class car. Her laugh is throaty with a hint of sexy. Her hair is thick, curly and as brown and shiny as polished wood. She spends all her time pushing it back over her shoulders or wrapping it up in a ponytail. Her dress sense is a bit mad. She wears these long patterned skirts and fringed tops, multicoloured bracelets, big rings and dangly earrings. If Danny was in a roomful of guys and you had to pick a husband for her, he'd be the one you'd settle on. He's tall too, wears Docs, drainpipe jeans and rocker T-shirts. He's totally bald and it doesn't suit him. When I met him first he had an eyebrow ring, a nose ring and three ear piercings. Age has dictated that all that's left is one hoop in his left ear. He divests himself of his biker jacket and settles down onto a chair.

'That idea is so Kate,' Marie says, grinning. 'And it's such a—'

'Good idea,' Danny chimes in.

'It's a terrible idea.' I'm a bit grumpy at their upbeat attitudes, but they're always like that. And normally I like it because despite the fact that they had their hearts broken over and over by Marie's many miscarriages and their failed IVF attempts, they can still laugh and tease and generally enjoy life.

'Oh, you're in a bad mood.' Marie winks at me now. 'Negative Nick, that's what we'll call you.'

Danny finds this really funny.

'I don't think,' I sit down opposite Danny, 'that it's right for me to be going out with anyone. It's sort of,' I wince as I say it, 'inappropriate.' I think I'm just scared.

'Now hang on.' Marie looks stern. 'Inappropriate my arse. Was it appropriate to leave Kate in the first place?'

I flinch.

'Aw now, Marie,' Danny interjects. 'Come—'

'No, it's true.' Marie flattens me with her gaze. 'Don't get me wrong, Nick, I know you were mad about her but you left her. She has a right to do this. I mean, come on, she must have worried that you'd introduce all the Jacks of the world into the kids' lives.'

For one mad moment I want to tell Marie to go home, to get out of my kitchen. I open my mouth to say it, I even half stand up, but because her gaze is steady, her eyes totally without rancour, reason settles on me with a thump, almost pushing me back into my seat. She's right. She is so right. And what's more, she's had the courage to say what no one else but maybe Larry might have said. I dip my head so I don't have to look at them. 'You're right.'

Marie reaches out and grabs my hand, squeezing it. 'Sorry, but it had to be said.'

I bring my eyes up to hers. 'Unfortunately, it did, yeah.'

She pats my hand, then releases her grip. I hear Danny sucking in his breath. He throws me a 'sorry for my big-mouthed wife' look and I flash him back a grin. Then, in an what I believe is an effort to change the subject, he asks, 'What is that god-awful stench?'

'Buns,' I answer. 'Me, Emma and Liam made them.' I open the oven to reveal enormous quantities of buns that we'd made on Friday. They sort of exploded and went black and gooey. 'Want one?'

They look at each other.

'I'll take one for tomorrow when I want to purge myself after dinner,' Marie quips.

Danny snorts out a laugh.

I pick up a bun and fire it at him.

Emma arrives into the kitchen at that moment. She observes me like I just crawled out of the gutter. 'It's not nice to throw good food out, Daddy,' she admonishes, to a laugh from Danny. Then to Marie, Emma adds, 'They got burnt and they went all crispy on top so they don't taste good. Me and Liam hate them.'

'Cooking with your kids,' Marie says as she rummages in her bag. 'That's sweet, Nick. A great start.' She finds a packet of sweets and hands them to Emma, telling her to share them with Liam.

I roll my eyes. 'It's like a minefield, this whole looking-after-the-kids thing.' 'Minefield' is putting it mildly. I mean, in the garage, if I fixed something and I did it right, it worked. With the kids, it's all flipping guesswork.

'Must be lovely, though.' Marie looks longingly after Emma as she hurries in to Liam. 'I'd have loved a little boy or girl.' Her voice has grown wistful. 'You're lucky, Nick.'

She's right. I *am* lucky to have them but sometimes I feel like running away. I feel like telling Emma to shove it. Just last week she'd accused me of being mean because I only gave her friend a tenner for her birthday present and not twenty like all the other mammies. Twenty flipping quid? For an eight-year-old?

'You can borrow them anytime,' I say. 'It'd be a relief to have Emma talking about you and Danny instead of Marcy.' I lower my voice to make sure Emma can't hear. 'All she talks about is Marcy this and Marcy that. And how much Marcy knows and can Marcy take care of her. Jesus, if I hear Marcy's name again, I'll brain the child.'

'She's good to the kids, though, isn't she?' Danny asks, sounding cautious. He doesn't spit at her name when Marie is there.

'Yeah, but we don't need her.'

'I like Marcy,' Marie says.

There is a silence.

'And so does Danny. He always teases me by saying how sexy she is.'

'I do not.' Danny flushes. 'Anyway, that is not the same as liking.'

'I never knew you thought hammerhead sharks were sexy, Danny.' I try to deflect Marie's words.

'Yes, well, I married Marie, didn't I?'

He and I laugh loudly. Marie picks up a bun and plants it squarely between his eyes. Then she looks at me. 'We're having this conversation again,' she says. 'This whole "we hate Marcy" is ridiculous. Just ask—'

'Who hates Marcy?' Emma interrupts from the door. Then before we can answer, she says to Marie, 'She bought me my Communion dress. Do you want to see?'

Marie hops up and, catching Emma's hand, lets herself be escorted from the room.

'Sorry about that,' Danny whispers. 'You know Marie. Always shouting her mouth off.'

Before I can reply, the doorbell rings. I stiffen. This is it. I'm glad Marie has Emma and Liam occupied.

Danny gives me the thumbs up. 'Hope she at least looks good.' He grins.

'Yeah, you and Larry both,' I grin back as, shoving my arms into my denim jacket, I cross into the hall. I haven't exactly gone all out to impress, wearing jeans and a white shirt, though both are washed and clean. I smell like a florist's, though, as Emma insisted I buy some fancy conditioner for clothes. Apparently, Kate loved it. Through the glass, I can see a big red shape and as I pull open the door, the shape is revealed as being an enormous red mac being worn by Jean, from the Parent and Toddler.

She is so not what I was expecting.

'Surprise,' she says weakly. Her face is a mass of running raindrops and her hair is plastered to her face.

So much for Larry jokingly predicting good-looking women. Not that it matters, as I'm not interested in any woman, good-looking or otherwise. I'm doing this for Kate. That's all. Whatever her motive is, whatever she thinks it'll achieve, I'm just doing it for her. And Jean is easy to talk to.

She smiles a little nervously at my open-mouthed non-responsiveness. 'I hope you were expecting me. I know today is six weeks since …' She studders to a halt. 'Well, Kate asked me to do this ages ago, she said six weeks after she died I was to … Anyway, she asked me not to tell you. I don't know why, maybe she thought you'd leave the country or something.' She laughs a little hysterically and pulls her coat around her like a big superhero cloak. 'It's all a little bizarre, isn't it?'

I feel a stirring of sympathy for Jean. 'It is,' I agree, 'but as I haven't exactly won any husband-of-the-year prizes, I guess when Kate asked me to do this I figured it was the least I could do for her.'

'Kate never said a bad word against you. Never to me, anyway.' Jean sounds a little surprised, which is gratifying.

I find it hard to believe, though. 'Well, she should have.' Saying this causes a lump in my throat. I shut the door behind us. We stand there in the porch, neither of us moving.

'Oh.' Jean's face flares as red as her mac. 'You'll have to drive. I don't drive. Kate said you'd drive.'

That's a relief. Driving will relax me. 'Sure.' I pull my keys from my pocket and 'blip' open the car. Jean and I make a dash through the rain towards it. It's a normal-sized car, but as Jean squeezes into the front, struggling to push the seat back, I wish it was bigger. I pretend not to notice as she does battle with it.

'OK?' I ask.

'Yes.' She nods, unbuttoning her coat.

'Where to?'

'Rith Running Track in Dundrum.'

I put on the wipers to swish the rain from the windscreen. Kate. Oh, Kate …

'She said the place meant a lot to you,' Jean continues. She's fluffing up her hair, which has curled disastrously.

That place means nothing to me at all. It's beside the fire station where I used to work up until I took a career break three years ago. I'd train there after a quiet shift. Kate used to meet me sometimes and we'd go on a run together. 'Dunno why she said that.'

Jean flushes, then rummaging in her bag, she pulls out a piece of paper and reads aloud from it. 'Rith Running Track,' she pronounces, 'Dundrum.' Nodding, she adds, 'That's where she meant all right. Maybe she knows something you don't know?'

I have a horrible vision of all the lads from my team waiting for me when I get there. I couldn't hack anything like that. The car stalls. Hands sweating, I start it up again. My knuckles are white on the wheel. I thought this was just going to be … well, I don't quite know. But I hadn't expected a trip down bad memory lane.

Jean, oblivious to my mounting unease, returns the paper to her bag and starts flapping her green top up and down in an attempt, I suppose, to cool herself off. A mix of sweat and heady perfume reaches me. I switch on the radio, unable to concentrate on making conversation.

Eventually, after what seems an endless drive, I pull up. The track is a little walk up the road. Jean takes a while to extract herself from the car as I busy myself getting an umbrella from the boot. I hand it to her. 'I have this,' she says, pulling up a big red pointy hood on her coat. She looks a little odd.

'Now.' She consults a map. 'Where to?'

'Here,' I say quietly, pointing up the street. 'This way.'

To get there, we have to pass my old place of work. The fire station. I can't even look at it as we go by, though I get a sense that

Jean is glancing at me and about to ask me a question. But wisely, she decides not to. I keep my head down and walk rapidly by. It's three years since I was last here.

The track is accessed through a little laneway which has been tarmacked since I ran here. The walls on either side of the lane are heavily graffitied. After a short walk, which has Jean puffing and panting, we come to a gateway at the top of the lane. Beyond it is the track and small stadium. There used to be a security number for the gate, which I don't have, so this will probably be as far as we'll go.

'One, four, nine, five,' Jean reads from her piece of paper. Then she looks up at me. 'That's how you get in.'

Reluctantly, I press the code and there is a click as the gate swings open. I let Jean go through and follow her in. It is a truly beautiful facility. A red asphalt track with a grass insert, stands that can accommodate up to five hundred people. The seating has been changed and is now the blue and white of club colours. In front of us, two runners are jogging around the track.

I so don't want to remember, but just standing here I can remember the hypnotic spell of running around and around. Of speeding up and slowing down. Of winning and losing. I ran track until my early thirties and ran it well. I ran longer distances to keep Kate company, or just to be in Kate's company. Taking the lead, Jean makes her way to a seat under a shelter and I follow her. I watch the two runners train as rain drips down from the roof.

One of the runners stops and bends over, taking deep breaths. He glances at his watch, decides he's had enough for the night and begins to leave the track. To my mounting dismay, he is walking in our direction. I try to turn away, but it is hard for him to ignore Jean and her red coat. He sees us.

'Nick?' he says. 'Nick Deegan?'

I consciously relax my shoulders and, taking a deep breath, bring my gaze up. Despite my whole life flipping over, it hasn't changed the way I look to others. 'Yes.' I manage a grin. 'Joe?'

The man nods.

'How you doing?' I hold out my hand and Joe, who worked in the same station as I did, pumps it enthusiastically.

'Long time no see,' he says. 'Were you in visiting the lads or what?'

'Not at all, just in the area, you know how it is. So how have you been?' I think I might vomit.

'Good,' Joe says. 'Still running, you know.' He pauses. 'It was terrible about Kate. We heard. I was there. At the funeral. But you probably don't remember.'

I manage a nod. 'Thanks. It's a bit of a blur.' Then I remember my manners. 'Joe, this is Jean. She was Kate's friend. Jean, this is Joe, we were workmates.'

He shakes Jean's hand and says to me, 'You're missed, you know.' With that, he fists my shoulder, says he's sorry about Kate again, and leaves.

'Are you OK?' Jean asks, once he's out of earshot. 'He seems nice.'

I nod but I'm shaking. 'He's nice,' I confirm. 'It's just …' I close my eyes, not sure if I can tell her. I mean, I want to, otherwise I look like a neurotic idiot, but the words … Words are always hard to find where I'm concerned.

'I'd leave,' Jean says, cutting through my tangled thoughts, 'but Kate said we had to stay at least thirty minutes and it's only ten.' A pause. 'Sorry.'

Her 'sorry' makes me smile a tiny bit. 'Don't be,' I mutter. A sigh escapes me. 'We came here a lot, Kate and me. I worked next door. I used to be a fireman.' I guess I still am. My career break is up in two years' time. In the meantime I'd taken a job in a garage fixing cars. 'Being here just brings back memories. I really did not want to run into any of my old shift.'

Jean studies me but doesn't ask why. Probably she knows anyway. It was all over the papers at the time.

It's not such a bad half hour. Jean has brought along some cakes and a flask of tea. The cakes are soggy but great and Jean is good company. Her little boy Kyle is four next week, she says, and she hopes to have a party for him. She tells me that she works part time in insurance. It's a good job, she gets paid well. 'It's OK to yawn.' She giggles, and she sounds so girlish when she does. She describes her house, her garden and her neighbours. And it's not so much what she says but how she says it that is so likeable. Her voice is like a warm blanket, safe and secure. You could imagine being wrapped up in it. All that changes when I ask about her husband.

I recognise the dipped head, the tensing up of shoulders, the massaging of temples. 'He died too,' she admits quietly. 'I miss him so much.'

'Sorry.' It's all I can say. Words are a bit meaningless anyway in situations like that.

'I know,' she says. 'Thanks.'

I wonder if she'll say any more. I hope she doesn't.

'He just went to work one morning. He said he had a pain in his chest but sure, he was as healthy as anything. He ran too, you know. He spent days in the gym, all the stuff you're meant to do. He was dead by lunchtime. It was like this awful dream that I couldn't escape. Everyone was saying he was dead and I knew he was dead, but I kept thinking that he wasn't really dead.' She takes up another cake and bites into it. 'That was the shock, they said. I'm not sure I ever got over the shock. To die like that was good for him, but sometimes I wish he'd been sick, so I could have been prepared, you know?'

'You're never prepared.' I think of how Kate was given eight months and of how she'd died after two. None of us had been prepared for that.

'Yes, I suppose when Kate died, you got a shock all the same.'

'I did.'

She shrugs. 'Anyway, that's me.'

The conversation stalls a little then but soon resumes when someone else jogs out onto the track and proceeds to run around it at an unnaturally fast pace. We both stare in admiration.

'This is so the wrong place to bring me,' Jean giggles. 'I'm not exactly a healthy person.'

I grin back, not exactly sure how to respond.

We leave after the thirty minutes. When we hit the street, the cold night air slaps me about the face. Jean pulls her hood up and shivers. I shove my hands into my pockets and hunch my shoulders up against the cold.

A group of young men pass by on the opposite side. One of them shouts something but I can't quite make it out. Beside me I feel Jean stiffen. I glance at her.

'Will we call Greenpeace to put you back in the ocean?'

There is no mistaking that. I stop. 'Is he shouting at you?' I ask incredulously.

'Just forget it,' Jean says.

'Forget it?' There is no way I could let that go. How dare he. Who does he think he is? I know part of my anger is fuelled by the unfairness of life, by Kate being dead and by the way I messed up, but most of it, it has to be said, is at the twisted humour of this boy. I know what it's like to be vilified. Leaving Jean standing in the street, I cross the road. 'Oi!' I yell. 'What did you just say?'

'Nick!' Jean calls. I hear her hurrying after me.

The lads stop. There are at least five of them. And in the light from the street lamp, I see how respectable they all look. Neat, well turned out guys from the right side of town.

'What did I just say?' The middle guy wearing the Lacoste jumper and expensive-looking jeans shapes up to me. 'What's it to you?'

'That woman is a friend of mine, that's what it is to me,' I say, moving forward. I've a good two inches on him, and he has a good twenty pounds on me. 'And you just insulted her.'

'So?'

'I want you to apologise.'

As a group, they laugh. I feel my fist curl up of its own accord. I take another step forward. I'm not normally so gung-ho. Normally I'd run in the other direction.

'Nick,' Jean says from behind me, 'just leave it.' Then she adds, 'They can't help it if they're idiots.'

It's her deadpan delivery, it makes me laugh. And then Lacoste's fist connects with my chin and I fall like a felled tree. They all run off, catcalling. I sit up but it's no use, they've fled. I rub my chin and wince.

'Oh, oh, you poor man.' Jean bends over me. 'Are you OK?'

'I'm great.' Jesus, I hurt. I'm glad they've run off, though. It's a relief.

She offers me her arm and I stagger up. 'You?'

'Fine.' But to my absolute horror, big tears stand out in her eyes. She turns away and swipes her face.

'Can I join you?'

I'm rewarded with a hiccup of a laugh. She turns back to face me. 'No one has ever stuck up for me like that before,' she says. It's still raining and her face is covered in droplets, so I don't know which are tears and which aren't. 'Thank you.'

'People have done that to you before?' I am genuinely shocked.

'They think it's funny.'

'Come on.' I nod towards the car and we start to walk. My jaw is aching; I reckon I'll have a massive bruise by tomorrow. That'll take some explaining to Emma.

When we're in the car and the wipers are on and I'm about to fire the engine, she says suddenly, 'I wasn't always this big, you know.'

I'm not sure what I'm expected to say to that, so I just indicate and pull out of the parking space.

'It was after Matt died, that was my husband. I just started to eat. And I just ballooned and I can't stop now.'

I still don't know what to say.

'I know I look awful.'

'You don't.' I say that with conviction.

'Nothing looks good on me.' She sniffs a little. 'I bet when you saw me standing there tonight, you weren't happy. I could hardly fit into your car, for God's sake.'

'So do something about it.' I glance at her in the dimness. 'Get fit, join a gym.'

'I've tried all that. All I want to do is eat.'

I'm not sure what I can say to her. If Kate was there, she might have known. Suddenly this woman's anguish shimmers in front of me like a small sun, hot, painful to touch. 'I killed two men once,' I tell her.

'Well, now, you didn't exactly—'

I know what she is about to say, so I interrupt. I am tired of people telling me that I didn't kill anyone. I did. 'The awfulness of living with it made me a bit crazy. But there comes a time when you realise that you have to live with the pain and move on. You can't eat it away or drink it away. You just have to live with it like it's the worst neighbour you ever had.' I don't look at her as I say it, I just drive in the direction of my house and I realise that I don't even know where she lives.

A pause. 'And does it get easier?' she asks.

I shrug. 'I'm still finding out.'

'I'm in Vanessa Way,' she says, 'just two roads up from your house.'

We say no more about her eating habits or my awful history. A silence descends on the car and when I eventually pull up in front of her house, she gets out. Just before she leaves, she pokes her head back in and says, 'Thanks, Nick. I'm glad Kate asked me to do that. You're a good man, she was right.'

And she hurries off before I can say any more.

It's been a long time since I've been called a good man.

I don't know if I believe it but I like it.

* * *

Shortly after Danny and Marie went home Emma fell asleep in the hall, refusing to go to bed. I swear that kid stretches my patience sometimes. She got it into her head that she and Liam were going to stay the night with Danny and Marie. She was howling when they left. After they drove off, she said, 'Mammy is watching you and she is not happy. She is not happy. She said that.' I tried to reason with her, I even offered to make her French toast but she said that all she wanted was to go to Danny's. 'I'm not moving until you let me,' she said, and crossed her arms and slouched against the wall. So I said fine, went into the kitchen and shut the door on her.

She's in the hall now, fast asleep on the floor.

Softly, so as not to wake her, I pull Kate's book from the drawer. 'After the First Date' is written on a pink tag that sticks up. I flick to the page and see a newspaper cutting. I catch my breath, half-smiling. I remember it well. My mother must have given it to Kate.

It's just a small headline.

NICK DEEGAN SURPRISES WITH A SUB 1:48 800M WIN.

Nick Deegan (Rith AC in Dundrum) was the surprise winner of the day in the Senior Men's 800m final in

Santry. He has been making steady progress over the last few seasons, with his dedication paying off in fine style.

Underneath Kate has penned: *Hey, you.☺ Your coach told you to go up a distance and you wouldn't. You knew you could do a sub 1:48 and you did. You kept going. Happy memories. x*

It was my best race ever. I'd never run as fast again. Whatever happened on that day, I was on fire. It could have been the fact that Kate was there, cheering me on. It had been the best feeling in the world.

Happy memories indeed.

THE SECOND DATE

LARRY

It's a terrible business, Kate dying. I liked Kate, everyone did. She used to scare me a bit when I met her first, like. I think it was the way she dressed – even in her twenties she was all in black with spiky hair and a spiked collar around her neck. It looked cool on her and she was kind of cool and I just felt … well, I'm useless with cool people. Nick and me weren't cool at all. Nick tried to be, and in fairness, he was pretty good at it, but he had the Gothic looks to sort of pull it off, all pale face and dark eyes. Plus he was a fireman, which gave him some street cred. Me, well, I just looked like someone trying to be cool, which, let's face it, is pretty uncool. And I had a job that no one understood or cared about and was mainly carried out by nerdy types. My ex-wife, Shelly, she was a nerd. A very intelligent, quite pretty nerd. I met her at a conference run by an electronics giant on the viability of … well, anyway, I met her there and we clicked. It was a pity she turned out to be a lesbian.

Obviously, being gay wasn't her fault but she didn't have to marry me. But as she said later, both of us wanted the whole family thing so we never really looked at each other. The three years we were together was like some elaborate play where we both had a role. I used to look at Nick and Kate and wonder how they were so easy with each other, they just *were*, if you know what I mean.

I was so pissed off when Nick and Kate split. It was like the people I looked up to to teach me about family had disintegrated. I tried to put them back together and probably made things worse. Plus, Nick was my friend but Kate was right, if you know what I mean, so I was totally stuck in the middle. Now Kate is gone and Nick is on his own and he's coping. Just about. The kids are gone a bit wild, but as Nick says, they're bound to be upset and his job is to make them not be upset, so I guess he has a point. What do I know about kids?

I'm thinking all this stuff as I approach Kate's grave. The day is nice, for a change. It's actually warming up a bit and the sky is the clear blue of a sky in spring. About a week before Kate died, she asked me to come up once a month at noon to put flowers on her grave. She loved flowers and the garden and all that kind of stuff, like. The first time I came, Marcy was here. That's another scary woman, only she has got better over the years. It's mainly because of that night, the one we've never talked about. It lies between Marcy and me like common ground. In my experience, a secret between people either brings them closer or drives them further apart. In Marcy's and my case, it brought us closer, maybe because what we did that night was for the best, even though it meant that I had to lie to Nick. After that night, Marcy has seemed more approachable to me, a lot more human. Then when Kate was sick, we spent a lot of time in each other's company, Marcy minding Kate and giving me progress reports so I could tell Nick, and me minding Nick and giving her progress reports so she could tell Kate. It wasn't that Nick didn't try to see Kate, but a lot of the time Kate didn't want to see Nick. Nick blamed Marcy. He was convinced that Marcy was keeping him from Kate, but Marcy told me that Kate didn't want to see Nick because it upset her too much. She said that he wasn't the guy she married. It's true that Nick is not the guy he used to be. Not at all.

Anyway, the last time I met Marcy up here at the grave I invited her for a coffee. Then I plucked up the courage and asked for her help in choosing something special for Emma for her Communion day. This present was playing on my mind a lot. I'm not great at presents for kids. The last time I bought Emma a digger. I thought it was a good present, let Emma know that no one expected her to play with dolls. Liam has the toy now and I'm not sure Emma has forgiven me. Kate thought it was a great gift, but then again, Kate was probably just saying that. This time, I want Emma to be so happy with her present it wipes the sad look that she sometimes has from her eyes.

Anyway, a couple of weeks ago, Marcy came shopping with me and picked out something for Emma and so I bought her a drink to say thanks. Then we both got a bit drunk but nothing happened.

That's kind of the story of my life.

I put the flowers on Kate's grave and jump as someone shouts out a 'Hello'. It's Marcy, looking pretty damn fine, it has to be said. 'Hey, are you here again?' she calls out.

She has the huskiest voice. It sounds like she has an incredibly sexy cold. 'Yep. I think you're following me.' I wish it was true.

'Kate told me to come up once a month to do the flowers for her,' Marcy says.

'Oh.' I shrug and attempt to casually unzip my jacket so she can see the nice mustard designer jumper I bought. Marcy likes designer clothes. My zip gets stuck in the jumper. I decide to forget it. 'She asked me to do that too.'

'Well, I guess we've a date up here every month so.' Marcy bends over and my heart clatters against my ribs.

'Good,' I say, and we grin at each other.

I think I might pass out.

EMMA

I have a little bag under my bed. Marcy bought it for me last Christmas. She buys the coolest presents. This bag is one you can put on your shoulder and it has a big padded strap that runs sideways across the front of your body. It has one big zip and lots of small zips and secret places to hide things. Today I hid some of Liam's nappies, even though he's nearly three and should be toilet-trained by now. I hid some of his cream. And some crisps and an apple that Daddy gave me for my lunch which I didn't eat. Then I pushed the bag far under my bed.

Daddy won't find it. He doesn't clean like Mammy did. He just hoovers the parts of a room that you can see. He says that's sensible. He never dusts anything and our house still looks OK. He likes washing, though. Every day he washes clothes and our clothes smell all fresh because he uses conditioner, which I always wanted Mammy to use but she said it was a waste of money. Daddy uses it and Liam and me smell like Amy Murphy now.

I was liking Daddy a bit more until he came home the other night after Danny and Marie minded us. I was up when he came in because I was afraid that he might not come home and I wanted to be up to make sure that he did. Also I have bad dreams and I don't like going asleep.

I was glad when I heard Daddy's car coming up the driveway but then when he came in he had a big lump on his face. Marie gasped and Danny said, 'What have you done?' and Daddy gave them a funny look, the kind that means that he will tell them later. Then he said, 'I banged into a wall.' Only it was a lie because he looked the way he used to look when him and Mammy were fighting and he was trying not to fight.

I was not staying with Daddy with a big lump on his face. And Liam wasn't either. And Marie said I could go home with her and Daddy wouldn't let me. Mammy would be very cross about that.

Once before he had a big lump on his face only it was on his cheek and it made his face swell up. It was when smelly Jack hit him. Then Mammy had to pour cold water over it and dab it with a cloth and she was cross that time too.

I'm going to watch him real careful now.

NICK

Two weeks pass, days running into each other. Time moves on and it has such a weird quality. Seconds can go on forever and days pass by in a flash. It all depends on what's happening. Parent and Toddler, for instance, is like being suspended in formaldehyde. I go because Liam genuinely seems to love it. Philip, like the heat-seeking vile little missile he is, keeps sussing Liam out and giving him a belt when he thinks no one is looking. I've told Liam to hit him back the next time. The place is wilder than a David Attenborough documentary and no one seems to notice. Jean has stopped eating the soggy biscuits at break and I wonder if she's trying to cut down, or if she's just avoiding them. I've decided to bring a fresh packet along with me the next time. I even write it up on the board on the fridge.

Emma has gone to a few more houses to play after school and when she comes back it's usually with other people's dinners and home-baked cakes. That's pretty good, I have to say. Kate's friends are very thoughtful like that. I would never think of doing that for someone but I would now. For the First Communion on Saturday, Marie has organised Larry, Peter and Davy to bring cakes. She and my mother have made all the salads. The plan was that Emma, Liam and I would make a contribution too but I haven't been able to impart any cooking skills to them, not having any of my own, though the buns last week turned out quite well. We diligently followed Kate's recipe from the book this time and I didn't let the kids add any extra eggs or sugar. It wasn't as much fun for any of us but the buns worked out much better.

While we had the book out, I saw a 'First Communion' tag. My heart studdered to a halt, wondering if I was about to read a list of instructions on what I should have done for the day, but when I flicked to the page, there was just one phone number that Kate had scribbled down. Beside it, she had penned in caps: *RING IT!*

So I did. And it was for a 'Monster Bouncy Castle'.

How did she know I always wanted one of those?

EMMA

Mammy's room is gone. Well, the room is there, all clean and big and smelling like Flash wipes. Daddy brings me into it one day after school and tells me that Nana did it, that Mammy wanted her clothes to be given away and that she told Nana what to do in a letter. He shows me the letter in a book Mammy left for him. It's the same book where we looked at the photographs that night. The book with me and Liam on the front of it. A big book with bits hanging out of it all over the place and lots of tags. I walk around the room and I try to think of Mammy in it and of all the hugs me and Liam got on the bed and it won't come. I even climb on the bed and hug the pillow and Liam tries to climb up too and Daddy puts him up and me and Liam lie there but Mammy's arms don't come around us. It makes me sad.

'She left you this, Em,' Daddy says then, and he sits on the bed. I don't like him sitting there but in his hand is an envelope with writing on it. It says, 'For Emma'. 'It's a present for you.'

I like presents. I sit up on the bed and Liam sits up with me. He copies whatever I do, which is so cute. I take the envelope off Daddy and open it up. There is jewellery inside. It's not new jewellery, it's all Mammy's jewellery. Things she wore. Rings and bracelets and necklaces. And her engagement ring. It's like a big diamond all flashing.

I can't wait to wear that to school. I put it on my finger but it's very big, but if I hold my hand in real tight and curl my fingers up it won't fall off. Everyone will be so jealous.

'You like that?' Daddy asks me.

'Yes,' I say. I hold my hand out and look at it. It's like it's winking at me. 'You bought that for Mammy, didn't you?'

He takes my hand and stares down at the ring. I think he will never let my hand go. I have to pull it away then.

'Tell me the story of the ring,' I say.

Daddy is good at telling stories. He makes me and Liam laugh and when he tells us stories he pulls us in real tight and we can all smell each other's nice fresh clothes. Sometimes when Daddy does that, I don't look at him and I pretend it's Mammy holding us and I don't feel sad.

Daddy puts Liam on one knee and he puts his arm around my shoulder and he says, 'The story of the ring, eh?'

'Yes!' I say back.

'Yes!' Liam says, and claps his hands.

Daddy always told us this story before smelly Jack came. He is smiling at me and I like my daddy when he smiles. He has a nice smiley smile and Jane said that her mammy thinks my daddy is like a film star and we laughed and laughed, thinking of my daddy in a film. Daddy tells the story of getting Mammy her engagement ring and that he brought my mammy away to a fancy hotel for a weekend, one where they leave chocolate on your pillow at night. He was going to ask her to marry him after a race they were going to run. He said he knew what ring she liked because she was the kind of lady who dropped hints about things like that. I don't know what hints are. Anyway, Mammy dropped hints whenever they were outside the ring shop and Daddy just knew what ring she wanted so he bought it and they went away to the hotel and he had the ring wrapped up in some tissue to give to the waiter so he could put it in a drink for Mammy at dinner, only Mammy found the tissue and flushed it down the toilet. And then Daddy had to tell her what was in the tissue and the hotel had to get men to dive into all the toilet stuff to see if they could find the ring and they looked and looked and the smell was terrible and then Daddy realised that the ring was actually in his pocket all the time and he just pretended that it wasn't because he was so embarrassed.

The way he tells it makes me and Liam laugh and laugh.

Daddy kisses us on the head and squeezes us tight and tells us that he loves us very much. He does that loads, our daddy. He tells me when I get in trouble in school that I am not to worry, that it's just my personality shining through. That I am who I am. That he loves us.

Sometimes when he does that, I forget about the bruise I saw on his face.

Mammy's room is full of our laughs.

NICK

The following Saturday is Emma's Communion day. When I wake, the day is clear and bright. Liam is curled into me and I lie for a second in the silence of the morning and I think what an incredibly sad day today might be. Kate would have loved this, she would have loved getting Emma ready, doing the child's hair and fussing over her. It's the kind of day when a girl needs her mother. And then I think of Emma, of the way she's been looking forward to today, of how she keeps sneaking peeks at her dress and wearing her veil up and down the room. I think of how she has to say a prayer in church and of how she's been practising it over and over and I vow that there is no way she will feel sad today. Yes, she will remember Kate but in the right way.

I gently shake Liam awake and make him be real quiet as we tiptoe down the stairs. 'We are going to make Ems a Communion breakfast,' I whisper, and Liam, who hasn't a clue what a Communion breakfast is, cheers.

And Emma hears him and hops out of bed.

I grab Liam and shake him and tickle him and tell him that he's just spoilt Emma's surprise and both my kids laugh and laugh and we sit on the stairs and I wrap my arms around them and tell them that I love them.

*　*　*

It's ten thirty and Marie is bustling about like a loud-mouthed God, berating Danny for leaving the cream cake in the window. Upstairs, my mother is getting Emma ready for her big entrance. I'm fixing up some balloons and admiring the bouncy castle in the garden.

Larry arrives by coming around the back. He's holding a small rectangular package in his hand, all wrapped up in silver paper and tied with a white ribbon. 'Where is she?' he grins at me as he waves the box in the air.

This is his elusive gift. Emma has managed to contain her excitement admirably as Larry, despite his generous spirit, is the most shit present-buyer ever. I hope for his sake that Emma can feign delight as he looks as thrilled as a kid on Christmas morning with his gift.

'She's up with my mother,' I tell him. 'She'll be down in a second.'

And just as I say that, my mother's voice cuts through the room. 'Here she is!' she announces with a slight wobble on the end.

I've told them all that I won't tolerate any tears today and they're all doing well.

Emma, looking ridiculously holy, but beaming like the sun, appears at the end of the stairs. I have to catch hold of myself before my heart burns right out of my chest. I watch as, to the 'oohs' and 'awws' of all my friends, she does a little twirl, her veil flying out behind her. My mother catches my eye across the room.

'Thanks,' I mouth.

She blows me a kiss and I manage a smile. We had a bit of a tiff earlier when she gave out to Liam for shoving his hands into a cake.

Pushing through the crowd, I crouch down and enfold Emma in a hug. 'You look beautiful, beautiful,' I whisper into her ear.

Her little arms hug me tight. 'And you look nice too, Daddy,' she says.

Larry gets down on one knee. 'I bet you'll be needing this for your big day,' he says, presenting her with his gift. Both Emma and I look at him, without much hope.

'Can I open it later?' Emma asks. I can see the fear on her face that Larry might spoil her look by giving her something truly woeful.

'Nope.' Larry doesn't take the hint. 'It has to be now.'

'You can open it and then decide if it'll match,' I say diplomatically.

'Of course it'll match.' Larry's grin grows wider. 'Go on, you'll see.'

'Go on, I'm dying to see what it is,' my mother coaxes.

Emma smiles politely and I'm proud of her for that. She slowly unties the ribbon and pulls off the wrapping paper to reveal a grey rectangular box. Opening it, Emma gasps, and when she looks up, her mouth is agape and her eyes are shining. 'Larry,' she breathes as she once again looks inside. 'Wow!' Her voice is a mix of stunned amazement and gratitude. It seems my friend has hit present pay dirt with this one.

'What have you got?' I ask.

Emma looks at the present again. 'I wanted this charm bracelet for ages. How did you know?' She shows me the present but asks the question of Larry. 'How did you know this was the very thing I wanted?'

Larry plants a soft kiss on her cheek. 'A little bird told me. It said, "Emma Deegan is the best Communion girl in the country and she would love this." So I bought it.' He stands up.

'A bird didn't tell you,' Emma giggles. She turns around and hands the box to my mother. 'Nana, can you put it on, please?'

'And I put one charm on,' Larry says, 'and inside there's a voucher for you to buy two more, any ones you like.'

'This is so cool.' Emma hops from one foot to the other.

'It's gorgeous,' my mother breathes. 'I'd like one of those myself.'

'Next time, Violet.' Larry winks at her.

My mother laughs.

I look at my watch. It's ten to eleven, time to go.

'OK, everyone,' I call out. 'We'd better go.'

To a chorus of goodbyes, I usher Emma, my parents and Larry into the hall. A communicant can only bring parents, grandparents and godparents.

'Where's Marcy?' my mother asks.

Oh, shit. Too late, I realise that I never invited Marcy to the house. Still, she'll be at the church. 'I think we're meeting her at the church,' I hedge.

My mother shoots me a look. 'Did you not invite her to the house?' she whispers.

'I can't remember everything,' I hiss back.

'Nick, she is an important part of Emma's and Liam's lives. You cannot forget about her.'

'Can we get going,' I say out loud, and my dad unlocks his car.

'Come on, Voilet,' he calls.

'She is a lovely girl,' my mother says firmly. 'Just remember that.' Then she totters away on her very high heels to catch up with my dad.

'She thinks everyone is lovely,' I mutter.

'She's right, though.' Larry nods. Then adds hastily, 'Not about Marcy being a lovely girl, obviously, but about her being included in your lives.' A pause. 'I have her to thank for pointing me in the right direction for Emma's present.'

'What?' I am gobsmacked.

'Daddy! Come on!' Emma shrieks in a most unladylike manner. 'Hurry up!'

Larry tips me a salute and grins before running off to his car.

* * *

Marcy is at the church, alone. I'd invited her and a guest. It's obviously over with macho man. Marcy is dressed in a short red tight dress that comes to just above her knees. Her coat is fake leopard skin. She doesn't look like she's going to a church, that's for sure.

'Oh, Ems,' she says as she sees my daughter, 'you are beautiful, good enough to eat.' She hands her a card. 'Don't open it now, leave it for later.' Emma tucks it into her Communion bag.

I nod a hello to her and she nods to me and says a bright 'Hi' to Larry, who mutters a response at which she seems taken aback.

Greetings are exchanged between my parents and Marcy and my mother links Marcy's arm and together they walk into the church. Larry hoists Liam into his arms and I take Emma's fine-boned hand in mine and walk her up to the seat that has been reserved for us. I smile down at her and tell myself to keep it together.

The ceremony starts off with all the girls marching up the church, holding a rose. They're singing as they walk, and as I watch my Emma, I have to bite the inside of my cheek. Beside me, Larry is breathing heavily, so I know he's finding it hard. Up from him, my mother and Marcy are in tears and I'd like to shake them, tell them to stop, but I can't because I can't blame them either. My da just looks as if he'd ransom his house for a cigarette.

The ceremony goes on. Most of it washes over me, until Emma does her little piece. Her voice is like a clear bell and she is truly the best of all the readers. She says, 'Thank you, God, for this wonderful day,' then steps down.

'Brilliant,' Larry whispers to me, and I'm so proud that a huge smile makes its way across my face. And then, a while later, another little girl gets up and says, 'Let's all pray for Kate Deegan, Emma's mammy who died earlier this year.' As one, everyone mutters the response and looks are flung in our direction. I smile down at Emma, who whispers to me, 'That's Mammy they're praying for, Daddy. Our teacher thought it would be a nice thing to do. I didn't tell you so it would be a surprise.'

'It's a very nice surprise,' I say.

I'm rewarded with a squeeze of my hand. 'In a sad way,' she adds perceptively.

'Yeah, honey pie.'

After the ceremony, tea and biscuits are served in Emma's school and I fear we might never get back to the house. Marie had said that all the food would be on the table by three and it's now two thirty but I can't deny Emma anything, not today, not ever really.

She's happy as she runs in and out with her friends while all us adults stand about drinking coffee and making small talk. Sue comes over to us and compliments Emma's dress. Her little boy starts running about helter-skelter with Liam. Jean arrives over too, minus any food, and jokes that the Communion wafer filled her up. Sue looks a little appalled at that and also at me and Larry as we laugh loudly.

I spot Emma's teacher in the crowd and, leaving Larry talking to Marcy and my dad, I make my way over to her. She's young, in her late twenties I reckon, and dressed in a way that would impress Emma very much, short skirt and high heels. It's no wonder Emma thinks she's great. She's talking to another person and turns as I tip her on the back.

'Hiya.' I hold out my hand. 'Nick Deegan.'

'Emma's dad. Yes, I recognise you,' she says, shaking my hand. 'Wasn't she great at her little piece? I wasn't sure she'd do it.'

'She was fantastic,' I agree, delighted that she has recognised how brilliant Ems is. 'But I just want to say thanks for including Kate, my wife, in the ceremony.'

Her expression softens. 'Not at all. Of course she should have been included. I know Emma adored her.'

'She did,' I agree, and we realise that we've nothing else to say to each other so I make my excuses and go back to Larry. He seems to be getting on well with Marcy, she's laughing at something he's said and I'm glad he's making the effort with her for the day.

And then it's back to the house. Emma insists on travelling with Marcy because Marcy hadn't been at the house that morning. As Emma says that, I see a flash of hurt cross Marcy's face and I feel guilty, though I didn't deliberately omit her. I wonder if maybe I should apologise about forgetting her but then that just might make it into a big deal. Instead, I just ignore Emma's comment and say that of course she can travel with Marcy. Larry opts for that too, saying that Emma has to travel with her two godparents.

* * *

It's about three thirty. The day has brightened into full-blown summer. I'm watching Larry as he staggers about my back garden with a bucket on his head and a cushion up his shirt. He's a monster and he's chasing all the kids. Apparently, the idea is to kick him so that he falls over and then to run away before he catches you. I can see Larry being fatally injured before the day is out. I stand at the door, a plate of salad in my hand, smiling at the excitement.

Marcy tips my arm. Immediately, my shoulders stiffen and the grin dies. I try to get it back in place. 'Yep?'

'I think I'll go on now,' she says.

I hadn't expected that. 'What?'

'I'm just going to head home now.'

Emma spots her across the garden and calls out, 'Marcy, come on over and play, come on!'

Marcy shakes her head and Emma, who has changed into another dress to save her Communion one, runs over and begins tugging on Marcy's hand. 'Come on, it'll be fun. You can kick Larry.'

'I might play that myself,' I grin at Emma.

'No. Marcy!' Emma is insistent.

I say nothing, wondering if Marcy will have the nerve to leave now. Annoyance bubbles up in me. How dare she leave, I think, how dare she.

'Hey, hon,' Marcy says, bending down, her tight dress straining. 'Just let me talk to your daddy for a second and I'll talk to you then.'

Emma hesitates, her smile wobbles. 'Be nice, Daddy,' she warns, before running off again. I could kill her. How does she know I don't like Marcy? I've been really careful and actually quite mature about saying nothing in front of the kids.

Marcy flushes.

'So, you're going, are you?' I try, and fail, to sound casual.

'Yes, thanks for having me.'

I don't know how to respond. All I know is that I'm so angry at her. I want to tell her to go, to do a runner, but what comes out is, 'Don't make this about you.'

She looks startled. 'What?'

'We're all missing her, you know.'

Her head dips. 'That's not why I was leaving,' she says quietly. Then adds, 'But you're right, this is Emma's day. I'll stay as long as she wants me.' A pause, then a muttered, 'Sorry.'

It is the first time she has ever apologised to me for anything. I can't exactly say I am happy about it, in fact I feel as if I've been waiting for something to happen for a long time and finally it has. And it just isn't as great as I'd hoped. I shrug her apology off and ask instead, 'So why were you leaving?'

'Doesn't matter.' But it must because there are tears in her eyes. Jesus, I think in semi-despair. She flaps a hand towards Emma. 'I'll just go and join in the fun.'

She doesn't look like a woman ready to have fun.

'Was it something I said,' I blurt out. 'Because if it was, I didn't mean to.' Then after a beat, I add, 'I am trying, you know.'

Up the garden, Larry has been toppled by a humongous kick from a very stocky kid. I have no idea who the kid is. I think he lives in the house behind us. Both of us turn to look as Larry howls.

'I was hurt,' Marcy says, her eyes still on Larry, 'that you didn't invite me to the house.'

'I forgot.'

'I know.'

'Is that why you were leaving? Because I forgot to invite you to the house.'

Marcy shrugs. 'Yes. I don't like feeling like a museum piece.'

'A what?' I'm confused.

The stocky boy from over the wall kicks Larry again. Everyone is cheering. I have to damp down my smile.

'I'm a relic from Kate's life,' Marcy goes on, all intense. 'I'm only here because of what I was to Kate. Not because of any relationship to you or your friends or anyone else. If Kate was here, the two of us would have organised it. I'd be doing what Marie is doing now.'

'If you wanted to contribute, you should have offered, everyone else did.'

She flinches at that.

'And you're here because of Emma,' I say. 'Emma wants you here. You have a relationship with her.' Am I actually trying to make Marcy feel better?

As if she has some kind of telepathic ability, Emma calls over, 'Come on, Marcy! We have to kick him.' She aims a kick at Larry and connects with his bucketed head.

'Ouch!' Both of us laugh together.

'Now there is an offer you can't refuse,' I say, joking.

'I'd prefer if it was you on the ground,' she says back.

And I suspect it's the truth too, but we laugh like it's a joke.

* * *

The day ends, the castle is collected and people go home. I reject offers of help and tell everyone that I'll clean the house the next day. There's no point in spoiling a good party by cleaning up after it.

Emma and Liam are knackered and they get ready for bed without any fuss.

'Thank you, Daddy.' Emma smiles sleepily. 'I bet that was the best Communion party ever.'

'Only 'cause it was yours.' I rub my nose against hers.

They fall asleep pretty much immediately.

I stay looking at them both for a bit, at their perfection. At the way, when she's asleep, Emma has a look of Kate. At the way Liam buries himself underneath the covers, hugging his pillow, just like she used to do.

It's been a hard day but I've survived it. I think that if I can survive my daughter's Communion day without my wife, I can pretty much survive anything.

It's like a small slice of hope has taken up residence in my heart.

And I realise as I look at them, at the way they resemble her, that she'll never be gone, not really. That all the possessions in the world won't recall her to me as clearly as her children.

I love that.

* * *

A week later, I pull a few cans from the press and put them on the table. I hastily leave the room to get the door before the lads ring the bell and wake the kids. Larry had offered to have the poker session in his place but I said no, that I wanted it in mine so that I wouldn't have to get a babysitter. I'd have had to ask Marcy, and while the Communion was a little bit of an icebreaker, it's like trying to melt the polar ice cap with a blowtorch. I'll take any excuse not to have to deal with her. I open the door to Larry, Danny, Peter and Davy.

Telling them to keep the noise down, I lead them to the kitchen. They go as silently as they can, carrying bags of takeout lager and packets of crisps. We've been playing cards together for years. Sometimes the five of us go to poker tournaments and competitions. I tend to do OK, I find it's easy to read people. It's real life that's hard. In the light of the kitchen, Larry looks a bit odd. 'Did you do something to yourself?' I ask him.

'No.' He sounds defensive.

'He got a new haircut.' Danny winks at me. 'Is there a woman on the horizon, Lar?'

'Well, if there is, she's probably running back over it,' Davy grins. 'Into the arms of another woman.'

'Oh, fuck off!' Larry snaps, but he's grinning.

His marriage break-up, while traumatic at the time, is fodder for a lot of humour nowadays.

I open a window. 'Hope you don't mind, but I don't want the house filling up with smoke. Not good for the kids.'

They all murmur that they don't mind and we slide into our usual positions.

I'm dealer.

'So who is she?' Danny asks Larry, taking a peek at his cards. 'This mystery woman.' He immediately lights up a cigarette.

'There is no one.' Larry glares at him. 'Most people go for haircuts, you know. Or maybe you don't know that. Maybe Marie likes your hair looking like shit.'

We laugh loudly and I have to say, it's great to be doing something normal again. I peek at my cards. An ace and a two. *Great*. Cans are opened. Davy lights a cigar. I change three of my cards. I can't believe it when I get a king and two fives. We place our bets. I pull out and try to predict who has the best hand. Larry is looking good, he has a thing where his shoulders hunch forward if he has a great hand. He's well hunched forward now.

Davy is the hardest to read, the quiet ones always are. I find I don't know what he has.

The bets pile up. Davy pulls out first. Then Danny. Peter lasts another round before Larry triumphantly claims his win.

'Lucky in cards,' Danny laughs, 'unlucky in love.'

'Well, you should have won so,' Larry sniggers.

Danny promises to relate Larry's comment to Marie.

***

The thing about card playing is the way it steals your time. One minute it's eleven at night and the next it's four in the morning. And you just don't feel the time passing. The drinks relax you, the smoke goes deep into your lungs and life becomes all about the fall of the cards and the jingle of money and the flare of a match. I only smoke when I play cards. It's hypnotic. It makes you almost forget who you are and you just become part of the whole game. Like running, you can zone out for a while. And then a scream can shatter the silence.

'It's Liam!' I jump up as if I've been scalded, upending my chair. For a second I can't breathe but the scream turns into a wail and I'm gone. Out the door, up the stairs, my heart hammering, fit to burst.

Liam is in my room, running around – looking for me, I think. I can't believe that I forgot him tonight. What sort of a parent am I?

'Liam,' I say. 'Hey, buddy!'

He's bleary with sleep, but when he sees me, he dissolves into tears. 'No Daddy,' he says, and I feel my insides churn.

'I'm here, I'm here,' I say, and I lift him up and press him to me and kiss his sweaty hair. His body shakes with sobs.

'What's going on?' Emma, dressed in bright yellow pyjamas, observes us from the doorway. Her hands are on her hips and she's glaring at me. 'Why is Liam crying? Was he looking for you? Were you not there?'

'I was downstairs with Larry and my friends,' I tell her. 'We were playing cards.'

Emma's eyes widen in disbelief, mirroring my own annoyance at myself. 'And poor Liam was looking for you,' she says. 'You don't deserve us, Daddy, you really don't.'

From downstairs, I hear a snort of laughter. I think the lads have heard her. I can't laugh, though. She is so bloody right.

'Emma, just go to bed,' I say, 'I've got Liam now.' I look into his face. 'Do you want a sip of milk, Liamo?'

He nods without answering, sobbing silently.

I walk past Emma. 'Bed,' is all I say to her.

Behind me I hear a deep sigh and I know I've been judged and found wanting. Yet again.

'Go to bed,' I say, an edge to my voice. 'Now.'

There's a bit of a pause, but finally I hear Emma's feet padding across the landing back to her room.

I head down to the kitchen, Liam wrapped up in a blanket. The child is half-asleep. 'Sorry about that,' I mutter to the lads. 'I forget Liam comes in to me at night.'

'Well, you won't forget again.' Danny smiles. 'Emma will keep tabs on you.'

I know he's joking. I know all that, but God, I can't laugh. I feel so inadequate and Emma's criticism has gone in deep. I grab one of Liam's cups from the press and fill it with milk. Then I sit us both back down on the chair and I concentrate on his small hands as they wind their way about the handle and he starts to sip. I bow my head and tip my forehead towards Liam's. He depends on me.

There's silence for a bit. I just can't speak. Now that I know Liam is OK, relief is washing over me in waves. I feel a bit sick.

'Eh, your deal, Nick,' Peter says.

What if something had happened him? What would I do?

'Do you want to opt out of this?' Peter sounds uncertain.

'Lads, can we take a rain check?' I strive to stop the shake in my voice. 'Just … just call a taxi for yourselves or whatever.' To my shame, I think I'm about to blubber. Jesus.

'Taxi, right, I'll … eh … go call.' Davy hops up and whips out his mobile phone.

There is a silence as Davy waits to get through.

'Are you OK?' Larry asks, and then the others start chiming in with the same question.

'Say yes,' Danny snorts. 'We won't know what to do otherwise.' It garners a laugh.

'Sure. Fine. Liam got a fright, that's all.'

'We all did,' Danny says. 'Nothing worse than hearing a child scream, eh?'

At that my shoulders start to shake. Jesus. Jesus. Jesus. I am crying. Oh, Christ. I've held it together so well. I haven't got upset in front of the kids at all.

'I think I speak for all of us when I say that we feel that fight or flight panic thing they talk about in disaster movies,' Danny says.

'Shut up!' Larry hisses.

'Sorry,' Danny apologises. 'It's just—'

'I can't lose another one,' I say, my voice all jagged. 'I just can't. I thought—'

'Jaysus, women are never around when you need them,' Peter says, and they laugh nervously.

I hold Liam tight and look up. My friends are darting nervous glances at me and at each other. Even when Kate died, I didn't cry in front of them. Truth be told, we were all kind of relieved. Now here we are, stranded in the wasteland of my emotion. 'I don't think I can do this,' I say, and the admission is like being forgiven. 'Emma's right, I don't deserve them.'

'It doesn't matter whether you deserve them or not, you're all they've got,' Larry blurts out.

A silence.

'Well, that's helpful, Dr Phil,' Danny says, rolling his eyes at me. 'Fucking hell.'

'Oh, and what would you suggest, huh?' Larry asks.

'No one loves those kids like you, Nick,' Davy chimes in. 'You'll be great.'

They all chorus a 'Yes'. What they really mean, I think, is, 'Please stop it now, Nick.'

'My folks love them as much,' I say.

'For feck's sake, you're their dad!' Larry sounds cross.

'Bloody Marcy does,' I say again.

'Marcy's a bitch,' Davy contributes. 'Forget about her.'

The others all chorus their support for that statement.

'If only I could,' I say. 'They love her minding them. She knows what to play, how to make them laugh, she—'

'Nick,' Danny interrupts, crouching down beside me. 'So you were playing cards and forgot the time. Big deal. It was a mistake. Give yourself a break. It's not undoable. Some things are, this isn't.'

A silence descends. I know they're all thinking of the undoable mistake I made four years ago.

But he has a point. 'I guess.'

'I mean, once I lost track of time and forgot to pick Marie up from the train. Gigantic mistake.'

The tension eases as we laugh quietly.

'Marie is one scary woman,' I grin.

'Once I forgot the time and my runny egg turned hard,' Peter contributes. 'And it was the last egg I had.'

'I forgot the time and left the immersion on,' Davy says. 'Me ma killed me when she got the bill.'

They all look at Larry. 'I married a lesbian,' he offers. It's his winning hand, his trump card. The 'my life is way shittier than yours' sympathy vote. It's a crock of shit, though, because Larry loves his life.

'A hot lesbian, though,' Davy reminds him.

'Yeah.' Larry nods. 'I should've known she was way out of my league.'

'Thing is,' Danny says, 'we all learn from our mistakes.' He smirks a tiny bit. 'Larry will never, ever again go for a woman way out of his league. Will you, Larry?'

'Like you did, you mean?'

Now everyone laughs. In my arms, Liam stirs a little.

'Yeah, like me,' Danny says. 'I had the personality to carry it off, though.'

Larry sneers at him. He sneers back.

I envy them their lives. Mine was once like that, now it's taken this whole other direction.

'Look,' I say, 'sorry for all ...,' I shrug, '... that.'

They all wave my apology away, only too glad it seems to be over.

'But I'm struggling,' I go on. 'Like, I'm trying hard, but every day here is like groundhog day. And when I think I've everything right, something else comes along and fucks it up.'

'Like what?' Larry asks. 'I think you're doing well.'

They all agree that I am.

'Emma is not happy,' I admit. 'Sometimes I think she hates me.'

'She lost her mother,' Danny says. 'How the fuck would she be happy?'

'She doesn't hate you,' Larry adds. 'She just thinks that you don't deserve her. The kid's got great self-esteem, I'll give her that.'

They laugh. 'We're here, though,' Larry says then. 'Like, if you want a hand. You know we are.'

'Yeah, Kate told us to be here,' Davy says.

'But we would've been anyway.' Peter nods. 'It's not every day your wife dies.'

That shuts us up for a second.

'Thanks. I appreciate it.' And that's when we've all had enough. 'So, cards?' I say.

'Just don't go and take advantage of our good nature, though,' Danny admonishes. 'We're not supermen, you know.'

And with that, after Liam falls asleep and I tuck him up in my bed, we sit back into the table and play another few rounds. No one smokes and I lose every hand.

I wonder if it means that, despite everything, I was lucky in love.

I think it does.

* * *

It's the following Tuesday. Parent and Toddler time. I'm dropping Emma off to school and she has run on ahead with her best friend, Saoirse. Emma is the sort of kid that seems to have a different best friend every week but Saoirse is a girl whose house she has gone to a couple of times after school. And when Abby, her mother, dropped Emma back the last time, she even offered to mind the kids if I wanted to go out some night, but I haven't taken her up on it. Today she bounces over to me. She's small, round, looks like she could be a good laugh on a lads' night out.

'Nick, hi.' She smiles. 'How are you getting on?'

'Not so bad. Haven't been late for school yet,' I grin. It's getting a little easier to talk to these women, though the conversations tend to be quite generic. Usually of the 'how are you managing?' variety. I'm happy with that.

'Go, Daddy!' Liam kicks his legs about.

'Parent and Toddler,' I say, rolling my eyes. 'He loves it.'

'Oh, I remember that,' Abby chortles. 'Kate and I set it up. We were both so lonely at home with the babies.'

Lonely? Kate had never said. She'd wanted to give up her job to stay at home, which had been a surprise as her job paid more than mine. 'Yeah?'

'Do they still sit in a circle on the floor and sing?'

'Unfortunately.'

Her laugher is like a wheezy car starting up. 'That was Sue.' Her voice dips and she glances around furtively. 'She came along and convinced us all to do it. Said it was an American thing that was very beneficial to children. Kate used to change the words of all the songs. One time she sang, 'Old McDonald had a harem, uh, uh, uh, uh, uh. Sue went mad. Told Kate she'd ban her, but as Kate had set it up …'

My laughter joins hers. I'm so glad Abby told me that. The more I sat and sang, the more I felt that I didn't know Kate. I feel a reconnection with her now, the fact she hated it too. 'He loves the singing, though.' I nod to Liam. 'I'm very disappointed in him for that.'

Abby laughs again and falls into step with me. She's quite fit and is well able to keep up with my strides. Her whole personality fizzes with energy. I can easily see her and Kate being friends.

'Hello!'

It's Jean. She's come from behind us at quite a pace. She's wearing a grey tracksuit with the Nike logo and a 'Just Do It' scrawled across the top in big purple letters. She's pushing her son in a buggy and she looks as if she's just climbed Everest, that much sweat is pumping off her.

'Hi, Jean,' Abby says. 'Looking good.'

'I look terrible, but I *will* look good,' Jean announces breathlessly. She bends over and takes deep, gasping breaths. 'I've lost five pounds so far this week.'

'Brilliant.' Abby gives a little cheer and I smile. It's great to see

Jean being so proactive. Touching my hand, Abby says, 'You know where I am if you need me.' Then she turns off into her estate.

'Mind if I walk with you?' Jean pants. 'Only you have to walk fast, I'm making every movement count.'

'Sure.' I start to push Liam along too and he and Kyle jabber to each other. 'Jogging will get you in shape a lot quicker,' I tell Jean.

Laughter wheezes out of her and she flaps a hand at me. 'Oh, I couldn't. I'd never manage that. I can barely run ten feet.'

'Well, you start off by running eight feet and build it. Exercise is better than starving yourself,' I say. I used to be fit, I knew all the rules, all the things to eat or not to eat. I don't know why I stopped running.

'I'd feel stupid jogging along.'

'I'll go with you.' I don't know what possesses me to say that except that in some weird way, Jean reminds me of me. Trying to do what seems bloody impossible. And when I'd seen that guy fly around the track that night, something in me had yearned to do it too.

'Oh, you'd be faster than me.' She waves me away.

'Well, I'd slow down, try and get you to go faster.'

'You wouldn't want to be doing that.' Her face goes red and I think I've embarrassed her.

'Why not?'

'Look at me!' And she stops walking. She stands in front of me and indicates herself. 'Look at the state of me.'

'I am. And I think jogging will do you good.'

She swallows hard. I wonder if that was the right response. Maybe I should have said there was nothing wrong with the state of her, or something.

'We could go at night,' I blunder on. 'I'll get my friend to mind the kids for an hour or so and we could meet up.'

'I'm not a jogger.' She sounds very firm.

'And I'm not a great parent but I'm trying it.'

That floors her. 'You are a great parent, don't be silly.'

I realise then that I should have said that she wasn't a state. 'I'm really not, Jean. I'm sure Kate filled you in.'

She reddens up again. 'No, Kate didn't,' she says.

'Anyway, the offer's there. I'm unfit too. Might be good to get out and about.' I turn back to push Liam, who has begun to whinge about the delay.

'I will never walk with you again.' Jean catches up and laughs with a wheeze. 'God knows what you'll have me doing next. Running the marathon, probably.'

'So, you're on for a run, then?'

'I'll try it out. I can't promise anything.'

I grin. I'm beginning to realise that promises are for complete optimists or gobshites.

'Me neither. Let me sort something out with a friend and I'll get back to you in a couple of weeks.'

***

The Parent and Toddler is mental as always and I manage to offend Sue by presenting her with a biscuit tin to keep the biscuits fresh. It makes me grin thinking about it. Molly and Jean had spent the time sniggering away at Sue's reaction, telling me that Sue would have it in for me now.

At three I collect Emma. Weekdays are good like that, they give us all structure. Structure is good, Kate wrote in the book, so we're all timetabled up now. Well, except for bedtimes, that's still a problem.

Liam likes to stand up in his buggy to see if he can spot Emma coming out of her school. Sometimes I put him on my shoulders and I keep asking him, 'Can you see her, can you see her?' and when he spots her he starts to wave and clap. People around always laugh.

I hope he'll always love her as much.

Today, Emma wanders out alone, her bag strapped tightly to her back, her coat slung over an arm. She looks a little cross over something but brightens when she sees Liam waving at her. 'Hello, cutest little boy in the world,' she says in a baby voice. Then she flicks a glance at me. 'Hi, Daddy.'

'Hey, munchkin.' I rub her head and she immediately smoothes her hair down. 'I thought we could drop in and see Marcy, give her her present from Mammy, what do you think?'

Her pout broadens into a smile and she agrees immediately.

The walk to Marcy's beauty place takes about fifteen minutes and is only slightly out of our way. Marcy is a walking advertisement for her job, long fake nails, long fake eyelashes, fake skin colour, fake hair colour. I've never seen the woman without makeup. Her salon is in the local village, just on the corner of Yellow Halls Road. It's not a big place. Marcy's name is painted in blue over the door.

Today, as we near, the place looks a little grubby. Maybe it's just the way the strong sunlight highlights the smears on the half-cleaned windows or the fact that the premises beside hers has been freshly painted. Whatever the reason, it looks more run-down than I've ever seen it before. Pushing open the door, I'm surprised that it's empty save for Marcy and a lone man at the counter. I'm even more surprised when the lone man turns and it's Larry.

He jumps, looking a little guilty. 'Hey,' he says, avoiding my eyes, before turning to the kids. 'How are my very favourite people today?'

'I didn't know you'd be here,' Emma says. 'I thought you hated Marcy.'

Oh, shit.

Larry flushes. I flush.

Marcy looks a little hurt.

'No,' Larry splutters, 'I don't hate her. Sure if I did, why am I here?'

'Yeah, why *are* you here?' I ask. For one mad moment, I wonder if Marcy and Larry have a thing going. But there is no way, he's not her type and vice versa. And Marcy has just broken up with her boyfriend. I think.

Larry winces at my question and he and Marcy look uneasily at each other.

'I'll bring you up to the shops for an ice cream,' he says cheerfully, holding his hand out for Emma to grasp, which of course she does. 'How 'bout that?'

Is he bailing?

'OK.' Emma gleefully forgets that she was the one who insisted that she wanted to give the envelope to Marcy. An offer of an ice cream and she's anybody's. But I underestimate her. 'Can it wait until we get back, Daddy?' she asks, stressing the 'it'.

'Go on,' I grin.

Marcy says nothing until they are gone. Then she heaves a sigh and says, 'I guess your friend has left it to me to explain what he was doing here.'

'None of my business.'

She ignores that. 'I guess he didn't want to say it in front of Emma and Liam but he was here asking me what sort of flowers to get tomorrow.'

'Flowers?'

Marcy bites her lip. 'Kate asked us to tend to her grave,' she says quietly. 'Well, she asked me but she also asked Larry for some reason and for the last two months we've met each other up there, both of us carrying flowers. Today, Larry thought one big bunch would be better than two separate bunches and …' Her voice shakes and trails off. She absently traces a finger along her appointment book, which looks pretty empty.

'Right,' I say in a matter of fact voice. 'I see. Grand.'

Then we spend a few seconds in silence, both of us praying for the kids to come back.

'So,' she says after a bit, when the silence has stretched beyond comfortable, 'are you ever going to go to the grave?'

I flinch, the question like a shot of shrapnel. 'Dunno.' What's the point in going to a place where the only memory is of burying my wife?

'Oh,' Marcy says, not meaning 'oh' at all. Meaning something far worse.

'What?' I say, irritated.

'Nothing, I said nothing.'

'You have a way of saying nothing.'

She holds up her hands and barks out a laugh. 'You have a way of misinterpreting everything.'

I let it drop.

'So what are you doing here? Kate always called on a Wednesday with the two and I'd shut up shop and we'd go for a coffee.' The memory makes her smile and her face softens.

'I'll let Emma tell you.' I find myself smiling a little.

'Can't wait.'

It takes a very long few minutes for them to arrive back. I watch Larry as he swings Liam by the arms up and down. Liam has a massive ice cream in his hand. He'll either be sick or drop it. But he's laughing so hard, it makes both of us smile.

'They love him, don't they?' Marcy remarks affectionately. 'It's so nice he can make them laugh after …,' her voice dips, '… everything,' she says softly.

'Yeah, it is,' I agree.

Larry bounds into the shop, Emma pushing open the door for him. She eyeballs me. 'Did you tell Marcy?' she demands sternly.

'I did not.' I hand Emma the envelope and she hands me her ice pop.

'Me too,' Liam pipes up, and Emma lets him hold half of the envelope in an ice-creamy hand. 'For you,' Emma announces, 'from my mammy.'

Marcy's mouth forms a perfect 'o' and she blinks rapidly. 'Really?'
Emma nods, and Marcy takes the envelope from them.

'Will I open it?' Marcy asks, hunkering down to the kids' level.
Over their heads, Larry grins at me.

Marcy carefully tears open the flap of the envelope and empties its contents onto her palm. It's Kate's sapphire and ruby bracelet, along with a little note. Kate had bought the bracelet as a treat to herself on holiday one year. 'I always loved this,' Marcy says as she holds the bracelet up so that Emma and Liam can see it, before clipping it around her wrist. 'I am never going to take it off.'

'It might get wrecked in the shower,' Emma says seriously.

'OK, well maybe I'll take it off in the shower,' Marcy concedes.

I have a sudden image of this woman in the shower and I have to banish it. Marcy was never someone I looked at in that way but I think lack of sex is really catching up on me. I can barely remember the last time I was with a woman. But God, do I need it. Even just comfort sex.

'Daddy.' Emma is pulling at my arm. 'Marcy is asking you something.'

'Huh? Yeah?' I glance at her. 'What?'

'I said can I take the kids to a movie on Saturday, maybe let them have a sleepover.'

I dread being alone in the house. 'Liam likes to come in to me at night.'

'Well, I'll mind him good. You know me, don't you, Liamo?'

'Liam know you,' he says.

'We could go out,' Larry says. 'Might be good, Nick.'

I wonder if they've planned this but it seems unlikely. Maybe I do need a night out and I could crash in Larry's and not have to go home. Me and Larry on the tear. Getting drunk, forgetting for a while. A date with Larry is bound to be preferable to the date I'm going to face the following week. That's one I'm trying to forget.

Marcy looks from one to the other of us.

'Well, if Liam gets upset, call me.'

'I'll mind him, Daddy,' Emma says.

'OK so.'

Emma cheers and Marcy joins in.

* * *

Marcy collects the kids pretty early on Saturday. She arrives just as dinner is over and I've banished Emma upstairs to get changed. The doorbell rings as I lift Liam from his high chair. He's managed to get red sauce all over himself and he thinks nothing of smearing it over my face. I'm pretending to chew his fingers off and he's laughing in the way kids do, chuckling and infectious.

'Have I come too early?' Marcy looks at the state of us. I'm in a T-shirt and shorts. 'I thought five would be late enough.'

'Marcy!' Emma calls from upstairs. 'Quick, help me pick what to wear.'

Marcy glances at me.

'You heard her. I wouldn't cross her if I were you,' I joke.

Marcy click-clacks across the hall in her too-high shoes. I don't know why she wears them, she's tall enough as it is.

It takes about forty minutes to get the kids ready and then I pack their overnight bags. Emma can't find the one Marcy gave her a while ago, so I'm forced to hand her a recycle shopping bag. Marcy bundles them into her car, promising to give me updates about how they're getting on, and then I wave them off.

The door closes and echoes in the emptiness.

* * *

Larry and I have decided to do a pub crawl. It was something we used to do years ago, before everything went wrong for both of us.

We'd aim to have a pint in every pub in town if we could. By the end, we'd stagger home to either his place or mine. Life was fun.

It's ten o'clock and we're in our fifth pub. The alcohol buzz is kicking in. This pub isn't too crowded, obviously not being one of the 'in' places. I like it. There's a new millennium vibe off it, a little dated, a little modern. The thing about being with Larry is that it's easy. We can just sit there and appreciate a good pint. Kate used to joke that we were like two auld fellas off a sitcom. Maybe we are.

Then I think of something I should say. Something I should've said ages ago. 'Sorry.'

'What?' Larry looks at me.

'Sorry for the time I hit you. I've felt bad ever since.'

'I figured you would. I was kind of enjoying your suffering.'

'Fuck off or I might hit you again.'

He laughs.

The silence descends again.

I'd hit him when he asked me why I was leaving Kate. He'd called to the house the morning I was packing, maybe Kate rang him, I don't know. As I tried to leave, Larry had barred my way. Kate was shouting at Larry to let me go, I was shouting at Larry to let me go, Larry was refusing. The kids were bawling and Jack was calmly smoking a cigarette in the front garden. Larry did the thing no one ever does, he got involved. He probably shouldn't have. I tried to push past him. He pushed me back, quite hard. I hit him, right in the face. I had no idea that he wouldn't move out of the way.

'I thought you'd move out of the way.'

'I thought you'd chicken out.'

More silence.

'Why'd you do it anyway? It wasn't your business.'

Larry shrugs. 'You had what I never had, Nick. You had a great family. I wanted you to keep it.'

'Well, thanks for trying.'

We drink and move to another pub.

In the next place, I buy the pints. I'm a little unsteady on my feet, way out of practice. Larry takes an appreciative sip. 'This is my all-time favourite place for a beer,' he says.

'Hey, hi,' a friendly, chirpy voice says.

I turn and see a girl, late twenties, early thirties maybe, with a funky-looking hairstyle, wearing jeans and Docs and a green-fringed top. I have no idea who she is, though I know I've seen her somewhere before. I think that she might be a friend of Larry's from work, though he's looking at me. There's another girl behind the first, with a long fringe that obscures one eye. I know I definitely haven't seen her before, I'd recognise that fringe.

'Oh, God,' the first girl says, 'this is embarrassing, I thought you were someone I knew well, and now I realise who you are!' She dissolves in a laugh. 'And I hardly know you at all.'

'So where did we meet?' Yes, I definitely know the voice. I find I'm smiling.

'Your daughter bought a dress from me for her Communion.'

And that's it. 'Clara!'

'Yep. Wow, you remember, impressive.'

'Very,' Larry mutters, giving me a sidelong glance and a smirk.

'You were very good to us,' I say to Clara. I turn to Larry. 'She was dead nice to Emma.'

'That's my job.' Clara smiles. It's like she radiates sunshine. 'Did she have a good day?'

'She did. Had a great day.'

'Well, good to know.' Clara nods. 'Nice to bump into you again. You know where to come if you have any more Communions.'

'Do you want to join us?' Larry says. 'We're just here for the one but at least you can have this seat when we leave. It's pretty packed.'

I wish he hadn't asked them. I'm tired of talking to women. I talk to women every day of the week now. With blokes there is no need to chat. And with the next date looming, my head is a bit all over the place wondering who it will be and where will they take me. For a week after the first date, I had dreams about running, of flying along a track on the tops of my toes. Then I'd wake up and feel all heavy-legged again, ground down by the responsibility of trying to do stuff right.

'Well?' Larry asks the girls again.

Clara looks at her friend, who shrugs. 'Great.' And she hops in right beside me, her friend beside her. She introduces her friend as Jamie. Jamie's one-eyed look is a little unnerving. And her baggy clothes cover her right up, so there is no idea of a woman in there at all. She peers into her glass.

'So, you on a lads' night out or what?' Clara asks.

'Yep.' Larry sinks half his pint in one go.

'Just the two of you? Are you secret lovers like in *Brokeback Mountain*?' she giggles.

She has a nice giggle.

Her friend gives a guffaw and her one eye glitters.

'My ex-wife was that way inclined,' Larry confides in a mock-wounded tone. 'So jokes about that sort of thing tend to hurt me.'

Clara makes a face. 'Your wife was a lesbian?'

'Yep.' And Larry is off. He gets great mileage out of his lesbian ex-wife. Women love it. They feel sorry for him. They laugh at his self-deprecation. Hell, even though I've heard him a million times before, I laugh. He has a way of describing how Shelly used to leave his newspaper and slippers out for him when he came home from work because she was trying to be a real wife to him and she thought that's what wives did. 'I thought I'd been blasted back to the nineteen fifties,' Larry chortles.

Even the friend laughs.

'And you two?' Larry is in full flow now. 'Married? Single?

Divorced?' Then before they can answer, he holds his hands up. 'Doesn't matter. Me and Nick, we're not choosy.'

The girls laugh.

A few pints and Larry becomes a comedian. One more and he'll be snoring. It's a fine line.

'Well, we're pretty choosy,' Clara says. She leans towards Larry and her arm brushes off mine. It's like a bomb going off under my skin. 'First of all the men have to be good-looking, so you're both out on the first hurdle.'

'Awww.' Larry feigns devastation.

'I'll live with the disappointment,' I grin. A lot relieved. For a second there …

Talk then turns to films and music and other stuff. I try to contribute but my mind is falling into an abyss of watching Clara as she leans forward, chin cupped in her hand. Kate did that very thing. I see the outline of Clara's breasts through her top and it turns me on. I hope Larry doesn't ask me to get the pints in. Clara keeps brushing up against me, her thigh, her arm, her foot, all unconscious but achingly frustrating for me. It takes a huge effort not to touch her back. I am so turned on I think I will explode if she doesn't stop. Eventually the two girls do that thing that women do – they head to the jacks, with their handbags – and my head expands again.

'You are well in there.' Larry winks at me.

'What?' I'm still reeling.

'She can't take her eyes off you. You should go for it.'

'What?' I stare at him. 'Go for what?'

'Nick,' Larry says patiently, 'when was the last time you had sex?'

I grin. 'Thanks, but no. I just want to be your friend.'

Larry smirks. 'You know what I mean. That one, Clara, she's into you big time. You should go for it.'

'She hardly knows me.'

Larry laughs so hard, he almost chokes. 'Hate to break it to you, Nick, but it's not your devastatingly witty personality she's after. She doesn't have to know you to do you.'

I laugh but then I gulp out what worries me. 'And what about Kate?'

Larry leans across the table. He's well on, he'll be asleep in ten minutes. 'You loved Kate. But she's dead, Nick. And you haven't been with a woman in ages. I don't know if you're punishing yourself or what but you need a good fuck. You really do.' He leans back in his seat and takes a gulp of his pint.

I feel a flash of irritation. Of hurt for Kate. 'Do you not care about Kate at all?'

'Of course I bloody do.' Larry stuns me with his anger. His voice is low but seething. 'Of course I do. I'd never have left her. That's for sure.'

The cruelty of his words paralyses me.

'Sorry,' Larry says immediately, 'I shouldn't have said that.'

'It's fine.' I wave him away. 'I deserved it. It's fine.'

'It's not.' He heaves a sigh. 'You are my best mate, Nick, the best guy in the world and you've had a shitty time. Give yourself a break. Have a bit of fun. That's all.' He looks up. 'Kate told me to take care of you. I'm doing it. Have some sex, for Christ's sake.'

I take a drink. I don't know how to put it without sounding disloyal. 'My head wants to,' I say, 'but the heart …' I touch my chest.

'Forget about the heart. It's broken. It doesn't work right any more.'

And he's right. It is utterly, utterly broken. 'Thanks, Lar.'

'I'll entertain the Cyclops, you go and get that girl.'

As usual, he makes me smile.

***

It's taken ten minutes. Clara sits down, her foot touches mine under the table and I bring my eyes to meet hers. She stares back fearlessly. Very deliberately, while still talking, I touch my sneakered foot off hers under the table. She doesn't resist, just leaves her foot where it is. Then she leans forward and brushes her arm off my shoulder, and when she moves back, she is closer than before. The length of our arms are touching through fabric.

My head is spinning with desire. She allows the back of her hand to touch mine. Her hand is warm.

I stand up and I can see the shock in her face. 'I'm heading outside for a smoke,' I say. 'Anyone coming?'

'I'll join you.' Clara hops up, her face is flushed, her eyes bright.

'But you don't—' Jamie says, then clamps her mouth shut.

'You'll have a pint, will you?' Larry asks her.

She nods, though it's obvious she isn't happy.

As casually as I can, I pick up my jacket and, trying to hide my massive erection, I walk out, aware that Clara is following. Outside, the air is warm. Groups of smokers huddle in the doorway, drink in one hand, cigarette in the other.

'You don't really want to smoke, do you?' I ask Clara.

'No.' She holds up her jacket and bag and grins. 'You?'

I hold up my jacket and she laughs. I'm almost detached except for the ache in my groin. She stands on her toes, her body inches from mine, and kisses me, just once, very softly. To one sex-starved man, it's totally erotic. Then she pulls back and looks at me.

I smile slowly. I am so turned on.

'I live just around the corner,' she says. 'D'you want to come for a drink?'

'Great.' My voice is a little ragged. We walk, glued to each other, back to her place. She lives in a small apartment and she fumbles with the key. I am caressing the back of her neck and she moans a little. It's a long time since I've made a woman do that. She unlocks her door and we tumble inside. I kick it closed with my foot and I pull her hard against me. Our mouths lock and she is gasping.

Should I tell her that this is a one-off. Does she know it?

'Come on,' she gasps. 'Bed.'

We take two steps towards the bedroom before we fall to the floor in a tangle of limbs and half-strewn clothes.

It's great. It's frantic. It's fast.

Afterwards, we lie on the floor and her arms are around me, her leg over mine, my arm about her shoulder. I realise how long it has been since I've been held, touched, loved. It's been a long time and I've missed it. I've missed someone telling me how great I am.

I know it's a one-off. I know I've used her, I hope she used me. But it feels so damn great.

And kinda sad.

I walk home through the brightening air. The sun is rising and the sky is streaked all sorts of fantastic colours. Light bounces off windows and the city begins to awaken. The noise of traffic increases, the hum of pedestrians, all making their way to work. Last night, in the main, was great. No strings. Today will be better, I think. Having sex, actually feeling something like that, reminds me that there is a big wide world out there, something beyond my own grief.

If I can hold on to that, it'll be the raft that will carry me through.

EMMA

I love Marcy's house. It is just the right size for a small amount of people. When we came back from the film, she let me and Liam sit in her bubble chair and she swung it for us. The chair is big and round and see-through and she has it hanging at her gigantic window and we could see the sea from her window. She made us pose for some pictures, then she gave us some hot chocolate and put on a DVD for us.

There is a picture of my mammy on her wedding day on Marcy's windowsill. Marcy is in it too, she is in a blue dress and my daddy is there and Larry. Daddy has a big smile on his face. He looks like he did in the photo album. Marcy and Mammy look like fashion models. I ask Marcy why she didn't get married yet and she said that her Prince Charming never came along. I tell her that Daddy isn't a prince and that he isn't very charming but he can be funny sometimes and she says that she meant she never met anyone she was really truly in love with. The boyfriend that she had, the big one with the muscles, he is gone off with another girl. Sometimes that happens, Marcy says.

She looks sad when she says that so to cheer her up I say that she can marry our daddy if she likes, then she'd be able to live with us or we could come and live with her. And that my daddy wouldn't go off with any girls, only maybe smelly men, so that would be OK, wouldn't it?

She laughs and laughs so I have cheered her up. Then she says that she doesn't think she will marry Daddy but that she'll always be around us.

That's not the same, I don't think. Daddy says that Mammy is always around, all I have to do is ask for her, but me and Liam said we'd prefer if we could actually see her. Well, I said it but I knew what Liam was thinking. Daddy says we could maybe have a picture of her to carry around and then we could see her sort of. So I have a picture of her beside my bed and so has Liam. It's still not the same.

Daddy says he knows that but it's the best he can do. But he's used to not seeing Mammy much. We're not. I told him that and he said that the picture was the best he could do. I think I made him sad or cross then. Good.

The rest of Marcy's apartment is this: a cool bathroom with a bubble bath and a see-through sink and a cool toilet that even if you slam the lid down real hard, it stops and goes down real soft. It's the best bathroom in the world, I think. Then she has a kitchen in her bubble chair room. That's a bit small and she has a small table with four chairs and a big bowl of fruit on the table. She eats lots of fruit as she says it's good for people but I tell her that me and Liam prefer chocolate. Also on the table there is a cross letter. It looks cross but I can't read it well. It's red and black and has big letters in the middle of it. Marcy puts it in a drawer when she sees me looking at it.

Also, she has shiny presses that you can sort of see your reflection in. And it's all neat and tidy, not like our house now that Daddy is in charge. But Daddy is good, he lets Liam fling all the stuff everywhere then he just tidies it up. He doesn't get mad. Mammy would have got mad. But Mammy just wanted a nice house, Daddy doesn't care.

Still, I like Daddy sometimes 'cause he lets us have the pancakes. He said first off that we couldn't have them. He said that in the book Mammy said we were not to have them, that they were bad to eat. I got real sad because I like the pancakes, so Daddy said we can have them on Tuesday for dinner instead. It's better at dinnertime, he said, 'cause we don't have to rush them. That was a good idea because we get to eat more of them and for longer now. I think it was mean of Mammy to put something like that in a lovely colourful book. Then I slap my arm because I don't let myself think not nice thoughts about Mammy. We go to bed very late. Marcy says we can all sleep in her bed if we like so we do, only Marcy comes in later on. Liam is asleep but I am not. I wait for Marcy. She has pyjamas like a princess. She gives me a hug and we snuggle into each other.

We have a whisper. That's what Mammy used to call it when she and me talked late at night. Whispers are better than talking during the day. I like talking in the dark. I tell Marcy all about my class in school and how everyone was being real nice to me when Mammy died but now they have sort of forgot. Marcy says that Mammy wouldn't mind that but I think she would. It's not nice to be forgot. I tell her that I get mad with the girls in my class sometimes. Then I tell her about Daddy having bad dreams that make him shout out at night. I tell her that he tells lies. He always says he is happy when he looks sad. I tell her how he can't cook right. How he bought a cookbook and how his cakes are always hard and how his potatoes are always mushy. He curses sometimes when stuff goes wrong. Marcy says that he's probably doing his best. I say that I hope it isn't his best. I hope it's his worst and that he will get better. Marcy laughs. But I mean it.

Today we went to Mammy's grave with Marcy and Larry. Marcy rang Daddy to see if she could bring us and Daddy said that if we wanted to we could go. Liam doesn't know what a grave is but I do and I wanted to go. I want to see where my mammy is now. When we meet Larry, at the front of the graveyard, he has big black circles around his eyes. Like glasses, only drawn. He looks funny and we all start to laugh. 'What happened?' Marcy asks.

Larry goes red and starts scratching at his face. He has red patches on his face sometimes. He says he gets nervous and that his face gets itchy. I wonder if he is nervous going to the grave. He says that a girl got cross with him and drew on his face.

Marcy tells him that in all these years, he hasn't changed.

That's a weird thing to say as everyone is always the same. But he did look funny. And then he says that he's learned a thing or two. Probably in school.

Larry carries a big bunch of flowers and we all follow behind him. Marcy is holding Liam's hand. When we get to the grave – I don't know how they know it – Marcy starts to arrange the flowers in a vase and Larry cleans up the dead ones and the weeds and puts them in a bag. Then he says he will put the bag in the boot of his car and bring it home for recycling. Larry has a nice car. He has lots of money. Daddy says he is really clever and that he invented things for engines and that people think he is great and that he is kind of famous. Famous people don't wear brown trousers though or have itchy skin. They wear shiny things and use L'Oréal. Larry never wears shiny things so he's not that famous. It is sad seeing Mammy's grave. I said a prayer to her in the sky. Liam didn't but he is only a baby. So I said one for him too.

After we say prayers and Larry looks at other people's graves, he brings us to lunch to a nice restaurant. Marcy tells Larry that she likes his car and Larry says that it gets him around and then Marcy copies him, saying, 'It gets me around', and she calls him a show-off. I think she is having a joke but Larry itches his face even more so I think he isn't happy with that. In the restaurant, Liam and me get chips and ice cream and Larry and Marcy get a boring dinner and some ice cream. Larry can't eat his dinner as he went out with my daddy last night and sometimes when grown-ups go out they don't eat the next day. Marcy asks him where they went and Larry says just a few pubs and then they went home. Then Marcy asks about the girl he offended and Larry says that he fell asleep and that the girl drew circles on his face. And Marcy asks where Daddy was and why didn't Daddy stop her drawing on Larry's face and Larry says that my daddy left early as he wanted to go to bed.

Marcy says that Daddy should go out a bit more, that he needs to relax. Larry looks at us and so does Marcy and they say no more about it at all.

NICK

'Now,' Larry advises me jokingly on the Saturday of the second date, 'don't go getting into fights, right?'

'I reckon it's still better than falling asleep.'

Larry sneers at me. 'Yeah, it took this whole bloody week to get the ink off my face. The lads in work had a great laugh.' He rubs at his face as he says it, before asking, 'I wonder who it'll be this time? I was talking to Violet yesterday—'

'Voilet? My mother? You were talking to her about this?'

'Yeah.' Larry looks surprised. 'Course.'

'I wish you hadn't.'

'Well, someone has to, you hardly ever go to see them.'

'I suppose she said that.'

'Yeah.'

I'm about to say something else when Emma arrives in with a photo album tucked under her arm. 'Will you look at these with us, Larry?'

'I will.' Larry pats the seat beside him and Emma hops up. Then she peers at him before standing up on the seat and pulling at his hair. 'What happened your hair?' she asks.

'Nothing,' Larry mutters. 'Just had it styled.'

'Styled?' I gawk at him. 'What do you mean, "styled"?'

'I mean that I got something done to make it look like it's in a style. Marie suggested it.'

'Marie? Danny's wife? What are you doing talking to Marie?'

'If you must know,' Larry looks at both of us, 'having my hair styled is an attempt at launching myself at the female market. I've decided to dip my toe in the water again.'

'Do you mean you're going to get a girlfriend?' Emma asks.

'I do,' Larry says.

'Well, that hair is not very nice,' Emma says, making us both laugh. 'I have some combs and some gel upstairs and I'll fix it for you, OK?'

'OK.' Larry nods.

Emma hops back down and runs off upstairs.

'Go you.' I grin.

'Yeah, we can't all be sex gods picking women up in pubs.'

'It was a one-off.' I feel a bit ashamed of myself for that. But I don't regret it.

The doorbell rings.

'Off you go. Enjoy!' Larry tips me a salute just as Emma appears back laden down with hairdressing paraphernalia. Liam toddles in behind her carrying some pink fluffy rollers.

'He's my assistant,' Emma says.

'Besistent,' Liam parrots.

I watch for a second as Larry obligingly sits cross-legged on the floor to be their customer.

The doorbell rings again.

'See yez,' I call. I kiss Emma and Liam, who absently kiss me back.

The doorbell rings a third time and I wonder who can be that impatient. I hurry to answer it and just as I'm about to say hi, Molly pushes by me. 'I have to go to the loo, hang on a second.'

I wait for her and she appears a few minutes later, looking embarrassed. 'Sorry if I rang the bell a little too much but it's the curse of being pregnant.' She pats her stomach. 'So sorry.'

'It's fine.' Kate was the same when she was pregnant with Emma.

'Right, I'm ready to go now.' Molly rattles her keys and, calling out another 'Goodbye' to the kids, I follow Molly to her car. As we sit in, she says cheerfully, 'Right, this is all very odd. I'm so glad you came to the Parent and Toddler or I wouldn't know you at all. OK, this is the deal. I bring you to this place and you have to tell me why.'

'What?' Her directness is in startling contrast to Jean's shyness. I wonder if all the Parent and Toddler women are going to be ferrying me about. The thoughts of going anywhere with Sue scares me.

'Only joking.' Molly chortles as she starts the car with a jerk. I'm thrown forward. She pulls out onto the road. 'Though it would be nice to know. Kate rang me when she was diagnosed as …,' she pauses, ' … terminal,' she adds gently, 'and asked if I'd do this. She wanted people she thought you'd like because she said you were useless at small talk.' Molly studies me. 'I hate small talk.'

'It comes in useful sometimes, though. You know, for discussing the weather.'

She laughs.

'So, enough of the small talk,' I say. 'How's your husband's underpants?'

It turns out that Kate has asked Molly to bring me to The Rock Place. It's a small, well-regarded music venue in Swords. I used to come here a lot with Kate and Larry, but more importantly, it was where our fledgling rock band had their first gig.

Even now, just like back then, the music blaring out seems to make the walls pound.

'Oh, God, I feel way too old for this.' Molly makes a face. 'What is this place anyway?'

The old affection for the shabby exterior wells up in me. The green door is still the same, a small entrance belying the cavern inside. Rad had secured a booking for us and, full of excitement, convinced we were on the cusp of the big time, our band had eagerly taken to the stage. I remember I wore one of my many pairs of skinny denims, so tight it was almost painful to walk. I also wore a T-shirt with the name of our band emblazoned across it, along with the carefully thought-out image of a rotten apple and a lollipop. My hair was long and unkempt and I had carefully contrived designer stubble adorning my face. Larry and Rad were much the same. Kate, I remember, was stunning. Her dark hair was streaked with pink, which matched her shiny lips. I remember she wore a bright blue pair of jeans that clung to her the way I so longed to. I dropped my guitar twice, just looking at her. Larry teased me, told me loudly to go for it. But he'd been telling me that for months and I still couldn't get up the nerve. I fell properly in love that night.

'Nick?' Molly says, and I'm aware that she's tugging my arm. 'Hello?'

'Sorry, just remembering.'

'What is this place?'

'It's a music venue.' I would have thought that was obvious. 'Years ago I was in a band with Kate. We played here.'

'Wow!' Molly's freckled face scrunches up in a huge smile. 'Kate never said she could sing.'

'She couldn't.' I laugh. Then add quietly, 'But she looked great.'

Molly smiles and squeezes my arm.

Once again the heavy sound of bass music pumps onto the street and I feel a sudden yearning to go inside and see if it's still the same. 'Will we go in?'

Molly nods and gives my arm another squeeze.

'I hope they have a toilet in here,' she says.

Of course the place has changed. Nothing stays the same. The last time I was here was with Kate, Larry and one of his weird girlfriends. Back then there was just the manually operated spotlight and bare stage; now though a brilliant new lighting system is in place and the sound is a lot better. After a bit of a tussle I persuade Molly to let me pay for her at the door and lead her into the darkened room with the bar at one end and the stage at the other. There's a band on, a three-man outfit, young, so terribly young, with enough energy to power Sellafield.

Molly heads to the bathroom, asking me to order her an orange, and I take a seat at the bar, throwing my jacket over another stool for Molly. The place is fairly packed but most of the crowd are around the stage. I wonder if agents still come to suss out new talent. We managed to attract one that first night. He told me, Larry and Rad that we were fine musicians but that we had to lose the singer. I turned him down; I was more interested in making it with Kate than I was in making a career in music. All I ever wanted to be was a fireman. Larry of course had decided to stick with me and Kate. He was never interested in making it either. He just wanted the craic and he wasn't prepared to lose his two best friends. Rad ditched the lot of us without a backward glance. I don't know where he is now; I hope it worked out for him.

Of course, Kate was upset and I had to sleep with her to cheer her up. It was my idea. She asked how she would ever feel better and I said that sex with me would cheer us both up. It was a joke but it worked.

The band onstage finishes and the MC announces that there'll be a five-minute break as the other band sets up. Molly arrives back and I help her up onto the stool. She looks uncomfortable and she takes a grateful sip of juice.

'I think your Kate was a masochist,' she jokes. 'This is so the wrong place for me to come.'

I like the way she says 'your Kate'.

She looks around and remarks that she has never gone to a place like this before. I tell her that it was where I always went for a night out. When had I stopped going, I wonder? Probably around the same time I stopped running. Only I'm taking up running again, albeit in a smaller way. Maybe I might resurrect my guitar, if I can bear it.

I signal the barman for another couple of drinks just as the lights dim and straggly clapping starts. A duo take to the stage. A man on guitar and a girl with an amazing voice. Molly, who has been telling me about the difficulties of her last labour, mercifully stops mid-sentence and both of us look to see who the singer is. We're quite far back so it's difficult to see them at first, but as the joyful, beautiful first song peters out, I am hooked. It's a long time since I've been caught up with a piece of music.

'Thank you,' the singer says, to applause. 'It's so cool to be back here after all this time.'

A cheer goes up.

'They're wonderful,' Molly says. 'Who are they?' She directs this question to the barman.

'Aren't they?' he answers as he polishes a couple of glasses. 'They're called Locust. It's their first night back in six months. Telling you, they were badly missed by the punters.'

'Were they touring?' I ask. I can't take my eyes off them. Obviously a couple, they're laughing with each other as he strums a few chords getting ready for the next song. I like their laid-back, casual approach. They remind me of the way Kate and I used to be before everything went wrong.

'Nah. Leah wasn't well.' He grins as she hits a high note. 'The crowd love her.'

All I can do is look and think how bloody brilliant they are.

After they finish, Leah ends up beside me and Molly at the bar.

'You were brilliant,' Molly says.

Leah grins. She must be in her mid-twenties, pretty in a fragile way. 'Thanks,' she says, nodding, 'Oi! Clive, vodka. No ice.' Her speaking voice is rich with a Dublin twang. Nothing delicate about that. 'And a Carlsberg for Richard.'

'No problem.' Clive gets the drinks for her.

'I'll get that.' I put a tenner on the counter. 'The songs were worth it.'

'Nice one.' She nods. 'Cheers.'

We leave after the next set. Molly is tired and I am too, but in a good way. There are memories of Kate wherever I look. The seats we sat on, the places we stood, the part of the bar where the agent made his pitch. I'd forgotten the way The Rock Place made me feel: alive, in touch, happy. That duo, singing on despite everything, humbled me. Why did I never go back? I loved music once; I've a massive CD collection. I used to go to every gig going, but in the last few years, all that disappeared, like smoke in the wind. Music for me has always been about beauty, celebration, joy. Even the sad stuff could shape itself into something wonderful by the way it was sung. And I let that go. I lost the happy among the sad. What should have saved me was ignored. I think I was determined to lose myself.

I almost did. If Jack hadn't disappeared, I think I would have. If Kate hadn't got sick, I would have. If the kids weren't there, I certainly wouldn't be. These thoughts flit through my head like fireworks across the sky as Molly drives us home.

No amount of time in a hospital could have given me so much clarity.

* * *

Heart pounding, wondering what I will find, I pull out the book once more. 'After the Second Date' is a darker pink tab, almost red. I flip to its page and I actually laugh out loud when I see the old playbill. Where had Kate found it? It's on white paper with menacing black lettering. It's old and faded and curled at the edges. It makes my heart sing.

The Black Forces of Destruction

The Rock Place: June 23rd.

See this band before they go global.

Underneath, Kate has written: *Hey, you.*☺ *We never did go global. Sometimes when stuff doesn't work out, it's for the best, isn't it? I think we rocked, just not in the way we'd planned. Happy memories. x*

'You're right,' I whisper. 'I wouldn't have changed a thing about us.'

Not a thing.

THE THIRD DATE

MARCY

Kate's bracelet is beautiful. The night I get it from Emma, I cry. I stand in my apartment at the big picture window and watch it glitter under the lights of the room. I see it reflected double back to me in the window and tears start sliding down my cheeks. I miss her, it's that simple. Nothing is the same without her. She was my best friend, my confidant. She'd be here now, advising me what to do about my non-existent love life, she'd be laughing at the way I'm deftly avoiding my landlord every time he calls in to the salon looking for my rent. She'd be telling me to stop doing my neighbours' nails for free. But, I'd say, the woman is eighty and it's her only pleasure. Yes, Kate would say back, and fleecing you is her other pleasure.

My eye falls on a picture of the two of us taken when we were in our late teens. I love this picture because in it I do a fair job of looking as cool as my friend. Kate beams out of the frame, skinny as a rake with shocking pink hair and wearing a rocker T-shirt. I'm beside her, a big towering heifer of a girl with a faceful of makeup and matching pink hair. I have no idea if Kate ever knew how inadequate I always felt beside her, how her smallness seemed to mock my largeness, how I tried so hard to match in with her. Sad as it was, I think I was impressed by the fact that she lost her parents early. It gave her, in my eyes, a tragic air, an air of someone who'd lived.

When she started going out with Nick, I was dead impressed that he was in a band. I thought, that's the exact person Kate should marry. I could see her as a pop star's wife; I had visions of her hanging onto an arm of a laconic young man, both of them looking ever so slightly bored. Then Kate made a suggestion that I meet Larry, Nick's friend. She thought we'd get on and wouldn't it be great to be a foursome? I desperately wanted a cool boyfriend. And, even though I'd never met them, I couldn't think of anyone cooler than Kate's cool boyfriend's friend. And so I got all dressed up. Probably I tried too hard. I managed to bore the guy so much that he had to get drunk to endure my company. In fact, he actually fell asleep. It was the worst date of my life.

Then Kate married Nick, who still intimidated me because I thought he was cool. Then she had kids and decided to leave work to be at home with them. Nick never became a pop star.

In all the years I'd known Kate, I never guessed that ordinary was what she wanted.

It's a pity I don't get on that well with Nick. I reckon he'd go mad if he knew that Kate asked me to keep an eye on him. I'm betting she's asked Larry too. But I can understand why. Kate was so worried leaving the children. I told her Nick was a good man and though she knew it, the fact that he'd had such massive problems scared her. I don't think Nick ever saw himself at that time in the way we all did. In his mind, what he did with Jack made sense. Maybe after being in hospital and all, he knows it was mad. Kate told him that he wouldn't get to mind the children without treatment and even though he was managing all right and getting his shit together, he did go for help. I look at him sometimes and while most of the time I want to thump him, other times, especially when I see him with the kids, I just want to hug him and tell him it'll all be fine.

EMMA

Daddy cooks us all a big fry for breakfast. 'Us all' means Larry too. Larry stayed the night, he does that sometimes. I like when he does. It makes me feel safe. Fry is my favourite thing and Mammy only let me have two sausages but Daddy lets me have as many sausages as I want once it doesn't go over eight. Liam has five and so have I. Larry and Daddy have three but they have rashers and eggs too. Then Larry goes home.

On the TV there is a movie about a kid who is a spy. Liam and I watch it and Daddy goes out and I see him bringing a ladder in from the shed. Then he carries it upstairs and I hear him pushing open the attic door. I don't like the attic. It's dark and has a funny smell and it scares me. I think that I will stay at the end of the ladder just in case something gets him up there. At least I can run to Angela next door and tell her to phone the police. It's important to be safe and to think ahead.

I ask Daddy what he is doing and he tells me to wait and see. There are a lot of sounds of him pushing things about and every time I hear a sound I jump. Liam is lucky, he is too small to worry and he is enjoying the movie. Next thing, Daddy climbs back down the ladder with a guitar case in his hand. He closes the attic door, which is good, and holds out the guitar case, which is all dusty and makes me cough. Daddy says, 'Do you know what this is?' I say it's a guitar.

Daddy says that is right but that it's not any old guitar, it's his very first one. The one he bought with his very first wages. It was a really expensive guitar, Daddy said. Then he goes down to Liam and I follow him. Daddy is smiling and acting a little weird and I feel a bit sick.

Daddy sits on the sofa and takes the guitar out of the case. Dust goes everywhere and Liam laughs and points at it and Daddy says that it is dust. Liam says 'dust' real clear and Daddy winks at him and calls him a great fella.

The guitar is a red guitar with a picture of an eagle on it. Daddy plucks some strings but it isn't right. It hurts my ears and Daddy says that he needs to tune it up. So as Liam and me try to watch the film, Daddy makes a lot of noise, which is annoying as we can't hear the film. So instead I decide to play hairdresser and so I make Liam sit down and I tell him that he's my customer and that I'm doing his hair 'cause Liam's hair is real long now and all curly. Liam says no. I say yes. Then Liam says no and he sort of squeals a bit but in the end I tell him that I won't play with him any more if he doesn't be my customer and Liam is just about to be a good boy when Daddy begins to play the guitar.

He stops and starts a little bit but even that is good. It is real proper music and he's smiling at the way the guitar is sounding. He closes his eyes and he sings Liam's favourite nursery rhymes and Liam and me stop playing hairdressers because Liam is clapping and saying 'more, more' and me and Daddy are laughing at him. Then Daddy asks me what I want to hear and I say, 'Bringing You Home, Kathleen', which is Mammy's favourite song and she used to sing it to us all the time.

Daddy starts to play it and sing some of it and he is a way better singer than Mammy. I never knew he had a nice voice before but then his voice sort of goes a bit weird and he says that he has to stop, that he isn't able to remember the words and could I give him another song. So I say a One Direction song and Daddy doesn't really know that either so I hum it for him and the next thing, there he is playing it and I'm singing it and it is fun. He's laughing at me, telling me I'm a great little singer. Mammy used to say that too.

Then he says do we want to hear a song he wrote once. I say OK, and what a surprise it is. It's all about me and Liam and I can't quite remember all the words but it's sort of, 'Oh, Emma, don't you know, even though you're eight years old, I love you as much as I can. Oh Liam, don't you know, even though you're barely grown, I love you as much as I can.' Then it goes on about how we're going to grow up and have fun and the end is funny. It's like, 'I know, I'm just your dad, but hey guys, I'm really glad to love you as much as I can. But that doesn't mean I give you sweets or endless chewy treats, I'll just love you as much as I can.' There's more but I can't remember it right.

Me and Liam are dancing and Liam looks funny 'cause he has fuzzy pink rollers in his hair. And we join in the chorus and 'cause Liam can't sing it right, it's funny.

Today is my very favourite day since Mammy died.

NICK

Jack. I suppose I'd better exorcise Jack before I go on. Jack was a seventeen-year-old drug addict with his whole life ahead of him. He was rail thin, jittery as hell. He spoke in the slow drawl of an addict, as if tongue and brain were at permanent war with each other, and he shambled when he walked. He looked about fifty with his bad skin and matted hair. I met him when I did a soup run for the homeless. I was into doing good deeds for a while. My life seemed to be fragmenting all around me and the only thing that seemed to keep me stable was helping everyone else and so I became part of the soup kitchen brigade. It didn't involve much, just driving around in a van, late at night, delivering food to the homeless. And there were a lot of them. Some of them liked to chat when we showed up, others just took the food without a second glance. Jack struck me as different, somehow. He was the youngest I'd met, I guess. And even though he said he was seventeen and he looked fifty, there was this innocence behind his eyes, a fear. He hated the streets, I could tell. Some of the other guys chose the street rather than live a normal life, but Jack, he was only a kid, for Christ's sake. Something in me had to put him back together.

And so I'd chat to him, night after night. Sometimes he was high and zoned out, other times he made perfect sense. He told me he couldn't live at home, that his dad had thrown him out. He said he didn't blame his dad but that he was scared. He'd talk about art and sport and school. He'd tell me about the friends he used to have. He told me about his girlfriend and how he loved her and how he wasn't able to get her back. Stuff that he would never have told an older guy like me unless he was desperate. And so, I dunno, I decided that I could help him. I brought him home one night and let him sleep on the sofa. Kate found him the next day and thought he was a burglar. She hit him with the knife block and he ran off.

I brought him back, though. I kept bringing him back. He came back when he was off his head, he came back when he was on a downer. He took over the living room. He ignored the kids. I refused to believe he could steal from us but things did go missing. Kate and I rowed and rowed. I accused her of only caring about herself. She said I only cared about myself, which was ridiculous, I thought, when I was the one doing the good deed. Jack stayed out of it. I remember one row when Kate and I were laying into each other and Emma and Liam were upstairs. Jack calmly came into the kitchen and took a yogurt from the fridge. He sat there watching us. Kate turned on him and told him it was his fault. Then she turned to me. There was this awful silence. I remember it like a blanket, pressing down. Then she said, her voice only shaking a tiny bit, 'It's us or him, Nick, you have to choose. I can't have you going on like this.'

'Marcy put you up to this,' I remember saying.

'No, Nick, you did,' she snapped. Then she folded her arms and looked at me. 'Well?'

And for me there was no choice. I chose Jack.

At the time, the way I was thinking, it made sense. Now though, I'm horrified by what I did and yet I still understand *why* I did it. I needed Jack to save me. To prove to me that I was good. That's why I chose him. Making sense and doing the right thing are not the same. Larry came over to talk to me. I think Kate must have rung him. I hit Larry. My best mate, and I planted him such a dig that he landed on his back in our garden.

I rented a shitty apartment, moved Jack in with me to fix him up and told myself that this was my life now. A few months later, Jack disappeared. No note. Nothing. And not only had I failed to save Jack, I'd also failed my kids and my wife. How could I go back and ask forgiveness when I felt I didn't deserve her? When I had nothing to offer her. When I was a loser in every respect. And then when she got sick and was diagnosed as terminal, I offered to move back but she refused. I told her I loved her, that I always had. That I regretted everything. That trying to save Jack was like the mirage in the desert and I'd missed the oasis under my nose. But she said no.

She said I wasn't well enough.

She was right.

As always.

***

'Hey, we've been expecting you,' Marie says in a really weird accent as she opens her door to us. 'How's everyone?'

Before I can answer, she scoops Liam up and plants kisses on his face. 'Hi, cuteness. How are you?'

Liam babbles something and Emma says, 'He says he's fine and can he ride the horse?'

'Yes, he can.' Marie opens the door wide to let us in. 'Come on in, folks. Nick, give the door a good slam, it won't shut properly otherwise.'

I slam the door and make my way into the kitchen, climbing over boxes of flat-pack furniture and sports equipment and, amusingly, a book on how to win at poker. Danny obviously hasn't read it yet.

Danny and Marie's house is in a permanent state of chaos. My kids love it, seeing it as an obstacle course. As Emma used to say when she was younger, 'Daddy, their house is full of everything,' and it's true.

I suppose there's no point in assembling things when three enormous dogs keep bashing into everything. One of them, a Burmese Mountain Dog, stands in the middle of the small kitchen, tail wagging madly. He jumps up on Liam as he enters and knocks him down.

Liam is about to cry when the dog, with one lick, covers his face with slime. I scoop him up, laughing to make him laugh, and give him a scrub as Marie berates the dog. The dog whimpers, then lies down. 'He's saying sorry,' Emma says delightedly.

'He's saying you can brush him, Liam,' Marie says, holding out a brush for Liam to take.

Liam approaches the animal with caution. Emma instructs Liam sternly on what to do. I'm proud to see that she holds his hand to protect him if the dog jumps up again. God, I love them. It catches me out, that feeling, like sunlight through cloud. It blinds me suddenly. Even though I know the love is there, it doesn't always show itself. I can't take my eyes off them as Emma babbles off a list of instructions and Liam listens intently. I wish he listened to me like that. Marie opens a press and pokes around for a second before extracting a saddle and harness. She orders the dog to stand and straps it onto him.

'Do you want to ride him, Liam?'

He nods, not looking too sure.

Lifting him up, she sits him in the saddle and puts his feet in the stirrups. She had it made for my kids. Emma used to use it but she's too big now.

'Now, Ems, you can lead Liam around the garden. If the other two dogs get in your way, just say, "Off" and they'll go, OK?'

'I know,' Emma says. 'Come on, Hunter.'

I have no clue how she knows which dog is which, the three of them look the same to me.

Liam, looking equal parts thrilled and terrified, holds on for dear life and I suppress a laugh.

'Coffee?' Marie fills the kettle.

'Yeah. Ta.'

I sit down and watch as she flicks on the kettle.

'Danny says he'll be back in about twenty minutes. He got called out on a breakdown.'

'No worries.' I don't mind being alone with Marie, she's easy to talk to.

'Now, he might ask you back to work,' she warns me as she spoons some coffee into two mugs. 'If you're not ready, don't go back. He'll keep your job open anyway.'

'Thanks, Marie.'

As we wait for the kettle to boil, she sits opposite me and studies me. In the end, on a laugh, I'm forced to ask, 'What?'

'No chance of you ever going back to the fire brigade?'

The air is sucked from my lungs and lodges in my throat. I can't even answer, just shake my head.

'It's OK.' She reaches across and pats my hand. 'Just asking.' A pause. 'You loved it, though. You were different then.'

I don't need reminding. Instead, on a very deliberate change of subject, I pull an envelope from my pocket. 'Kate left this for you.'

'Oh.' Marie takes it, looking sad for a second before smiling across the table at me. 'I bet I know what it is too. Can I open it?'

'Sure.'

It is taking me ages to hand these envelopes over. I keep forgetting them. Maybe, on some level, I know that when they're all opened, that'll be it. There won't be any more effortless ways to bring Kate up in conversation. I watch Marie as she tears open the flap of the envelope and laughs in delight. 'I knew it!' she says. She empties some seeds from the envelope onto her palm. 'They're from a plant I admire in your garden, Nick, you know the big pink one that blooms in the summer?'

'Nope.'

'You can't miss it.' She sounds appalled. 'It's huge in your garden. Beautiful thing.'

'Oh yeah, that one,' I say, not having a clue. Our garden is a bit of a mess at the moment. I will have to do something with it.

'Well, she left me some seeds. Every time I was over, she'd give them to me and I kept leaving them behind.' She hops up, makes us a cuppa, then beckons me outside. I take my mug and follow her.

In contrast to their house, their garden is pretty orderly, despite the dogs. Marie finds a pot in a corner and fills it with some compost. 'She told me to grow them in a pot first,' she says as she pushes the seeds down. 'And to place them in a sheltered spot.' Marie looks around, decides on a space and places the pot there. 'I hope they grow,' she says.

I do too.

'I need a favour,' I say, sitting beside her as she takes a seat on the patio. 'But only if it suits, right?'

'Go on.'

'I found a note in Emma's bag looking for a cake for a cake sale. Emma is insisting that I bake it despite overwhelming evidence that my strengths lie in other directions.'

Marie laughs. 'Well, don't do buns, that's my advice.'

I grin. 'Any chance you could? I know you're a professional so I'm happy to pay. I want something really special.'

'Pay? Will you get lost!' She flaps her hand. 'When do you need it for?'

'I can send Larry over to collect it tomorrow night. I have an idea that I think will be a bit of a laugh.'

'What idea?'

I tell her and she stares at me, her mouth open. Then to my horror, tears brighten her eyes.

'What?' Jesus, what have I done now?

'That's something the old Nick would have done,' she says. Then she hugs me, hard. 'You are a lovely, lovely man.'

'You can't marry my daddy!' Emma shouts over. 'You have Danny and Marcy has no one.'

'And that doesn't surprise me at all,' I say but just loud enough for Marie to hear.

'Hmm,' she says, with a bit of a grin, 'that's mean. Maybe you're not such a lovely man after all.'

* * *

Danny comes back a while later. Marie has asked us to stay for dinner, which she always does, and Emma is peeling the potatoes and Liam has the unenviable task of scooping the peelings into a compost bowl. I'm chopping the carrots.

'There is nothing I like to see more than my wife hard at work making my dinner,' Danny calls loudly as he slams the door shut behind him.

Marie fires a potato at him, which one of the dogs neatly catches in his enormous mouth.

Danny elbows his wife affectionately out of the way and washes his hands at the sink. I envy them suddenly. 'When are you coming back to work?' he asks me. 'Or are you going back to the fire service?'

My carrot falls to the floor and is eaten by one of the dogs.

'Can we leave this for afterwards?' Marie says sharply. 'Let's have our dinner and then you and Nick can talk. I'll bring Emma and Liam off to the shops for a treat.'

'Now?' Liam asks, eyes wide.

'No, silly,' Emma chides, 'after dinner when Danny and Daddy can chat about Daddy having a job again.'

'She misses nothing.' Danny winks at me.

* * *

Afterwards, I hand the keys of my car to Marie as it saves her moving the car seats into her own. I'm not too worried about the state my car is in as she never notices things like that. Emma and Liam kiss me goodbye while Danny and I watch the last few minutes of a football match.

'I need to know,' Danny asks, 'are you coming back to the garage? Sorry for pressuring you now.'

'I'll be back as soon as I get someone to mind the kids for me.'

Danny sighs. 'I was talking to your mother, she said she'd do it.'

Does everyone talk to my mother?

'And you know Marie,' Danny goes on, 'she's only dying to mind them whenever she's off.'

'Yeah, I know,' I say, a little miffed. 'But it's hard leaving them, you know?'

'No. No, I don't.'

I flinch. 'Sorry, Danny, I didn't mean … I just meant that I left them before and it was all wrong. It's …' I sigh and shrug, unable to explain it right.

'I know you didn't mean anything by it,' Danny says. 'And I know you had a raw deal, Nick, but stop beating yourself up over it. You need to earn a living for them too.'

Danny and Marie. Mr and Mrs Practical. 'I know.'

'And in some ways, you're bloody lucky. Me and Marie, we envy you. You've two gorgeous children. We never had that.'

There is no self-pity in his voice, just raw honesty. And I

remember their struggle. Danny drowning in despair at Marie's moods. Marie crying to Kate. They dragged us all in. 'I know I'm lucky to have them,' I say. 'I just want them to be happy.'

'Getting on with your life will make them happy,' Danny says. He takes a sip of tea, chomps on a biscuit and waves it about, crumbs falling everywhere. 'Me and Marie, we had to leave the idea of happy kids behind to be happy ourselves, but you don't. You need to get back to work, Nick.'

His words pierce my skin like an injection. I find myself saying, 'Give me one more month with them, then I'll come back.'

'OK. This time next month, I want you rocking up in a pair of overalls to the garage.'

We shake on it. On the drive home, Emma asks, 'Daddy, why aren't you a fireman any more?'

I feel that involuntary clenching of muscle that always happens whenever someone mentions the words 'fire brigade'. 'Just prefer to work in a garage, honey.'

She's asked me this before, I've always told her this answer, but there is something in her silence that unnerves me. 'Why?' I ask.

'No reason.'

I should have known there was a reason, there is always a reason why Emma asks questions. But my relief at not having to talk about it makes me accept her answer. I steer the conversation around to boy bands and crushes and enjoy it when she tells me I'm a dork.

* * *

'Daddy, I need a cake for the cake sale on Tuesday,' Emma says, as I knew she would. 'I told the teacher we'd bring one in. And you can't have cream in it because there is nowhere to store it for Tuesday. Only special people are making the cream ones.'

'OK. Well, I think you and Liam should do it yourselves.'

Emma gives me one of her looks that would wilt poison ivy. 'And how are we supposed to do that?'

I hunker down to their level. 'Did you never hear of wishes?'

'I did!' Liam's hand shoots up.

'Tell me what they are so.'

'Eh …' Liam's face screws up and his mouth moves as he tries to find the words to articulate what he knows. 'Wishes,' he says.

'They are when you want something to happen and you think about it real hard to make it come true and it does come true. That's what a wish is,' I say. 'So, we are going to make a wishing cake. We will make it up as we go along and throw it into the oven and see what happens.'

'No one will buy that at the cake fair,' Emma says wearily. 'Daddy, that won't work.' Then, in dawning horror, she says, 'People will laugh.'

'Can we not just try?' I say gently. She really is way too young to be so cynical. I look at my watch. 'Right, you have thirty minutes to put in whatever you think this cake needs.' I open a press and pull out an enormous bowl that I bought especially for tonight.

'Wow!' Liam's eyes are round at the size of it.

Emma looks less excited.

'I try,' Liam says. 'I know how to make cake.'

His first full sentence makes me laugh and Emma squeals. I hope Kate, wherever she is, heard it too.

'How?' I look puzzled.

Liam toddles over to a press and drags out some flour. He knows where everything is because he spends his day flinging most of it around. I reckon he thinks everywhere is a giant Parent and Toddler group. Then he takes out a wooden spoon and some sugar. He dumps the whole packet of flour into the bowl.

'Eggs,' Emma says grudgingly.

'How many?'

'Five?'

I take five eggs and break them into the bowl.

'Anything else?'

'This!' Liam yanks a tin of pepper from a rack in the press.

'You can't use pepper.' Emma is appalled.

'You can. This is a wishing cake.'

She watches wide-eyed as I pour it over the flour and eggs.

Encouraged, Liam hands me some peas and some paprika. I pull over a chair so he can stand and add the ingredients himself. Emma, getting into the spirit of it, adds margarine. Liam adds half a turnip which I have to peel. It's been in the press a while and I'd been wondering what the smell was.

'A tea bag,' Emma says, opening it and scattering the leaves everywhere. There is a hint of a smile on her lips.

'Coffee?' I offer.

'OK.' She nods.

'How much?'

'Half a jar.'

It's expensive coffee but I can't back out now.

Liam fires some biscuits in and some crisps and Emma adds jelly, tinned fruit and milk. There is nothing else in the house to add. They take turns mixing it up and bits of the cake fly all over the place. The bowl is big but not big enough. The whole thing is a gloopy, smelly mess. I scoop it into a tin and turn the oven on low. 'Now, lads, close your eyes real hard.'

I smile as they do so, Liam clenching his fists for good measure. 'And wish for the best cake ever. It has to be a proper wish. Eyes closed, Emma, or it won't work.' I leave it a second or two. 'Now, wishes take ages to work so we'll leave it real low in the oven all night and see what it looks like in the morning.'

They open their eyes and I carry them both up to bed, one in each arm. Emma has grave doubts about the cake and she tells me that if it doesn't work out, she is not bringing it in.

She asks for a story. I make up one called 'The Rat and Nick' about how I defeated a King Rat. At first Emma said she didn't want a story about a rat but I told her she'd love this one. In truth, I think Liam is pretty sick of Ballerina stories. Anyhow, I made up a song in the middle of it and they loved it. I made up actions for them to do and *I* loved it. I tell them that the wishing cake won't work if they don't stay in bed. They promise that they will.

It was a good night.

* * *

Later, after they're asleep, Larry calls over with the cake from Marie. It's exactly like something a kid would imagine, decorated with mad colourful icing depicting spaceships and stars, dolls and fish. I place Marie's cake in an identical cake tin and slot it into the oven which I've turned off. Larry brings the crappy cake out to his car to dispose of it without the kids seeing.

'Kids are great,' he says, when he comes back, 'they just believe everything.' He forages about in the press and finds a packet of biscuits that somehow escaped the cake cull. We share them between us. 'Danny says you're going back to work next month.'

'Do you do anything other than talk about me when you go places?'

'Well, I didn't tell him that you had a one-night stand with the woman who sold you a Communion dress.'

I laugh, then tell him about taking my guitar down from the attic. 'The kids loved listening to it,' I say. 'When was the last time we went there?'

'Your attic?'

'The Rock Place, you thick!'

Larry laughs easily. 'Dunno, but I met every one of my girlfriends there. My social life has been shit since.'

I notice then that his hair has been 'styled' again. It's floppy and highlighted. Kate would have had a field day teasing him. His clothes too look a step up from the usual thick cord and mustard jumper club. 'You're looking mildly fashionable there, Lar,' I take another biscuit and sit back, eyeing him up and down. 'What's the story?'

'Like you'd know what fashion was.' He scoffs, indicating my worn jeans and black T-shirt.

I refuse to be sidetracked. 'So? You got someone or what?'

'Nope.'

'And?'

'What?'

'Who is she?'

'There is no one, but I'm working the Larry magic.' He moves his hands in a weird way.

'Oh, right. Well, good luck with that.'

He laughs. 'Any chance I could crash here tonight? I'd love to see the kids' faces in the morning.'

'Go on.'

'Great.'

He would have been so much better at this than me.

EMMA

When Daddy gets us up in the morning, I am worried. I was lying in bed last night and I thought that Daddy is a bit silly if he believes in a wishing cake. And if I have no cake to bring to school, some girls will laugh at me because I said I was going to bring a great cake and it didn't matter if I had no mammy to cook it. Now I don't know. I think I might pretend to be sick if it looks horrible.

Larry stayed last night and we have to wake him up before we go into the kitchen. When we tell Larry about the wishing cake in the oven he says that it is not true. He says no way. Daddy says that Larry is a septic, which means that Larry doesn't believe in things. But Larry still says no way. Larry says if it is true then he will pay me and Liam ten euros each.

Daddy says that the oven turned itself off, like magic when the cake was ready. He tells us to close our eyes. I peek but Daddy and Larry have their eyes closed. We all wish really hard.

Then Daddy tells me to open the oven. I pull it open real slow, just to give the magic extra time to work.

'Is the oven cold?' Daddy asks.

It is. I am scared now in case it didn't cook.

'That's part of the magic,' Daddy says. 'It means you can just reach in and take the cake out.'

So I do and the tin is cold.

And the cake!

Oh. My. God.

OMG is what the big girls say. It's like a party. It has fish on it and spaceships and dolls. It's pink and yellow and blue and green and red. I can't even talk when I show everyone because it is a miracle, like when we learned about Jesus and the loaves and fish only a much better miracle because it's cake. The cake is transformed, like me on my Communion day. Nana used that word and it is a good word. It means making something so beautiful you can hardly see it.

Liam gasps and gasps.

Larry says there is no way it can be true but it is, so he has to give us money.

'Can I bring this to school?' I ask Daddy, and he says yep.

Larry pokes the cake to see if it is real. Even though he paid us our money, he says it is a trick. That we must have tricked him. But no.

Larry goes to work then and he says he is going to tell everyone about the magic. Daddy walks Liam and me to my school. Liam is a bit mad because he wanted to eat some of the cake but Daddy says he will buy Liam a nice cake afterwards.

School term is nearly over now, which is good. I will be glad to have holidays away from all my class.

When I show teacher my cake, she says it is the best cake she ever saw and some of the girls agree. Teacher asks me how we made it and I tell her that Daddy said it was a wishing cake and that I just talked to my mammy in heaven and she came down and made it all up nice last night. It is only a small lie.

Some of the girls start to cry and say they are scared of my cake.

I say who could be scared of my cake?

The teacher says that it is a lovely cake and that it is time to do maths.

At break, Jane, who I don't talk to any more, comes over and says that I am a liar. But she is really the liar so I say no, that she's a liar. And she pokes me and says, 'Liar, liar pants on fire' and I say, 'Well, at least I have pants.' I saw that answer on a TV programme and some of the girls laugh.

Then Jane says that her mammy made an even nicer cake than my angel mammy and I said no way. And then she says – and this is what she keeps saying and it isn't a bit nice – she says that at least her daddy didn't kill someone. And I say that my daddy didn't either and she says why isn't my daddy still a fireman so and that she heard her mammy say it and I said that my daddy is just tired of being a fireman and Jane says that my daddy is a great big fat liar so I push Jane real hard and she hits her head only a tiny bit but she pretends it's real bad and now I am in trouble.

**

When my daddy comes to the school, he talks to my teacher without me being there. I don't know what the teacher says but Daddy tells her that I will be a good girl. When he comes out of the teacher's room, he says, 'Emma is a good girl' and I like that he says that. Then he takes my hand and we walk home. Only he doesn't say much on the way and I think he is sad.

'Did I make you sad, Daddy?' I ask. I don't want to make him sad because Mammy said he was sad when he left us.

He tells me that I could never make him sad. He says he is proud of me. He says I should always, always just be myself but that he is worried why I pushed Jane. And why I keep hitting some of the other girls. He says that that is not a nice thing to do and that I shouldn't do it any more.

I tell him that Jane was laughing at my cake and he tells me she is probably just jealous. Then I tell him that sometimes the girls say that their mammies are better than our angel mammy and he says that is rubbish, that everyone thinks their mammy is the best. Then I say that Jane said that he killed someone. Daddy stops walking then. He stops right in the middle of the street and crouches down. 'What?' he says.

I can tell he is angry at that. It is not a nice thing to say.

I say it again. I say that Jane said her mammy said it.

'And do you believe it?' Daddy asks.

'No!'

'So what difference does it make what she says?' He takes my two hands in his and squeezes them. His hands are warm.

That is a good point. But I tell him I don't like when she says it.

He says that I can't stop her from saying it. But that I have to just be happy with the fact that our wishing cake was the best in the class.

That is true.

He gives me a hug and I hug him back because he is being so nice.

It's nice to know that there are such things as wishes.

When we get home, Daddy takes out Mammy's book that she left him and I watch TV with Liam.

NICK

I have an urge to yell at Sue when I see her in the Parent and Toddler group the following day. I feel like going up and asking her why she had to discuss me in full earshot of her daughter. I want to ask her what the hell she knows about what happened that night. Does she have insider information? I fantasise about doing it but of course I won't. Maybe I'm too much of a coward. I'm sure most of the women here have heard some version of the story about me, but whatever they've heard, they've either forgotten or managed to ignore and I don't want to go dragging it back up. But poor Emma, to have to listen to it. I looked through Kate's book last night but I couldn't find anything on how to deal with horrible kids in school. Maybe it's because Kate never thought anyone was horrible.

Damping down my anger, I disgorge Liam from the buggy. Sue is in the kitchen and I see her busily putting fresh tea bags into the press and pulling out cups, shaking her head at the way they've been washed. God help the poor sod who messed that one up. She spots me looking and calls out, 'Hi, Nick. I see our two girls were in trouble during the week.' Her cheery tone grates and I can't believe she's brought it up. I cross into the kitchen. I don't return her smile and am gratified to see her own dimming. 'I've told Emma to hold her fire and I hope you've told Jane to do the same.'

'Well, I …,' she makes a face, then straightens up and gives me a bit of a glare, '… I'm not sure Jane is to blame, quite frankly, but I've told her to stay away.'

'I'm not sure Emma is to blame, quite frankly, either.'

'Right, well …' Sue shoots me an uneasy look and then dismisses me by walking past and clapping her hands, saying in her high-pitched kiddie voice, 'Who wants to do some drawing?'

She leads the kids towards the art table and I watch her for a second as she lays out paper and art supplies. Then taking a seat beside Molly, I mutter a 'Hey.'

'Are you in trouble with Sue again?' Molly gives me a playful dig. 'Honestly, if this keeps up you'll have to sit in the bold corner.'

I laugh and give her a rundown on the activities of our two offspring, leaving out the bit where Jane called me a murderer.

Molly laughs. 'We should get Emma in here to sort Sue out too,' she says, before adding, 'though really, Nick, Sue can be bossy and annoying but her heart is in the right place. She'll do a good turn as quick as anything.'

'The day I need her for a good turn, I'll be desperate,' I say back.

There must be something in my voice that stops Molly from saying any more on the subject. Instead she starts talking about how she's packed her bag for the hospital because she has a feeling that this baby will be early due to the pressure on her bladder. Just as I'm praying for someone to save me, Jean arrives, panting and red-faced, chomping on a health food bar. 'All set for tonight, Nick?' She elbows me quite hard in the ribs. 'Oh, sorry.' Then adds, 'When I'm tired like this, my limbs just go and do all sorts of things. I can't control them.'

'Lucky the man that gets you, then.' I grin, rubbing at where she elbowed me. It bloody hurts.

Jean snorts with laughter. 'So what time did you say we're meeting again?'

'Seven. Eat about two hours to ninety minutes beforehand.' It's the first running session tonight. Jean was only free after her night course in Mandarin Chinese ended. I've arranged to meet her in the local park and we're running a loop which I reckon will be about three kilometres.

'I got my feet tested,' she confides, 'like you said, for the good trainers. I'm a pronator.'

'I like a good pronator.'

Jean giggles and flaps a hand at me. I've discovered that Jean will giggle at absolutely anything. It's quite an attractive quality to have. 'Stop it! Anyway, the runners cost me about a hundred euro. I asked the guy who sold them if they have a turbo drive in them for that price.' Another giggle. 'And I hope you don't mind, but I've asked a few friends to come along too. Nothing like some moral support.'

'Are they going to be cheering you on?'

'No.' Jean shakes her head as if I'm thick. 'They're running too.'

'Hiya.' Philip's mother passes by, dragging Philip by the arm. Philip is not walking, just dragging his feet along. His mother doesn't bat an eyelid. 'See you tonight, Nick.' Then she laughs. 'Ever since you got here, I've been wanting to say that.'

'Sorry?'

'See you tonight? At the running! Jean is telling everyone. I like running. Philip,' she turns to her child, 'if you don't stand up, I'm going to let your arm go and you will fall flat on your face. Right. One, two, three.' She drops him but Philip, with the agility of an acrobat, breaks his fall and skids off towards the art table. 'Feck's sake.' She runs off after him.

'I didn't tell everyone.' Jean gives me an over-bright smile. 'Just a few people. And I didn't want her to come. She's far too skinny, she doesn't need running lessons.'

I shift about, suddenly uneasy. 'So how many people do you think are coming?'

'I don't know,' Jean says airily. 'I just put up a notice.' She makes big motions with her hands in the air as she says, 'Keep fit. Tuesday. In the park with Nick.'

'But it was just meant to be me and you,' I say. Holy Jesus. Me running with a whole pile of what will probably be women. I'm going to look like a tool.

'I know it was,' Jean says sympathetically, 'but try to get over the disappointment of not having me all to yourself.' She giggles and pats her belly. 'There's a lot to go around, you know.'

'I'm not sure I really want to be with a whole load of women,' I mutter.

'You're the first man ever to say that,' Molly remarks caustically. Then, 'Adam! Stop!' She runs over to where Adam, her four-year-old, has just fired a whole box of paint at Philip.

Philip, covered in green and red poster paint, has an armful of blocks and is firing them with gusto at all who approach. One little girl gets hit on the head and tells him to 'fuck off' before picking up a fallen block and firing it back.

Liam, I notice, is gamely joining in the chant of 'fight, fight, fight' which has started up.

Sue keeps trying to approach Philip, but as a brick wings its way towards her head, she flaps away like an agitated hen.

'Philip, stop it or I'll brain you!' his mother shouts.

'Who wants a game of football?' I call out over the noise. The lads here need to be run around. I remember the frustration of sitting in school as a child and all I wanted to do was to be up and out kicking a ball or kicking one of my classmates. When I was a kid, I'd rather have eaten my arm off than paint and play Lego. I pick up a ball that has lain idle in the corner ever since I've come here. Any time one of the kids attempts to kick it, Sue takes it away from them, telling them there is no space. 'Football!' I shout again. 'Who's playing?'

'Me!' Liam's hand is the first to shoot up.

Four or five more boys do the same.

A little girl drops her crayon to put her hand up.

Philip says that he hates football.

I pick up the ball and, throwing it up and down, ask them to come with me.

'Oh, you can't go out,' Sue twitters.

'Why, is there a magic lock on the door?'

My insolent tone makes the kids laugh, though some of the mothers look a bit taken aback. I feel suddenly ashamed.

'We are not insured for children going outside,' Sue says stiffly.

'I'll take the risk,' I say. I look around the room. 'Any mothers object to their children having a kickabout?'

'I'll go with you.' Jean hops up. 'Help keep an eye on them all.'

'I would too, only there are no toilets outside,' Molly says.

Adam, Molly's boy, bounds towards the door and pulls it open.

'See yez later,' I call.

I ignore Sue's frosty look.

We're soon out in the open, on a big grassy stretch, in front of the community centre. The sun is shining. Ten eager little kids all look up at me. 'We're going to divide you into teams. Who wants to be goalie?'

No one volunteers.

'OK,' I say, 'what's your best position on the pitch?'

'Striker,' someone says with a casual air. 'I'm great at scoring goals.'

'Yeah, me too,' another little boy says.

They all agree that, yes indeed, they are all good at scoring goals.

Jean and I share a grin.

'OK, well, you'll have to take turns doing that,' I tell them. 'And you'll have to take turns in goal.'

They groan but I divide up the teams anyway and ask for

volunteers to give me their jumpers to make the goals. Then I give them tips on how to play, which are lost on the younger ones but which make them feel important, and I show them a few tricks on how to dribble the ball. And we're off.

It's a hilarious match, with every one of the kids running after the ball like the Three Wise Men following the star. The goalies spend most of their time centre pitch too. I haven't laughed so much in ages.

Someone tips me on the shoulder. I turn around to see Philip's mother there, Philip all contrite beside her. 'Can I play?' he asks.

''Course you can, bud.'

He smiles at me.

'Only no one is allowed to get too rough or trip people up. They'll be put off if that happens, OK?'

'OK.'

'You're on the team playing left to right, Liam's team.'

Philip runs on and stands uncertainly on the pitch. 'They're all running after the ball,' he calls to me. 'No one is there to receive it.'

'Whoa, football brain or what?' I call back, impressed. 'Well done. Get stuck in.'

Philip waves at his mother, who waves back, and off he trots.

'Thanks,' his mother says. 'He loves kicking ball. That place in there drives him mental but I like bringing him 'cause the kids there are a bit normal, you know. The kids on our road would eat him for breakfast.'

'That's one scary road you live on so.' I grin.

'Too right,' she says.

And we turn back to the match and spend the rest of the time laughing.

* * *

The only person I could get to mind the kids is Marcy. She arrives straight from work, smelling of chemicals and perfume. Her too-tight trousers and her too-high shoes and her too-shiny hair all depress me. Something about her drives me to despair.

'Hello, my little chickens,' she calls out, her arms wide as my children throw themselves at her.

She stands back and surveys them. 'Good, in your pyjamas already. I've brought a DVD for us to watch. It's only ninety minutes long so it should be over by eight thirty. Is that OK, Nick?'

'Grand.' I don't tell her that the earliest they go to bed is ten. It is pretty late, I realise now, only I have no way of backtracking. Even though Kate listed their bedtimes, Emma cries when I try to make her go earlier and I can't bear it, so I just leave it.

'Half eight is nothing.' Emma ruins it. 'Daddy is fine about bedtime. Once we go up and don't come down again, he is fine.'

'So where are you off to?' Marcy asks. She eyes up my shorts and T-shirt. 'Running?' There's a silence.

She has a weird look on her face.

'I decided I'd get fit.'

'A whole load of women are joining him.' Emma again. 'All my friends' mammies.'

Marcy raises an eyebrow. 'That's nice.'

I have no idea what she means by that. I have no ability to read her. If I was to play cards against Marcy I'd lose every time because she wrong-foots me. So I go down the aggressive/defensive route. 'What do you mean, "That's nice"? What's so nice about it? It's only a run.'

It's like my words suck the warmth from the room.

Marcy gawks at me, struggling to form an answer.

'Daddy,' Emma says, sounding confused, 'why are you cross?'

'I'm not.' I smile, wide and unconvincing. 'Why would I be cross? It's only a run.'

'Come here and show me how to work your DVD player.' Marcy expertly distracts the kids and I stand like a spare, watching them yapping away to her. I should apologise but I can't. I just can't. This is the woman that cut me out when Kate was dying. She was there all the time, minding her, advising her, and I couldn't squeeze in. Oh, everyone else was allowed to help out, but when I asked what I could do, Marcy kept telling me there was nothing. Just give the kids a good time, she said, like I never normally gave the kids a good time. I was left feeling even more useless than I already was. I find that hard to forgive. This is the woman who told Kate to ignore my phone call that terrible night and …

'See yous,' I say, before the thoughts can crowd my head. The kids absently kiss me.

I've just opened the front door when I realise that Marcy has followed me out. 'Yeah?'

She looks a bit upset. 'Don't talk to me like you just did in there,' she whispers. 'I'm tired of it.'

'Talk to you like what?' I feign innocence.

'I was trying to make a joke and you turned it into something else. You have no right to cut me down like that.'

How many times did she cut me down? 'There are loads of people queuing up to mind my kids,' I say. 'Think about that now.' Even as I say it, I know it's low. Feeling like a heel, I turn away.

She catches up with me in the driveway. She grabs my sleeve. 'You will not stop me seeing those kids. Not ever.' She sounds a little panicky.

I know I won't. I wouldn't do it to them. Or do it to Kate. I say nothing. I climb into my car. Marcy, of course, doesn't give up. She hammers on the window. Feigning boredom, I roll it down. 'Kate would hate you if you did that.'

Why couldn't Kate have had a nicer friend? Someone I could get on with.

'She might hate me if I ran you over too, so you'd better get out of the way.'

Marcy moves aside.

I have to grin.

***

When I see a load of women in garish running gear at the entrance to the park, I do not believe that they are waiting for me. When Jean announces loudly, 'Here he is, girls!' I realise that the only running I want to do is in the opposite direction.

I freeze, unable to take another step, and Jean hurries over as quickly as she is able. 'Now, Nick,' she wheezes, 'isn't this a wonderful turnout?'

I smile like I'm drowning with no hope of being saved and I've just been shat on by a pile of seagulls.

A wonderful turnout is my worst nightmare. As Jean propels me rapidly towards them, I see that there are at least thirty women of all shapes and sizes, ranging from 'Jean size' to anorexic. Some of them look quite professional with their branded gear, while others have clothed themselves in heavy jogging pants and big sweatshirts. All of them look to me expectantly, as if I'm some kind of thinness guru. I have no clue what I'm meant to do. I was just going to run.

'Nick!' Jean announces, like she's saying, 'Christ has risen.'

'First of all,' I gulp out, sounding a little panicked, 'I am not an expert.'

They all assure me that that doesn't matter.

'Second of all, running is tough.'

They all agree that that doesn't matter either. I assure them that it *will* matter. No one leaves.

'Third of all, tonight, we'll … eh … start with a warm-up, then run gently, speed it up and then hopefully run a loop of the park. Is this OK with everyone?'

This is so OK with everyone. Their optimism is endearing.

'Right,' I say a little bit more confidently, 'form a circle.'

Cars with no engines could form a circle quicker than these women. They have to chat about it, greet each other, adjust their clothes. Finally, after about ten minutes we're assembled into a square.

I make up some rudimentary exercises for them to do. I get them to jump and flap their arms about. People going by look, and I cringe and try to conceal myself among these women. I'm a man's man, always have been. Being the only man among a load of women, nice and all as they are, is my idea of hell.

'Oh, me bladder,' someone shrieks as she jumps.

People laugh.

I stop the jumping pretty abruptly.

A woman at the back puts her hand up like it's school. 'Can I ask you a question, please?'

'I'm not an expert.'

'Where is a good place for a sports bra? Can you recommend any?'

'No.'

'How would he know that?' Jean snorts. 'For God's sake.'

Someone else offers advice and more time is taken up. Then someone asks if the time of the month can affect performance. I pretend not to hear.

I think they're doing it for a laugh now because someone sniggers.

'OK,' I say loudly, 'let's get going. Gently now.'

'As my husband said last night,' someone else squeaks, amid much laughter.

I start off slow. It is not a success. Half of the women complain that I'm going too fast. I go even slower. They catch up. The other half say it's too slow. I tell everyone that three kilometres is a long way, that slower is better. 'OK, come on, keep up if you can. We'll all wait for each other at the end.'

I start to run.

Philip's mother is leading the pack. She looks good, her hair is tied back in a ponytail and she's got a youthful energy which is missing when she's in the Parent and Toddler group. Her running style is good to watch. 'You're going well,' I tell her. I'm beginning to pant a bit. My calves are tight.

'I used to do it in college,' she says. 'About eight years ago.'

That makes her about twenty-six. She looks older. 'And what did you do in college?'

'Got pregnant.' She laughs ruefully. 'I know, I'm a fucking eejit. Never finished my degree, never did anything after that. But it's not so bad, I have Philip, don't I?'

That's the good part? Her life must be shit. 'You run well.' It's embarrassingly hard keeping up with her.

'I was a track champion over fifteen hundred.'

'No way.' I think I might tell her of my one glorious eight hundred but I don't. It was a long time ago.

'I loved your warm-up.' A cheeky grin.

I grin back. 'Could you tell I was winging it?'

'Totally.'

We laugh.

'You take the warm-down, you must know what to do.'

'Aw, no way. I couldn't.' She blushes, looking unsure.

'You could. I was only meant to come with Jean, to help her exercise, and somehow she told everyone.'

'She put posters up.'

'So I heard.'

'Your football was great today. Philip was knackered after it. His own dad fecked off. But even if he had stayed, I wouldn't say he'd have played with him. Bloody disaster, he was.'

I don't know what to say to that.

'I'd love a good man in his life,' she goes on a little sadly.

'I haven't been great myself,' I find myself admitting. It's easy to own up to not being perfect when someone else has been through the mill too.

'My arse. Philip thinks Liam is dead lucky to have you.'

'Really?'

'Defo.' And with that she ups the pace and speeds away from me. I try to keep up. I was a good runner too but this girl is just better.

I tail her right to the end and then put on a final spurt. But unfortunately so does she. She beats me by twenty metres or so, and while she looks remarkably fresh, I need every ounce of strength to flop onto the grass. I think I'm going to puke.

Philip's mother folds her arms, looking down on me. 'Better luck next time,' she sniggers.

'It wasn't a race,' I say offhandedly. Kate would laugh. She knew I hated it when she beat me.

'Course not,' she says.

Most of the women are walking by the time the session ends. A few of them have stripped down to T-shirts. Their faces are heart-attack red.

'I'll never walk again,' someone complains as she arrives back on wobbly legs.

'You will,' I say, not really believing it myself. My legs are ferociously heavy. 'The thing is to keep at it. Now, this girl,' I point to Philip's mother, who gawks at me, 'she'll be showing you a warm-down.'

'Fuck off,' she says in horror.

'If I had the energy, I would,' I quip, and people laugh.

Philip's mother gulps a bit and mutters, 'Hi, everyone, I'm Chantelle.'

I realise I hadn't known her name until then.

'Hi, Chantelle,' the rest of them chorus.

'I ran for years, so I can show you what I learned. These exercises should help you not be so sore tomorrow. But if you are, the best thing is to get out and run it off.'

Someone moans.

'And also,' Chantelle says, 'I see some of you in cheap trainers. Get fitted for proper ones. Your knees and all will get wrecked otherwise.' She names a few shops where they can buy good runners.

Chantelle starts to do some stretches with them and I have to say, to my shame, that for a guy who's not getting a lot of sex, being in the centre of a load of women who are bending over to touch their toes kind of rocks.

* * *

When I and my erection get home, Larry's car is outside the house. He'd said he might call over and eat a takeout with me, seeing as he was working late and I was forgoing dinner in case it came up all over the park. Marcy is still here too but chances are that she'll go once I come in.

To my surprise, the kids don't come to greet me. From the kitchen, Marcy is laughing. Entering, I can't believe my eyes. Marcy is lounging on a chair, holding a cup towards Larry as he solicitously pours her some tea. 'Cosy, eh?' I say.

Larry looks a little startled, I think.

'Larry is just telling me about the wishing cake,' Marcy says, smiling up at him. 'I got a garbled version from the kids but his makes much more sense.'

Larry smiles weakly.

'Where are the kids?' I ask, ignoring both of them.

'Bed.' All traces of our row have been erased from Marcy's voice. But, then again, when she talks about the kids, she reminds me of me. It's the one thing I like about her. The world could make me angry but they just wipe it off. 'Poor little things were knackered. The DVD was a bit of a rollercoaster.'

'Are they asleep?' I'm kind of amazed. It's only nine thirty.

'Yeah, I think so. You should go up and look at them. Liam looks dead cute sucking his thumb.'

'I'll grab a shower while I'm there. Larry, are you getting takeout?'

'Yep.' Larry nods. 'I thought Indian?'

'Indian is grand. Get my usual.'

'Marcy?' Larry asks.

For fuck's sake. Why has he asked her?

She looks a little surprised herself. 'OK. Thanks. I'll have a beef korma.'

'Korma,' Larry scoffs. 'Lightweight.'

'OK, I'll have the vindaloo.'

'Oh-ho.' Larry rubs his hands and whips out his mobile. Then he glances back at me. 'Well, hurry up, will ya. The food might arrive and you'll still be showering.'

I stomp upstairs as best I can with my sore legs. I'm in a bit of a mood, though I can't say why. I should be glad they're both making an effort to get on, but I'm not. The first thing I do is peep in on Emma. Her room is such a pretty place, all pink with fairies and ballerinas. Every time I walk in the door, the sheer prettiness and innocence of it grabs my heart. She is curled up under her pink covers, her thumb in her mouth. She stirs as if she senses me there and her face scrunches up like she's having a bad dream. I touch her forehead, tell her it's OK and she calms down. I stand looking at her for a few more seconds before heading in to Liam. The poor kid is a typical second child. His room is a bit of a mishmash. I guess we had run out of steam for him and the idea of doing up his room seemed so trivial at the time. He's in his cot bed, already too big for it, sucking his thumb. His face is round and baby fat still, his hair too long for a boy, but Kate liked it long and I can't bear to cut it, not yet.

I press a kiss to his forehead with my fingertips and leave.

Showered and changed, I head back downstairs. Larry is paying the delivery man for the food at the front door. One thing about our Indian, they deliver quickly. 'Why did you invite her?' I whisper, nodding to the kitchen.

Larry gives me a puzzled look. 'Because she minded your kids all evening, that's why.' He makes it sound quite reasonable but he knows how she rubs me up all wrong.

'Well, it'll put me off my food.' I'm only half-joking.

Larry grins mildly. 'I don't mind finishing it.' He takes the food from the delivery man and, closing the front door with his foot, he heads back into the kitchen, me following.

While I've been upstairs, they've set the table, poured three glasses of water and heated up the plates. It must be Marcy's doing because Larry and I never think of stuff like that. We usually eat out of the cartons. I like eating out of cartons.

Larry gets busy laying the food on the plates while I refill the jug of water. Marcy does nothing, just watches us from her position at the table. Well, watches me, actually, as if I might bite her.

'How'd the running go?' Larry asks.

I fill him in. If Marcy wasn't there, I could be a lot more entertaining, but she'd probably object to something I'd say.

'Oh, so you're the Nick on the poster then.' Marcy grins at me and I'm unnerved. I feel like she's a cat and I'm a mouse. Why is she grinning? Does she have a motive? Where are my card skills when I actually need them? 'Someone came into the salon yesterday and asked me to hang one up.'

'Well, take it down, for God's sake.' I pick up a fork and start to eat. God, it's good. 'I'd feel a lot better with a few men on board.'

'Well, it won't be me,' Larry says, holding up his arms. 'I get enough exercise chasing women who keep running away from me.'

'No!' Marcy says, like it's a big shock. 'From what I remember, we had such an entertaining date.'

Now that's low, I think. Dragging up the past like that. But Larry laughs loudly. 'I have money now and I can bring a girl anywhere she wants but the only place most of them want to go is home.'

'I'm sure that's not true.' Marcy smiles, forking an enormous quantity of vindaloo into her mouth.

We both watch her chew and are quite impressed, it has to be said.

Larry scratches a patch of red on his face. 'To be honest, a person doesn't tend to date much when they've gone through the trauma of having a gay wife. My life was like an episode of *Friends* there for a while. Only without the funny bits.'

'Kate always suspected she was gay,' Marcy says.

'She did?' Larry looks to me.

'Lar,' I break it gently to him, trying not to smile, 'we all kinda did.'

He raises his eyebrows.

'She was always with that other girl, Tanya. And she was into football and weightlifting and, you've got to admit, she wore a lot of suits.'

Marcy suppresses a laugh.

Larry waves her on. 'Oh, laugh. It's fine. I'm over it. I was blinded because she was like the ideal woman. Gorgeous and into guy things.' He dips some naan into his curry and chews morosely.

'I wonder why she married you,' Marcy says.

'That's lovely,' Larry says dryly.

'No.' Marcy is quick to placate him. 'I mean why marry you if she was gay.'

Larry chews some more. I know the answer to that even if he doesn't. But he surprises me. 'She wanted the package, the whole family thing. And so did I. My parents died when I was a kid and all I ever wanted after that was a real family. So we blinded ourselves to reality and dived right in.' A pause. 'I learned that in couples therapy.'

I never knew he'd gone to therapy. 'Therapy? Like a shrink?'

'They're called counsellors,' Larry says, like I'm a dork. 'And it was good. I only had to go once.'

'Oh, yeah, because you are as stable as an Irish bank.'

'Says the man who's just come out of St Michael's.'

The way he says it makes me laugh. And I never thought I'd laugh at being in a psychiatric hospital. I flick a spoon of rice at him.

He fires some back.

Issue closed, we start eating again.

'So, your parents died?' Marcy gets us back to what we'd been discussing. 'That must have been terrible.'

'It was, yeah. In my teen years I virtually moved in with Nick's folks.'

'He did,' I confirm. 'They had to build an extension for him.'

Larry almost chokes with laugher on his chicken.

'Yeah, they are great,' Marcy says. 'My parents are disasters. I couldn't get away fast enough.'

Kate had told me once how horrible Marcy's mother was and I think I'd said something along the lines of, 'like mother, like daughter', and that had been the end of that.

'I'd say in those heels, you had problems getting away fast,' Larry teases, and Marcy laughs. Huh, if I said that, she'd accuse me of being flippant. But Larry gets away with stuff like that all the time. No one can take offence when he's so self-deprecating, I guess.

'Tell you one thing,' Larry says approvingly, 'you're well able for your vindaloo.'

Larry likes women who like spicy food. His ex-wife could drink Tabasco sauce and was only hospitalised the first time.

'I'm well able for lots of things,' Marcy says, and it sounds very suggestive. Larry thinks so too as he gulps audibly.

I grit my teeth and get another glass of water. Why is she turning it on like that? Marcy is not like your average woman. OK, she's fanciable, I'll say that. But like a Mercedes, she's all gorgeous on the outside, but look beyond that and it's clear she's overvalued and would be a nightmare to run. Surely Larry can see beyond the tight clothes and the throaty laugh and the large breasts. Where is the guy that spits at the sound of her name? Why isn't he scared of her any more?

I sit back down with my glass of water and observe, trying to figure out what is going on. I see that Larry is at his sparkling best. OK, he has a few red patches on his face but it's like she has him in a spotlight and he can't even look away to scratch them. If he was a ship, she'd lure him to the rocks.

I think of the horror of them getting together. I'd have lost my best ally. He'd be on her side, just like Kate was.

'Hey.' Larry clicks his fingers in front of my face. 'Are you still with us, Nick? I'm just telling Marcy the stunt you pulled when we went to that Indian restaurant years ago?'

'Oh, yeah.' Why is he telling her that?

'D'you want to tell her?'

'Nah, you do it.' Larry loves this story.

Larry looks a little disappointed in me but he says, 'OK.' He turns to Marcy and crouches towards her the way he does when he tells a story. 'Years ago, oh, I don't know now, before we even knew Kate, I reckon, me and Nick and some of our mates used to eat at this Indian restaurant. It was like a novelty back then. It was probably the first Indian restaurant in Ireland or something.'

Marcy grins.

'Anyway,' Larry goes on, 'this night Nick and me ordered the korma.'

'Lightweight,' Marcy teases.

'We were,' Larry grins. 'We were suspicious of spices. Anyway, there we are eating our kormas and in the middle of the meal, Nick calls the waiter over and doesn't he tell him that the korma is off. The poor fella nearly drops his Indian accent he's so upset. What can I do to make it up? he says. Then Nick says, real serious,' Larry adopts my voice, quite unsuccessfully as it happens, "D'you know what, don't worry about it, I knocked down a guy on the way here, so …" Larry splutters on a laugh, "… it's probably just bad korma."'

Marcy joins in Larry's laughter.

I smile a little, remembering. 'What can I say, I'm hilarious.'

'You were, though,' Larry says.

There is an awkward silence.

Marcy looks from one to the other of us. I don't know what she senses but she obviously decides to get going. 'I'd better be off.' She's all false cheer. She pulls on her tight leather jacket and shakes her hair out over the collar. 'It's past my bedtime.'

I'm glad.

'Thanks for the curry, guys.'

'No worries.' Larry bids her a cheery goodbye and both of us watch her as she sashays out of the house.

'Well, that went well.' Larry grins at me.

'What?' I ask grumpily, slugging back some water. 'Well for who?'

'For us all.' Larry looks a little bewildered at my tone. 'You know, we all have to get on now.'

'Well, you're certainly doing that.'

'Pardon?'

'Do you fancy her?'

'Oh, for Jaysus' sake!' He laughs a little, a mirthless sound. Then he leans his hands on the table, his face almost shoved into mine.

I have to pull back a bit. 'Do I fancy her? The girl is in your kids' lives. They're mad about her. They've lost their mother, they don't need to lose her too!'

'I wouldn't be so bloody lucky!'

He pulls away and sighs in exasperation, then turns back to me. 'She was upset when I got here, d'you know that? Apparently, you told her she wouldn't be able to see the kids again.'

I wish I had a bottle of wine in the house.

'Did you say that to her or not?'

'Have you morphed into my dad?' It's a feeble attempt at humour.

'So you did.'

'Yes.' I pause. 'She knew I didn't mean it.'

'Well, she was scared you did,' Larry says, his voice low for the sake of the kids upstairs, but he is pretty furious, which is a bit of a shock. 'You'd want to cop on, Nick. Tonight, that was about cheering her up. That was about letting bygones be bygones. I meet that girl every month up at Kate's grave. We chat. We go for coffee. She—'

'That's cosy.' He has no idea how much that hurts.

'She is lost without Kate.' His voice rises above mine. 'Lost,' he repeats, 'just like we all are. Just like you are. So just cop on. Now.'

The air quivers with so much tension that I can almost touch it. I hate falling out with Larry. And of course he's right. 'Sorry!' The words wrench themselves from somewhere. 'Sorry.'

Larry pulls away. He sinks into a chair. He thumps my arm. 'Yeah. I know. But a bit of perspective, Nick.'

'Well,' I manage a grin, 'you're better at all this perspective shit, you've had therapy.'

And I know if Kate were alive she'd have gone mental, but when Larry flicks his last morsel of rice at me, I fist his arm and he fists mine back, and before we know it, we're wrestling and laughing like when we were kids.

* * *

I take out Kate's book that night after Larry leaves. I do it most nights now. It makes me feel close to her, to think that she touched those pages and thought those thoughts. And I want to get through it; I don't want to feel that there is something she wanted that I missed. Finding the Communion page was the shock I needed. Imagine, I almost missed hiring that castle because of my reluctance to read the book. That won't happen again. Tonight, I see a section marked 'Christmas' and read the type of things she thinks the kids would like from Santa. There is another section on books they like and ideas on what ones to buy for them. Then I come to a page she has marked 'The Garden'. There are pictures of what our garden used to look like at various times during the year. I glance out the window, and though it's dark, I know what lies beyond is an unloved wilderness. Kate has written down in meticulous detail what has to be done with it. I vow to give it a go the next sunny day.

EMMA

When I made my Communion, the priest said that our mission this year was to say our prayers and make Jesus our friend. Imagine being friends with the son of God, that'd be like being friends with someone in sixth class. It's a bit hard to make Jesus your friend, though, when he is invisible, but at least he can't say mean things about your daddy being a murderer or, even worse, just forget about your mammy.

I am going to make Jesus my best friend. Even though Daddy forgets to say prayers with me, I say them myself. First off, I say a proper prayer like the Hail Mary full of grapes one or a Oh My God, which is shorter but really a confession one, then after that, I talk to Jesus in my head. It's the same as talking to Mammy only Jesus is the son of God and Mammy is just the daughter of a nana we never even met. I ask Jesus if my mammy is OK up in heaven and for him to tell her that me and Liam are fine. I tell him to say that Daddy plays his guitar to us at night-time when we ask him and that Larry makes him laugh. I tell him to tell her that yesterday Daddy dug a big hole in the garden and planted a tree. I ask Jesus to make Daddy better at cooking dinner and also, and most importantly, not to let my daddy go away on us. I sometimes think that I will wake up in the morning and Daddy will not be there, that Jack will come and Daddy will go away. So that makes me be all nice to Daddy so he will stay, but sometimes I just get so mad at him, like when he does things different to the way Mammy did them. Sometimes Daddy gets mad back at me and that makes me afraid that he will go. And then I think that maybe Daddy will get sick and die and go off with Jesus the way Mammy did. I sometimes think that maybe Mammy just wanted to be with Jesus more than she wanted to be with us, just like Daddy with Jack. Even though Daddy tells me and Liam that he loves us, he said he loved Mammy too.

Then I say A Men, which means 'so be it' or 'I'm done'.

And I bless myself.

* * *

We go to Nana's and Granddad's at the weekend. Just for a visit. Nana must think that Daddy is not able to remember stuff because she says, 'I thought you'd forgotten us,' and she doesn't sound happy about that but no one likes to be forgotten about. Daddy tells her not to go on about it so I wonder if maybe Daddy is forgetting things.

It's ages since we've seen them and I like their house. It's real small, not like ours which is big and has echoes and ever since Mammy went off with Jesus, it feels bigger. Nana's house has a little kitchen and you sit up on high stools at a bench to eat. She has yellow sunshine presses that all her food is in and it is up high so Liam can't pull things out. In her back garden, there is an old swing that Daddy used to play on when he was little. It still works but is real creaky and Granddad brings me and Liam out to play on it. The swing is at the end of the garden and to get to it, me and Liam have to run through real high grass because Granddad has no pride and never bothers cutting the grass. I wonder if pride is a type of lawnmower.

We take turns on the swing. First Granddad sits with Liam on his knee and I have to push them. It's hard. Then I go on my own and I hold on to the chain and Granddad pushes me real high. It's nice being up in the air, seeing all things looking small.

Then Daddy spoils it by knocking on the window and telling Granddad not to push me so high. I say that I am fine, that I want to go high, but Daddy doesn't hear me. Granddad stops pushing me so high then and I am a bit cross but then Granddad says he will bring us to the shops. His back garden has a little gate at the end that you can go out and you are on a road. He holds both our hands because this road is dangerous with lots of cars and trucks. I would like to live with Nana and Granddad on their dangerous road or with Marcy in her apartment. Not with Larry, though, 'cause his apartment is quite messy and he plays a lot of Playstation and he has big charts all over the place and lots of computer stuff. He has a basketball hoop on his wall, which is only fun twice. I think Liam could live there.

Granddad asks us how we are. I say that Liam and me are fine, thank you very much. That's what Mammy told us to say when someone asked us. When I was small and someone talked to me, I used to hide behind Mammy's legs and I don't know why now. Liam is never shy like that.

Then Granddad bends down and asks but how are we really? Do we miss Mammy? I don't know how to answer this sort of 'how are you' question. We are not at the shops yet, only halfway, and Granddad is looking at me because he knows that Liam can't talk.

I tell him that Mammy is with Jesus and that we can talk to her in our heads. I don't want to talk about it any more because I think I am going to cry. But Granddad is still looking at me so I tell him that Mammy gave me all her necklaces and jewellery and that I wore a ring into school last week and everyone was jealous. I nearly lost it too but I don't tell him that bit. I tell him about the wishing cake and he likes that story and he says that we must be good at wishing for things. I tell him that I'm not because Mammy hasn't come back yet and he says that some things you just can't wish for, that our wish came true when we had such a lovely Mammy and that wishes for Mammy are probably used up a little bit. That maybe we should wish for other things instead.

I wonder is he forgetting Mammy too.

You can still wish anyway.

* * *

When we get back from the shops, Nana has made us a lovely dinner. In the middle of dinner she tells me and Liam that when Daddy goes back to work she will mind us and would we like that? I say that that will be good. I tell her that Liam feels the same.

Daddy says that he will be off on Tuesdays as he will have to work on Saturdays so on Tuesday he will be able to bring Liam to Parent and Toddler group and collect me from school. He says that even though he will be at work, nothing will change for us at all. He will cook us pancakes that day too.

After dinner, me and Liam go in to the television. Nana puts on a DVD for us to watch. She has a small TV, not like our big one. While Liam is watching, I look at all Nana's ornaments. I am looking for the black cat one. Nana has lots of ornaments that she swaps about all over the place so that sometimes sheep are on the windowsill and other times elephants. Daddy says Nana's room is downright creepy. We are not allowed play with the ornaments because ornaments are not toys. Other things in the room are flowery cups and saucers that she never uses in a cabinet. Probably like the animals, the cups are not for using. Her room smells old. Then I see it. It is a black cat with green eyes and he is all shined up. He is a bit high for me to reach but I stand on my tiptoe and get my fingertips to him. Then I curl my hand around his body and I look at Liam, who is looking at the TV, so I take the cat and put it in my pocket.

Jesus won't mind, I don't think, as it will be worth it in the end.

Nana won't either when she sees what I want it for. It will be a surprise.

NICK

Before I know it, the third date comes around. The weeks have picked up pace, the way they do coming into summer. The numbers of women attending the running have expanded. Two men mercifully materialised last week so that was good. I've started running myself too in between times and I can feel my fitness coming back. It's good, like I have some control over something.

Parent and Toddler is coming to an end in the next week and I've proposed a little football insert for when it resumes in September, which hasn't gone down well with Sue at all.

It's weird how the season is changing: the weather is growing milder, the leaves are back on the trees and Kate is gone. That's the hard part of death. The fact that the world goes on but that yours has stopped for a bit.

The dates are a connection to Kate, I think now, and as the other two haven't been so bad, I'm banking on this one being OK too. In fact, part of me is kind of looking forward to it, mainly because I can read something from Kate afterwards.

I've asked my folks to babysit mostly because my mother is annoyed with me as I haven't called up to them in ages. Apparently, I only call over when I want something, which I guess is shamefully true. When Kate was alive, she made it her business to call over a couple of times a month with the kids, but I think women are good at that. I don't need to call over to be thinking of them but my mother seems to think I do. Her house isn't exactly kid friendly anyway, it is the kind of place where if you turn too quick, you'll knock something down. She is obsessed with ornaments and knick-knacks. She even has things I brought home for her from school tours years ago. It's embarrassing to walk into a house and see a big banner proclaiming 'To My Mammy, I Love You!' hanging up on the wall.

Anyway, tonight she arrives over with a huge bag of sweets for the kids and a bottle of expensive wine for herself. 'I'll just have the one glass,' she says. 'It'll be nice to have wine in peace. I left your dad at home and told him if he didn't cut the grass I was leaving him.'

'Well, good luck finding some place to stay,' I joke, and she laughs and says, 'Oh, Nicholas,' so I know I've been forgiven and I make a mental note to call over more often.

At that moment Emma and Liam charge into the room and my mother enfolds them in a big, squashy hug. She's a hugger, my mother, which is great when you're a kid but not so good at fifteen. Though Kate loved her hugs and so did Larry.

My mother settles the children on each side of her and gets them to close their eyes and hold out their hands. Then she pours a river of sweets into each outstretched palm. The two squeal in delight. 'Right, that's another twenty euro a week I've to save.' I grin.

'What?' my mother says, looking over her shoulder at me.

'Don't mind him, Nana.' Emma dismisses me with a toss of her fine hair. 'He always says that when someone gives us sweets. He says it's for fillings.'

My mother laughs and I wink at her and she goes, 'Oh, Nicholas' again. I've been truly forgiven now.

The doorbell rings, and amidst much kiss-blowing and 'goodbyes', I leave the room.

My heart drops like a stone at the all-too-familiar silhouette outside the door. Still, I knew that it had to happen sooner or later. If Kate wants me to meet her mates, then of course her best mate is going to feature.

'Marcy,' I say, as pleasantly as I can, pulling open the door.

She's dressed for attention, that's all I can say. Plus, she smells like the botanic gardens in full bloom.

'Nick,' she says back. To give her credit, she does attempt a smile. It sort of looks nailed to her face.

'I've been expecting you,' I tell her, and she laughs.

It's an unnatural sound.

'We better get going before the kids see you, or they'll make you stay.'

I half hope that'll appeal to her, but nope, she nods and strides before me down the drive, all ass and hips.

Marcy drives a mini, a yellow one with yellow and black trim. I feel totally ridiculous as I climb with difficulty into the tight front seat. Big furry cats glare at me from every conceivable pocket in the vehicle. Marcy opens her door and flings her purse onto the back seat.

The car smells of lemon.

'I know you'll hate where I'm bringing you,' she says, 'but Kate wanted it and I agreed.'

It sounds like a warning.

As we drive to wherever we are going, Marcy is oblivious to the number of guys that do a double take as we stop at traffic lights. There's always some fella in the car beside us that nudges his mate or just plain gawks. She is an imposing figure behind the wheel, it has to be said. Her profile is determined; over-large sunglasses fail to dominate her aggressive-looking face. Overall she gives the impression of being a highly successful businesswoman, which I guess she is, running her own business and all. Neither of us say much on the journey over; I don't know how we'll spend an evening in each other's company. When we eventually park in Drury Street, in the city centre, I have the uneasy feeling that I know where we are going.

'OK,' she says as she locks her car. 'Here we go.'

I walk beside her, my hands shoved into my jacket, head down. She's good at walking in the stilettos; I almost have to jog to keep up with her. I wonder if she's walking this fast so that we can get this night over with. I think she is.

My phone bleeps. Because it's Marcy, I'm rude and take it out. 'Anyone nice?' Larry texts.

I grin and shove it back into my pocket.

'I'm betting that was Larry,' Marcy says, without even looking in my direction. She hikes the sunglasses into her hair; the evening is a little dull. 'He said he was going to text you and it was killing me that I couldn't tell him it was me.'

'You and Larry seem to be getting on well,' I remark, as casually as I can.

'He's a really nice guy,' Marcy says, as if this surprises her. Then it's my turn to be surprised as I notice we've arrived outside Langton's, the super-expensive restaurant where Kate, Larry, Marcy and I once had our disastrous foursome.

'I think this is Kate's way of telling us to get along in future,' Marcy says, turning to smile at me.

The smile wrong-foots me. My lack of a smile wrong-foots her. It's all a bit awkward.

As far as Marcy and Kate were concerned, the night of the foursome was the start of the rot. But I'm not that petty. In the beginning, I enjoyed teasing Kate about her friend. I liked the way she'd get all fired up and then dissolve in giggles at whatever smart remark I'd throw out. I'm sure, in time, we would all have rubbed along just grand. In fact we were doing OK until all the crap happened to me.

We were doing fine until Marcy showed her true colours and turned Kate against me. And Kate didn't know that I heard what I heard that night on the phone. I couldn't tell her. I don't know exactly why, maybe because I felt Marcy was right, maybe because I didn't want Kate to see how much she'd hurt me. No man likes anyone to have that much power over them. Well, not me anyway. And so I resented Kate and blamed Marcy. And the blame has built up like an infection that hasn't been dealt with properly.

'We can only get on if we're honest with each other,' I say, without knowing that I was going to say anything. I flick a glance at Marcy, who shoots me a quizzical look. Maybe now is the time to clear the air, to show her that I'm not bearing a ridiculous grudge over a dinner date gone wrong.

I pull open the door and let her go in front of me. I wonder, when I ask her, will she even remember the incident? If she does and she successfully explains it away or says she didn't mean it the way I took it up, then I know I'll let it go. Or I'll do my best. But until then, it'll eat away at me like a cancer. I've never held a grudge against anyone before. Larry was right when he said I used to be fun. I used to be a really nice guy to know. All I want to do is find my way back there.

The head waiter or whatever he is scurries out to meet us. He's better dressed than I am. He's clutching a rake of black leather-bound menus close to his chest. His eyes appraise us, settling finally on Marcy. 'Ello?' he says in a French accent.

'I've booked a table for two, please.' Marcy's husky voice makes his eyes widen even more in appreciation and he looks at her the way I'd look at a great hand of cards. 'Name of Marcy Kirwan?'

'Tees way, s'il vous plaît,' he says, ushering us along. 'I teenk you request tees table?' He gestures to a table set in a recess.

It's set for two, but many years ago, it had been laid for four. My heart twists.

'Thank you.' Marcy smiles at him, and if he could combust with desire, I reckon he would. He lavishly pulls out Marcy's seat and hands us each a menu. Marcy orders a water and I order a beer. I'll need it. I'll need all the courage I have to ask her. Asking her will reveal … I dunno … my desperation, I guess. Vulnerability, even. Better than asking Kate, though.

'It hasn't changed, has it?' Marcy looks around. Her neck is long and slender and she has small neat ears, which she has pierced all the way up. 'I've never been back.'

'Me neither.'

The waiter lays our drinks in front of us and tells us he'll be back for our order.

Marcy leans towards me and her eyes are … I can't even describe them. They're not hostile, is the only way I can put it. 'Look, Nick,' she says, and I bristle, feeling I'm in for a lecture. 'Your loyalty to Larry is commendable but he's managed to get over the fact that we all got off on the wrong foot that night, so maybe you should too?' She gives a bit of a laugh. 'I tried too hard, I know that. And it was years ago.'

She tried too hard? She hadn't tried at all.

'And I know now Larry was nervous,' she goes on, her voice all syrupy, like as if she's explaining something to an eejit. 'He told me. And I know he has some sort of nervous skin thing, he told me. And I know I look like a horse at a rodeo, he told me that too.'

Wow, Larry has certainly told her a lot of things.

'I was nervous too that night.' She looks hopefully at me. 'Can we put it behind us?'

I lay my beer on the table. My heart is thumping and I feel a bit sick. Maybe I should just leave it. But I might as well drink poison and hope not to die. It bugs me, it confuses me. It bloody hurts me. 'I have something I want to ask you,' I say.

'Yes?' She looks politely interested.

How do I say this without appearing weak? I take a while to phrase it and all the time Marcy is studying me, with no idea what's coming. 'That night was a mess, you're right. But I'm not that petty.'

A faint smile lights her face. 'Oh … well—'

'I want to ask you about something you said to Kate a few years ago,' I interrupt, trying to keep the shake from my voice. I harden it, make it sound as if I just need this little thing to be cleared up.

'Yes?' Now she looks puzzled. 'What did I say?'

'You see, you probably didn't think I heard you, but I did.'

'And?' Nothing. No clue.

Fuck, I hoped she'd remember without me having to explain. Explaining only makes me sound as hopeless as I felt back then. Perhaps I've been hopeless ever since. 'It was about three months, well, maybe more, but after …' I swallow, '… after Tom and, eh, Alan died.' It's the first time I've said their names in four years. I feel sick.

There's a cautiousness in the way she pulls slightly back from me, almost as if she's protecting herself. She says nothing, though.

'I, eh, well, I rang Kate from work one night.' I don't say that I had a panic attack. That I was so paralysed with fear when the lads got a call out to a fire that I had vomited. 'I asked her to pick me up. You were there with Kate.'

Marcy still says nothing.

'And she was about to collect me, you know, but in the background you told her to look after herself and to rethink coming out to me.' My voice cracks. 'I heard you.'

Marcy opens her mouth, then closes it again. She stares at me as if she's about to run but can't decide where to.

'Kate said she couldn't make it. I was …' I inhale sharply and plough on, '… I was in bits and she never came. She sent Larry and he made me come home with him, said Kate was out with you. But you told her not to come. Why would you do that?' A pause. 'And why would she leave me?'

'Reedy to order?' The waiter arrives back.

'No,' I say rudely.

'In a few minutes.' Marcy gives him a wobbly smile and, a little placated, he moves off.

'Why?' I ask. Please just let her give a good reason, I think. Then I can let the anger go.

'It was nothing,' Marcy says, but she's shaken. 'She was there all the other times you needed her.'

'Why would you do it? I just want to understand.'

'Kate was stressed with everything. She wasn't able. I was minding her.'

'I know she was,' I say, 'and if there had been another way, I'd never have rung her. But I …' I stop. I drink some beer. I can't say it. I can't say that I was cracking up, that I needed her like I needed air, that I don't think I ever got over the fact that she didn't come. That she never explained. 'You should have minded your own business.'

Marcy goes to say something, then stops. It's as if she's physically restraining herself.

'What?' I say. I go to drink more beer but it's gone. I drank that very fast.

'And you should have minded your wife,' she hisses, leaning across the table and startling me. It's like something out of *The Exorcist* and I flinch. Then she pulls back and says, sounding bitter, 'You and your bloody self-pity made your wife and children miserable—'

'Stop,' I say to her. 'Don't.' I say it quietly but her words are sticks, beating me.

'I was there to help them. Where were you? Off with some young lad you were trying to fix to shore up your pathetic self-esteem.'

'That's not why I did it.' I don't sound convincing, not even to myself.

'Truth is, Nick, you never deserved her.' Tears form at the edges of Marcy's eyes and roll down her cheeks. The silent way it happens is worse than her shouting at me. 'She was my lovely friend and you hurt her.' Then she gets up. 'This was a mistake,' she says as she furiously scrubs her eyes. 'Let's not bother.'

'You still haven't said why she never came that night,' I say.

'Because you are a worthless piece of shit,' she whispers.

The waiter is hurrying over.

'It's OK, we're going.' I throw twenty euro on the table and follow Marcy out. She strides with confidence towards the car park. I follow behind, just to make sure she doesn't get mugged. I don't need that on my conscience. When she ascends in the lift, I turn and walk away.

I walk and walk and I must look pretty scary because not even the drug addicts approach me for money. There's no point in heading back as my mother will be full of questions and I won't be answering them. I pull my phone out and dial Larry but he doesn't pick up. I leave a message for him.

After about three hours plodding in the gathering darkness, I realise with some surprise that I'm near The Rock Place. Maybe I'll go in, have a beer, listen to some tunes. It was great the last time. I wonder will that duo be singing. I hope so. I'll let the sound of their extraordinary vocals wash over me, and the beer will relax me and take away the comment Marcy hurled at me as she left.

She was lying, though, that much I could tell from her. That's not the reason she said what she did to Kate and I don't know if I should take comfort in the fact or not.

The street where The Rock Place is is incredibly quiet. I can't even hear the dull thud of music as I walk up the narrow road. As I approach the door, I see with some surprise that it's closed. How can it be closed on a weekend? There is a notice in Cellophane taped to the door.

Closed due to the death of Leah from Locust. Locust played
here for the last six years. Leah will be sorely missed. She
lived by her own words, 'Cling on hard to the good days.
Sing on hard til the light fades.' RIP, Beautiful.

The notice hits me hard. I didn't even know the woman, I only saw
her once, but the memory of her music is sharp as shrapnel in my
mind. She must have still been ill six weeks ago but you'd never
have known. What a waste, I think. What a bloody waste.

But she had kept going, one song after another until the end.
Fair play to her.

* * *

It takes a lot for me to open the book that night. I know I've let
Kate down by not finishing the date properly, but I was prepared
to give it a go and that has to count for something. I turn to the
book because I need to believe that despite Kate not coming for
me that awful night, she did not believe that I was worthless. 'After
the Third Date' is indicated by a brilliant red tag, and when I open
the page, there are pictures. Pictures of Emma, Liam and Marcy.
Lots and lots of pictures. My children looking so happy with this
woman. This woman looking so happy with my children.

Kate has written: *Hey, you.* ☺ *Need I say any more?*
Maybe the memories aren't happy but at least you and
Marcy have time left to start over.

PS: I hope you paid. x

I smile. There is no choice. I have to make my peace with that
woman.

And at least I did pay.

THE FOURTH DATE

EMMA

It happened like this.

Daddy was sad. He sat in his room a lot and Mammy used to go up to him with his food. I was only nearly five, just after starting school, and when Mammy came to pick me up from school, she would have to rush back home because she was worried about Daddy. I was sad about Daddy too because he was fun before he got all sad. He brung me to the zoo lots of times and he swung me around and around and he played with me when he came home from work to give Mammy a break. We went on holidays to the beach and Daddy was scared going down the waterslide and so even though I was too I showed him how to do it. When Daddy was sad, he stayed in his room every day for days and days. He came downstairs sometimes and he would hug me and tell me that he loved me in a sad voice. But most times he stayed in his room. Then one day Danny came over and whispered with Mammy and then he went upstairs and Daddy got cross and told Danny to go away. I was scared then and I hid in my room. Daddy never talked like that before.

Then after a bit, I don't know, lots of time, Daddy went to work in Danny's garage. But now Mammy was getting sadder and sadder but she pretended that she was happy. So I did too, because if you put on a smile the whole world smiles with you. Nana sings that song. Then Mammy said Liam was going to be born only I didn't know it was Liam at the time and Daddy decided that working at night-time would be good and he went out at night-time and when he came home he would smile and it looked like he was happy again. And one day we went to the zoo for my birthday and Daddy saw someone and that person had to run away. Then he started to get real tired working at night-time. I know this because when he came home he kept banging into things and waking me up. And when I woke up I could hear Mammy crying because Daddy was so tired. Then Mammy got fat and then Liam was born and he made everyone happy for a tiny bit and I told Liam that I was going to be the best big sister ever and would always mind him and it made Mammy and Daddy laugh. And Daddy gave me a hug and told me that I was brilliant.

Then one day I got up and Smelly Jack was there. He was old like Granddad and he had a very sore arm, Daddy said. His teeth were all dirty because he never brushed them. And he talked in English only sometimes. The rest was a mumble. Daddy said we had to be nice to him.

I tried but Smelly Jack didn't. And Smelly Jack was there for days and nights. And Mammy was all cross and shouting at Daddy. And Daddy had to mind Smelly Jack so he stopped working for Danny because Danny had to keep ringing looking for him.

I liked school better then. I just wanted Smelly Jack to go home to his own home and Mammy said she did too but that Smelly Jack was Daddy's project. And she said that I was not to call him Smelly Jack.

Then one day I went into my room and my piggy bank was

all smashed open. It was a pink pig with a smiley face and long eyelashes and Marcy had given it to me and I went into my room and it was broken. Daddy said I must have broken it only I didn't. He said I must have put the money somewhere else only I didn't. And I cried because Daddy got cross and it wasn't my fault. Them Mammy got cross with Daddy and said was Daddy blind and stupid. Daddy didn't like her to say that and they got mad and they shouted at each other and I said it didn't matter. I didn't need the money really. And baby Liam was crying real loud. And I was crying and Mammy hugged me and Daddy didn't. I didn't like Daddy then because he was cross with me and I did nothing and it was my piggy bank.

Then another time Mammy's ring was gone. Mammy said that Smelly Jack took it, which wasn't very nice of her really. You should never say someone took something without knowing for sure. Mammy told me that when I said that a girl in school took my sandwich. Anyway, Mammy said it to his face and he said that he didn't and he looked like he didn't and I felt a bit sorry for him because Mammy was real mad at him then. I don't know what happened after because Mammy told me to leave the kitchen but she was not nice to Smelly Jack after that, I noticed.

Then the big row happened. I don't know what started it but I was standing outside the door because I was hoping Mammy would help me with my homework – it was maths and I am no good at maths – only I was too scared to go in when her and Daddy were talking like that, sort of hissing at each other. I was about to push down the handle when I heard them so I didn't. Then Smelly Jack came into the hall too only I didn't look at him. He didn't mind fights. He just said nothing most times. Then Mammy yelled and made me and Smelly Jack jump. She said something like that Daddy was ruining us all for Smelly Jack. And Daddy got mad and he said Mammy was ruining everything. And why couldn't she just stop yapping. And to stop calling Jack Smelly Jack. I looked up at Jack then but he was gone. And Mammy said that she couldn't take it any more. Daddy said that if Smelly Jack went then he would too and Mammy said fine. And Daddy said fine.

Then he came out of the kitchen and almost knocked me down and went past me and I just stood there in the doorway and saw Mammy at the table crying. I didn't know what to do.

I wish I had hugged her but I didn't know what to do. At least I got to hug her lots when she was sick.

Then the next day or maybe a few days later, Larry came and he stood at the door and Daddy was there. Larry asked Daddy was he mad and then Daddy hit Larry and Larry fell in the garden and he tried to get up and I screamed and Mammy helped Larry up and shouted at Daddy to just go. Just go, she said, and her face was red.

I was scared of Daddy then.

I was glad when he was gone. It was like there was sunlight back in our house again, even if Daddy wasn't here. After a while he came back one day. He asked to see me and Liam only I didn't want to see him. After another while he came back again and Mammy brought me into the kitchen to see him. I hoped he wouldn't come back because there was no fights when he was gone and no smells. And Larry and Marcy and all Mammy's friends could call in and it was a happy house. Daddy brought us out sometimes after that but we didn't stay in his flat.

Then Mammy got sick and Daddy wanted to come back. He said he was so sorry. He told us all he loved us. Mammy said she would think about it. She asked us what did we think. I said no. I cried and everything. So Mammy told Daddy no. I heard Daddy asking what did Mammy want? Mammy said maybe he should have treatment and Daddy said OK so he went off to a spa.

Marcy moved in for a while. I love Marcy.

But then Mammy died and instead of Marcy staying or even Larry or Nana taking us, Daddy did come back. I was scared but he is nice but it's not like having a mammy.

Plus he was nice before he went all cross. He is nice now and when he is nice, I love him again but he gets cross, especially with Nana when she tells him what to do. One day, I think he will get so cross that he will go. That's why I'm going to get Nana's ring.

NICK

It's great being back at work. I miss the kids, sure, but there's something solid about taking a car apart, assessing what's wrong with it and then fixing it.

And Danny is good company. He's been a great mate too, giving me work here. At first I thought it was a sympathy job, but judging by the amount of work on, it was the real thing. In the beginning, being out of practice, I kept it simple. I did the oil changes, the brake pad replacements, wheel alignment, stuff like that. But now Danny leaves me with the more complex stuff, as the busier the place gets, the more administration there is. I love the smell of diesel that permeates the place, though Emma will not let me cuddle her after a day at work.

Today, Danny leans against a car I'm working on. He's chewing on a bar. 'Want some?' he asks.

'Nah.' My head is buried in the engine. It's an old car, a pleasure to work on. I hate all the computer stuff in the newer models.

'I've a bit of news for you,' he says, and there is something about the way he says it that makes me look up. He's been in a bit of a funny mood all day, sort of jittery, and he's made a few mistakes with the bookings. Right now, thanks to him, there are two cars I have to finish before five.

'Yeah?'

'Marie's pregnant.' He says it as if he's trying to sound casual. As if it's no big deal.

I almost drop my wrench into the body of the car. 'Say again?' I'm sure I've heard wrong and congratulating him on a new baby would be so insensitive.

'She went to the doctor the other day, she was late and feeling sick and he told her that she was.' Danny gulps hard. His eyes are bright, almost shiny. He looks emotional. 'Pregnant,' he finishes.

'Aw, Dan.' I feel a burst of happiness for him. For them. I can't even articulate it without embarrassing us both. 'Aw, Dan.' I shake my head. 'After everything …'

'Yeah.' Danny nods 'All we had to do was wait. Like if only we'd known …'

'Well, in fairness, you had to do a bit more than wait.'

He laughs loudly. 'Trust you to drag everything down!' he chortles.

I laugh too and clap him on the arm and he claps me back and we do a sort of hugging thing.

* * *

On the way home from work, I decide that today is the day I'll bite the bullet and drive over to Marcy's beauty place. Five days have passed since that disastrous Saturday night and she hasn't been in touch at all. I was hoping that she'd ring so I could take the easy way out and make my peace with her over the phone. But her silence has kicked that plan into touch. Normally, she'll call the kids to talk to them or invite them somewhere, but this week – nothing. Emma and Liam haven't noticed yet but they will and they'll miss her.

What I've decided to do is to let Marcy see the kids and I'll stay well away. It's the best I can offer. If we stay out of each other's way, we'll tolerate each other. I'm sure Kate would have wanted more for us but I just can't do it. And neither, I fear, can Marcy.

So I park around the corner from Marcy's place and feed the parking meter. I've got twenty minutes.

I take my time walking around 'cause I'm nervous. I'm tempted to have another go at asking her why she told Kate to ignore my call that night but I decide not to. It's a long time ago now and I have to let it go. Get a bit of perspective. She'll probably just call me a useless shit again anyway, I think wryly.

I approach Marcy's from the side. It's six and she should be closing up by now and yep, the place looks deserted. Taking a deep breath and ordering myself to be calm, I push open the door of the shop. Marcy looks up from the reception desk and both of us stare at each other. Her eyes are red and bloated. I think she's been crying and I feel a flicker of guilt because I'm sure I'm responsible for the tears. I'm a bit of a wuss; I've never been able for tears. Emma's crying just about breaks my heart.

'Hey,' I say, in a much nicer tone than I'd intended.

'What do you want?' She picks up a diary and pretends that she's too busy to look at me.

Her voice gets my hackles up again. She sounds cross and irritated and annoyed.

I grit my teeth and run a hand through my hair. 'I came to say that just because we had a row it doesn't mean that you can't see the kids.' It comes out sounding like I want to strangle her.

'I know that,' she says.

I honestly don't know how to respond.

She's still looking at her damn diary. 'I just hadn't time to ring them this week,' she says as she turns a page. 'I'll call on Saturday.'

Then she glances upwards. Her face is puffy. She's not an attractive crier, I think with a bit of satisfaction.

I nod and turn abruptly away. The idea is to stomp out of the place but I pull the door instead of pushing it and it takes three attempts to get out of there.

I ignore her giggle.

EMMA

The first day of the summer holidays today and Nana is bringing us to a film because even though we were meant to go to the park, it is raining and so now we are going to a film. I think it's better. It's hard to pick a film that Liam will sit right through but I tell Nana that he might like a Disney one about a princess who has to save a prince. I know I will like it.

Daddy goes off to work real early. He is even up before us and it is Nana who gets us up. Daddy comes home from work in time for dinner. I don't really miss him much because I am in school all day usually but I think Liam does because he keeps asking where Daddy is and I have to tell him all the time that Daddy has to fix cars with Danny. At least he has stopped crying over it now.

Nana is fun except she makes us clean the table after our breakfast and bring our dishes to the dishwasher and she gets Liam to wipe up any of his spills even though he is only a baby. She won't even let him mush his toast up between his hands the way Daddy does. He has to eat it properly and not make a mess. Then she cleans the kitchen. I tell her that Daddy never bothers until we are in bed at night and even then he sometimes forgets, especially if Larry calls over, and Nana says that we should remind him to clean up as it is good to have things tidy.

Nana is different when she is minding us to when she is visiting us.

Nana is able to drive us to the cinema in her car as Daddy bought her two child seats; that way she won't have to keep swapping with him. Nana called it an extra vance, which means you spend extra money you don't need to spend. She is not able to figure out how Liam's seat clips into place so I tell her I will hold his straps and not let them go. Nana says that is dangerous and she knocks on our next-door neighbour's house and asks her how can she strap Liam in. Angela comes out and even though she has no children she fastens Liam in and tells Nana how to work it and then they have a big, long chat where Angela asks Nana how Daddy is coping and Nana says he is coping fine thank you and Angela says what a shame it was that Kate died and that she was such a lovely woman and so I climb into the car beside Liam because I don't want to listen any more. Nana talks for ages and then she remembers that we are going to a film and so she has to say goodbye real quick and she starts the car and says what a lovely woman Angela is and that we are lucky to have such a nice neighbour and I say that Mammy says Angela was a person you would never suspect of having a fair. I said that I never saw the fair but Mammy said to Marcy once that Angela had one.

Nana says nothing to this at all. I tell her I am not making it up and Nana says, 'What film are we going to again?'

The cinema is packed and because Nana didn't know how to work the internet she has to queue up for the tickets. She tells me and Liam to stand by the wall and not to move an inch. I hold Liam's hand and then I see Jane from my class and she has two girls with her going to the cinema too. I wave at them and they wave back and then they come over. Jane is all brown because she was on holiday.

Her mammy is all brown too and she smiles at me and asks me are we here with Daddy and I say that we are here with our nana now that Daddy is working. Then Jane asks me when are we going on our holiday and too late I remember that I told her that our mammy had booked a holiday for us before she died and that we were going on it for all summer. I go all red. Then Jane asks if Mammy really did book a holiday. But Nana comes back and saves me, phew. Then her and Jane's mammy walk together to the cinema and Jane and the two girls from my class say to me that I am a liar and I say that I am not, that my mammy did book a holiday only I got the dates wrong and that it is later on and that me and Liam are going. Liam is all excited at that and I say to Liam to tell the girls that we are so going on a holiday and Liam says that we are and then the girls have to believe us.

Nana already brought sweets with her so we don't get any popcorn, which she says are too dear. Jane's mammy buys her and her friends a combo and I try not to look at them as they get it.

The film is a very funny one and we all laugh, except the part where a caterpillar dies is very sad. I look and no one else is crying so I keep my sniffs real quiet. But then Nana takes my hand and squeezes it and I look at her face and she smiles at me. Anyway, then a lovely surprise. The caterpillar doesn't die at all but changes into a butterfly and Nana leans over to me and says that that is what happened to Mammy when she died, she changed into something even more beautiful.

That is a nice thing for Nana to say.

I picture Mammy flying over us with pretty wings always being there.

I hope Mammy is as beautiful as Cheryl Cole. That would be great.

NICK

Because it's summer and Emma is on her holidays, it's almost eleven when I manage to get the kids off to bed at night. I don't mind because I love listening to them. Liam's shiny new vocabulary provides a constant source of laughter. He repeats everything Emma says and somehow the word 'arse' has sneaked into his lexis.

'I didn't teach it to him,' Emma says, going all red. 'Probably it was Nana.'

'Nana does not say "arse".' I am firm. 'You can't teach Liam to say things like that, Ems.'

'Bold Emma,' Liam says, dancing around in his too-big pyjamas. 'Bold arse.'

Emma clamps her lips together and tries not to giggle. Liam is the bridge between us, making her forget that I am a source of annoyance for her. As Liam continues to chant 'bold arse' and I fail to look cross, Emma's giggles grow louder. I take the opportunity to entertain her with funny stories about my work; mostly I make them up. I tell her about Marie and Danny's new baby. I ask her how her day went. Anything rather than put a stop to her big smile.

Larry calls over just as I'm putting them into bed. I use the word 'putting' very loosely. They basically go when they're too tired to stay awake. Up until then they run around and play, but in fairness, they don't come downstairs.

'You will never get them to bed when school starts back,' Larry says, as if he's been doing fatherly things all his life. He lays a six-pack of lager on the floor.

'I will.' I take a can and break open the tab.

We sit down in the TV room and I flick through the channels. We settle on some late-night poker. 'So what's the story?'

Larry is gawking around the room.

'My mother,' I explain. 'She's done a bit of a cleaning blitz.'

'Looks good,' Larry says approvingly. 'Is she for hire?'

I laugh and we get to talking about Marie and Danny and how great it is, though he says that Marie is a little scared she'll lose the baby again. Then, as I knew he would, he asks me about the Saturday with Marcy. 'So you and Marcy had a blow-up, yeah?'

I told him this when he rang me back on Sunday but I never went into details. 'She called me a worthless piece of shit,' I say, 'which pretty much ruined the atmosphere.'

Larry doesn't laugh as I expect. He looks as if he can't believe it.

'I asked her about ...' I pause, take my time, '... that night when I rang Kate and asked her to pick me up from work. D'you remember?' I hesitate again, before muttering, 'I wasn't in great shape.'

'And I came instead?' Larry puts his can down and gives me a look that I can't quite gauge.

'Yep. Well, I never told you this before, but when I rang Kate, she was with Marcy and that ... that ...' I can't think of a word to adequately express how I feel about Marcy, so settle on 'cow', '... cow told Kate to stay where she was and not to pick me up.'

Larry says nothing for a second. 'And that's why you're so cross with her all the time, is it? I always thought it was because of our dinner that time.'

'Oh, Lar, give me some credit, for Christ's sake. You were a bit of a crap date yourself that night.'

He grins a little, then takes another slug of beer. Upstairs the place has gone silent. I excuse myself and tiptoe up, just to make sure they're all tucked in and haven't fallen and conked out. Liam is asleep, sideways in his cot bed. Emma is under her covers but her head pops up when I come in. She jumps as if she gets a shock.

'Go to sleep.' I cross over and kiss her forehead. There is a lump under her bedclothes and I go to pull it but she puts her hand on it.

'No, Daddy.'

'You better not be playing with toys under there. Go to sleep. I mean it.'

She nods. 'Sorry.' She smiles charmingly at me.

I blow her a kiss and close the door.

'All sorted.' I sit back down again opposite Larry. 'They'll be asleep soon.'

Larry makes no response and, glancing over at him, I see that he's studying me. There's a nervousness in the way he's staring at me and I feel fingers of apprehension play my spine like a piano. 'What?'

Larry runs his hands over his face. He hunches towards me and seems about to speak but stops, and picking up his lager again, he gulps it.

'What?' I ask again.

More silence.

'Lar, have you something to tell me?'

A small pause before he admits, 'I'm in a bit of a shit place.' Then he drops his can and rubs his face again. 'Tell me something,' he blurts out. 'If you were sworn to secrecy about an event but by keeping the secret someone else was being blamed unfairly for something, would you break that secret?'

'I'm having trouble understanding the question.' I crack a grin.

He heaves a sigh and swills his can around. The drink sloshes inside. 'I know why Marcy said what she said that night.'

My body feels as if someone has just shaken it real hard. Larry knows. Why? How could he know? 'You never said.'

'Well, first off you never asked, and second off …' he hesitates, '… no one wanted you to find out.'

'Find out? What?' I feel as if the room has tipped a little and I'm off balance.

'You've got to remember, you were in a bad place, Nick. You were distraught over those two guys—'

'Obviously.' I'm snappy.

'And Kate was distraught over you. We all were.'

'I was fine,' I say back. 'I lived, didn't I?'

'Part of you died, Nick,' he says.

I stand up suddenly. 'Yeah, well, maybe if two people died in front of you and you were to blame, part of you would die too, Lar.'

'I know,' Larry says calmly. 'But I'm only trying to explain what our thinking was that night.'

'So, what?' I turn to face him, my palms outstretched. 'Why did that …' I'm about to describe Marcy as a cow for the second time, but eventually settle for 'woman', '… woman say what she did? Why did she force Kate to choose between us?'

The quiet stretches. I think Larry is battling some inner voice that's advising him against telling me. 'She wasn't forcing Kate to choose,' he says eventually.

I look at him. He dips his head. 'Larry, if this is about me, I have a right to know.'

He makes a frustrated noise somewhere deep in his throat and turns to me. 'You're gonna go mad,' he says, and he sounds so sad. 'But Kate isn't here and Marcy is and I think you need to stop blaming her. She was only trying to help and it wasn't about you.'

I feel suddenly uneasy. Marcy has always been the hostile friend of my wife, or at least that was my thinking. Anything else would make the last few years senseless.

'Kate was pregnant, Nick.'

At first the words don't register. Yep, Kate was pregnant, she had Emma and Liam. 'Sorry?'

'That time, when you were really bad, Kate found out she was pregnant.'

'What?' I'm shocked in a totally stunned way.

Larry speaks really slowly, like he's walking through a burning house and afraid the floor will go from under him. 'She was a few weeks gone apparently and that night, the night you called, she was miscarrying. She was in the hospital. Not in Marcy's at all. Your mother had Emma.'

I don't feel anything for a second. Like the aftermath of seeing death. Then the anger and the horror of what they kept from me rushes in like some kind of satanic possession. But my voice, when it comes, is dazed. 'Kate lost our baby and no one told me?'

'She didn't want anyone to. You had enough to cope with, she said. Marcy had to stop her from picking you up that night.'

Kate lost a baby and I never knew. I can't even articulate the betrayal, the loss, the fury at not being told. So I just say, real quietly, 'Get out.'

'Aw, Nick—'

I walk towards him. 'Get the fuck out. Take your drink with you.'

'Nick, come on!' Larry stands up.

'You were my mate. Mine!' I thump my chest. 'You should have told me. I would have taken care of her. I would have helped her. She must have been so upset. Oh, Jesus.' I clamp my hands to my head and groan. 'Oh, Jesus.'

'There was no point. There was nothing you could have done.'

'Get the fuck out!' I roar now and upstairs Liam starts to cry.

'Out!' I pick up the cans and shove them into his chest. 'Don't come back.'

He stands there uselessly.

'Just go.' I shake my head and turn away. She was my wife. Mine. She lost our baby and I never knew. And I walked out on the baby she did have.

From behind, Larry says, 'I'm going. I'm sorry, Nick.'

I hear him walk out. Upstairs, Liam is still crying, so I head up to him to find him climbing out of his bed. I wait until he stumbles a few short steps across his room before scooping him up and covering his face with kisses.

EMMA

In my bag now, I have some beans and some fruit, only the fruit is getting smelly. It stinks up my room and I have to get rid of it. I don't think bananas are meant to last three weeks in a bag. When I take them out, they are black and squishy.

I try to make Liam try one but he screws up his face and says 'yeuch'. In the end, when Nana is busy cleaning the TV room, I sneak them into the bin in the kitchen. I am clever because I cover them up with other rubbish like paper and plastic. Only thing is that they start to smell in the kitchen too.

'What is that smell?' Nana asks when she is giving us our lunch. Nana gives us horrible lunches like brown bread and cheese and apples. Daddy used to let us make our own but Nana said eating crisps and jam sandwiches is not a proper diet. Nana likes proper diets. Me and Liam don't. Nana starts to sniff like one of those dogs on the TV when you see them finding drugs in airports. She sniffs us, which isn't very nice, I don't think. She even lifts Liam up and sniffs his bum. Then she sniffs in all the presses, then she sniffs the bin and she jumps back as if it has shouted at her. She opens it up and makes a face. The smell is not nice at all. 'Nana,' Liam calls.

'In a minute, honey,' Nana says.

Only I think Liam is trying to say 'banana' so I pinch him and he starts to cry.

When Nana takes the bin outside, I tell Liam that I am very sorry but I had to do it.

He glares at me, his bottom lip all pushed out and big tears in his eyes. I try to ignore him. It's for his own good. But then I hug him because he is my brother and I have to mind him.

In my bag, I also have some pretty things like my favourite hair bobbins and Liam's first baby picture, which I took out of an album. He was not a cute baby, his face was all red and he had a big face that would make you want to squeeze his cheeks real hard. Now he is nice. Well, for a boy he is nice. I also have half a tube of toothpaste and some tissues. You never know what comes in handy. That's what Mammy always said.

When Daddy comes in from work, I tell Liam that he has to be real good because Daddy had a row with Larry the other night and sometimes when Daddy has a row with people, he goes away. Me and Liam don't want our daddy going away, first of all because we love him very much even when we fight with him and we love his lunches and we love when he lets us stay up late and we love that he buys us an ice cream with sprinkles every Saturday and that he sings songs on the guitar for us. If we are real good, I tell Liam that Daddy will stay in a good mood. Only Daddy isn't in a good mood when he gets home and I think he's mad at Nana. He comes in and me and Liam are sitting at the table. Liam is eating his dinner because he still gets a baby dinner, and even though it is real small, he still takes ages to eat it. He likes using his fingers to make all the potato squish out. It makes Nana mad but Daddy says he is just exploring texture. Anyway, Daddy sits down and he says to Nana, 'I saw Larry the other night.'

Nana smiles and she says what she says every time Daddy talks about Larry: 'He's such a lovely boy.'

Larry is not a boy!

Then Daddy tells me to take Liam into the TV room, that he wants to talk to Nana.

I know Daddy is in a bad mood because normally he smiles at me and Liam but he didn't. I feel sick and I don't want my dinner any more. Nana tells Daddy that children must not eat in front of the TV. Daddy just says again, 'Emma, take Liam inside and bring your dinner in. I want a word with Nana.'

So I open up Liam's high chair and I lift him down and get all covered in his goo.

'Let me at least wipe the child's hands,' Nana says.

'He's fine,' Daddy says.

I just hurry me and Liam out. I hope it's not starting again.

After a few seconds, I sneak out of the room and try to listen at the door. I'm not sure if there is a row now because it's not a shouty row but it sounds like one of those talks that grown-ups have when they're cross with each other and don't want you to hear. Like what Mammy and Daddy used to have, all whispery. Anyway, I didn't hear what they talked about but Nana went home soon after and didn't have her coffee and biscuit with us, so there was definitely a row.

When Daddy puts me to bed, I decide to ask him even though it makes me feel sick. He is tucking me in and when he goes to kiss my forehead, I say, 'Did you have a fight with Larry and Nana?'

His kiss doesn't meet my forehead. He pulls back and pushes my hair behind my ear. 'Why?' he says.

'Because you shouted at Larry and you were angry whispering with Nana.'

Daddy stays real still. Then he says, 'Everyone rows, sweetheart.'

'Was it a bad row?'

'No,' he says. But he is telling lies. The row with Larry was real bad. If Daddy is telling lies, he will have to go to confession or he will not be forgiven. Then he won't be able to get into heaven and meet Mammy when he dies.

Marcy didn't ring us. Well, maybe she did only maybe we missed her call.

* * *

Today, which is Sunday, Daddy brings me and Liam to the playground. When Daddy takes out Liam's buggy, Liam runs around the house screaming his head off. Daddy laughs, and when he catches Liam he tries to get Liam into the buggy but Liam goes all stiff like a board and squeals and squeals like a pig and Daddy says, 'I'll have to snap you in two to get you in.'

But Liam still screams and in the end Daddy tells him that it's OK, that he can walk instead.

I tell Daddy that he will spoil Liam if he gives him everything he wants.

'Do you think so?' Daddy asks me.

I nod. Mammy would have made Liam sit in the buggy.

'Will we try to get him in?' Daddy asks me.

Liam is dancing about trying to reach the door handle. He is jumping up and down.

'Out!' he keeps saying. Then when Daddy unlocks the door, he laughs.

'He looks happy to be walking,' Daddy says then. 'Let's just leave him.'

I tell Daddy that of course Liam is happy, he is being spoiled. But Liam does have the cutest little smile.

NICK

At Parent and Toddler this week, after the football, Sue greets me with her usual tight little smile and asks me when we're going on holidays. 'I thought you'd be gone by now,' she says.

I have no clue what that woman is on. Maybe it's just her way of making conversation. I guess it would be nice for just the three of us to get away, somewhere with a beach, but I can hardly ask Danny for any more time off. When I asked him if he knew anything about the miscarriage, he said no. I choose to believe him because he and Marie are so happy and I can't spoil it for them.

Sue is still yammering on about her own holiday and telling me that if I am going foreign with the children to make sure I lather the sun cream on. 'I can lend you our bottles,' she says. 'In fact—'

'Sue, Sue.' Molly lumbers up. I swear, I have never seen such a big pregnant woman in my life. Sweat is standing out on her forehead and I realise quite suddenly that she doesn't look good.

'The baby is coming.' Molly clutches her stomach. 'Call an ambulance.' Then she screws up her face and clenches her teeth and moans.

Sue looks to me in alarm. 'Molly,' she says, placing her cup down, 'sit down.'

'I can't. The baby is coming.'

'Oh, you can't have the baby here, the children—'

'It's coming now,' Molly gulps out. 'Oh, Jesus, Mary and Joseph, call an ambulance.' She clenches her stomach as if she can somehow stop the labour and falls a little forward. I catch her.

Some of the kids stop playing and glance over.

'Ambulance,' I snap at Sue, who whips her mobile out.

Molly's nails dig into my flesh. I wrap an arm about her waist. A cluster of women gather around. 'Oh, God,' Molly pants, 'it's coming now. I have to lie down.'

There is instant chatter. Someone suggests bringing the kids outside, someone else says Molly should go, another woman volunteers to drive Molly to the hospital.

She screams again.

Some of the kids start to cry.

'Get the kids into the fresh air,' I order loudly. 'Get them playing outside.'

'But the in—'

'Forget about the damn insurance, OK?' I snap at Sue.

'I never said anything about the insurance,' Sue sniffs. 'Honestly, you are a very grumpy man and—'

'Get the kids out now!' I roar as Molly virtually collapses in my arms. 'Take them home!'

More kids crying. Liam howls. A huge exodus ensues. 'Jean, Chantelle, stay here!' I yell.

I lay Molly gently down on the floor and order someone to get me a cushion for her back.

'I'll need you to boil a kettle, Jean, use it to sterilise a scissors in case we need it. Chantelle, go in search of clean towels and something warm.' I glance around. 'OK,' I peel off my jacket, 'this will do. Now get towels. If there aren't towels, newspapers will do.'

'Jaysus,' Chantelle says. 'It's like a film.'

Liam runs towards me and I heft him up. 'You have to go out

now, bud,' I tell him. 'I'll see you in a few minutes, OK? Will someone take Liam, please?'

Sue has come off the phone and she holds her arms out for him. I have to peel him off me and he shrieks as Sue carries him out the door. Poor little guy.

Molly cries out and I hunker down to her and say, 'I used to be a fireman ...'

'And he never killed anyone,' Chantelle offers, which makes me flinch. 'I googled him. He was exonerated.'

She earns a thump from Jean.

'... and we've paramedic training. I've delivered a baby or two,' I go on in as steady a voice as I can, 'so let's just do the best we can here, eh?'

Molly nods and groans deeply again. She reaches out to catch my hand, and God, she has some grip.

I ask Jean to remove Molly's leggings and underwear and as she does so, I extract my hand from Molly's grip and open a window. I pray to any god out there to let this go my way. Saving people from fires was never as scary for me as being responsible for bringing a new life safely into the world. So perfect, so undamaged.

Eventually Jean tells me that Molly is ready and I turn back.

'Oh, Nick,' Molly says breathlessly, attempting a small smile, 'I won't be able to look you in the face ever again.'

Chantelle laughs loudly as she carries over a bowl of hot water in which a scissors is immersed. She also has a pile of clean-ish tea towels.

She earns another poke from Jean.

'Right, ladies,' I say, 'just do exactly what I ask and we should be fine.' I lick my lips, take a few deep breaths and tell myself to just remember my training. Which was so long ago ...

'An ambulance is on its way,' someone shouts from the doorway. 'We're ringing your husband now, Molly, OK?'

'OK,' she says. 'He was on night shift so he should be at hoooome.' She writhes around in pain and Chantelle declares that she can't look.

The ambulance is not going to get here on time, I don't think. 'You'll be fine,' I tell Molly. My heart is thumping. I hope I can do this. 'I need to see how far gone you are, OK?'

'Nick, do what you have to do.'

'I've always wanted to say that to a fella.' Chantelle offers a feeble joke.

Molly manages a laugh before another contraction takes over. The baby's head appears.

Jean gasps. 'Is that the head?'

'Yep. Molly, I can see your baby's head so at least it's not breech.' I'm down on my knees and I order Jean to have a towel ready. Babies can be slippery.

Molly moans again.

'OK, Molly, you're going to have to push on this next contraction. I'm going to get the head. OK?'

'OK.'

'You're doing great.'

'It's a month early. Isn't that bad?'

'This baby is coming. Doesn't matter.'

She screams and I immediately go into action. It's as if the years fall away and I'm back, working away with the lads on the shift. I'd loved my job, I'd loved the craic we all had. All my life, that's all I'd ever wanted to be. In the beginning as a kid, it was the uniform, later on it was the idea of being a hero. And then when I finally got in, it was the camaraderie and the work itself. I liked helping people. Kate used to tease and call me a do-gooder and maybe I was. Maybe I got that from my folks, who were green before it was ever fashionable. I'd loved my job until I'd made a mistake and people died. I can't think about that now, I push it away. My world narrows right down to this woman on the floor and her baby and the ticking of the clock and the occasional expletives of encouragement from Chantelle, who has decided that, in actual fact, she can look.

Little by little, the baby arrives. The head, one shoulder, then the other and finally the skinny, slippery body. She's small, blue, fragile as a feather. Eight months is not ideal for a child to come into the world. I scoop her up into my jacket, which is the warmest thing in the room. I clean her nose with a towel dipped in hot water. I check her breathing.

'It's very blue,' Chantelle says, her voice high-pitched and yet wondrous.

I swallow hard. I will not lose you, I think. I tap its little chest. For a long couple of seconds there is nothing, then a tiny little whimper, a gasp, a grasping for air, for life. I am weak with relief.

Jean is sobbing openly. Chantelle hugs her.

Molly holds out her hands, crying. I tell her not to let the baby get cold. It's so small. I tell her that the cord is still attached and to be careful. If the ambulance gets here in the next ten minutes they can do it. I don't want to risk infection.

Just then a man bursts into the room. He's tall, dishevelled, as if he just got out of bed.

'Molly?' he calls, and before I can say anything, he's down on his knees.

'You have a baby girl,' I say, leaning back against a chair. 'Tiny but alive.' I'm exhausted from the stress, the adrenaline. Elated. I glance at my watch and just then the wail of sirens comes from outside.

Behind me, mother, father and baby are all together.

It's one of the most perfect images in the world.

It's the way it should be and it's so bittersweet.

I leave to brief the ambulancemen.

* * *

It's the following day and as I make my way to work, my mobile buzzes. It's on the passenger seat of my car and I'm tempted to pick it up, just in case it's my mother ringing about the kids. But I've only left the house ten minutes ago, so it's probably not that; I'll be at work in five minutes anyway and I'll check it then.

The phone buzzes off but starts back up again. Then it stops and starts again. The traffic lights go red in front, so I reach across the seat and flip open my phone cover. I don't recognise the number so it can't be too important. Probably just someone selling something. Then another unknown number calls me. Weird.

Five minutes later, I pull up in front of the garage and Danny is just rolling up the door. Hopping out of the car, I signal to him that I'll be a minute or so on the phone. Dialling message minder, the incredibly posh woman with the sexy voice tells me that I have four new messages.

'Hi, Nick Deegan? Tom Smyth from the *Irish Independent* here. Just looking for a quote from you about your delivery of a baby girl yesterday. Bit of feel good. Wondering if we can get a picture. Thanks.' He leaves a contact number.

'Hello. This is Robert Reilly from the *Star*. Any chance of an interview about the drama yesterday in the Abbeylands Community Centre?' Again he leaves his contact details.

'Hello, Nick, this is Sue. I've had journalists on to me about what happened yesterday. I have no idea how they found out. Anyway, I hope it was OK to pass your number to them. Let me know if not and I'll ring them back. But I thought you wouldn't mind and that it would be best for them to talk to you directly.'

'Hi, this is a researcher from RTÉ 1 *Daily Dose* radio programme. Is there any chance you could come on and chat to us about your heroic deed yesterday? I believe you saved the baby's life.'

Even as I hang up, the phone is ringing again. I cannot believe it. I switch it off. There is no way I'm doing any interviews or getting in the paper. It was bad enough the last time. I could happily brain Sue.

'Anyone important?' Danny asks.

'No one, boss.' I manage a grin. 'So, what's on for today?'

* * *

It's lunchtime and I switch on my phone so I can ring my mother and ask after the kids. I stare in horror as message after message piles in. Apparently, I have twenty missed calls. I rub an oily hand through my hair and decide that if I don't talk to the media, there is nothing they can say about me. I ring my mother and, as ever, Emma gets to the house phone first.

'Hello, this is the Deegans. How can we help you?'

'I'd like two children, lightly toasted, with some garlic please.'

'Daddy!' Emma giggles. 'You can't have that.'

'Why? Is there no garlic?'

More giggles.

'So how's my girl?' I ask.

'I'm very good. And Liam is good, only for he said,' her voice dips, '"fuck you" today.'

I have to stifle a bit of a shocked laugh. 'No. Where did he hear that?' Where *did* he hear that?

'Nana says it has to be at the toddler group. Oh …' a pause as she remembers, '… Liam says you had a baby there yesterday and someone asked Nana about it in Lidl. Is it true?'

'Well, I didn't actually have the baby, but a lady did. You know Molly, your friend's mammy?'

'Oh, *she* did.' A pause, then Emma yells, 'Nana, there was a baby born in the toddler group yesterday!' I have to hold my phone back from my ear with her screech.

My mother enters the room and I hear her talking to Emma as the phone is handed over.

I'm still not really talking to my parents, but it has to be said, daily interaction does tend to soften even the most gigantic betrayals. As for Larry and Marcy, I can't even go there yet.

'A woman in Lidl said you had the baby.' My mother sounds anxious. 'What on earth did she mean, Nick?'

'I delivered the baby,' I say.

'You delivered a baby?' Danny walks over, chewing on his egg and onion. The man has never heard of privacy. 'When?'

'In the middle of the floor, in front of children?' My mother sounds horrified.

'You've had a baby, Mam,' I say shortly. 'You know how it all works. It's not a case of crossing your legs until you get to the hospital.'

Danny snorts a laugh out and then starts to choke.

'Nicholas,' my mother snaps, 'there is no need to be so crude. Honestly. I know you're still annoyed with me over the whole ...' she flaps about a bit, '... other thing, but honestly.' She leaves it at that.

'Anyway,' I say, 'are the kids OK?'

'They are fine.'

'Kiss them for me.' Danny is still choking so I belt him on the back.

My mother says something that I can't make out and I hang up. In between Danny's coughing, I fill him in on yesterday. 'You need a cheap gynaecologist, I'm available,' I tell him.

My phone starts to ring again. I shake it in front of Danny's face. 'It's just media,' I say casually. I pass the phone to Danny. 'Tell them I'm not taking any calls until I see Max Clifford.'

Danny laughs again.

* * *

Just after dinner, Emma says she's going to bed. I hope she's not sick. 'I don't want to talk to anyone,' she says, and I don't know if it's my imagination, but she seems to be eyeballing me.

'Are you sick?' I ask her.

'No. I just want to be on my own.'

My mother makes a face at me.

'What if I want to tell you some really good news?' I tease. 'Or offer you your very favourite sweets?'

She gives me a funny look and shrugs. Emma's looks can make me feel about as high as a worm and I instantly feel bad for joking with her. 'Off you go so.' I blow her a kiss, which she doesn't return.

'She has been very quiet this last couple of hours,' my mother says, after Emma disappears up the stairs.

'She's probably knackered. They go to bed late now that Emma's on holidays.'

'That can't be good for them.'

I ignore that.

My mother clucks and then starts fussing about, wiping Liam's hands constantly, arranging dishes in the presses and, oddly enough, smiling over at me.

'What?' I ask, sausage poised on my fork.

'I'm so proud of you,' she says then, 'saving that baby's life.'

'I didn't save it, I just delivered it.'

'That's not what all the reporters who called here have been saying.'

'They called here? How did they get this number?'

My mother shrugs. 'Phone book, I'd imagine.'

'They just like a story.' I put my fork down, my appetite gone. 'I'm not talking to them. They hung me out to dry the last time.'

Her smile dips a tiny bit and she crosses over and rubs my shoulder. 'I know.' A pause. 'At least you can mention it now.'

It's true. I can mention that fire. At the time, I let the newspapers talk, I let the guys in court talk. 'I should have seen how sure Tom was,' I blurt out.

My mother inhales sharply, then asks, 'Did you do what you thought was best?'

'Yeah. Course.' What a stupid question.

'Well, that's all you should have done,' she says, and gives my shoulder a squeeze.

* * *

Liam is ready to go to bed at nine. Without Emma, he has no one to impress by his cheeky words or his death-defying climbing. It's like he's half the boy without her. He yawns widely at nine.

'Tired, bud?'

'Tired,' he repeats, rubbing his eyes with his fist.

I lift him up and nuzzle his neck. He giggles. He smells of soap and clean hair. My mother obviously bathed them that morning. He wraps his arms around my neck and peace briefly settles in my heart.

Behind me the phone rings but I ignore it. It's probably another journalist.

I pop Liam into his cot and he joins his hands and closes his eyes and we fumble out a prayer about God looking after Mammy in heaven and blessing us all. I'm not religious but Emma, since making her Communion, has us praying every night. She's not keen on mass but that's fine. We only go when she wants. Liam curls up on his side and obediently closes his eyes. I leave his door open to let the light from the landing shine in on him.

Emma's door is closed and I rap on it before pushing down the handle and walking into her room. She is curled away from me and, crossing towards her bed, I peer down on her. Her eyes are closed but they're scrunched up real tight, so she's not really asleep. I sit down alongside her. 'Hey, Ems, what's up?'

She doesn't answer.

'You can tell me. Even if you're cross with me, you can say it.' A pause. 'I know you're awake.'

Nothing.

I lean over and kiss her cheek and she moves away. Standing up, I tell her I love her and leave the room.

* * *

Davy calls in about ten. He's got a box of sweets, some crisps and a packet of jellies with him. It's an unexpected visit and I think I know what it's about. I pull two cans from the fridge and we open the sweets. Davy shifts about on his seat.

'So,' I ask, ignoring his unease. 'How's the ma?'

'Never better. She's visiting her friend down the country next weekend.'

'I thought she was sick.'

'She's better now.' He says it grimly and I suppress a smile. A pause. 'She's annoyed with me. I'm getting my own place.'

'Good for you.'

He nods and then there is silence. I let it build. I'm waiting …

'Eh, I was talking to Larry,' Davy says eventually. He stares at the unopened bag of jellies. 'D'you mind?'

'Open it.'

I watch as he opens it. He takes a handful of sweets and chews them all at the same time. He says something else that I can't make out.

I make a face.

Davy swallows. For one awful second I think he'll choke. 'He told me about your row, Larry did.'

I take a deep breath. 'Yeah?'

'He told me to call over and, well, he *is* my boss.'

Oh, Davy, Davy, I want to laugh. 'Larry told you to call over to me. Did he tell you what to say as well?'

'No, he didn't.' Davy sounds indignant. 'He just said to tell you he says hi to the kids. That's all. And anyway, I came to tell you that I think Larry was right not to tell you at the time.' A pause. 'And so was Marcy.'

The words out, he looks defiantly at me.

'Yeah, well, see if you feel the same when you get married, Davy.'

'Larry was married, so he knew what he was doing keeping it from you.'

Davy, normally so meek and impressionable, has the big guns out tonight.

'Let's not go there, OK?' I hold out the box of sweets. 'Another one?'

Davy peers inside and picks out a purple one. 'He's pretty cut up that you won't take his calls. And, like, it's gonna affect the mood at the poker sessions.'

'I'm cut up he didn't tell me about Kate. I'm cut up to think that she went through what she did and I wasn't even given a chance to be there.'

Davy takes another sweet. He pops it in his mouth and makes loud sucking noises. 'No one knew you'd never have another chance, no one knew Kate was going to die, Nick.'

'Exactly,' I say.

Davy makes a pained face. 'Aw, shit, I'm meant to be sorting this and I keep saying the wrong stuff.' He chews his sweet. 'Let's just watch some telly, yeah?'

I allow myself a grin and flick on the TV.

EMMA

Today I feel not so bad as last night. The reason I felt bad was because of a message on the house phone that I heard yesterday. I got to it too late and pressed the code and heard the message. I deleted it real quick as I didn't want Daddy to hear it and I didn't like hearing it myself.

Now it doesn't seem so bad. Mammy used to say a good night's sleep is like medicine and I think she is right. Daddy is gone to work and me and Liam are dressed and ready to go to the shop down the road with Nana. We go every morning after Nana gets us ready. She brings us for a walk because it is healthy and also to buy her paper. Then we walk home and Nana has a quiet cup of coffee and some biscuits and some 'me' time in the kitchen and me and Liam are allowed watch TV and have a biscuit too. Today is sunny so we don't need our coats. When we get to the shop, Nana asks me to run and get the paper while she chats to the shop girl, whose name is Lisa. Lisa's boyfriend smokes dopes she said once. I wonder will Clare in our class be smoked when she grows up. Smoking dopes is a bad thing and Nana told Lisa to get rid of her boyfriend ages ago. I walk past the sweet counter and the special offer tins of beans to the newspaper place. Nana gets a proper paper, not the ones with the nude girls and the celebrities in them. I go to pick up Nana's paper and there, right on the front, in a tiny little space, is a picture of Daddy. Only it is an old picture because in it, Daddy looks dressed up and clean. He never looks clean normally, he's always sort of scattered. That's the word Mammy used about him when she was teasing him when they used to be happy. In this picture, Daddy has a suit and tie. I pick up the paper and the words are real small and some of them are big words and even when I read the words, I can't understand them right but the word 'fire' and 'died' are there and it makes my heart kind of jump because yesterday on the answering machine message it was a man. He said he was a journalist, which means he writes for the newspaper. He said that he was writing about Daddy saving this baby's life and was my daddy the same Nick Deegan that was involved in the fire where two firemen were killed. I got a shock when I heard that and now, in the paper, they talk about a fire too.

'Emma!' Nana calls. 'Come on.'

I take up the paper and I fold it so that Nana won't see about Daddy. But when I hand it to her, she unfolds it for Lisa. Then she looks at the picture of Daddy too and I see her eyes grow wider and she shakes her head and she folds up the paper and pays for it.

I wait until we are out of the shop before I ask, 'Is that Daddy on the front?' I am pushing Liam along.

'Yes,' she says, and she is smiling, which is strange. 'It's a story all about how he saved that baby the other day.'

Liam is hard to push because he's getting heavy and sometimes, like today, he drags his feet all over the ground when Nana isn't looking. All Liam's shoes have the tops scraped off. Daddy says he will stop once he realises that it hurts him to do it but I think Liam won't.

'When did Daddy get his picture taken?' I ask. I really want to ask why are the words 'died' and 'fire' there but I don't want Liam to hear.

'They had it from before,' Nana says.

That is a surprise. 'Daddy was in the paper before?'

'Yes,' Nana says.

'Why?'

'Oh,' she waves her hand about, 'I can't remember. Maybe they think he is a handsome man.' She laughs.

I won't ask her about Daddy killing people now because maybe she doesn't know.

I keep pushing Liam. Scrape, scrape, scrape go his shoes. Nana notices and pulls him up and straps him in tighter and Liam yowls really loud.

'You'll ruin your shoes,' Nana says. 'You're sitting arseways in that buggy, you'll have to sit up straight.'

'Daddy let me!' Liam yells.

Nana shakes her head. 'Well, Nana doesn't!'

Nana doesn't let us do lots of things that Daddy does. Nana is like Mammy, that's why. When Nana is there, Liam can't pour milk on his own breakfast cereal or draw with chalk on the wall or I can't just take out my paints and start painting. She makes me put down newspapers and everything. It's not worth the trouble then.

'Do you believe in God?' I ask Nana.

'Of course I do,' she says. She sounds a little cross that I've asked her.

'I don't know if Daddy does,' I say. 'If you don't believe in God, can you get to heaven?'

Nana stops walking. A man bangs into her from behind. They both say, 'Excuse me.' Nana pulls me in from the street, away from people walking up and down 'You get to heaven if you're a good person and do your best,' she says. 'And that's what your daddy is and that's what you and Liam are.'

'And Mammy?'

'Oh, yes, your Mammy is definitely in heaven.'

I can't wait to be grown up so that I'll know all these things. I'm just not sure. Even though I made my Communion and I'm making it my mission to know Jesus, it's just not working out so good. I still don't know things for definite the way Nana does. But I like that she's sure.

After lunch we go to visit Marcy. Nana brings us. She told Daddy that we had a right. Daddy said he knew that and to stop nagging. Today, Marcy's shop is closed. It is after lunch so it should be open and it is not a Wednesday so she is not on a half-day. Nana walks around and peers in the windows. I do the same as Liam screams really loud from his buggy. He makes me laugh but Nana makes a tisking sound. Then she pulls out her new mobile phone from her bag and spends a bit of time just staring at it. Daddy bought it for her when she said she would mind us so that he could contact her wherever she is. Nana told him she knew how to use it but I don't think she does. She presses a button and the phone makes a singing sound and Nana goes, 'Oh.'

'Cool,' I say. I stand on tiptoes to look at it. Nana passes it to me. 'Can you get the screen where I can call someone, Emma?' she asks. 'You know, the number pad thing your daddy showed me.'

I take it from her and examine it. Amy Murphy in school has a mobile phone. She is the first in our class to have one and she let us all have a hold of it. I got extra long because Mammy had died. I offered her a lend of my rubber again for a go of it but she wouldn't. She said if I gave her my engagement ring I could have it but I said no.

I think I remember how to get the screen up. I press on a picture of a telephone. A keypad pops up. 'Now.' I hand it to Nana.

She stares at it for ages, then she presses in a number. The keypad must be a funny one because she seems to press it really, really hard. No one answers her call. She says, 'This is Violet. Why is your shop closed? I hope everything is all right. Emma and Liam say hello.' Then she hands me the phone. 'How do I switch it off?'

I show her the button that says 'end call' and she laughs.

When Nana goes to wash Liam after he has taken a packet of biscuits from the press and eaten loads of them, I find her newspaper. I stare at the picture of Daddy. He doesn't look happy in it. I stare at the words beside the picture. Gobbeldy Gook is what Mammy called things she didn't understand. But the word 'died' is there. Why would the word 'died' be in with a report of Daddy saving a baby? And then what the man on the phone said yesterday.

I wish I could ask someone but I can't.

Nana has left her ring on the table. She always does that but this time I take it. Just in case I need it. If I don't, I'll give it back.

Nana won't mind.

NICK

If I thought that meeting a load of women in the park for a run was embarrassing, it's even worse when the load of women break into a cheer and start whooping and clapping. The two lads who have joined us laugh at my embarrassment.

'I know I look great, but honestly, girls, keep your admiration to yourselves.'

I'm not sure if the laughter that follows is exactly flattering.

'You're a celebrity,' Chantelle says.

'Yeah, get me out of here!'

They laugh again.

'There I was,' Chantelle goes on, at the top of her voice, 'reading the paper the other day and there you were staring out at me. Have to say, it put me off me breakfast.'

I grin but, to be honest, it'd put me off my lunch. Because I hadn't given any interviews or posed for any pictures, the papers had used an old picture of me from their files. One that I hoped never to see again. In it I look shell-shocked; that day had been one of the worst days of my life.

'I hardly recognised you,' one of the women says. 'Did you have to go get dressed up for it?'

I consider lying. I consider telling her that yes, I had. But I can't. For one thing, a lot of the women would know when it had been taken. 'That picture is an old one.'

'You were in the paper before?' the woman says with a smile. 'Do you make a habit of delivering babies, then?'

Does she not read the papers? Does she not know who I am? In a way it's reassuring because for years I'd thought everyone talked about me. But on the other hand, there is a terribly awkward silence as I consider how to answer.

Chantelle saves the day. 'It was taken when his friends got killed, wasn't it, Nick?'

'Yeah.'

'Oh.' The woman flushes and looks around at everyone. 'Oh,' she says again.

'But it wasn't Nick's fault,' Chantelle says. 'Do you not read the papers?'

'I just glanced at the piece, that's all,' the woman stammers out.

'Technically, I was responsible for the deaths,' I say to them all. Sweat coats my palms and I find myself rubbing my hands down my strides. 'But I was found not guilty.' I'd wanted to be charged, though.

There is a chorus of nodding and chattering and the woman who initially asked the question looks a bit miserable and I feel sorry for her. 'Now, can we do some warm-ups?'

Everyone moves into a circle.

'I'd like to say something, if I may?' It's Jean. She has her hand up in the air and is waving it about.

'Well, it's not school, so go ahead,' Chantelle says.

Jean shoots her a sour look. 'I just want to say …' Jean looks around and flushes from her neck up, ' …and I hope I speak for us all when I say it. I want to say that, well, while all that stuff about those firemen was tragic and sad, you survived a terrible thing, Nick, which can't have been easy, and I for one am eternally grateful.'

And they break into applause. Some of them whoop. A couple of women clap me on the back.

Not so long ago, if someone had said this to me, I'd have walked away. I'd have said I didn't deserve those words, but now I find a lump the size of a turnip in my mouth and I'm really scared I might cry. So I just make a face and croak out, 'You lot would do anything to get out of warming-up.'

By popular vote, we do a longer run that evening. We head out of the park and loop around its outer ring. It's just under four miles. I stay at the back, to keep an eye on the stragglers. Well, that's my excuse. Charlotte is bouncing high on her toes tonight, her feet flying along. I'm not in the mood for a race. Well, I would be if I thought I'd win.

I join Jean at the back. She's panting, but at least she's managing a run of sorts. 'I'll make it or die trying,' she says. Or at least I think that's what she says, she's so breathless.

'Thanks for what you said.' I trot beside her. 'It meant a lot.'

She manages a nod and a gasp.

'Keep going,' I say. 'Come on, even if you slow down a little, just keep moving.'

And together, even though we're last, we get to the end.

* * *

Marcy and Larry are waiting for me in the kitchen when I get back. I hadn't noticed either of their cars outside, so they must have parked further up the road.

I feel ambushed.

The sounds of the TV drift out from the living room. The kids are laughing at something. My mother, Larry and Marcy are gathered in the kitchen.

'We just want to talk to you,' Larry says.

He looks terrible. I'm kind of glad. He looks like how I feel when I think about him.

Marcy is without her usual swagger. In fact, she's all sedate in jeans and a jumper. Her face looks really weird and I notice that she doesn't seem to have any makeup on. She looks so different without makeup. Freckly, pale and younger. Not so scary.

I shrug.

'Now hear them out, Nicholas,' my mother says, as if I'm twelve.

'You can go now, Ma,' I say to her. 'Thanks for minding the kids. I appreciate it.'

My mother hesitates, but, after giving us all a look, she picks up her coat and click-clacks out the door.

There is silence as she leaves.

'We want to apologise for not telling you,' Larry says quietly. 'Probably we should have.'

The relief of him saying that floods right through me. I open my mouth to tell him that it's OK, when Marcy chimes in, like the bum note in a choir, 'Kate didn't want us to. And to be honest, Nick, I'm really annoyed that Larry did. I was used to you hating me.'

'Marc—'

'Oh, don't worry,' I say, without even looking at her. 'I still hate you.'

'Aw, Nick!' Larry snaps. 'Jesus.'

And in an instant, all my goodwill towards him is wiped. 'What? How would you feel if I didn't tell you about your wife, when you had one, huh?'

'You never told me you knew she was gay,' Larry says, like he's laying down a hand of poker.

'Suspected,' I clarify. 'And that was different.'

'Yes, it was.' Marcy nods. 'Very different. Larry could have handled that news. He wasn't going off the deep end, he wasn't facing into a massive court case, he wasn't having a breakdown and acting all crazy.'

Larry gasps and says, 'Fuck's sake' to her.

The words cut deep. Through sheer force of will, I stay standing. The worst thing is, I have no defence to what she's just said. I see Larry elbow Marcy but she eyeballs me unrepentantly.

'We came to apologise,' he says to her.

'We came to sort it out,' she says back. 'But not at any cost.'

'Oh, Jesus.' Larry rubs his head. 'Nick, what Marcy means—'

'Don't tell me what I mean,' Marcy says. 'The guy was nuts, we all knew it. He couldn't handle anything. Now—'

'Thanks for that,' I interrupt. I look at both of them. 'I don't see how this conversation is helping things so can you both just go.' I push past them and sit down. I have to sit down. All the good that the run did is leaking out of me. I was crazy, I did mad things and I am so very, very sorry. Only the person I have to say it to is dead.

'Nick, look—'

'She was my wife. Mine.' My voice breaks a little and I reign it in. 'She lost our baby. And I didn't know.' I look at Larry. 'Thanks for your apology.' I turn to Marcy. 'You have a disastrous track record with relationships and I can see why.'

Marcy flinches and I can see I've struck a nerve. I turn away before I feel too guilty.

'That was uncalled for.' Larry again.

I say nothing.

'And for the record—'

'Larry, now is not the time,' Marcy snaps.

'Oh, I think it is.' Larry comes around the table and leans in towards me. His face is inches from mine. 'For the record, Nick, Marcy went out with me last night, so be careful what you say to her.'

Larry. And Marcy. I should have known really. And yet, I can't believe it. I feel as if I've lost him now. 'Just go,' I say wearily.

'I don't want to,' Larry says.

'You told me you were being nice to her for the sake of the kids,'

I say. 'It was just so you could get a leg-over, wasn't it?'

'I could hit you for that.' Larry sounds a little hurt.

'Go on, then.' I stand up.

But I know he won't.

'Nick—' Marcy begins.

'You.' I turn to her. 'You took my wife away, now congratulations, you've taken Larry too!'

'I have not! It's about time you took responsibility for the damage you keep causing.'

'Stop!' Larry says.

'Daddy?' Oh, damn. Emma is standing at the kitchen door. Cute and fearful as a bunny.

'Hey, Ems!' I try a smile.

'We're going,' Larry says. 'Bye, Nick.'

'See you munchkin.' Marcy bends down and hugs Emma, who stares at me over Marcy's shoulder, her eyes big and wide.

We all say cheerful goodbyes and I even manage a wave after them as I close the door.

'Were you fighting?' Emma looks a little confused.

I feel cornered. I can't lie to her. 'All adults fight,' I tell her. 'It's fine.'

'OK.' She nods, like she's not swallowing it.

'Can I have a hug?' I hold out my arms. 'I'll even throw in a special swing-around?'

'It's OK,' she says, 'maybe later.'

She turns around and walks back in to the TV.

* * *

It's over a week later and Marie arrives ten minutes before I'm due to go on the date. She's wearing a big floaty dress that screams 'pregnant'. It makes me grin because the woman has nothing to show yet. 'Where are the kids?' she asks, waving about some DVDs that she's taken from her bag. Then she peers out my kitchen window. 'Oh, Nick, would you ever do something about your back garden, it's a tip. Kate would have killed you.'

'I did,' I say glumly. Marie looks like she doesn't believe me, but I had dug out a flower bed and planted some things Kate had written would bloom and they hadn't. I've bought a gardening book now and downloaded some tips. I will get the garden back to what it was. Eventually.

I indicate the stairs. 'The kids are up there. I'll go say goodbye and tell them to come down. Emma, from what I can gather, is playing a game she's invented in which Liam plays a humiliating role.'

Marie chortles. 'Poor little squirt.'

'One day he'll turn around and thump her,' I say reassuringly as I leave the room. Climbing the stairs, I can hear Emma loudly instructing Liam to get into bed and pretend to be asleep. The patter of footsteps lets me know that Liam, as usual, is doing exactly as instructed. I wish I had that power over him.

I creep nearer her bedroom door to have a sneaky peek before saying goodbye but they seem to be in Liam's room.

'Now!' Emma says. 'You're asleep.'

I grin as, through a crack in the door, I see Liam obligingly curl over on his side and stick his thumb in his mouth.

'That's really good, Liam,' Emma says. 'Now imagine it's real late at night and suddenly you hear a noise.'

Liam sits up.

'No! Just listen to me first.' Liam lies back down again. 'Suddenly you hear a noise,' Emma's voice dips like the way mine does when I tell them a story, 'and you sit up and look in the corner of the room. Then you get real scared. OK. Go.'

I hold in a laugh as Liam pretends to hear a noise, then sits up. He's either a terrible actor or hasn't a clue what 'scared' means because he gives a delighted laugh. I can't see what he's laughing at but it's obviously something Emma is doing.

'Do not be afraid,' Emma chants over Liam's chuckles. 'I have come back from the dead. Jesus said that I can come for a visit.'

My stomach lurches a bit.

Then Emma, wearing all Kate's jewellery and Kate's birthday coat, glides across and plucks her brother from his cot. He's a heavy guy and she has a bit of hefting to do before he is in her arms. Then she attempts to glide across the room with him.

Liam is clapping his hands and hugging Emma. Is this right? Healthy? I have no idea what to do. Should I go in there and ask, or should they be allowed play like that?

I take a few quiet steps back from the door and call out, 'Hey, Ems, Marie is here. Come on down. I'm heading out.'

There is an immediate scuffling. Emma shouts out that she and Liam will be down in a minute. I stay where I am, wondering will she still be adorned in jewels when she comes out of the room.

Someone rings the doorbell.

'Emma, Liam, I have to go now. Come on, say goodbye to me.'

Her head appears around Liam's door. 'Bye, Daddy.'

'Aren't you going to come out?'

'Nick! Door!' Marie calls from downstairs.

'You better go, Daddy. Bye.'

'Come and give me a hug,' I say.

The bell rings again.

'Will I get it?' Marie calls up the stairs.

At that moment, Liam pushes past Emma and throws himself at my leg. Emma, clinking and jangling, strolls out after him.

'Is that all Mammy's jewellery?' I feign surprise.

'It's mine,' she says, with admirable composure. She gives me a dutiful hug. 'Bye, Daddy. See you tomorrow.'

She's been in a weird mood for a while now.

Downstairs I hear Marie telling someone to step inside. The voice is familiar, though I'm so bewildered I can't figure out who it is.

'Love you, Daddy,' Emma says, and as usual, the endearment gets me in the gut. I'll tackle it tomorrow. I kiss her soundly on the forehead and give her an extra squeeze. 'Ow,' she says.

'Sorry, hon, I'm just kissing you harder to make up for Mammy not being able to do it.' I watch her for a reaction but her eyes are their usual serious blue. Then she smiles.

'Thank you. Give Liam one too.'

So I do and I tickle him as he tries to wriggle away. Then I tell them both to head down to Marie. There is no way I want them playing that game again.

They bound ahead of me down the stairs and gawk at the woman in the hallway. I gawk too. I haven't seen this woman in over two years at least and I wince as I remember the last time I did. What is Kate trying to do to me? It's Lucy, the woman who ran the homeless shelter I worked in. She's in her early forties but looks younger because she's slim. Narrow shoulders, skinny legs, child-like wrists. She dresses like a twenty-year-old in skinny jeans and biker boots. And even though she's not classically beautiful, she's pretty in a china doll kind of way. She's the kind of woman that men want to take care of. Only Lucy's large eyes and generous lips are misleading. This lady is one tough cookie. Kate had liked her a lot.

'Hello, Emma.' Lucy smiles. 'You have really grown up into a lovely girl. And who is this?'

'I Liam.' Liam proudly sticks out his Ben 10 pyjama-ed chest.

'Who are you?' Emma asks suspiciously.

'You probably don't remember me. I was a friend of your daddy's and your mammy's. I'm Lucy.'

'No, I don't remember you,' Emma says. 'Why are you going out with my daddy?'

'She just wants to show me something,' I say.

'OK.' Emma nods.

Lucy holds out her hand to Marie. 'Hello.'

Marie eyes her up and down. 'Hello yourself,' she almost growls, which is a bit of a surprise. Marie normally loves meeting new people, and then I wonder if Danny told her. Or if Larry did. I'd sworn them to secrecy. I should have bloody known better.

Lucy seems oblivious to the hostility, though working where she does, this is no surprise. Hostile and violent people come in all the time. 'OK, Emma, can I borrow your daddy for a while? I promise I'll bring him back.'

'I hope you're a girl that keeps her promises,' Marie says with fake sweetness.

'Oh, I am,' Lucy says back.

'You can only borrow him.' Emma takes my hand. 'Only for a little while.' She looks suddenly anxious.

'I'll be back before you know it.' I ruffle her hair. 'Now, you and Liamo be good for Marie and make sure and watch all the DVDs she brought you. Thanks, Marie.' I flash her a smile.

'Come on, guys.' Marie ushers them into the room.

'Nice to meet you too,' Lucy calls after her, and I see Marie's shoulders stiffen, which makes me smile a little.

Lucy, despite the small frame and the sweet face, is no pushover. She jangles her car keys. 'Ready?'

I'm not sure I am, actually.

'I was so sorry to hear about Kate,' Lucy says as she pulls away from the curb. 'She was great.'

I say nothing, just nod.

'She rang me and asked me to do this, how could I say no?' Lucy looks me full in the face, then adds, 'And anyway, nothing ever happened.'

I loved Kate, I never would have cheated but I came pretty close to it with Lucy. It's no excuse but I was all over the place at the time. Like Marcy said, I was nuts. I wasn't thinking straight and Lucy is the kind of girl that messed-up guys like me go for. That's why she's so popular and brilliant at running The Dinner Club Soup Kitchen. The punters love her. They trust her. They tell her all their secrets, their fears, and she never judges. I even told her my stuff as I worked alongside her. Then, a week after Kate threw me out, after Kate had told me that I wouldn't see the kids until I stopped drinking, I went banging on Lucy's door. I was drunk but not that drunk. Lucy let me in, fed me coffee and listened to my rambling tales of woe. Christ, I was full of self-pity. She listened to the crap I'd put everyone through. Then she told me that I had to get over the guilt. If I didn't get over the guilt, I'd have no chance of getting over anything.

And I had leaned in and … I shake my head. Better off not thinking about it.

'It's good to see you again,' Lucy says. She drives like a Formula One racing competitor. I have to hold on to the door handle as we take a corner. 'How long has it been?'

'Two years, I guess.'

'Long time.'

I shrug. Then say, 'Look, Lucy, this is all a bit awkward. I was a mess the last time we spoke. I let you down. I'm sure you remember.'

'Of course I remember.' She gawks at me. 'You were a complete shit. I had to do all the rotas again when you walked out.'

I bow my head. 'Sorry.' I pause. 'I really am.'

Almost on two wheels, she yanks the car into a lay-by and turns off the engine. In the sudden gloom, she turns to me. 'This is not a conversation we can have while driving,' she says, and she sounds a bit firm and scary.

I have a feeling this is not a conversation I ever want to have. 'I'm finished,' I say, 'you can drive on.'

'You came to my house to sleep with me that night, didn't you?' she says bluntly.

'Not at first.'

She almost smiles.

'And I'm glad it didn't happen.' It would have been just another stick to beat myself with. 'And I'm sorry for even chancing my arm.'

'Good. So you understand why I walloped you across the face, then?'

I touch my eye which had swollen up like a balloon. I manage a grin. 'Totally.' And at the time, I think it was what I wanted her to do too.

'And have you got over the guilt?'

A beat. 'Of what? Of trying to seduce you with my alcoholic breath and self-pity?'

'No. The guilt of thinking you were responsible for those men dying?'

'I *was* responsible.'

'That's a "no", then?'

'It's not something you can get over,' I try to explain.

Lucy sighs as if I'm the stupidest guy on the planet. 'You're not even trying, Nick.'

'You don't know that. It's been two years since we saw each other.'

She doesn't respond. Instead she fiddles with an enormous watch on her slim wrist. 'Do you know why I set up The Dinner Club?'

'Because you are a wonderful, caring woman.' I quote a newspaper piece that had been written about her.

'Wow, good memory.' She smiles. Then her smile dips and she turns to face the windscreen. There is silence for a second and I realise that I'm not enjoying this date. Way too much history here. I'm about to tell her to drive us to where we're going when she speaks. 'I set up The Dinner Club out of guilt. Plain and simple.'

I'm unsure how to respond. 'Guilt? Why, did you accidentally not eat your dinner one day?'

'If you're going to make a joke, at least let it be a funny one.' She glares at me.

'Sorry.' Now I'm really stuck. If I can't joke, then my repertoire is empty.

'A guy came up to me in the street when I was going to work one day, young, smelly and desperate. He asked for some money for a hostel. I told him no. I thought he'd just spend it on drink, but really, who was I to judge? He begged me. Said please. I pushed him off.'

I say nothing.

'He was found in the canal next day and no one knew who he was. I saw his face in the paper. I kept thinking, what if I'd just given the money? What if he had got a hostel that night? It went around and around my head.'

I know what that's like.

'So I set up The Dinner Club, to make amends.'

It was the reason I'd volunteered. It was the reason I had to save Jack. It doesn't work, though.

'And while it can't change the past, it's changing the future.'

'Well, unfortunately I'm a guy who wants to change the past.'

She smiles a tiny bit. 'Really?'

I don't know why she's smiling but she is.

'Let's go so,' she says then.

We drive and drive. It's a long journey, we seem to be heading west. If she keeps going, we'll end up in America and I have serious doubts whether we'll be back by morning. We don't talk much; I sit back and enjoy the sight of the motorway whizzing by, inhaling the scent of her perfume, which is nothing like most women's perfume. It's not exactly pleasant or feminine. Lucy keeps darting glances at me but I pretend not to notice.

After I'd made my ill-fated pass at Lucy and been soundly turfed out, I'd staggered on over to Larry's. He hadn't been talking to me at the time because of the thump I'd given him. But he'd taken me in, iced my eye and called me every horrible name under the sun. It had been like bathing in cool water; I felt I deserved every one of them and I welcomed it. I'd been such a mess. I don't agree with Lucy; I have crawled back from the brink and with Kate gone there's a huge hole in my heart but I'm a lot happier than I was. The kids make it so, of course. They're proof that I have some worth. And my mates make it worthwhile. Even Larry, who I don't know how to talk to right now. I don't think of that awful night when two good men died. And I survived. Maybe in some ways I'm still only surviving.

* * *

After about two hours, Lucy pulls up in front of a small building. It's a dinner club, I realise. Inside, through a steamed-up window, I see volunteers piling food onto plates as people queue up before taking it down to a table to eat.

'This is the fourth dinner club,' Lucy says, hopping out of the car with the grace of a ballerina. 'Sorry it's so far away but it suited this person.'

What person? I climb out after Lucy, but sheer, I don't know, fear roots me to the spot.

'Come on,' she says.

My palms are sweaty but I sternly tell myself not to be such a wuss and I make my feet follow her. I haven't been inside a dinner club in two years, not since I told Lucy I didn't want to be involved again, which was the day after she slapped me across the face. As

I draw closer to the door, the hearty smell of stew assails me and I feel like I've been plunged back in time to when I first volunteered. It had been Kate's idea. She said it might make me feel better and for a time it had. I purged my guilt like confession. I listened to other people's tales of woe and felt a little blessed.

Lucy pushes open the door and calls out, 'We're here.'

There is no change in the hubbub. As Lucy enters the dining room, I see that many people have taken their seats and are busily eating away, others are queuing up. Lucy walks past, greeting the volunteers by name, and leads me to another door, set at the very end of the room. 'In you go,' she says, as she pulls the door open.

I glance at her and she grins. I walk in and the room is empty save for a table, a pot of coffee and a plate of biscuits. 'I just want you to know that I never agreed with what you did, Nick, but I know whay you did it. OK?'

I have no clue what she is on about.

Then she closes the door and a few minutes later a man comes in.

'Hey,' he says.

I nod.

The man pours us both a coffee and hands me a cup, then he takes a seat opposite me. There is silence for a few seconds. 'It's me,' he says.

'Sorry?'

'Don't you recognise me, Nick?' He smiles.

And it's the smile that lets me know. His teeth are in bits and there is a chip in one of the front ones. The room takes on an unreal quality as my heart whumps in disbelief. And my head tries to catch up with what my heart knows. It's like when Kate died, only the opposite.

'J-Jack?' I stammer out.

'Yep.' His hands are white on the mug. I feel his leg jiggle under the table. His face has gone beetroot red. 'I wanted to write to you, but Lucy said it'd be better this way. She said your wife heard me on the radio and rang her and asked that it be this way.'

'You were on the radio?'

He nods. 'I was trying to find you, to thank you. I'd been so messed up I couldn't remember who you even were. Couldn't remember Lucy.'

'Hard to forget Lucy.' I attempt humour and he smiles.

His smile fades then. 'I heard she died, your wife. Sorry about that.' His voice is crystal clear, the voice of a man. He must be about twenty now. He's put on weight, he looks good, aside from the teeth.

'Thanks,' I say. Of all the people who have offered condolences, his means the most and hurts the most. I feel like I'm looking at someone I know and yet it's someone I've never seen before in my life.

'And sorry for allowing you to do what you did for me. I should never have let that happen.'

'You let nothing happen. I did it all myself.'

'Nah, you were in bits and I took advantage. We addicts tend to do that.'

There is a pause. I blurt out, 'I thought you were dead.'

'I was.'

I take a drink of coffee. My hand shakes. The room smells of disinfectant and damp.

'I'm getting on better now,' Jack says. His voice, middle class, cultured, breaks the silence. He shifts about a bit, crosses his legs and leans in towards me. 'I'm doing lots of apologising, grovelling. And thinking.' He holds out his hand. His nails are clean and strong. 'Thank you, Nick.'

'I did nothing.' I can't shake his hand. It'd be wrong.

'You saw that I was worth saving,' he says. 'No one else did, not even me.'

'I used you to save myself,' I answer.

Jack keeps his hand held out. 'I'm glad about that.'

'All I did was—'

'It wasn't just what *you* did.' Jack shakes his head. He drops his hand. 'It was what *I* did. I left.'

'I know. I—'

'I left so you could go back to your wife and kids. It was the first unselfish thing I ever did and it made me feel good and it helped me climb back, despite the drugs and everything else.'

I hadn't thought of his disappearance like that. 'You sound like a counsellor.' I attempt a crappy joke.

'I'm training to be one,' he says. He holds out his hand again. 'Now shake my hand.'

And I do.

'It's … good to see you,' I stumble out. 'So good.'

'If it wasn't for you, I wouldn't be here.' And he really means it.

* * *

I get back at two in the morning. Poor Marie is conked out on the sofa and I gently wake her and tell her that she can sleep in my room if she likes. 'No, I'll head on home.' She sleepily stretches and yawns and I see her to the door.

'Good night?' she asks, before she turns to leave.

'Yeah.' I nod. 'Really good.'

'Kate knew what she was doing, eh?' And without waiting for an answer, she kisses my cheek. 'Get some sleep, you look wrecked.'

I watch her drive off, then after locking up, I take the book out and find a blue tab that says 'After the Fourth Date'. My heart aches as I see the pictures on this page. Tom and Alan, both smiling. Tom looking so impossibly young I could cry.

Kate writes: *Hey, you.* ☺ *If those poor men hadn't died, you would never have done what you did for Jack and he would be dead instead. That's what I want you to know. x*

It's like finding a tiny bit of gold in a heap of dirt. And though it doesn't make the deaths go away, it helps me to feel that those awful years were in some way worth it.

THE FIFTH DATE

VIOLET

I'm not one for interfering, though sometimes the urge is so strong, I have to take the phone off the hook and go out into my garden to distract myself. Take yesterday, for instance. Nick told me, quite clearly, that if the children misbehaved, they would be going to bed at nine. Nine! They should be well in bed by nine. But I said nothing.

So, Liam drew all over the walls with crayon, pulled his toys out of the box and refused to put them back. Kept saying, 'Feck, arse.' Emma refused to tidy her room for me because she thought it wasn't messy. She said that her daddy would think it was fine. I told her that I was her nana and that I didn't think it was fine. She told me, cheekily, that I didn't live there.

When Nick came home, I told him what had happened. Nick nodded and made his face all grave. 'Nine o'clock bedtime,' he said, and he sounded as if he didn't mean it for a second. So I pointed out where Liam had drawn on the walls.

Liam started to cry. Emma backed him up. She said that all little boys drew on walls. That her friend's little brother had painted the walls. That it was just a baby thing to do. I said that Liam had to know it was wrong. I told Nick to go and look at the mess Emma's room was in.

So Emma started to cry.

Don't get me wrong, I don't think it was manipulation. They were genuinely sad that they were in trouble. Sadder than they should have been, in my opinion.

Nick looked at me. I shrugged, and repeated what they had done.

Nick scooped them into his arms and said, 'I'm sure they didn't mean it. Say sorry to Nana.'

I had to leave. I can't even say I was cross with him for backing down. In a way, I understood and I wanted to wrap my arms around him but he just flashed me a quick, guilty-looking smile and said that the kids were just 'acting out'. Wherever he heard that, I don't know.

It's just one incident in a long line of them. Nick undermines me all the time, which is why I'm a little afraid to tell him about my suspicions that Emma is stealing things. I can't prove it, but a while ago I left my ring down on the table in Nick's kitchen and when I came back, it was gone. Emma was the only one in the kitchen and when I asked her, innocently, if she'd seen it, she went red and got upset and said that she hadn't taken it. It didn't even occur to me that she had until she said that. I still haven't found it. I think I'll just have to drop a few hints when Nick is around and hope he notices Emma's reaction.

I feel if he just showed them some discipline, things would be better. Kate even gave Nick rules to follow but he can't do it. Oh, he reads the book that she left him all the time. He looks at the pictures she pasted in, he studies the garden ones and the cake ones and he looks up instructions on how to use the washing machine, things like that. He even reads the rules for the children and I think he thinks that he's following them. It makes me want to shake him and hug him all at the one time. Henry tells me to leave it alone. He says it'll all come right in the end. Henry never stresses about anything. I wish he would. Our back garden would be a lot nicer if he did.

NICK

Dad and I are in the pub, two creamy pints of Guinness in front of us. Sun is streaming in through the stained glass window, making dust dance in the gloomy air. It's my dad's local and is a shrine to everything seventies, from the swirly carpets to the dark wood interiors. My father likes old things, things no one else tends to bother with, and his custom, along with the custom of his few friends, keeps this place afloat. I realise suddenly that I've never actually shared a drink with my dad. We occupied the same house for twenty-two years, he drove me to school every day, cheered me on when I ran track as a youngster, came to my early gigs with the band, gave Kate away at our wedding, babysat my kids, and I have never once had a pint with him until today. He's aged, I think as I glance across at him. His hair has whitened and the lines on his face have deepened. He's wearing old-man clothes, brown trousers and a check shirt. Sadly, they suit him. But I wonder when he started to look so old.

'Sláinte,' I say, clinking my glass off his.

He nods and drinks deeply.

The thing about my old fella is, you never feel you have to fill the silence. In fact, I think he's glad when you don't. All he's ever wanted is a quiet life, so why he married my mother is beyond me. She flits about the place dusting, cleaning, talking and endlessly socialising. She picks up friends like other people would bargains and then invites them to parties or girly get-togethers in the house. My mother has a heart of gold and is brimful of unwanted advice. My dad just sits and observes and nods. At the moment, she and two friends are minding my kids as she cooks Sunday lunch. Her friends are people she's organising a sale of work with.

'I believe you met Jack,' Dad says after a while. Up at the bar, one of the regulars is watching the racing on a tiny TV set high up on the wall. From his expletives, I think he has placed a bet on the horse which is coming in last.

'Yep.' I assume my mother must have told him.

'So, what now?' My dad has to shout a bit to be heard over the yelling punter.

I shoot him a look. 'What do you mean, what now?'

'You have to leave Jack be,' my dad says. 'You know that, don't you?'

Of course I know that. What does he take me for? 'Yeah.'

Dad nods and lifts the pint to his lips. 'Good.'

I angle my body towards him. 'What did you think I was going to do?'

He stares at me, really hard, and despite myself I drop my gaze. 'That doesn't matter,' he says.

I'm about to press him but I realise he's right. What he thought doesn't matter because while I'm glad Jack survived, I know I will never allow anything to come between me and my kids ever again. My feelings of guilt, my urge to make amends, cannot override the fact that I owe Emma and Liam the best of me, however inadequate that may be.

'Jaysus!' the guy at the bar yells. 'I'd have run faster myself!'

He's a twenty stoner at least with a massive beer belly. Dad and I share a grin. After a bit, Dad says, 'We are proud of you, your mother and me, you do know that?'

They always trot this out. 'Yep.'

'Good.'

We both lean back in the seats and watch the hands of the clock over the bar tick away until it reaches one o'clock. Dad takes his coat from the chair and stands up. 'Well, your mother will be looking for us. She'll go mad if we're late. Come on, son.'

I pull on my rain jacket, one Kate bought for me years ago when we used to run together, and follow him from the pub.

* * *

My mother is surrounded by the smells of roasted chicken and steaming vegetables. Emma is dutifully setting the table, while Liam has been secured in his high chair and is screaming blue murder to be released. My mother's friends are attempting to sing nursery rhymes to him as they try to placate him.

'Arse,' Liam screams, like a tiny Father Jack.

My mother's friends recoil as if shot. My dad laughs.

'Spirited little man,' one of the friends remarks.

I go to take him out.

'He can't come out,' Emma says sternly, 'he's causing a lot of trouble.'

'Out!' Liam screams. 'Want to help!'

I grab some bread from the press and hand it to him as my mother looks on in deep disapproval. Liam quietens for a bit as he munches on it.

'He always likes to help set the table at home,' I tell everyone. I don't add that he usually spends his time throwing spoons at Emma.

'He throws the spoons at me, though,' Emma says.

Oh! I wish I could glare at her but she deftly avoids my eye.

My mother says nothing but I know from her grim silence that she doesn't approve. She hasn't actually told me that I'm too soft with the kids but I know that's what she'd love to do. Last week Liam drew on the walls at home. My mother went mad over it but all kids go through that phase. When she gets cross with them, I tell her she should try giving out to them if they ever smile at her the way they smile at me. That stopped her. She actually touched my sleeve and said, in a funny kind of voice, 'You always were a big softie, Nicholas.'

Today, she hands me the bowl of veg and I put it in the centre of the table. She tells Dad to cut the chicken.

'Olive, Valerie would you like to stay?'

Olive and Valerie demur and hurry off.

My mother places a few potatoes on each plate and tells us to sit down. Liam quietens once he realises that everyone is now doing the same as him. I mash his food up and leave it in front of him.

'I was wondering if you ever came across my ring,' Mam asks after we've all helped ourselves to the veg. 'I can't imagine where it could have got to. Em,' she chastises gently, 'careful, love.'

Emma goes bright red as she's dropped a spoon of veg all over the floor. 'Sorry!' Jumping from her seat, she hunkers down and pops the dropped vegetables into her mouth.

'Oh, Emma,' my mother says, 'you'll get germs. Don't eat things from the floor.'

'Do you not have a clean floor, then, Nana?' Emma asks, and my dad chuckles.

'I do have a clean floor but everybody has been walking on it so it's not as clean as it was.' My mother shoots a look at my dad. 'It's the back garden I need cleaned up.'

'I'll do it for you one day, Ma,' I offer. It's the least I can do for her after all her help with the kids. 'Next week or whatever.'

My mother looks doubtful. 'You made a bit of a mess of your own garden, pet,' she says. Then with another look in my dad's direction, she continues, 'It's your father who needs the exercise.'

My dad smiles mildly and in a terrible attempt at changing the subject says, 'This chicken is delicious, Violet.'

'Well, eat up, you'll need all your energy for digging.'

'If my mammy was here, she'd do your garden, Nana,' Emma pipes up.

My heart lurches. Whenever one of the kids mentions Kate, I feel their loss so keenly.

'Yes, I know, petal.' My mother's face softens and she leans across and kisses Emma. 'She gave me loads of cuttings. Do you remember one summer you helped me plant them all?'

Emma nods. 'And she gave some to Marcy, only Marcy has to put them in pots 'cause she has no garden.'

'Oh, talking about Marcy,' my mother says, before mouthing something silently at me.

I have no clue what it is. 'What?'

Mam shoots a glance at Emma, then mouths something quickly to me again.

I shrug. 'Mam, I am a man of many talents but lip-reading and telepathy are not among them.'

My mother rolls her eyes. 'I don't want the child hearing,' she hisses.

'Hearing what?' Emma asks.

'Nothing.'

I suppress a laugh.

'Marcy's business went bust,' Dad announces.

'Henry!' my mother snaps.

'Oh, bust! Oh, Granddad, you said bust, that's like saying tits!' Emma almost chokes on her potato.

'It most certainly is not.' My mother looks offended.

I'd laugh only I'm shaken at the news. 'Emma, eat up. When?' I ask my mother.

'About a week ago,' my mother says, in the tone of the bereaved. 'It's so sad, her shop is all boarded up. She's devastated.'

I think of how horrible I was to her that night she called over. Well, in fairness, she had been horrible to me too. But she must have been under such stress and I know from Kate that running that place had been her dream. I remember now walking in on her to apologise and she'd been red-eyed. She'd probably been upset over the shop and not me. How bloody arrogant I'd been thinking she'd get upset over what I'd say. The woman has never taken any notice of me, why should now be any different? 'Well, I wish someone had told me,' I grouch.

'I'm telling you now,' my mother answers. 'Oh, Liam, look, you're making a mess again.'

I sigh in exasperation as my mother hops up and, wetting a cloth, proceeds to wipe Liam down. Can she not understand that the child loves mess. Liam wriggles and screams and yowls.

'Will you leave the child alone, Violet,' my father says.

'Daddy never wipes him.' Emma wrinkles her nose in disdain and I have to smile.

'Thanks, Ems,' I tease.

She doesn't smile back and I realise that she'd actually been criticising me. She's been a little off with me recently. Maybe she blames me for Larry and Marcy. Having heard about Marcy, I feel I'll have to bite the bullet on that one and apologise. Again.

'Have you spoken to Larry or Marcy?' My mother vigorously scrubs Liam's face and his shrieks grow louder. 'I heard there was another row.' She looks at me in annoyance. 'Honestly, you are like children the way you're carrying on.'

'They're coming over next week.' I don't know where the lie has sprung from.

My mother's eyes narrow. 'Really? Marcy never said.'

'When did you see Marcy?'

'She called in yesterday when you were at work.'

Oh, so she and Larry are sneaking around when I'm not there and visiting the kids that way. I'm kind of glad about that. Though it doesn't explain what's up with Emma, then.

'Maybe she forgot,' I lie again.

My mother now wets her fingers and starts patting down Liam's hair.

'Ugh,' Emma says, 'I hope you never put spit in my hair, Nana.'

'No spit!' Liam echoes, screwing up his face.

Mam takes her place at the table, having ignored both my children. 'You wouldn't want to fall out with them,' she says to me, 'you don't find nice friends like that every day of the week.'

'*You* do,' my father comments dryly. 'Every day of the week you find new friends.'

'Thank you, Henry.' My mother rolls her eyes but she smiles. 'It makes up for your lack of them.'

He smiles back, unoffended. 'I *have* friends.'

'Oh, yes, I forgot about the invisible ones.'

'You have invisible friends?' Emma is agog.

I smile as my parents laugh. I wonder if Kate and I would have lasted as long as they have. I'm sure, given the chance, we might have.

After dinner my mother asks me about her ring again. I tell her I haven't seen it. The house is so clean at this stage that if she'd dropped it on the floor anywhere, I would have found it.

'She's lost one of the cats too,' my dad remarks. 'Spent the last few weeks going through every ornament in the place to find it and no go.'

My mother has about a hundred cat ornaments scattered about the house. When Emma was younger, they'd frighten her because my mother kept them all together in a bunch on the sideboard. It was a truly disconcerting experience to walk into the room and find a hundred pairs of green eyes glaring at you.

When my dad takes the kids off to the shops and I'm helping with the washing up, my mother brings the subject of the missing cat up again. 'I wouldn't mind,' she says as she vigorously dries a plate, 'I was going to leave it to Emma when I died and now I can't.'

I am stacking the plates and the glasses. 'I'm sure Emma will live with the disappointment.'

'She loves that cat. Kate loved that cat.'

I say nothing to this. Kate had hated my mother's house, and her cat collection in particular, but would never have said this of course and instead had overcompensated by admiring everything effusively.

'Why are you smiling?'

'I'm not.' I try to damp it down.

'You're laughing at me!' But she's smiling too.

'Ma!' I hold up my hands. 'Would I?'

'Yes. But I don't care. It's just lovely to see you smile, Nick.' She puts down her tea towel and I feel a 'moment' coming on. Aw, Jaysus.

'I'm so proud of you.' Her voice cracks. 'Everything you've had to cope with.' Then she hugs me.

'Jaysus! Ma!' But I hug her back.

EMMA

I am not scared of anything any more. I used to be scared of lots of things like spiders and birds and Daddy. I was scared of the dark and monsters and the way teachers have eyes in the backs of their heads. I didn't like loud noises or crunchy sounds, not even cornflakes. I was scared of the sixth class girls when they came to mind us in school. Well, they are really big and some of them even wear makeup like an adult.

I am brave now.

When Mammy got sick, she told us that she would need drugs to help make her better. The drugs would make her hair fall out and maybe make her sick. She sat us down, one on each lap, and she hugged us real tight and kissed the tops of our heads and Liam wriggled out but I didn't. I kept my arms around her neck and I hugged her extra hard and I told her that I would be a good girl and help her get better real quick.

Only she didn't get better at all. At the time I didn't know that she wasn't getting better, I just thought it was the drugs making her real tired and making her stay in bed. I thought it was cool to have people cooking for us because some of my friends' mammies make nice dinners and desserts. Sometimes when I go to my friends' houses now, I tell them that Daddy is not a good cook, that cooking makes him real upset, and then my friends' mammies say, 'The poor, poor man' and they make us special dinners and give them to Daddy when they drop me home. Also, when Mammy was sick, I thought it was good the way I could sleep over in different houses if I liked and I was glad Marcy was in our house because Marcy was fun. I liked people making me feel special. Mammy being sick was sad but it was fun too.

Then, the morning she died, only I didn't know she was going to die, Marcy took us in to see her. Normally we had our breakfast and played and Mammy just slept but this day was different and I think maybe I should have known it was different for a REASON. Mammy was lying on her bed and she looked yellow like the Simpsons. And even her eyes were yellow and it wasn't nice. It was like, all the time before this she looked like herself but now she didn't. There was a scarf on her head but I knew that she had no hair underneath. And there were big dark circles under her eyes like a panda. I thought someone had come in the night and stolen my mammy. Even when Mammy patted the bed for us to climb up to her, I couldn't. Mammy said it was OK. She said not to worry. Marcy lifted Liam up. Liam just snuggled in and I wanted to yell to him to be careful, that it wasn't our mammy there.

Mammy put an arm around Liam and then she looked over at me. My legs were shaking and I think I was going to cry but I told myself not to. Mammy said that she loved us very much. She said that she didn't think she was going to get better.

Then Marcy started to cry.

'You have medicine,' I said. I felt cross. I didn't like her making Marcy cry.

'It's not working, baby.'

'So get other medicine.'

'There is no other medicine,' Marcy said. She crouched down to me and put her arm around me.

'Well, you can't die and leave us,' I said. Mammies don't leave their kids. Only daddies.

'I don't want to,' Mammy said, 'but I might not be able to help it.'

'I'll say a prayer,' I said. 'Holy God listens to prayers.'

'That would be lovely.' Mammy's voice sounded funny. 'But could you give me a hug as well?'

I watched Liam cuddle her. He wrapped his arms real tight on her neck and I think Mammy didn't like it. Her face all creased up and Marcy had to pull Liam's arms off and he started to scream.

'Ems?' Mammy turned her head and looked at me.

I moved real slow to the bed. I was scared of the yellow face. I gave her a little cuddle but I didn't feel it like you do with real cuddles. 'I'll give you a big cuddle when you get better,' I promised.

* * *

Today, which is Wednesday, Daddy gets Liam ready for bed even though Liam won't go to bed for ages and I go to my room and remember that I still have the other cat that I borrowed from Nana's to put in my bag. I am lucky because if Daddy had seen it first, I think he would be mad and I don't want to make him mad, only happy, so he will STAY. I think what I am doing might make him stay, but even if it doesn't, it won't matter. I take the cat out of my jacket and run over to my bed to get my bag from under it, only too late. Daddy comes into my room, holding his guitar, and he doesn't even knock, which is very rude, I think. Liam comes in behind him and when Daddy sits on my bed, Liam starts sliding about on the floor in his socks. Daddy sits on my bed near me and I move away. He asks me if I want him to play a song.

'No,' I say. 'Go away.'

He asks me what's wrong.

I sit on the cat I took from Nana's so he won't see it. 'Nothing,' I say.

He asks if he has made me cross in some way. He says I am not myself, which is a silly thing to say. Who else am I? I don't want to fight with Daddy because if he gets too mad he might go away. But in the end, after he says he will listen, I tell him that yes, I am cross. And once I say this, my mouth won't stop. All the crossness I feel comes pouring out and I wish I could stop but I can't. I tell him that he is a liar. I say that he told Nana that Marcy and Larry are coming over and I know that they are not because when Marcy came over the other day she said to Nana that she wasn't sure what the story was with my daddy. Actually, she said, 'I am not sure what the story is about the ship.' Then Nana said, 'The ship is a good ship, it'll turn around.' Then Marcy said, 'I hope it turns around in time for the other ship because he's very upset. This ship here,' and Marcy pointed to herself, 'feels that she has come between them.'

I knew then what they were saying but it was a clever thing to do. Like in a spy movie.

Daddy says that his lie was only a little lie but that he is going to ask Larry over.

And Marcy? I ask.

Yes, he says. Only he can't get hold of Larry.

Then Liam takes off his pyjama top and flings it at my

dolls and they topple over and Daddy laughs. I don't mind Liam laughing as he is small and doesn't know any better but Daddy is big. 'And you told me you didn't kill two people and you did.'

Then Daddy stops laughing and he pulls a little away from me. Then he stands up and turns his back and scoops Liam up and kisses Liam's head. Then he says real quiet, his mouth in Liam's yellow hair, 'I never killed people, Emma. But there was an accident and two men died.' He sits back down on the bed beside me. He holds Liam real tight. Liam struggles to get out of Daddy's arms but then he gives up and just snuggles in. The guitar slides to the floor and no one cares.

I move up the bed away from Daddy and too late remember the cat underneath me. I reach to grab it but Daddy says, 'Is that one of Nana's cats?'

'No.' It's a lie but I don't care.

'Where did you get it?'

'From my friend.'

He believes me. 'Anyway, I never killed people, Ems,' he says. 'I was going to tell you the story one day but I needed to wait until you were older.'

I tell him that Jane knew and she is the same age as me. I am shouting a bit because I don't want to think of men dying. I tell him that the reporter who rang the house knew. Everyone knew. It wasn't a big secret. I tell him that not telling the whole truth is the same as telling a lie. That is what the priest said.

He tells me priests haven't a clue. Only he uses the 'f' word between 'a' and 'clue'. Mammy would be very cross with him. Liam starts to cry. I tell Daddy to go away.

He stands up. He looks down at me. 'Sorry, Ems, I'm sorry. Love you.'

I don't love him any more. I give him a cross look so he knows that.

Then, I don't know what, he says real loud for me to put my coat on.

Put my coat on over my pyjamas?

Then he shouts, 'Now,' which makes Liam cry a bit and me jump out of bed and put on my coat.

NICK

I've the kids in the car, Liam laughing and Emma asking where am I bringing them? I tell her nowhere. I shout it out. 'Nowhere.'

I know I'm frightening her so I bring my voice down. 'I'm just calling in to Sue, to explain to her about the men in the fire so she won't get it wrong. You and Liam should stay in the car.' My hands grip the steering wheel and I know I'm a little bit possessed, but really, how dare she. How dare she go and poison my daughter with her half-baked lies.

'I can tell Jane,' Emma pipes up. 'Daddy, it's very late.'

'It's not late. Sue knows I'm coming.'

A voice in the back of my head is telling me I'm going to look mental. It's telling me I should wait for a better time. But there is no better time. I am so cross about this, so cross that Sue's daughter has upset Emma yet again.

I find Sue's house, which is easy because it's the most manicured one on the road. All the flowers, in alternate colours, planted in precise rows. Garden ornaments gleam in the fading light. They're probably power-washed every week and it's the first house I've ever seen where the brass knocker on the door is actually polished.

I give the bell a good hard ring and ignore Emma peering at me from the car.

A man, obviously Sue's husband, answers and I ask to see his wife. He gives me a funny look before calling Sue. They've obviously got guests over because there is a lot of chatter coming from the kitchen. Sue emerges, closing the kitchen door behind her.

'Hello? Nick? How are you?' She sounds a little drunk. A lot happy. Then her face creases. 'Is there something wrong? Is that Emma in the car?'

'I'm a bit pissed off actually,' I say, with cheery sarcasm.

'Oh?' She sounds baffled. She takes a step back from the door.

'I believe you told your daughter that I killed people, and guess what? Your daughter told my daughter.'

'What? I never—' Sue gasps. 'I resent—'

'She never said that,' her husband says. 'She—'

'You can resent all you like,' I snap, cutting him off. 'But I resent having to explain to my eight-year-old how two men died under my care. I resent the fact that my daughter won't sit beside me because your daughter told her what happened. I resent that you can't keep your big nose out of other people's business. And your big mouth shut in front of your child.'

'That is enough,' her husband hollers, but Sue holds her hand up and he stops.

'Firstly,' Sue says, and her voice shakes a little, 'I did not say anything of the sort to Jane. Maybe I discussed you with my husband and Jane picked it up in a certain way, I do not know. But what I certainly do know is that I do not go about saying things about people to my daughter but yes, I do talk to my husband, that's what couples do.'

'Maybe next time make sure that your bat-eared daughter is out of earshot.'

'I resent—'

'Oh, shut up!'

'Now hang on a minute,' her husband says, his loud voice

drowning out mine. 'You do not talk to my wife like that. She would never say anything of the sort to Jane. In fact, if anything—'

'Paul, stop,' Sue says.

'I won't,' Paul barrels on, 'he deserves to know. If anything,' he continues, eyeballing me, 'I have heard Sue encouraging our daughter to be friendly with your daughter because she was fighting with most of the girls in the class.'

'That's a lie.'

'No, it's not,' Paul says.

I get a sudden flash of memory, Emma emerging from the school buildings alone, head down, bag trailing from her hand. I swallow hard. 'Why won't they talk to her?' I hear myself ask.

'I don't quite know,' Sue answers, then adds in a softer voice, 'I think Emma is crying.'

I turn around and my heart nosedives. Emma has her hands plastered to the window and her face pressed up against it and she is shaking with sobs. I stand there helplessly, not sure what I can do now. Whatever anger had possessed me to come here has now been extinguished as abruptly as fire in a vacuum.

'Shit,' I mutter to myself.

'Bring her in,' Sue suggests suddenly, 'and convince her that you were bringing her for a surprise sleepover.'

I turn back to Sue.

She offers a hesitant smile. 'Jane will be delighted, I'm sure she will. And come and have a cuppa too. You look like you could do with it.'

And so it is that I find myself scooping Liam and Emma up, trying my best to convince Emma that my driving over here in the late night was a ploy to make her happy and give her a surprise.

I'm not sure she buys it.

But I can't think of anything better to do.

EMMA

How can Daddy think that getting me to spend a sleepover with Jane is a surprise? I don't like Jane. And anyway, Daddy is telling lies. He was cross in the car. He shouted at us. You don't shout when you are giving people a surprise. You make a happy face and sing, 'Surprise.' Instead, he just lifted me out of the car and said, 'Hey, Jane is waiting for you to have a sleepover. Isn't that great?' And he didn't even look at me. And he didn't even pack some clothes for me to wear the next day or anything.

So I know he is telling lies.

NICK

Sue leads me into their front room. In the kitchen people are still chatting away and her husband goes off to join them. Sue tells me to sit on the sofa and I do. I am incapable of leaving. I fear she will think I'm mad and get the authorities on me if I just run off. I need to explain to her. I need her to understand that I am not mad.

Sue leaves and comes back a few minutes later and hands me a mug of tea and some biscuits. I wrap my hands around the mug. She sits opposite me in her perfect, clean-smelling, every-thing-in-its-place room.

'Sorry,' I mumble. I bring my gaze to hers. 'Sorry.'

She shrugs a bit. 'It's fine.'

'No, it's not,' I say. 'What I did was, well, a bit mad.'

'If I thought that you had said something to your daughter about me that was untrue, I'd be mad too.'

I bow my head.

'You are entitled to feel the way you feel,' she says.

'That night,' the words stumble drunkenly out, 'was truly awful. I just, well, it's something I'm still coming to terms with.'

'I'm sure.'

'I killed two people.' And I stop.

She says nothing, just stares at me across the room. Once I say

I've killed people, I feel a gulf inside as if I'm somehow separate from normal people. But I don't know what it is, her stillness, the order of the room, but I start to speak. Maybe if the house had been a bit more like mine, a bit chaotic, I wouldn't have been able to, but this place looks as if nothing, not even nuclear war, would disturb it. 'I was a fireman,' I say. Even now, the words cause a rush of nausea. It's impossible to escape feelings. They tidal wave over you.

'I know,' she says quietly. 'You don't have to tell me.'

But I feel I do because I've come knocking on her door in the late evening, shouting the odds, and she has been so good about it. The last time I told this story was to a counsellor and I never went back. I take the memory now, like a perverse gift, swathed in bubble wrap and I present it to her, all fresh and shining. As clear as it happened on the day. Giving it to her in atonement.

It was nine o'clock. A winter night so it was dark and cold, but crisp. We were playing cards, our team always played cards. There were six of us and I wasn't so good at card-playing in those days. I lost a lot of hands that I maybe could have won. I never studied people the way I do now. Reading people makes you win at cards. Not giving anything away, betraying no emotion, makes you win at cards. This time I had two aces and a king so I was fairly confident of winning something. I had just laid a bet down when the siren went and the cards were abandoned and we were out of there, pulling on hats and boots and whatever things we needed.

I loved the excitement of going to a fire. Sure it was tempered with anxiety and stress, but the idea of being able to do something, being able to influence an outcome, that was the adrenaline rush. Saving lives was the ultimate goal.

This fire, on the surface, didn't look too bad. A house fire, right at the end of a street. Smoke was piping from the windows, grey and slow and easy. The fire was either deep-seated, which didn't seem like a possibility in a house, or it hadn't taken hold yet. We prayed for the latter. It was coming from the ground floor, though it was rising, so there was a chance that, given time, the fire would reach the roof. Neighbours were standing around in excited little groups as we arrived. The fire control officer was asking if anyone knew of people inside. Someone said they thought there might be someone as they'd seen a light on earlier. A couple lived there, they said. The fire officer went around examining the building and making the area safe.

In those days, I was way better at reading smoke than I was at reading cards. You judge the severity of any fire by the colour, volume and speed of the smoke. But this was a dark night and even though the scene was lit up, it was a hard call. The smoke, like I said, didn't look bad, it was drifting lazily out of the vents with no agitation or turbulence. But if the fire was deep-seated, the smoke would obviously take its time getting out and would slow down and abate.

The priorities are people first and property second. As one crew were hosing down the building, we were getting ready to go in. I was sent, as I was the most experienced. Then Tom, aged twenty-one, who was a very talented newbie, and Alan, who had transferred from another station recently. The fire officer deemed it safe enough for the moment. He said to search for people and if we could, to locate the source of the fire. It might be in a basement, they'd had an extension with a basement done recently, a neighbour said. We had twenty minutes. The rules of the fireman are simple: you do not leave your team, you do not let someone leave your team to go off on their own. Everyone sticks together. In we went through the door and all appeared calm. Smoky, sure, but visibility wasn't too bad. And it wasn't too hot either. We called out for anyone in the building to make themselves known but there was no reply. It was a deceptive warren of a house with doors running off left and right and on two storeys. The place was around two thousand feet with an extension at the back. There was no fire anywhere, just a lot of smoke which seemed to be coming from the back of the premises. Cautiously, still calling out, feeling the ground with our feet, using our hands to protect our faces, we made our way through the gloom until we came to a set of stairs, which we passed. On, around a corner and into a kitchen. There was definite heat under us. Looking down, I spied a set of stairs leading to a basement.

Fuck, I remember thinking. This is where she is. Down here.

I pointed and began to climb down, taking the stairs cautiously, the others following and all of us calling out, spraying at anything we deemed a risk. It was hotter here. The fire was definitely on this level and the smoke was a lot thicker. We followed its trail, still calling out, still searching for bodies and the place was huge. It was the size of at least the ground floor. A massive square strewn with large objects. I think it was some sort of a games room. The smoke was thickest in front. I described things back to the fire officer by radio, who said that, judging by the velocity of the smoke, things were still under a degree of control. We hosed as we went. It was as we reached what I thought was the back of the basement that we saw it. Thick black smoke billowing towards us. It was a shock to have such a sudden lack of visibility and for the first time, I felt fear. But we had to hose it down; if we didn't, there'd be an explosion of some sort and we'd be trapped here either way. We had to stop the heat from igniting the smoke. And so, like a finely tuned machine, we got to work. The smoke was pouring out of what seemed to be an electrical box set into a wall and it had become thick and was descending towards ground level, a sure sign that everything in the room was heating up, ready to explode. The time in that room seemed endless but was probably only a few minutes until finally, almost heaving with relief, the fire was brought under control. But our time was almost up and we were under instructions to get out. We stopped for a moment to regroup, to assess the damage. And though it must have been going on all the time, we were too busy or too hard at work for it to have registered – there were unmistakable sounds of something shifting above our heads. The three of us looked up.

I sucked in a breath and motioned for the guys to leave. I told Tom to take care and stay calm. It was much harder to see now, the smoke had done its damage and while no longer dangerous, it was dense. We had started making our way out towards the stairs when I felt a tip on my back. I turned, and Tom was pointing to the right. I shook my head and kept moving.

'It's this way,' I heard Tom say. He sounded scared. Beside us the walls groaned, the ceiling shifted just a tiny bit.

I shook my head. I so clearly remembered coming down here. I said I knew where we were and for him to follow me. I looked at Alan. He said hesitantly that he thought I was right. Tom shook his head but because he was a good kid and he followed rules, he fell into line.

Slowly, slowly we inched our way back up the room, taking it easy, careful not to disturb anything. I radioed outside, told them that while the fire was under control, the walls were a danger. I kept up contact until I arrived at a blank wall. There was no staircase.

The panic was instant and it flooded every part of me. I'm sure the other two felt the same. I'm sure they were cursing me. I apologised to Tom over radio, so everyone would know he'd been on the ball. Tom slapped me on the back as if to say we all make mistakes and slowly we began inching our way in the other direction.

In my earphones, someone told me calmly to get the fuck out. Now. Only the noise from overhead became so much louder. Hearing a building collapse is pretty much like witnessing a murder. It's the death throes of a structure that was built to survive. And the world slowed down so that I could absorb every microsecond of that nightmare. I saw the walls buckle and shudder, I saw bits of plaster crash to the floor and spray into a thousand pieces, I saw the cracks running up the walls across the ceiling as if an invisible child had drawn on them with marker. And as Alan and Tom ran, I stood and watched and knew this was my fault. This was my fault. We would die because of me and my mistake. I heard the girders groan and clang and pull free and I saw one of them *crush Tom as if he were a spider under a foot. I saw Alan turn and try to pull him up and then Alan was gone. I saw him disappear like a snap of a photograph. And then everything was still, and smoke had begun to rise up from the rubble and I could see onto the upper floor through beams and twisted metal. And as sound returned, and the hail of stone abated, I heard a crackle in my headset. I was still standing. Still alive and whole. I ran towards where my team had been and began tugging at the cement girders and stone that had fallen in and yelling for help and saying that two men were gone and that it was my fault.*

And it was all my fault.

I had miscalculated.

I had fucked up.

And from then on, I had lost my way on just about everything.

When I finish talking, silence descends on the room like a shroud. It covers me up, wraps me tight and squeezes the breath out of me. I feel sick and relieved all at the same time.

'It was an accident,' Sue says softly. 'It's not as if you set out to kill anyone.'

I've heard that so many times. 'But I did kill people.'

'The falling ceiling killed them, not you,' she says.

'I led them the wrong way, they depended on me to know what I was doing.'

Sue doesn't reply, and I'm so used to people trying to batter me with their thoughts on how I did my best – how I was brave to go into the building in the first place, how I might as well blame the building for being so unstable as to blame myself – that her lack of response forces me to look at her.

'I guess no matter what I say it won't make a difference,' she says, sounding all matter-of-fact.

I nod. Consoling words are like hail on a window, they don't even make an impression. I've got self-blame down to a fine art.

'All I'll say is that you're doing a great job with the children. I love the easy way you have with Liam in the Parent and Toddler.'

The subject change wrong-foots me. 'Thanks.'

'I have to learn to relax like that. I'm too uptight.' She flaps her hand about. 'I grew up in chaos and now, sadly, I'm the opposite.' She smiles glumly. 'You struck a chord with me when you said Jane was like a Stepford wife that day.'

'I didn't mean—'

'She is, and it's my fault, but I'm trying to change. It's never too late to change.'

We smile at each other. Me and Sue. Who'd have believed it?

Out in the hall, I hear Liam laugh loudly, and Emma explaining to Jane that Liam is pretty good fun for a boy.

I look at my watch. It's eleven thirty. 'I'd better bring the fun boy home.'

'I'll drop Emma back tomorrow.'

We stand up. 'Thanks for being so understanding,' I say.

'What you're doing, bringing up the two kids after losing Kate, it's tough. Of course you're going to get upset.'

'Thanks.' I walk by her from the room and she pats my arm.

NICK

Danny hands me an invitation. It's in a yellow envelope with green writing. There's a big blob of oil in the place where the stamp should be. 'We're having a conception party.' He grins. 'Next Saturday.'

'A what?'

'To celebrate conception, obviously.'

'Obviously!' I fist my head. 'Right, yeah, 'cause I've been to so many of them!' Laughing, I open the invite. It's shaped like an egg. 'Lovely, very tasteful.'

'Aw, well, Marie said we have to celebrate everything about this,' Danny says. 'She thinks if we lose the baby after all this at least we'll have made it count in some way.'

'You won't lose it.' I have no idea why I say this. How would I know?

'We might.' Danny shrugs and rubs the bald patch on the top of his head as if embarrassed. 'Anyway, a party is a party.'

'Best idea for a party I ever heard.' I shove the invite into my overall pockets. 'Count me in.'

'Larry and Marcy will be invited too,' Danny mutters.

I murmur something to that. I tried to ring Larry again yesterday but he didn't answer. I plan on calling over tonight after work. I've told my mother that I have a job on and she's OK with staying on.

'How are things there, by the way?' Danny asks.

'Dunno.' I pick up a wrench, hoping to avoid talking about it.

'Youse all talking yet?'

'Nope, but you know … soon … hopefully.' I pop open the bonnet and stare at the engine. 'I'll call over tonight.'

There's something about Danny's silence that makes me look up. 'What?'

'He's … eh … gone on holiday with … eh … her. You didn't know?'

'Nope.' Jesus, he must be pissed off with me that he never said.

'He'll be back Friday night. Apparently, her business is gone belly-up and she's lost her apartment, so he's trying to cheer her up.'

'Right.' Emma is going to freak, I think suddenly. She'll really think I'm a liar. She didn't swallow the whole 'sleepover in Sue's' for a second, though by all accounts she had a great time.

And my mother must have known and she never said.

Danny sits on the rim of the bonnet, his arms folded, his legs stretched out in front of him. 'He's fancied her for ages,' he said. 'Only kept away from her because of you.'

I'm not sure I believe that. Larry was always on about the girls in his office and whatever girls he managed to meet on nights out. Not exactly many.

'Apparently, Kate told them both to visit her grave. Once a month at twelve noon they had to put flowers on it. Neither of them knew the other had been asked. That's how they got closer.'

When I look up, Danny adds, 'Or so they say.'

Larry would hardly lie about that. Maybe it is true but I doubt Kate wanted them to be together. She probably just wanted someone to visit her grave. The thought gives me a pang. Obviously she felt that I wasn't going to.

'Kate was always saying to Marie what a great couple they'd make.'

'Kate and Marie? A couple?' I try for a joke. Danny looks blank. I shrug. 'Yeah, well, Kate was a big romantic.' I say it with a mixture of grief and fondness. 'Look what she organised for me – going out on all these dates.'

'Yeah, but that's not about finding you someone, is it?' Danny says. 'It's more about you finding—' He stops. 'Anyway, back to work.'

'Finding what?'

'What?' Danny lifts himself up. 'What?'

'You said all these dates were not about finding me a woman, it was more about finding – what?'

'Did I?'

I quirk my eyes.

'I'd be more comfortable answering that question if you didn't have a wrench in your hand.' Danny grins. Then says, 'OK, I think Kate organised those dates so you could, you know, get your life back on track. Shock you into being who you were again. Not this,' he gestures at me, 'half-person.'

The radio is playing some upbeat tune in Danny's untidy office. In the yard someone drives up, slams their car door and shouts out a 'hello?'. The dates flash by – the running track, the music venue, the restaurant, the shelter. My history, our history. Who we were, who we became. My past, my present. I suddenly get it. She did it so I'd be fully alive for the kids. Just like she asked me to get treatment. I stare at Danny.

'Makes sense, yeah?' Danny says.

'Hello?' The voice from the yard is becoming impatient. A woman in tight jeans and stilettos, wearing overlarge sunglasses, totters up to the entrance and pokes her head in. 'Do you want my business or not?'

Danny claps me on the back and strides over to greet his customer.

Kate, I think fondly, I swear I won't let you down.

EMMA

We are going to a party in Danny and Marie's because they might have a baby. Daddy's friends are nice. They invite him to their parties. Amy Murphy had her party and I never even got an invitation. I will not do swapsies with her next year. I hate her now. Jane is my best friend. She is coming over tomorrow for a sleepover here. She agrees that Amy Murphy is a show-off, even though she went to Amy's party and everything.

I asked Jane if she knew I was coming for a sleepover that night in her house and she said no. She said that my daddy was shouting at her mammy and daddy and then they all got friendly again. She said that the sleepover was her mammy's idea.

My daddy tells lies but Jane says lots of people do. She says that her granddad used to tell her granny that he was working late and he really wasn't. He was spending all the money they didn't have. She says her mammy or her granny never talks to her granddad now. At least I have a nice granddad.

I took a few nice hair bobbins from Jane's house when I stayed there. I know Jane won't mind. I took them for the Virgin Mary.

NICK

Danny and Marie have a knack of throwing a good party. It's not that they provide amazing food or ply you with drink all night. They do that too but it's them, the relaxed vibe they project, the comfortable, messy house, the way they are as a couple, that makes for great occasions.

I get there around nine thirty, with the kids, carrying four bottles of wine and some cans. The house is jammed already and we have to shove our way into the narrow hall. It's not made any easier by the fact that one of the dogs has planted himself right in the middle of the space and is refusing to move. With much laughter, we climb over him and make our way into the kitchen to drop off the drink. The kitchen door is open and as I walk in, I see through the window that a marquee has been erected out the back.

'Hey!' Someone wraps their arms around me from behind. Turning, I see Marie, who enfolds me in a hug. 'Great to see you.'

I kiss her cheek. 'Congratulations on conception.'

She giggles. 'Ah, you know us, any excuse.'

'What's conception?' Emma asks.

'It means that I might have a baby,' Marie tells her. She reaches behind and finds some crisps. 'Now, you and your brother eat those and see if you can find some other cool kids to play with. I know Rosemary and Jake are somewhere about.' They are her niece and nephew.

Emma grabs the crisps, grabs Liam and shoots off.

Marie shakes a glass of water in my face. 'Can't drink. I forgot that bit when we were planning the damn thing.'

'Which means at least four more glasses each for everyone here.' I laugh.

She slaps my arm. 'I don't drink that much.'

'Where's Danny?'

'Outside, helping the girls set up their equipment.' She snorts a bit. 'Like he knows what he's doing.'

'Equipment?'

'We're playing music in the marquee.'

'Cool.'

'Yes. Larry recommended these two girls he saw on some work junket.'

Larry's name, so casually said, makes me flinch. If Marie notices, she ignores it.

Danny arrives in at that point. 'Aw, Nick, just the man. You know about music equipment, don't you? Come out here and give us a hand.'

Marie chortles. 'Aw, have you messed it all up, sweet thing?' She tweaks his cheek. 'Did you not know what you were doing? Does it not resemble a car at all?'

'I find that very patronising.' Danny sniffs. 'I've got most of it done, it's just not working and the girls can't figure it out. Nick?'

Both of them look expectantly at me. I leave my booze behind on the table and follow Danny outside.

The marquee is huge. A chef is preparing food in front of an array of tables and chairs. Large pink and blue balloons hang from the ceiling. A long buffet table has been set up with plates and cutlery. I spy Emma, Liam and some other kids already shoving the sweet stuff into their mouths. Right at the top is a small stage. Two girls are pottering about unplugging wires and tapping microphones.

'I have just the man to help you,' Danny announces as we approach.

Both girls turn.

I rub my hands together and feign eagerness. 'What's the problem here?'

'I think I've got it sorted,' one of the girls says, hunkering down and adjusting a lead. 'Danny, no disrespect, but you haven't a fucking clue.'

I laugh loudly as Danny goes fire-engine red.

'Well,' he manages a smile, 'disrespect taken.'

'Sorry about that.' The girl flashes him a cheeky grin, not sorry at all. Then she turns to me. 'So we won't need you. Thanks anyway.'

We are dismissed.

Danny and I are just walking back into the house when I spot Larry through the kitchen window. He is talking to Marie, and has his arm loped about Marcy, who is nestled into his neck. The sight of them being so couply when I'd always assumed they couldn't stand each other is disconcerting. I must make a noise or some gesture because Danny stops and asks if I'm all right.

'Sure, yeah.'

He claps me on the back. 'Come on, let's say hi.'

I follow in behind him. 'Hey.' Danny greets Larry with a fist to the upper arm and then he envelops Marcy in a hug. 'Sorry about your business,' he says to her. 'Total bummer.'

Marcy smiles a little. 'Larry reckons he can find a cheaper premises for me to rent.' She places her hand possessively on my friend's arm. 'It was the rent that was crippling me.'

I find it weird to see Marcy in the midst of my friends. For all the years Kate had been around, Marcy had always stuck with her. She'd never have been invited to a party at Danny and Marie's and

now here she was right in among them. I feel like the outsider all
of a sudden.

'Hey, Nick,' Larry says, with a nod. 'How's things?' His eyes are
wary, assessing me.

I manage a smile. 'Great,' I gulp out, 'the kids are asking for
you.'

'Are they here?' Marcy asks.

'In the tent.'

'Marquee,' Marie corrects, grinning. 'Tent! Jesus!'

We laugh awkwardly.

There is an uncomfortable silence. Marie and Danny look at
each other and then, in the way of couples who've been together
ages, by some signal they both move away. Now it's just the three
of us.

'Good holiday?' I stumble out. I wish Marcy would just go. If
things were normal, I'd be telling Larry about the last few weeks
and we'd find some way to have a laugh about everything.

'Yeah.' Larry shuffles from foot to foot. Marcy stands her ground.
'We had a blast, didn't we?' He looks down at Marcy.

'We did.' She looks up at him and I feel excluded. Maybe
that's the way Kate and I were around Larry, I don't know. But it's
something I envy.

'Good.'

More silence. Marcy looks at both of us before extracting herself
from Larry. 'I just want to go and see if I can find Emma and
Liam.' A pause. 'Is that OK, Nick?'

'Sure. They'll be delighted to see you.'

'I got them a brilliant present.'

We watch her go and then Larry turns to me. 'You going to
accept her?' he asks. He sounds blunt. Hard.

'Have I a choice?' That is so not what I meant to say. But, damn
it, we've been friends for so long. And of all the women he could

have, he picks the one who annoys me more than any other woman on the planet.

'No, Nick, you don't.' Then he picks up a can and walks off. Turning back to me, he says, 'I'm going to say hi to the kids too.'

My reply is to down a can.

Davy arrives and I spend some time with him, the two of us on the sofa in the sitting room, gradually getting a little drunker. Peter surprises us all by bringing a woman with him. He'd met her at a dancing competition for the over-fifties, he said. She is definitely over fifty, my guess would be late sixties, but she's pleasant enough. Her name is Cecelia.

'Peter is a fantastic dancer,' she raves. 'So smooth, suave and very sexy.'

Peter smiles at us as if he just can't help it, and adjusts his cardigan.

'And I know your mother,' she tells Davy. 'I went to school with her.'

Davy blanches and unsuccessfully tries to hide his can behind his back. 'Wow,' he says weakly.

'She was a right laugh, your mother.' She flaps a hand and giggles. 'All the boys used to be chasing her.'

'Wow,' Davy says again, and goes even paler.

'She says you've moved out of home.'

'Yeah, in the last few weeks.'

Just then one of the dogs bounds into the room, knocks over a table and hops up on Cecelia, who squeals. Marie comes in behind and drags the dog off.

'My tights.' Cecelia is examining a tear in a very stout, unsexy pair of brown tights.

'Sorry,' Marie, still holding the dog by the collar says. 'I've some upstairs still in their packets if you'd like to use them.'

'Yes, yes, I will, if you don't mind,' Cecelia says. 'I tend to get a cold in my kidneys if I don't have tights on. Think it's my age or something.' She follows Marie from the room.

'You can take the can out now.' Peter winks at Davy. 'Cecelia won't tell on you.'

Sheepishly, Davy takes the can out from behind his back. 'I know I'm a wuss, but honestly, my mother is better off in the dark about stuff. If she found out I was drinking and going back to an apartment, she'd have the fire service on standby.'

We laugh.

'I'm not joking,' Davy says. 'She came around to my apartment the day before I moved in and quizzed the builder on the security in the place. She says she didn't bring me up to lose me to a stray robber squeezing in through a window. I said, "Ma, I'm on the eighth floor." For fuck's sake.'

I laugh a lot at that.

'She's baked me about a hundred dinners and because my bloody fridge isn't big enough, they started to stink the apartment out of it. The neighbours thought there was a dead body in the place.'

We laugh again.

'They called the cops.' He looks at us. 'I'm serious. They called the cops.'

Cecelia arrives back down in a pair of incongruous fishnets and sits herself on Peter's knee. He wraps his arms around her waist. Davy excuses himself.

Later, I don't know how much later, I wander into the marquee. It's a testament to a good party that I have not seen my children once. The food has been served and it seems that I've missed it. I've successfully avoided Larry and Marcy all night or maybe they've avoided me. The singer at the top of the room is asking for volunteers and a man I don't know is belting out a terrible but good-hearted rendition of 'The Irish Rover'. I make my way towards the salads and nibbles, the usual party fare.

'Anyone else?' the girl calls, as the man takes his bow to cheers and shouts of 'encore'. 'Come on, there has to be someone else who wants to sing.'

'My daddy is a great singer,' a voice pipes up and my blood freezes.

'Yeth, Daddy great!' a second voice chimes in.

'And there he is!' Emma shouts loudly, pointing in my direction. 'His name is Nick!'

'A big hand for Nick!' the singer calls.

Heads turns to look, among them Larry and Marcy. Davy is there too. Of course, he, being as drunk as I was a few seconds ago, starts to whoop and cheer. I laugh it off, take a quick bow and start loading up my plate with leftover meat. 'I'm hungry,' I say. 'I can't sing on an empty stomach.'

'You can eat it later,' the girl calls.

'Nope,' I say.

She gets them clapping.

'I've drunk too much,' I say.

'So what?' the other singer says.

'So what, Daddy?' Emma says. She runs up and tugs on my hand. 'You are better than them all so far,' she whispers. 'Go on.'

I am unable to refuse her anything. I grin down at her. 'You think so?'

'Swear.'

'Will it make you smile if I do it?'

'Yep.'

'Then how can I refuse?' I dump my plate and stride up the room, Emma clinging to my hand and Liam cheering somewhere in the crowd. They part before me like grass blown by the wind. I climb up onstage.

'Nick, everyone,' the girl shouts, to loud clapping and whooping. At the back, I see Marie and Danny enter. Peter comes in with

Cecelia. Christ, it's like Indian smoke signals, the way they've all suddenly gathered.

'I'll just sing one,' I say. If I can bloody remember the words. I think about what song I should do and then I know. This is a party Kate should be at, she should have been with me, drink in hand, sitting on my lap, nibbling my ear as I surreptitiously have a feel of her breast when no one is looking. We'd have stared at each other until neither of us could have borne it any longer and then we would have gone home and hardly been able to breathe for desire. In my head, I say, 'This is for you, Kate,' and, after taking the guitar from the girl, I sing the song I used to sing for her at parties like this. Josh Ritter's 'Kathleen'. Only I change it to Katie. Anyone who knows me will know what it means. It's a bright, happy song, just like her. About love and desire.

As the words pour out into the room, the cheering and whooping stop. Larry wraps an arm about Marcy, who I think is crying. Marie is bawling down the back and I wonder if I've ruined the vibe. But I couldn't stop now if I wanted to. My fingers hit the right chords, the guitar is rich with sound, the music carries up into the roof and then slowly, slowly dies out. A final twang falls into silence.

I take a bow and they start to clap. From the back, Marie blows me a kiss.

Emma is smiling, fit to split in two, and Liam is gawking at me like he's never seen me before.

'Lucky woman,' the singer says softly.

'Naw, I was the lucky one,' I say back.

'That was great,' Larry says as I step down.

'Thanks.'

And we leave then, me, Emma and Liam. It seems right. As if by singing the song, I've brought Kate with us and now we're taking her home.

Danny and Marie will understand.

NICK

I'm out running with Chantelle and a few of the more dedicated runners the following day. The sun is high and bright and as sharp as a knife in my slightly hungover brain. I'd promised the group that we'd get out for eight miles and while I was tempted to pull out, as I'm sure they could have gone on their own, I realise that I would have missed the craic with them. Women are different to blokes, they talk about stuff that matters. Not that I'm saying football results don't matter or anything, but they talk about their lives and their problems and, listening to them, I don't feel as alone. Chantelle has told me all about not being able to finish her college course because she got pregnant. 'I wanted to do PE,' she says. 'I worked my ass off to get in and then, in my final year, I ended up in a maternity hospital.'

'And would you ever go back?'

She gives me a half-smile. 'Nick, I have never even got so far as a holiday in Kildare since. Heading back to Limerick is a stretch too far.'

'Aw, one day …' I let the sentence trail off. Then add, 'You never know what might happen.'

The irony of me actually thinking that's a good thing makes me smile a little.

'Was Kate a good runner?' Chantelle changes the subject. 'She used to say she wanted to enter marathons.'

'She was good,' I answer. 'She loved long-distance. Some days she'd go off for hours just running. I reckon given time she'd have been into all the ultra stuff. It was her addiction, I guess.'

Chantelle smiles. 'And you?'

'I was into short runs that were over quickly.' I grin. 'I never liked the pain.' I don't tell Chantelle about the marathon Kate had entered us both for and that we never got to do. I should have done it. 'Anything longer and I was crap.'

'Aw, you're getting better.' Chantelle grins. 'You'll never beat me, though.'

She increases her pace and I don't even attempt to follow. I tried the last time we were out and was crippled for the day. But it was a good pain, I realised. One that would go in time and would get better in time. But now I slow down and join the women at the back. Jean is a bit behind and I jog back to her.

'Eight miles is way out of my comfort zone,' she pants. 'I'm holding you all up.' She bends over from the waist, gasping, 'I have to stop.'

'No.' My tone startles her. 'Just slow up even more, don't stop, you'll never bloody start again.' I jog a little on the spot. 'Come on.'

She glares at me. 'Sometimes I hate you.'

'A lot of women say that.' I wait for her to smile before coaxing her to jog more slowly. 'Every time you go running it should be a little out of your comfort zone, Jean. It's OK to be slow, once you get there in the end.' I glance at my watch. 'We've two miles to go. You have just done 10K. That's great.'

'10K.' Jean says it like it's the holy grail. 'I have just run 10K!'

'Yeah.' I am enjoying the delight on her face when my phone rings. I unzip the pocket at the back of my strides and pull it out.

I keep running beside Jean as I take the call. It's my mother. 'Hi, what's up?'

There's a choking sound from the other end. 'Nick,' my mother says, her voice thick, 'Oh, Lord, come home, please.'

My heart flips. 'What's up?'

'Emma and Liam,' she gasps.

I feel my legs turn to water. 'What about them?'

'They're gone.'

* * *

Chantelle drives me back to the house. She'd been the one who'd talked to my mother after I'd handed her the phone in puzzled bewilderment. What did she mean my kids were gone? Gone where? And how? And when?

Jean, who sits in the back of the car, keeps telling me that there has to be an explanation for it but I know that most of life doesn't have an explanation. It's just a random series of events, some good and some bad, and it's learning to live with it that's the main thing.

If anything happened to them, I couldn't live with it.

There's a Garda car outside the house. My heart lurches like a drunk.

'It doesn't mean anything,' Jean says, but none of us really believe that.

The three of us hop out of the car and the front door is opened before I've taken my key from my pocket. My mother is wild-eyed and panicked. Behind her is a guard. In the kitchen, Angela and some of the other neighbours are flitting about.

'Nick.' My mother stares up at me. 'Oh, please, pet, I'm so sorry. I'm so sorry. I was outside in the back all morning trying to get your garden into shape and Emma came out and said she was going to play with Liam out in the front and I said OK and to close the gate to stop Liam getting out and now they're gone.'

It's all a mistake. The relief I feel is instant. 'Ma, they're probably in a neighbour's.'

I look up, the neighbours look back at me. My stomach lurches and I suddenly want to vomit. I have to sit down.

'Excuse me, sir,' a young guard says, 'can we ask you a few questions? It might help us find out where your children have got to.'

In a daze I stand up and follow the guard upstairs.

He goes into Emma's room first. 'Now, sir, could you have a look and see if there is anything missing from here, please?'

I stare at Emma's pretty little room. At her dolls and teddies and painted flowery pictures. At her duvet with ballerinas and her frilly curtains. She can't be gone. 'She has so much stuff.' I open a wardrobe. 'I don't know …' My voice catches.

'Take your time.'

I move around. My head is so jumbled with panic and puzzlement that it takes a few minutes for it to register. 'Her mother's jewellery,' I gulp out. 'That's missing.' At the guard's puzzled look, I explain about Kate leaving Emma her jewellery.

He asks me to describe the pieces and I do so as best I can.

'Why would she take it?'

'Well, she hasn't been abducted anyway,' he says. 'She's probably run off.'

'She's eight.' My voice is hard. 'Why would she run off?'

He doesn't answer, just leads me to Liam's room. His favourite teddy is gone. The policeman writes it down and then asks me to be as honest as possible. It'll be the quickest way to find my kids. He asks if there is anyone who would like to hurt my family.

His words take an age to make sense. 'No. No one I know of.' My voice breaks. 'Everyone I know adores the kids.' My head is pounding now. I want to get out and start looking for them. I want to do something.

'Those people who died in the fire with you a few years ago, you ever have trouble from their relatives?'

I'm too numb to be startled by his line of questioning. 'Nope.' In fact, Kate had told me they'd wanted to meet me at the time but I couldn't face them.

'OK, sir, I need you to tell me everything that has happened in your life in the last week or so. Leave nothing out.'

Twenty minutes later, I've been instructed to stay by the phone in case there are any developments. It's driving me nuts. I need to be out searching for my kids. They could be anywhere. My father has arrived to take my mother home but she won't leave. She is inconsolable.

'Will you have a word with your mother?' my dad says to me. 'This is going to destroy her.'

He looks older than before. Yet again.

I cross over to my mother. 'Ma, go home.'

'No. They're going out searching and we'll be going too, won't we, Henry?'

'Yes.' My dad shoots me a look.

'Mam.' I slide in beside her at the table. 'This is not your fault. You were only doing what you always do.'

It hits me then what I've said. On the night of the fire, I'd only done what I always did. I'd taken charge because that was my job and the lads knew it.

'I don't blame you,' I say to my mother, with renewed passion. 'I really don't.'

'But I blame myself.' She sobs. 'I blame myself.'

'Believe me, Mam, it's not a good idea.'

Her eyes meet mine and I catch her hand. 'You are not to blame,' I tell her. 'And anyway, we'll find them.'

'We will, won't we?'

'We will.'

EMMA

So many pretty things in my bag now. Two cats, Mammy's jewellery, Nana's ring, rubbers, cool pencils, Liam's first curl, my first tooth, bits of glitter and some ribbons. A CD that sings Mammy's favourite song, 'Kathleen', a picture of Daddy that Mammy loved. Perfume.

Liam has his hand in mine and he is eating a lollipop.

We are on an adventure like Dora the Explorer.

I am not scared, only excited.

NICK

As news travels, and the media run with it, people start turning up at the house. Marie and Danny, Davy and his mother, Peter and his new pensioner lady friend. People I know to say hello to, people I've never seen in my life. All the Parent and Toddler women arrive with their husbands. Molly enfolds me in a hug, tells me that whatever has to be done, she will do it. I gave her her baby, she will search for mine. The rest of our Sunday runners arrive, still in their training gear. Some customers from the garage arrive. The girl my mother chats to in the local shop appears. All these people, that a few months ago I didn't know, come as allies. I realise how large my network has grown, how small it was before. Lucy from the shelter comes. She brings others. About an hour later, I see Larry coming through the front door, Marcy, her face tight with worry, hurrying in after him.

Oh, God, I am so glad to see him. It's as if someone has reattached an arm I was missing.

He sees me and pushes his way through.

'Fuck,' he says. His eyes are bright with unshed tears.

We hug clumsily.

Marcy stands observing us. Suddenly, she no longer looks so scary, so judgemental. She looks frightened, she looks how I feel.

'Marcy,' I say brokenly, 'thanks for coming.'

'I've always thought of them as mine, d'you know?' Her face crumples up.

'Yeah. Yeah, I know.'

'I was never trying to butt in on you and Kate.' Tears run down her face.

I want to say, 'I know,' but we both know that'd be a lie. I never knew that.

'Let's just find them for now, eh?' Larry says. 'We can talk afterwards.' He lopes an arm around her and it looks so right. So right that I can't believe I never saw it before.

We turn as a strident voice tells everyone to be quiet. It's Sue. Sleek and shiny, even in a tracksuit and trainers, she is standing up on a chair.

'I'm going to divide us all up into groups,' she says, like a strict schoolteacher, 'and we're all going to take a section of the town and search. If there are two little children out there, we will find them before tonight is out!'

Someone cheers.

I never thought I'd ever be grateful for Sue's aggressive capableness but I am that afternoon. She has the ability to make people do exactly what she wants.

'Sometimes it's good to have a large pain in the ass around,' Jean whispers to me, before enfolding me in a hug. 'Oh, you poor thing. You must be out of your mind. They can't be too far.'

I can't even reply, my throat is too thick with emotion.

I turn to Larry, 'They won't let me go out searching,' I say. 'And I have to, Lar, I have to.'

'I can stay here,' Marcy volunteers. 'I'll stay with your mother, Nick.'

'No, you go, love,' Jean says. 'You're fitter-looking than me. I've run 10K this morning and I can't go another step. I'd only hold people up.' She points to my mother, who is standing at the kitchen counter looking dazed. 'Is that your mum?' she asks me.

'Yeah. She likes cats.'

Jean flashes me a smile and crosses over.

One by one the various search groups leave. Davy's mother can be heard loudly telling him to wrap up, that the weather is to turn nasty.

'Mam, I will turn nasty if you don't shut up.' Davy is mortified.

'You bring them up and this is the thanks you get,' his mother says, shaking her head. Rolling up her sleeves, she adds, 'I brought some bread to make a few sandwiches for people. This could go on for days.'

Davy shoots me an apologetic look before leaving.

Then Larry and I head off together, just the two of us.

EMMA

At least it's a sunny day. If it was wet, our map would get all wet and it might go soggy and fall apart and then we would have no map, but luckily, the sun is warm. It is a long walk, probably about a hundred miles; maps don't show the real distance 'cause if they did they'd be way too big. So I think about a hundred miles but it could be more. Or less. We can't get the bus because people would notice us on our own. When you are walking they don't notice so much, especially if you tag along at the back of a group of grown-ups.

I don't know if my idea will work. I don't know if anyone ever tried it before but I have made Jesus my special friend so if he doesn't do it for me, I won't be his friend any more, which means I won't go to mass.

I think it will work because Jesus is holy and everyone likes nice things and the bigger the thing you want, the more nice things you have to give in exchange.

I didn't tell anyone about my idea because all of them think once you go to heaven that is it. Marcy said Mammy didn't want to go, so I think it was unfair of Jesus. Maybe he just didn't understand what she wanted. Maybe he didn't listen right, like Daddy with Smelly Jack. Everyone makes mistakes. Even Jesus.

If Daddy leaves us, which he could because Smelly Jack is back (I heard Nana telling Larry about it) and Daddy is fighting with everyone again, who will mind us? Nana might mind us but she is no use at all. All she does is clean the house and clean Liam and go out with the girls who aren't really girls at all. Marcy might, but one day she could have her own baby with Larry and then she might want to get rid of us. I told Liam I would always look after him and I will.

I take out my map and study it. I know all the names of the roads now because I went over and over them in my head. Only when you are walking the roads they are bigger and some of the roads aren't on the map and there are cars and lots of people around. It's not as easy as I thought.

A lady comes up to us. She's old and has a hairy chin like my granddad. She asks us if we are OK.

Mammy told us never to talk to strangers so I ask her what her name is and she says Gertie.

I almost laugh but I don't. I tell her that my mammy is in the shop buying sweets but that I am looking at this map and where are we on it. I tell her we are doing a project in school. I thought of this lie just in case.

'Mammy in shop,' Liam says.

When he says this, it makes me feel that Mammy really is in the shop and it's nice.

Gertie takes my map and looks at it. She points to a red street. 'That's where you are,' she says.

I ask her where do we have to go to get to Mount Venus Road. That's where our mammy who is in the shops buying us sweets is bringing us.

She shows me where to go. She tells me to keep hold of Liam real tight as Liam is only small and might run in front of a car. She says do we want her to wait with us until our mammy comes out. I say, 'No, thank you.'

Then she is gone.

NICK

I sit, hunching forward in Larry's car, my hands clenched into fists as I peer out the window. It's a good day, really bright, surely someone will see them. It's been three hours since they told my mother they were going to play in the front garden; surely to God someone will spot them. How could you not spot an eight-year-old girl with her hair in two plaits, looking like a prim schoolteacher, holding the hand of a hyperactive two-year-old?

They must be hungry.

I wonder if they've got sun cream.

Where are they?

Larry is driving a four-mile radius from the house. We reckon that'd be about all the two could cover in three hours. We've covered Milltown, Ranelagh and Rathmines. We've asked people in shops and on the streets if they've seen the kids. No one has. When we're driving, my eyes keep sliding to the photographs we have of them. Emma, gap-toothed and in a pair of jeans and a top that says 'Sparkly Princess', has her arm around Liam's neck, hugging him as hard as an eight-year-old can. Liam is scowling at this headlock embrace. He's in the shorts I think he is wearing today and a T-shirt that says 'Here Comes Trouble' which Marie bought for him. My mother was appalled that he would wear something like that. Oh,

God, the need to see them, the need to hold them is a physical ache. I will go mad if I don't.

Larry flicks on the radio. I want to tell him to turn it off but the main news story is of Emma and Liam. In horror, not able to believe it's me and my kids they're talking about on national news, I listen as the newscaster dispassionately tells the nation that an eight-year-old girl and her two-year-old brother from south Dublin have gone missing from their home. The newscaster says a Twitter account has been set up and to please spread the word as a matter of urgency.

Larry looks across the car at me.

'Pull over,' I say.

He does, and I vomit.

* * *

At five o clock, the sun is still high. It's a dead heat, like a calm before a storm. Hot, oppressive and headachy. In Dún Laoghaire, all along the road by the harbour, people strut by in T-shirts and impossibly short shorts, displaying acres of white flesh. Do they know how lucky they are? Larry drives down narrow streets but I know it's hopeless. If Emma and Liam were walking, there is no way they'd have made it over this far. Larry thinks they might have got the bus but I think they would have been noticed.

'Let's go back over where we've been,' I say wearily.

Larry nods and turns the car. 'Why would they have run off?' he asks.

'I dunno. Emma wasn't happy these last couple of weeks. She called me a liar. Somehow she found out about the …' my voice stalls, '… the accident. Maybe she got scared of me. I dunno.'

'Poor kid,' Larry says.

'Yeah, finding out your dad was witness to two deaths can't be easy.'

'Nick, I swear, I will throw you out of this car if you start that self-blame shit again. I swear I will.' Larry sounds mad. 'You've been fucking brilliant with them. You always were but you've been great since Kate died. And you've been strong. Don't go saying Emma and Liam running away was your fault. You did your best.'

I heave a sigh. I *had* done my best. I know that. My best, like before, just hasn't been good enough. Is that my fault? I don't know. 'I just want to find them, Lar.'

'We will, we just have to figure out where she would go. Where would she bring Liam?' Larry sounds like I feel. Broken.

My mobile rings. 'Hello?'

'It's Detective Clive Brennan here, Mr Deegan. We've some news. Apparently, someone spotted two children walking through Dundrum earlier today. The little girl had a flowery backpack.'

'Emma has one. Marcy, her godmother, bought it for her. She might be able to describe it. Did this person talk to the children they saw?'

'No. Just thought it was odd.'

My heart sinks. 'What direction did they go?'

'They think towards the motorway. We're going to have a look at some security cameras in the area.'

Holy Jesus Christ. 'Larry, M50 please.'

Larry nods.

EMMA

Liam has hurt his foot. I think he really hasn't, he's just bored. I suppose he thought the adventure would be funner, like the way Dora's are. I keep telling him that at the end it will be funner but that we have to get there first. We have gone along a big road; it's windy and twisty and in a little bit we'll be onto Mount Venus Road and that's where we have to be.

'Want Daddy,' he says, and he sits on the ground.

He can't sit on the ground because then people will see us and maybe bring us home. Up to now, we have been pretending to go into gardens of people's houses whenever a car goes by.

'I'll give you a sweet if you keep walking,' I say to him. I take off my backpack and open the zip in the front. I have three sweets that I saved from ages ago. It was a whole packet only I kept eating them and before I knew, there were only three left.

Liam looks up at me. His bottom lip pokes out. 'No. Want Daddy.'

My face feels really hot and sore. 'I have an apple.' The apple is brown but I have two nice green ones for when we get there, like a reward. 'You can have a sweet and an apple.'

Liam thinks about it. He stands up. He holds out his hand. I give him the apple in one hand and I pull him along by the other. He walks real slow and when he is eating he walks even slower.

My legs are tired. It's a long walk and there are loads of hills. We are going up and up and up. But heaven is up in the air so maybe that is a good thing.

NICK

Larry drives and drives. Up and down the motorway. Up and down the slipways. We spot some people we know along the route and when they see us they shake their heads. We divert to Knocklyon, Tallaght, Rathfarnham. No one has seen anything. With every second that passes, part of me loses itself to panic. Where are they? They are out there somewhere. That's the frustrating thing. They haven't disappeared, they're there. Out there.

I think about Emma, how I told her about the accident. How did I not know what she was going to do? Awful as it is, the thought of her and Liam running away from me is preferable to thoughts of them being abducted, of them being loaded onto a van and being killed. I need her to have run from me, however awful that makes me as a dad. When I find her I'll tell her that she doesn't have to stay with me if she doesn't want to. She can go anywhere. She can do anything. I just want her to be alive.

The sun is dipping now and the sky is clouding over. Both Larry and I try to ignore it as best we can. One by one, street lights start to flicker on. It's growing dark rapidly. I think that a storm is coming and I feel like I'm lost in someone else's life. The feeling of being completely powerless swamps me.

Silence permeates the car.

Out of nowhere, to bat away the panic, I ask, 'Did you always fancy Marcy?'

The unexpectedness of the question makes Larry take his foot off the accelerator and the car judders. He shoots a sideways look at me. 'The first time I saw her, I was terrified,' he admits.

I give a short laugh. 'Me too. All that makeup, all those tight clothes.'

'It was only when Kate got sick that I began to get to know her really. I used to visit Kate, and Marcy was always there and she'd make me a cuppa in the kitchen and at first it was awkward and only done under sufferance.' He smiles a little. 'But bit by bit, as the weeks wore on, we'd talk about your kids and our jobs and it just became …' he pauses, '… easier.'

'And you never said?'

'I didn't think I had a chance. Come on, look at me.'

'Nothing wrong with you.'

Larry fists my arm. 'Thanks. Anyway, we both ended up looking after Kate's grave. And we'd go for a coffee afterwards and one day, after it was off with her creep of a boyfriend, I asked her to dinner.' He shrugs. 'And we just clicked.'

I nod.

After a beat, Larry says, 'But *we're* still good, right?'

I turn to him. 'We're still good.'

All the road lights are on now. Dusk has arrived.

EMMA

It's too dark now. I am lost. The map is wrong. We are on a
road like the country. Walls and big fields. Whenever a car
comes around the corner, I have to pull Liam into the hedge
by the side of the road. Parts of it are prickly. He does not like
it and he is crying a little. I tell him that we are on a camp
like in the movies only we have no camp. We just have to find
somewhere to shelter out of the night-time. The walls are too
big for Liam to climb and I can't pull him up. I have to look
for somewhere with a gate that I can open. Liam is tired, he
keeps rubbing his eyes and whingeing. Mammy used to hug
him when he whinged, and sing a little song to him. Daddy
does that too, only Daddy plays his guitar. I think of Daddy's
song and I start to sing it as we go along. 'Oh, Liam, though
you're only two years old, I'll love you as much as I can.'

Liam stops crying for a second. He puts his thumb in his
mouth. 'Want Daddy,' he says.

There is a rustling at my feet and something small runs
out from the hedge and scuttles across the road. I yelp. I hope
it wasn't a rat. Daddy isn't scared of rats. I start to tell Liam
Daddy's story of the rat and the man called Nick.

'Once upon a time, there was a rat,' I say. 'He was a King Rat and he lived deep under the ground. Every other rat in the whole world knew of him and was scared of him. If he didn't like you, bad things happened. If he did like you, bad things happened. Then one day, the King Rat heard of a man called Nick. Nick said he was tired of the bad things happening to everybody and he said he was going to put an end to it. And do you know what he did?'

Daddy always stops here and waits for Liam to answer.

'What he do?' Liam says, in a funny voice because his thumb is still in his mouth.

'He sang.'

'What he sing?' Liam asks.

'He sang a song and it went like this.'

I laugh as Liam sticks his foot out just like Daddy taught him. I stick my foot out, ready to kick the rat too. I sing,

'Sunshine and sunlight, things so bright,

Make the grey go away today.

Take that and that, Mr King Rat!

Take that and that,

I'll knock you flat!

Now, go away, you awful guy!

Go away, say goodbye.

This is Nick,

I'll give you stick.'

We punch our fists in the air. Liam laughs.

'And do you know what happened?'

'What happened?' Liam asks.

'That big bully rat went away!'

'Hurray!' Liam cheers.

And then, like the best birthday present, there it is. I see that we haven't got lost at all. There it is, through the gate.

NICK

Detective Brennan calls again. This time he sounds a little excited. Behind him, I can hear the hum of conversation, the clink of cups and plates. Someone called Gertie has seen the kids. The little girl asked her for directions to Mount Venus Road.

Larry and I look at each other. My hope is reflected in his face.

'Please let us check this out,' I say to the police officer. 'If it *is* her, I know where she'll be.'

'Where?' he asks.

'Her mother is buried there,' I say.

'We'll have to dispatch someone,' he says. 'But if they're there, we'll keep our distance.'

Larry presses his accelerator. His car responds instantly. We drive faster than I have ever driven before. I close my eyes and silently pray.

EMMA

It starts to rain. Big fat drops plopping on our heads. Liam is scared of all the shadows and the big slabs of stone. 'Don't you remember,' I say to him, trying not to sound scared myself, 'that we came here with Larry and Marcy before and that when Mammy died we came here too?'

Liam takes my one hand in his two and then squeezes his body into my legs. It's hard to walk with him like that. But I let him because I am his big sister and it's my job to mind him.

It's a really big graveyard. It seems to go on forever and ever. I know when we came with Marcy that we walked straight for ages and that Mammy's grave was right on the edge. She didn't have a stone so that makes it easier. Liam and me walk and walk. And it gets darker and colder and wetter. There are other people here too but they are far away and they are running for the entrance to get out of the rain. Liam and me can hide behind the headstones if they look at us.

Liam trips up and he almost makes me fall. 'Want Daddy!' he starts to cry again and then his crying turns to hiccups. He rubs his fist into his eyes and I have to crouch down to make him look at me.

'Just a little while, Liam. I didn't know the walk would take so long, a hundred miles is a long way. It's only a little way on the map.' I hand him one of the nice green apples. 'Eat this.'

He takes it but he just keeps it in his hand and won't eat it.

'Now, you have to help me look for where Mammy is, OK?' He looks puzzled.

'Remember Mammy?'

'Want Daddy.' Big tears come down his cheeks.

I am really cross with him. 'Mammy was nice. She made you buns, Daddy doesn't make buns. And she bought you all your toys and she played hide and seek with us.'

'Want Daddy!' His voice rises up real loud.

I have to pull him onto the ground. 'Stop.'

And there, just in front, is a grave with no headstone, right on the edge. It has a big yellow vase with sunflowers sitting in it and a picture in front of it. I take the picture and try to see what it is. Oh, wow! It is the picture Marcy took when we stayed over in her apartment. This is where Mammy is.

NICK

It's turned into a miserable night. The temperature has dropped and if the kids are out in this, they'll be cold and soaked through. I think of Liam in his little shorts and Emma in her summer dress and I have to physically stop myself from yelling at Larry to hurry up even more. I guess if he did, we'd both be killed. He's careering up those mountain roads like a mad man. It hits me, once again, how much he loves them. 'Thanks, Lar. Thanks for everything.'

'You can thank me when we find them,' he flashes back.

I start my silent praying again.

EMMA

Liam has helped me to lay out all the things. At least it stopped him crying. All my treasures look so colourful on the ground, even in the dark. Mammy's jewellery is the best of all. She has loads of diamond earrings and gold bracelets. I tell Liam to kneel down then. He likes that 'cause the ground is gone all muddy and the rain is real heavy and Liam likes mud. I kneel down too and feel my knees squelch into the earth. It's yeuch but it'll be worth it.

I join my hands and close my eyes and say to my friend, Jesus, 'Hi, Jesus, it's Emma. From Dublin in case you know lots of them. There are four in my class but I am the Emma whose mammy died and that is why I am talking to you. I was wondering if we could borrow Mammy from you for a little while and you can take all this stuff. Then we can swap back.' I'm not going to swap back, though, only he doesn't know that.

'Swap back!' Liam parrots.

'All these things are Mammy's favourite things and I thought you could give the jewellery to your blessed mother to wear. I also put in my favourite things and Liam's favourite things to show you how much we want our mammy back.'

Liam is chewing the ear on his teddy.

'I know Liam has his teddy in his mouth but he will give it to you when we see Mammy. It's only for a little bit and anyway my mammy didn't want to go with you.'

Up in the sky, thunder booms and makes us jump.

I think it's Jesus answering.

'Please, Jesus, just for a week,' I say.

Lightning flashes and the grave looks great but Mammy still hasn't come. The rain makes drumming sounds. Me and Liam are really wet and it is cold.

'I won't be your friend any more if you won't lend my mammy back!'

NICK

'Do you hear that?' I stop dead in the middle of the path. 'It sounded like Emma. She's shouting!'

Both of us start to run down the long pathway. I thank God I'm fit from the running. If someone has her, I'll kill them. I can feel the speed in my legs; it never left me, despite the years of neglect. I leave Larry far behind as my feet cover the uneven surface effortlessly. Wind and rain drive into my face. As I near the grave, my heart starts to hammer wildly. Not only for the kids but because I lied when I told Marcy I didn't visit as I had no emotional attachment to the place. I didn't go because I was scared, pure and simple. Scared of being taken over by the grief which I've somehow kept under wraps. Scared of seeing Kate reduced to being in a piece of ground.

With knee-buckling relief, I see two small figures at the grave. I have an urge to yell out but I don't want to frighten them. Liam has his thumb in his mouth and a bear dangling from his hand, while Emma is kneeling devoutly, her hands clasped.

'Emma? Liam?' I say softly.

Two heads swivel around.

'Oh my God.' I stumble to a halt, my head swimming. 'There you are. We've been so worried.'

Liam's face creases up into the most wonderful smile. He extracts himself from the mud and hauls himself upright. 'Daddy!'

I stoop down to scoop him up as he stumbles towards me and his chubby little arms find purchase on my neck and I close my eyes as he squeezes me.

Larry, panting heavily, comes up behind me.

'What are you doing, bud?' I ask. I cover his muddy face with kisses.

'Aventure,' Liam says. 'Like Dora.'

'Great stuff.' Over his head, I can see Emma studying me warily. Liam shivers a little. I stagger up, Liam clinging to me. 'Lar, will you take Liam back to the car? Dry him off?'

Larry emerges from the shadows.

'And ring the … you know … the guy who wanted us to ring him.' I don't want to say 'police' in front of the kids.

'Sure thing,' Larry says brightly. He pulls off his jacket and wraps it around my son. 'Great to see you,' he says, taking Liam from me and tenderly carrying him off.

I turn to my daughter. Both of us face each other, the rain just one of the barriers between us.

She is soaking, her dress clinging to her skinny body, her braided hair dripping onto her neck. I take off my jacket as I approach her. I walk slowly, like you would to a frightened puppy. 'Can I put this around you to keep you dry?'

She says nothing but doesn't protest as I hunker down and wrap it around her shoulders, zipping it right up to her neck. Something crunches underfoot and I glance down. The grave is strewn with all sorts of mad things. In a lightning flash I see Kate's jewellery draped over a vase. I am at a loss.

'You feeling warmer?' I ask.

She nods. Big bright tears stand out in her eyes. I want to hug her, scoop her up and never let her go, but I know it's not what she wants, not just now.

'Why, Ems?' I ask after a bit. 'Why did you need to run off, hey? Am I not a good daddy?' More lightning flashes across the sky, illuminating her sad little face.

Just at my foot, I spy a picture of me. I reach out for it and Emma says sharply, 'No. You have to leave it.'

'Why?'

She stares at me defiantly. 'I'm doing a swap. Jesus can have these and I can borrow Mammy back for a little while.'

Her words slam into me. The innocence, the hope, the utter futility of them. And more than that, the way she must miss her mother so much. And her sad eyes reflect mine, which was why I had just wanted to keep her and Liam happy all these months. I can hardly bear to meet her gaze. But I have to. I bring my eyes to hers and I feel my heart will crack with grief. 'Em, honey,' I say it as gently but as firmly as I can, 'it doesn't work like that. Mammy isn't coming back. Not ever.' My voice dips.

'You tell lies. You're a liar.'

'I would never lie to you about this.' My knees sink further into the mud. The rain is getting heavier.

'If you leave us, who will mind us? I want my mammy!' Her voice rises, tearful and lost. 'I miss her.'

'I am not going to leave you. Not ever. Aren't I here now? Haven't Larry and I been looking for you for ages? I will never leave you.'

'You left with Smelly Jack! Now he's back!'

I touch her shoulder and she doesn't pull away. 'I was wrong to do that. I am sorry. I was sick, Emma.' I tap my head. 'My head was not well. I wasn't able to remember who I loved most, but I'm better now. I'll never get sick again.' The wind whips the words from my mouth and flings them in her direction. I inject them with as much raw honesty as I can. 'I love you and Liam. I do. I will never leave.' I pause. 'I miss your mammy too,' I finally admit. 'I miss her so much.'

Her face, so sad, finally crumples. Her little lip wobbles. Huge tears drip from her eyes. 'I just want Mammy. I want to hug her just once more. I want to smell her hair and taste her buns just once more, Daddy.'

I grab her. I pull her to me. I let my own tears fall. I kiss her head. Her arms tighten around me.

'I just want Mammy!' Raw anguish.

'I know you do,' I say. I tighten my hold on her. 'And if I could give her to you, I would. I want her too.' Lightning forks down in front of us. 'But it doesn't work the way you want, Emma. We've just got each other now.' Then I say the words I suddenly realise she wants me to say. 'It's OK to be sad.'

Her body shakes with sobs. Into my T-shirt, she says, 'I never hugged her properly that last day, Daddy. She wanted me to hug her and I didn't do it right.'

'She won't mind that. That's why she gave you all her jewellery. So you could mind that instead and hug it too if you wanted.'

Emma pulls away a little and looks up at me. 'Really?' she sniffs.

'Really and truly.' I thumb her tears away. I stare into her face. 'Cross my heart.'

She hugs me again. I savour the moment, in the pouring rain. The feel of her hugging me. The feeling that I've said something right at last. It's like finding a key to a door in the dark.

Emma shivers suddenly and I realise how wet she must be. 'You ready to go?' I ask softly.

She looks at the grave, then looks back up at me and it's as if she makes a decision. 'Yes.'

'Will we bring the jewellery home so you can mind it for Mammy?'

In response she peels herself away from me and begins to gather it up. My jacket trails on the ground. I see my mother's cats among the mud and I decide to leave them there.

Emma holds up a ring. 'This is Nana's. Mammy liked it and I knew Nana wouldn't mind swapping it for Mammy. It wasn't stealing.'

'We'll give it back. Don't worry. Let's leave the cats, though.'

She smiles a small little smile.

Then as she clutches all her belongings and her muddy haversack, I hoist her up in my arms. I kiss the tip of her nose. 'I love you, Emmakins, and I'm going to make you a promise, OK?'

'What?'

'If you promise not to leave me, I won't leave you.'

'What if I get married?'

'Then I'll move into the house with you and your husband.'

Instead of laughing, Emma nods sombrely. 'You can even share our bed if you like.'

I bite the inside of my cheek. 'I would love that, Emma, thanks.'

And then she wraps her arms around my shoulders and snuggles in and I feel as if I've just been given a second chance.

NICK

Kids are resilient. They bounce back once they know that there is love out there for them. Adults are not so good at that. Or maybe it's just me. I never bounced back. I think I'm only doing it now.

I'm driving towards the coast of south County Dublin. The kids are with Larry and Marcy. For the first time in three years, I'm off to Dalkey, to the scene of the fire that claimed the lives of my two work colleagues. With every beat of my heart, I feel the vibration through my whole body. I flex my fingers, which are cramping on the steering wheel. In recent years, if I ever had to go near Dalkey, I took long circuitous routes rather than pass by any reminders of that night. Now, sweat slicking my palms, I indicate and turn down the road towards the house. Like an image seared on my brain, I recognise it instantly. Only now, there are no indicators to say that anything bad had ever happened here. The house looks like its neighbours, red-bricked and respectable. Even the trees and the hedging that surround it have matured once again so that they blend.

I park opposite and stare over. I take time to get my breathing under control before slowly climbing out of my car and walking to where I had stood that night after it had all fallen apart. The day is dull and a bit miserable, but in my head, there are bright lights and noise. Lots of shouting. Someone crying. The sound of crashing.

A glint catches my eyes.

Something gold.

On the pillar of the house is a rectangular plaque with black writing. It reads:

> *Dedicated to the two brave firemen, Tom Daly and Alan*
> *Fitzpatrick, who died while trying to put out a fire at this*
> *address. Also dedicated to Nick Deegan, their comrade,*
> *who dragged their bodies free despite risk to his own life.*
> *And to all in Dundrum fire station who were left bereft. The*
> *Crilly family.*

No one had told me to expect this. I reach out and run my hand along it. I swallow hard. How … thoughtful.

'Are you OK?' An old woman, clutching her cardigan around her, peers at me from the door of the house.

I straighten up. 'I'm fine, thanks.'

She cocks her head to the side. 'Nick Deegan?' Her voice has a sing-song note of hope in it, which is weird.

I think of denying it but I am tired of running away from who I am now. 'Yes.'

She smiles and looks, I don't quite know, as if something has finally clicked for her. 'Have you come to see our plaque?' Without waiting for me to answer, she pulls her cardigan tighter and approaches me, saying a little eagerly, 'We tried to contact you when we put it up but your wife said it was better to leave it, that you'd come to see it one day. In your own time.'

'My wife said that?'

The woman nods. Along with the cardigan, she's wearing slippers and thick red tights. 'She seemed very nice. And here you are.' She holds out her hand. 'I'm Margaret. I'm so pleased to meet you. The guilt has eaten away at me since that day. The plaque was the least I could do to put it right.'

I take her hand, feeling ever so slightly off-balance. 'You've been feeling guilty?'

'Oh, yes. Of course.' Her gaze dips to her slippers before she raises her head again. 'Substandard extension and basement conversion. We took the cheapest quote we could. That's why the ceiling collapsed, apparently. We were so grateful at least one of you survived.' A pause. 'I've wanted to ask your forgiveness for so long.'

My world tips a little.

'I've never blamed you,' I say quietly. 'Never.'

'Who else was there to blame only us?' she says.

'It's futile to blame anyone,' I say, and I know that somewhere Kate is laughing at me. 'No one set out to hurt anyone.'

Her eyes lighten, as if I've actually comforted her. I'm glad I came. 'I wish I could have told you that sooner,' I say. And I wish she'd told me sooner too. But maybe I wouldn't have been ready to hear it.

Stop two and three on the journey are hard. I visit Tom's parents who, three years on, are understandably still devastated. But proud. So proud of him. They have his picture up all over their front room. They even have a picture of him and me, arms slung about each other at a Christmas party. Another of him playing poker in the early hours of the morning as we waited to be called out. I can spot myself in the background and I know by the look on my face, I have a shit hand.

They don't blame me either. It was a risk of the job.

'And we still have your letter saying that he knew his way out and you didn't listen to him,' his mother says. 'But like we already told you, if it had been a choice of you leading us from a burning building or him, we would have chosen you too. His sense of direction was quite appalling normally.'

'Well, on the night, he was right, I was wrong.' It's important that that is acknowledged by them.

They nod. His arm around her.

'I should have come here before but I wasn't able,' I continue. 'I am sorry that he died.'

'We're sorry that he died too.' His mother touches my shoulder and with those words, she lets me know that I'm just another mourner, there is nothing to make me stand out from all those people who were sorry to see him die. I did not kill him, she seems to be saying.

'And Nick,' Tom's mother says as I leave, 'I'm glad you lived.'

I stare at her.

'I was so sorry about your wife.'

I dip my head. 'Thanks.' And I know what she means and for the first time since that night, I'm glad I survived. What would have become of Emma and Liam if both Kate and I had died?

Alan's wife, the woman half the lads in the station had a crush on, says that if he had to die young, she's glad he died on duty. It's the way he would have wanted to go. 'I love him and miss him every day,' she says. Then she looks at me. 'You know what I mean, eh?'

I nod. 'Yeah.' Then I ask, 'Does it get easier?'

'You come to a place where you're glad they were in your life.' She touches my arm. 'Take care of yourself, Nick, and those two kids. And call over anytime.'

We both know I won't be back. There is no need. We've both said what needed to be said.

And as the door closes behind me, I feel that I've somehow closed a door too.

NICK

The fifth and final date. I think back to the first one and how reluctant I was to go on it and now all I can feel is regret that this is the last. After this I have to go on on my own without Kate's guidance. I have come a long way since the first date, though, I think.

Emma legs it into the room, yowling, clutching her face. 'Daddy, Liam hit me. Look!' She peels her hand away from her cheek and I see the vanishing red of what is an unmistakable hand print.

Liam barrels in after her. He's got tall; his belly sticks out. He is all boy. 'Not wearing dress,' he shouts, in what I feel will develop into a foghorn voice. 'I am boy!'

Emma looks at me. 'See. He won't play with me any more.'

'He is a boy, Ems,' I say. 'You can't go sticking dresses on him.'

Emma narrows her eyes. 'I wear trousers,' she says.

I'm saved from arguing with her by the peal of a bell.

Liam dashes to get the door, Emma hot on his heels. I make it out to the hall on time to see her elbow him out of the way so that he slides to the floor and begins howling.

'Emma!'

She ignores me and pulls open the door.

Larry and Marcy come in bearing smiles and sweets.

'Oh, poor little guy.' Marcy stoops down, barely able to keep her balance in her high shoes. 'What happened?'

Liam gabbles out an indignant, incoherent explanation.

'Emma pushed him!' I say in his stead. 'Apologise, Emma.'

'I did nothing.'

'I saw you, you pushed him.' My voice is sharp. 'Apologise.'

She looks a little startled. Then out comes the most begrudging 'sorry' in the history of the universe. I can't figure out if Larry and Marcy look startled at my tone or the fact that Emma has actually listened to me.

It was my mother. After the kids had returned safe and sound, she had sat me down as if I was three and told me that unless I copped on to myself, I'd have two kids that were completely out of control. Boundaries, she said, you need to set boundaries.

'They're not foreign countries, Ma.' I grinned, but she wasn't having any of it. They needed a dad, not someone who felt sorry for them, she snapped.

Having got them back safe, I hadn't wanted any confrontation with them, but apparently, they are crying out for discipline.

My mother handed me a list of websites and a list of books to read. She recorded awful programmes like *Dealing with Grief* and *How To Help Your Child Behave*.

'I should have been firmer with you three years ago,' she said crossly. 'So should Kate. We let you away with murder.' The unfortunate choice of word caused her to flush, then she battled on, 'Children need discipline, it helps them feel safe.'

The word 'safe' did it for me. I took the books. I looked up the websites. I remembered with a guilty feeling Kate's instruction not to spoil them. I have started re-reading her book and I watch that video again and again, finally able to look at my wife without plunging into despair. So now, it's a braver me. But Pancake Tuesday night still stands.

We walk into the TV room, Larry doling out sweets as Marcy, having calmed Liam with a lollipop, shyly takes out some brochures. 'I thought the kids might like a day out next week. I've the choices here.' She looks up at me. 'You and Larry can take off somewhere yourselves.'

'Sounds good.' I smile at her. It's getting easier. I guess at the time of Kate's miscarriage, Marcy only did what she thought was right too.

The doorbell rings.

'Last date, eh?' Larry says.

I have made a real effort this time. I even went out and bought new denims. I'm wearing them with the jacket of a suit. It was a look Kate loved. I grab the kids and kiss them goodbye. Emma hugs me.

'Love you, Daddy,' she says.

I kiss the tip of her nose and wink. 'Loving you too.'

Then I'm dismissed but my heart is mush.

The bell rings again just as I pull open the door on a grinning, brightly dressed Chantelle.

She eyes me up and down. 'Wow, you scrub up well. Are you going out?'

'Yeah.' I look beyond her. There is no one. She's in her running gear, bright pink top, black strides.

'Right, well, I better give you this so.' She holds out an envelope, dancing impatiently from one trainer-clad foot to the other. 'Before Kate died, she warned me to expect a letter. It arrived yesterday morning from her solicitor with the instruction that it was to be delivered to you tonight at eight o'clock.'

I take it from her. Stare at the envelope. There's no USB this time. It's a real letter.

'Thanks.'

'She said that the page for After the Fifth Date is blank, that you've to fill it in yourself. Does that make sense?'

'No, but maybe it will.' I study the letter.

'Well, that's me,' Chantelle says. 'See you, Nick. I'm off for a run. Catch up with me if you feel like it later.' Then she turns around. 'Oh, sorry, forgot, you're crap, aren't you?'

I laugh as she jogs off.

Closing the door on her, I take myself upstairs. There is no way I can delay opening this and yet no way I can open it in front of Larry and Marcy. I go into Kate's room, because it seems right, even though all traces of her are gone. I sit on the bed and with one determined rip, I tear open the flap of the envelope.

It's a sheet of paper adorned with her spiky writing.

Hey, you.☺
Did you like the dates I sent you on? Your past, the present and this last one is for your future.

> *Do you remember that glorious day when we stood at the top of the Three Rock and we pretended to see into the future? Your arms around me, your chin resting on my head. We stunk of sweat and reeked of happiness. And then I ran off and you followed me and we ran down the mountain and across the car park and down onto the road and all the way home. And the sun was shining. And when we got back, we were so pleased with our times, because we were well on track for the marathon in Barcelona.*

> *But we never got to do it.*

> *It's like a picture, frozen in time. That very moment that you got back, Larry came to the door, waving the phone, telling you the station was on, that they were a man short in work and would you go in. And of course you would. You always did.*

If we had been ten minutes later, they would have called someone else in and our lives would have been great. Maybe.

I believe it was meant to be, Nick.

I believe you had to go in that night and I believe we were never destined to run that marathon.

But I want you to run it for me now. I want you to run it and feel the pain. Embrace the pain and keep going, Nick, that's what it's all about. I've booked two tickets, one for you and one for Chantelle, the girl who will give you this letter. I don't know if you know her, she's a woman in the Parent and Toddler group. She's never gone anywhere, never done all that she was capable of doing, so I want to gift her this chance and I want to give you the gift of knowing her. She's quirky, funny and a damn good runner. She loves her little boy and she will make you laugh.

You need to laugh, Nick. You're so lovely when you laugh. You need to run, Nick. You need to play music again. You need to get out there and help people again.

And don't be too mad at Larry, he can't help loving Marcy, nor she him. Keep them in your life.

Give thanks that you survived and you helped Jack survive.

Hug all our friends for me.

Live well.

Keep singing.

Love my children with everything you have.

Embrace the future.

And remember that day you ran the sub 1:48

800m. You said it was because I was there cheering you on. Well, guess what? I still am.

Just remember, when you can't go on ... go on.

Love always,

Kate. x

I use the palm of my hands to wipe the rogue tears that have fallen. Oh Kate, you surprised me in life and you're still doing it. And just like then, I'm still one step behind you.

I fold the paper up carefully, push it back into the envelope and stand up.

Downstairs, Larry is playing some manic game with the kids. They're shrieking and laughing. Marcy is telling him to calm down, he'll break something.

I cross silently into my room and change out of my jeans and shirt and into running gear. I do a quick warm-up and then I'm downstairs and out the door.

I'm running, running right out of the estate, down the road and my feet feel strong as they bounce on the pavement. I take a left. Run. Take a right. Run. I cross towards Marlay Park, passing pedestrians, cars in traffic, bicycles. I track around the walls, begin climbing up and up and up. I'm gasping for air but I push on. I cross into the car park, my feet are flying faster than they should, and I hit trail. Up stones, over rocks, slipping in mud and up and up. I'm short of breath, I feel sick, but I keep going. Keep pushing. Keep moving.

Seventy minutes later, I'm at the top. The view is panoramic. The light is beginning to change, making everything appear so much more beautiful. It was worth the run. The dying sun paints the world with vibrant colours. I stare out, beyond Dublin to the sea. I stare and stare until I feel the future.

And then I turn around and run back into it.

ACKNOWLEDGEMENTS

Firstly to my family. I love you all.

Thanks to Jules, my brother-in-law, who told me all I need to know about fire-fighting. All mistakes are mine!

For my friends – thanks for everything but especially your support in the last few years. (I won't name names in case I leave someone out – you know who you are!)

Thanks to Pete, who tells wonderful stories and from whom I stole the 'cake baking' episode for this book.

To all the single fathers I talked to – your insights were invaluable.

And to you dear reader – thanks so much for buying my book – I appreciate it. x the tamiacorey